CW01464963

CHURCHILL'S SHADOW
(Operation Longshot – Book 1)

by

Linda Stoker

First published by Beswick & Beswick Publishing House 2016
beswickandbeswick@gmail.com

Copyright © 2016 Linda Stoker

The author asserts the moral rights to be identified as the author
of this work

All rights reserved. No part of this publication may be reproduced,
distributed, or transmitted in any form or by any means, including
photocopying, recording, or other electronic or mechanical methods,
without the prior written permission of the publisher

BESWICK & BESWICK
PUBLISHING HOUSE

CONTENTS

BIOGRAPHY

Linda Stoker lives in a village on the Herts Essex border. She is married to Gordon Smith and has two daughters, Emma and Kimberley and two stepsons, Richard and Alex. She has four grandchildren, Charlie, Alfie, Lily and Albert.

Linda ran her own educational publishing and training company Dow-Stoker for 18 years. In 1990 she was a 'Woman of the Year' and presented to Princess Diana.

She speaks what she calls, 'reasonable French' and spends some of her time writing in the Aude region of France.

In 2015 she was diagnosed with breast cancer and has donated the royalties from this book to the Princess Alexandra breast trials charity.

PROLOGUE

17:00: 19 March 1941

Walter's service as Winston Churchill's personal bodyguard was officially over. As dusk fell, Walter rode his motorcycle for the last time along Downing Street. The bike stalled in front of the imposing black door of Number 10. He looked up at the brick townhouse to the Prime Minister's study. He touched his chest when he saw the silhouette of the Old Man - there in person as a final salute.

A shadow pulled Churchill back from the window. Walter smiled. The distinctive round shape of his chum, Sergeant George was a comforting sight.

Walter rammed his foot down hard on the old kick-start pedal, leaving his old life behind.

He slowed down at the corner of Whitehall. It stung his eyes – misery after fifty-seven nights of ceaseless bombing. The Luftwaffe had turned the elegance of Westminster into a traumatised landscape. Grey sandbags protected every doorway and buildings smouldered. He weaved the bike between gaping craters, scarring the road. It was rush hour and Lambeth Bridge was covered with the black shadows of resolute commuters, carrying gas masks and briefcases. He picked out the agitated walk of Downwood.

"Downwood…!"

Downwood looked at the pavement and pulled his lapel across his face.

"Look at me…. I'm not going to waste my energy popping you one – though God knows you deserve it. Just do your bloody job and look after the Old Man."

Downwood nodded.

"Well?"

"Y-yes Inspector, I'll make sure he goes to the bunker."

"You might have to force him at gun point. You know how wilful he can be. And be sure of one thing, if you let me down, I will kill you." Walter revved the bike. "And make sure you treat my Sergeant with respect." Walter sped off down the road until he approached Brixton Road. A council worker was clearing a mound of bomb debris. "You'll have to go around mate. Poor buggers got a direct hit on the shelter last night – 90 dead."

Walter grappled with the bike.

The council worker looked up. "Oh here, let me give you a hand." Together they wrestled the heavy bike over the boulders, sliding it down the loose concrete at the back of the mound.

***

18:00 As Walter neared his home, an air-raid siren wailed. With practiced speed, he clicked on his pocket watch alarm – *ting* – set for ten minutes. The ten precious minutes he needed to get home to Kate before bombs and fire would rain down from the sky.

This was his neighbourhood, but night and day no longer followed their regular course. He shuddered. A sudden loneliness, weighed on his chest, without the faithful Sergeant George by his side.

18:02 Beams of light were weaving crosses in the sky, searching for the first deadly aircraft. Giant, gas filled barrage balloons, tethered by steel cables covered the skyline.

The sirens shrieked louder. Walter tightened his grip on the handlebars. Smoke coughed from the exhaust as he opened the accelerator to full throttle.

The city shook when the bitter *ack ack* firing from the British artillery emplacements discharged shells at the advancing German bombers.

18:03 In the distance, a red double-decker bus blocked the road. He slowed the bike and stopped when he saw steam spewing from the engine. "May I be of any assistance?"

"Don't s'pose you've seen the relief bus on your way, 'ave yer guv?"

"Yes, I passed it away back at Gibson's Hill. Sir, the nearest shelter is a mile away in the park on the left. We have seven minutes. Hurry. Get all passengers off the bus now."

"Who are you then, giving yer bloody orders?"

Walter flashed his warrant card, "Inspector Thompson, Scotland Yard. Sir, we have no time – please."

"Oh, right you are then, Inspector. All change 'ere. Come on love – off yer get. Come on now, 'urry up darling – no, leave yer pushchair on the bus – Hitler's not gonna nick it. Give the little one to me…."

"Private…a word …." Walter called to a jumpy boy in uniform standing in line on the pavement. "Get on. You can alert them in the shelter – they've got a full bus load coming."

18:04 The boy climbed on the bike and clung to Walter. They flew past people laden with food and blankets, dashing along the pavement to spend another torturous night down in the damp, cold air-raid shelter. In an instant the ear-piercing wailing of the sirens stopped. The muffled booms advanced to a louder *crump, crump, crump*, of bombs tearing homes apart in the distance. A small boy stumbled and was left alone on the pavement. An elderly man at the end of the line took his tiny hand and guided him back to his mother.

The throbbing engines of the first wave of German bombers came grinding overhead, silencing the people of the city. All eyes peered at the moonlit sky now blackened by the silhouettes of hundreds of planes in close formation.

Walter slid the bike to a halt in front of the park gates. The conscript dismounted and ran towards the shelter – arms and legs flailing.

The might of the German air force had evaded the heavy British guns. There was a low intermittent drone as they smothered London, spreading wave after wave of fire and destruction.

***

18:06 Walter whistled his – cuckoo – cuckoo signal. Kate rushed to the parlour door.

"Walter!" She flung her arms around him. "You've come home." She pushed him away a little and marvelled at the sight of his handsome face.

Walter made a grab for her. "No time for this... Come on, we have to go."

18:07 She ducked under his muscular arms and picked up a flask of tea.

"Quick let's get to the shelter – I've got something important to tell you." He took her hand....

18:08 A flash! Kate's hand was torn from his grip. The air was ripped from their lungs and Kate's body was flung into an abyss.

"Kate – Kate". Walter saw her hand slip from his in slow motion over and over until the blackness took him too.

***

18:08 The relief bus left the ground with the blast. The passengers screamed. They were thrown from their seats and slammed down again, smashing heads and limbs on glass and wood. The bus slew to a halt in front of the park gates. The relief driver's head crashed through the windscreen - killing her instantly.

18:09 The Conductor stepped down from the bus. She saw her shattered friend in the driver's cab. She undid the buckle on her ticket machine letting it fall to the road. She balanced against the bus counting: One, two, three, four, five.... "That way.... O-Over there ...."

She held out her arm to help each passenger off the bus. "That's right, over there, see the man by the gate - follow on." Her words hit deafened ears as the bedraggled line of people hobbled off the bus in the direction of the park.

***

18:10 Walter's pocket watch alarm went off with small broken *tink-tink-tinks* as he lay motionless under the rubble. Tea dribbled out of the broken flask as it rolled across the floor.

***

St Paul's Cathedral stood alone while London was ringed and stabbed with fire.

1939
Two Years Earlier

CHAPTER 1
Walter - The Nazi Threat

1 July – The Duke of Windsor's home, Chateau de la Croe, Cap d'Antibes, French Riviera

Two men stopped outside the main gate.

Oberg, a tall balding German was an assassin. He was a clinical killer for an elite paramilitary group, the *SS* – Storm Troopers (*Schutzstaffel*). He was chosen for this job because of obedience, and loyalty until death to his *Führer,* Adolf Hitler.

It was a long walk up the hill to the villa and his guide irritated him with his constant nervous chatter. A pulse beat in his neck as he reined in the desire to kill him.

Frederick, a Frenchman was a local, hired for 50 Francs to escort Oberg to the villa. He was pushing a cycle with a box on the front advertising, *Frederick Criou, Artisan Boulanger.* He glanced at Oberg, who looked nothing like a delivery boy, and wiped sweat from his forehead.

Oberg put his hand on the handlebars to halt the bike. "This is it." He took a long look at the curving drive, sweeping up to the villa. "Wait here." He disappeared from view into the immaculate garden and headed for the back of the property.

Frederick hopped from one foot to the other.

The Duke of Windsor sat at his desk in the drawing room, facing the window with a view of the path to the back door. The Duke was a small, neat man, with the fine tailoring you would expect from someone who had once been King of England.

He gave a quick nod of recognition as the German passed the window. He picked up his pen and looked at his wife. "My dear, I want to invite the Churchill's to spend next weekend with us."

"That would be nice, David." Wallis looked up from her book. "I'll make sure we put chicken consommé on the menu. It's Winston's favourite, you know. Thompson, told me the last time we were together at Chartwell."

Wallis touched the Cartier diamond bracelet, a wedding present from the Duke and resumed reading.

The Duke finished his letter to Churchill and a short note for the German. "When I talk with Winston about Germany, I want him at his ease, in a relaxed atmosphere. I'm hoping to persuade him England and Germany can get along. His scare stories will do none of us any good."

The Duke was still angry he had been forced to abdicate so he could marry the woman he loved. He felt a stately duty to persuade Germany's loudest critic, Winston Churchill, the Nazis meant no harm. He rang the bell for the maid and got up to meet her in the hall. He closed the door to the drawing room and whispered. "Take this letter to the post office and give this note to the man at the back door."

The maid opened the door a crack. She stumbled back, gripping the hat stand on seeing Oberg, and the long raw scar traversing the length of his face. She thrust the note at him and shut the door.

***

Oberg glanced up at the high shrubbery, surrounding the villa. He had chosen his lair. Now to report to *Sturmbannführer* Schellenberg and wait for the orders to kill Winston Churchill. He smiled when he saw the Frenchman had cycled away; now he had a good reason to kill him too.

***

2 July 1939 – Himmler's office in Berlin

The second most important man in Germany, Heinrich Himmler the *Reichsführer* (Leader of the Third Reich) was watering the houseplants in his office.

His pallid skin framed by dark receding hair and glasses made him look more like a university professor than a military commander.

His secretary, a tall blonde with bright intelligent eyes and an immaculate SS uniform, knocked on his door. She waited outside, next to the youngest high-ranking officer in the *SS, Sturmbannführer* (Storm Troop Leader) Schellenberg, Himmler's personal aide. They waited in stiff silence for the order to enter. "HEREINKOMMEN!" She opened the door, followed by the young narrow shouldered officer, who hesitated at the threshold. "Excuse me, Reichsführer, SS Sturmbannführer Schellenberg is here."

"Good morning, Schellenberg. What have you come to tell me?" Himmler handed an empty watering can to his secretary for her to refill.

Schellenberg opened the file in his hand. "It's good news, sir. We had two meetings with the Duke of Windsor. Politically, he disagrees with the British government and his brother, the King. He is willing to collaborate with us and waits for the most favourable moment to make his decision public."

Himmler caressed the leaves of a large Aspidistra. "Ah, if only he had remained King. No Englishman could have ignored a king who was a friend of Nazi Germany and who sought peace. Will he come to Berlin and broadcast on our behalf to the British?"

"We've offered him 50 million Swiss francs, which will allow them to live in the luxury to which they are accustomed. Might I suggest we give him a little more time? He's invited *Herr* Churchill to his house next weekend to persuade him to support us – we will, of course be listening to everything they say."

"We will listen but understand one thing, Sturmbannführer, Winston Churchill is not to leave France alive." Himmler returned to his desk. "That will be all."

Schellenberg did not move. "Sir?"

Himmler looked up. "What?"

"If I may suggest…it has occurred to me… well, Churchill is just an old man who holds no political office. If the Duke convinces him of our good intentions, he may be able to return to England and convince others."

Himmler waved him away. "Our *Führer* considers Churchill his most formidable enemy. You have your man in position?"

"Yes sir, it's Oberg – a most reliable man. The Duke is comfortable with him because he thinks he's a diplomat."

"Then radio Oberg to let him know the operation has been approved at the highest level. We cannot afford to miss this excellent opportunity to eliminate *Herr* Churchill before he causes us any more damage."

Sturmbannführer Schellenberg snapped his heels together and performed a perfect Nazi salute. *"Heil Hitler."*

***

3 July – The Chateau St Georges Motel, Normandy, France

Miss Shearburn tapped on Churchill's bedroom door and entered without waiting for permission. Churchill looked up from his newspaper as she handed him his mail. She stifled a smile as Churchill wiggled to sit upright in the bed like a chubby, pink, baby.

"Good morning, sir, a man is here from the Secret Service."

Churchill beckoned the man forward. "Good morning, Downwood, this is unexpected."

Downwood touched his thin moustache. "Sir, you will find an invitation from the Duke of Windsor among your letters. I have it on the best authority; German agents will be waiting for you at his villa. I advise you return to England immediately." He twitched while he waited for a response. He saw his proximity to Churchill as an opportunity for promotion into the orbit of men with power.

Churchill grunted and put down his papers. He reached over to the side of the bed and rang a bell to summon the maid. He sat back upright in the bed. "Thank you, Downwood, I will follow your advice with all haste."

Downwood turned to leave, staring just a little too long at Churchill's young secretary. She was striking, her dark-blue suit revealing voluptuous curves and setting off her strawberry blonde hair.

4

Churchill slipped out of bed and walked over to the window. "Thompson, I need Thompson. Send him a telegram. Ask him to meet me at Croydon Aerodrome the day after tomorrow. Oh, and tell the staff we're leaving immediately."

"Yes, sir." Miss Shearburn gathered up her notepad and rushed downstairs to the reception desk of the hotel and asked to use the telephone. She got a connection straight away. "Hello, may I speak to Mrs Pearman, please? Good morning, Mrs Pearman, it's Miss Shearburn. I've been asked by Mr Churchill to send a telegram to a Mr Thompson. Can you help?"

"Ah yes, just wait a minute while I look him up." Mrs Pearman flicked through an index file on her desk in London. "Yes, here he is," she said, running a finger down the card. "Inspector Walter Henry Thompson, Special Branch, Scotland Yard, retired three years ago after serving as Mr Churchill's bodyguard for 15 years. Seems he might have had a change of career because his home address is Thompson's Grocers, Beulah Hill, Norwood. I'll take down the telegram and send it from here if you like."

Downwood stood listening at the end of the reception desk. "Thompson?" he mumbled to himself. "He calls for Thompson – a damn grocer."

***

Later, as she was accompanying Churchill in the car on the way to the aerodrome at Evreux, Miss Shearburn concentrated on tidying up the scribbled dictation she had taken. She was relieved when Churchill stopped talking and rolled down the window to look at the fields of grain undulating in the sunshine.

His eyes were moist, and his head dropped.

Miss Shearburn put down her notebook and looked at him. She waited for him to speak. She had become familiar with his *black dog* depression days, but this was different – worse. Her heart pounded as she waited a long 30 minutes for him to speak.

His voice was low like distant thunder. "Before the corn is gathered in, we shall be at WAR."

***

5

4 July – Thompson's grocery shop, Beulah Hill, Norwood, South London

The clatter from outside the shop alerted Walter to Bernie's return from making the morning deliveries. Walter's tall, freckly nephew had inserted pieces of stiff card between the spokes of the shop's bike to make it sound like the motorbike he imagined owning. Though Walter was a few inches taller than Bernie, their physical resemblance was becoming more marked every day. They both had handsome, symmetrical faces with high cheekbones and smooth skin. Local people often thought Bernie was Walter's son rather than his nephew.

Thompson's grocery store was on Beulah Hill, a road parallel to the main A23 London to Brighton road. The street was lined with large, red brick Victorian houses. Walter's store was in a parade of local shops in lower middle-class England.

Bernie fell through the door. "Uncle, Uncle – a telegram." He thrust the envelope at Walter.

Walter took the envelope and placed it on the counter, staring at it as though contaminated. This was the second telegram he had received in his life – the first, a few stark words to inform him his father was dead. From that day, he had stepped in as a father for his two younger sisters and nephew.

In his innocent excitement, Bernie pressed on. "Well… well…?" He was sixteen and had no idea telegrams only ever brought bad news. "Aren't you going to read it? I've never seen a telegram before."

Walter thought hard. He took a long breath, smoothed back his hair, and stood to his full six feet. "Who could be dead?"

"Dead uncle?"

"Did I just say that aloud? No, no one. Kate's in the parlour, Stella's at home getting ready for her wedding on Sunday, you're flapping around in front of me. Your mum is next door in the tobacconist. We're all present and correct…our little family. Well, all right then. Go and park your bike round the back of the shop and we'll take a look with your aunt Kate."

The smell of baking wafted from the parlour and travelled around the shop.

"I think it's time for tea." Walter smiled at Kate as he entered. "Young Bernie has met the postman at the top of the hill and brought me a telegram."

Kate, a petite, fair-haired woman of 47 with a flawless complexion and a heart shaped face was at the sink. "Oh, my goodness, I'll put the kettle on. If in doubt brew up, eh?" She wore a home-sewn cotton dress covered with a crisp white pinafore tied in a bow. She had been married to Walter for 25 years and now Walter was retired, they were enjoying their precious time together.

Kate placed three art-deco cups and saucers on the table next to a vase of summer flowers. "There, doesn't that look beautiful?"

"Ahh – but not as beautiful as you." Walter reached for his wife.

Kate knew his moves and slipped under his arm, stroking it as she passed. "Ooo... and you too, dear." She blew little kisses from a distance across the room. "I've got some scones in the oven, would you like one?" Walter winked at her and gave her his winning smile.

Bernie came in through the back door.

Kate stifled a giggle, hiding her flushed cheeks from her young nephew.

Walter waited until the tea had been poured before opening the telegram. Bernie's eyes widened.

Walter read the message aloud:
"MEET ME - CROYDON AERODROME 4:30 PM WEDNESDAY. CHURCHILL."

"Strange order for a grocer." Walter smiled, attempting to lighten what he knew would be a difficult moment.

"What does that man want?" Kate's hand shook as she took a sip of sweet tea.

Bernie gulped his drink and stood up to leave. "What Mr Churchill who used to show us films?"

"The very same." Walter folded the paper.

Kate sat rigid and narrowed her eyes. "But surely he knows you've retired from Special Branch. They can't make you go back now, can they?" She took a cotton handkerchief from her apron pocket. "And we've only just become a family again…. After all, it's Stella and Martin's wedding at the weekend. Your little sister will be Mrs Martin Gold."

Walter reached across the dining table and took her hand. "I feel like a proud father – young Stella married. Ah that reminds me – I've been talking with Martin's father…"

The shop bell rang and Stella, Walter's baby sister burst through the door with an orange crate full of linen serviettes. She entered the parlour and set them down on the dining table. "Morning family…" She was petite and pretty with long fair hair and bright blue eyes. "Sorry to barge in. I have to fold all these into swans for the wedding. Any helpers?"

Bernie cut in, not wanting to be late for his final day at school: "Ugh – not me. I'll be off then, Auntie and Uncle. Tell us what ol' Mr Churchill wanted when I come in on Thursday."

Kate opened the oven and took out the scones. "Any exams today, Bernie?"

"*Mais oui,*" called Bernie mounting his bike. "French oral. What good'll that be – waste of time …." He breathed in the aroma from baking. "May I take one of those to school with me?"

Kate put two scones in a brown paper bag and handed them to Bernie at the back door. "Try your best Bernie. You never know when a language might come in handy."

Stella folded a serviette. "See it's easy."

Walter picked it up, unfolded it and pretended to blow his nose on it.

Stella feigned a punch at him and laughed. "You beast. It's all that the Golds would let me do towards the wedding – so I'm going to do it well."

"I'll help you." Kate passed Walter a scone. "Would you like one of these first?"

"No, I can't I have to get to work. But I'll be back at six if you don't mind giving me a hand." Stella kissed Kate and feigned another punch at her brother before dashing out the door.

Walter buttered one of the hot scones. "Come and sit with me a moment. My love, I've been looking at the accounts, and frankly, the shop's not doing very well. When we went to Brighton to meet Stella's future in-laws, Mr Gold – Ludovic – made me a proposition. The upshot is there's a motor dealership and petrol station closed down next to his bus garage. I've just found out the rent is less than we pay here…for this shop."

"But if it's closed down, surely business can't be good?" Kate pulled away and began washing the teacups.

Walter walked over to her and held her around her waist while she clanked the cups in the sink. "Ah yes, but Ludovic has guaranteed us the sale of fuel for all his buses and taxis if we take it on."

"I'm not sure, Walter what about your sister? Emily and Bernie will struggle here without us."

"Ah, there's a very large car showroom, with two flats above it. Enough room for us all. I could mend and re-sell some second-hand motorbikes." He kissed her neck and she stopped her work. "No one can afford a car these days and I've always loved tinkering with my own bikes. Just think of it – you and I paddling on Brighton Beach after work each day, sharing a plate of cockles."

"Oh Walter, that would be a dream come true. I never liked the thought of Stella leaving us to live in Brighton." She turned and gave Walter a teasing kiss on the lips. "How big is that showroom? Could part of it be divided off for a café for the drivers and waiting passengers?"

Walter kissed her on the forehead. "What brains you've got in there. And with the two flats. We can take Emily and Bernie with us and make it a real family business. We've all been upset by the thought of losing my little sister. This way we can have a small business next to the Golds' successful transport company and keep the family together."

They were interrupted by the shop bell. "Customers, my dear, and I still haven't finished putting the new stock up on the shelves." Walter blew a kiss for Kate.

As he turned to enter the shop, she caught his arm. He stopped and pulled her towards him. He lifted her on to the dining table and planted the smallest of kisses on her lips before making his escape.

Four women shuffled around in the shop, looking at the unpacked boxes, waiting to be served.

"My apologies, ladies. May I help you?"

"No, no, Mr Thompson, we're quite content to wait and see what you've had delivered," said one of the women. "We know you're a very busy man."

Walter took off his tie, unfastened the top button of his shirt and removed the stiff white collar. He took care in removing his silver cufflinks and rolling up his sleeves, revealing his tanned muscular arms.

He climbed a wooden ladder to place tins on the high shelves. The women studied him. "Lovely day, Mr Thompson," said one of the women.

"Yes, very nice, Mrs Spencer." Walter climbed down the ladder. "May I serve you now?"

The women gave each other little nudges when he bent over to retrieve goods for them. Having made their purchases, one by one they left the shop and waited outside for each other.

"He's always so polite," whispered one woman.

"Huh, he's got no eyes for you," another replied.

"Why do you say that?"

"Oh, he never reacts to your little suggestive remarks."

Kate shut the door to the shop to drown out the giggling women. It was lunchtime and she turned the sign to read CLOSED and lowered the blind.

Walter pulled her towards him. Kate tried to wriggle free, but she was trapped within the circle of his arms. Walter nibbled her neck.

"How would you like a toffee apple on the seafront tonight? We could take a sneak look at the garage and take a proper look on Sunday, after the wedding reception."

"Oh Walter, can I please go and tell Emily and Bernie? They'll be so excited at the news." Kate kissed his cheek. "I'll just be a few minutes – back in time to make your lunch and anything else you may need." She blew him a second kiss as she slid from his grip and removed her apron in one smooth action to head for the door.

Once alone, Walter reached down and rubbed his shin, where the bone had been chipped in a fight with a thug. He had retired from the police force in 1935 with an annual pension of £207.07.

His career had begun in 1911 and had ended with the last fifteen years guarding Winston Churchill as his personal bodyguard. He took out the telegram in his pocket and reread it. *Perhaps the Old Man only wants me to run an errand for him.*

***

5 July – Croydon Aerodrome

Walter stood at the edge of the runway. He watched as the Paris plane came to a stop in front of him.

Out bounded, Churchill like a Bull Terrier. Walter noticed he had lost a little more hair, but his round face was rosy with health for his 65 years. Despite the glow of his skin, his expression was grim.

Walter held out his hand to greet his old boss as he walked towards him.

"Hello, Thompson." Churchill shook Walter's hand, without missing a stride. "Good to see you. Get the baggage together and bring it on with you to Chartwell, there's a good man." He opened the back door of a waiting car - clambered in and followed by Miss Shearburn in his wake. The car roared away.

A second car drew forward. Walter had his arms full of Churchill's cases and boxes and put them in the trunk. He slid into the passenger seat next to the driver. "George! By George – George." Walter gripped his former sergeant's large, flabby hand. "I thought you were living up in Scotland."

He noticed George's short brown hair was showing signs of grey at the temples, but his large brown eyes still flashed with mischief.

His wide face beamed as he slapped Walter on the back. "You've still got a handshake like a bloody vice, Inspector."

"How the devil *are* you, George, enjoying your retirement?"

"Well, thanks and no I'm bored to bits. So 'ow's the grocery trade going, then? Enjoying a booming business?" George pulled away from the aerodrome.

"Well… no good trying to pull the wool over your eyes, George. It's not been going well at all. But we are interested in a new business – a garage in Brighton."

"Blimey, you always were a bit of grease monkey with that ol' bike of yours."

"Yes, it's bikes I want to repair and re-sell. Kate and I are both very excited. What's all this about, then?"

George's face clouded. "Ah – well, it seems we're back in business."

"What? You mean you're working with the Old Man again?"

"Yep, he wants the old team back. And he wants his favourite son to take care of him – you, Walter."

"Well there's no need to be the jealous, little brother, because I'm not coming back. He doesn't need me anyhow. He's not even a Member of Parliament at the moment."

"Doesn't seem to bloomin' well matter to the Old Man's enemies. The Nazis want him brown bread." George drew his index finger across his throat, causing the car to swerve.

"George." Walter grabbed the wheel.

"What, lost the nerve for a bit of excitement, Inspector?" George swerved the car again.

"Ha, you're like a breath of fresh air."

George smiled. "Not changed too much then, 'ave I?"

"Well it looks like you've still been able to stuff yourself with apple pie while I've been away. If you're back working for the Old Man, I hope he's got a decent cook – or you'll be high tailing it back to Scotland."

"You cheeky basket. Think I've got a bit fat, do you?" George veered the car again.

"Still practicing your stunt driving, George." You could have been a racing driver with those skills."

The sun shone on the tree-lined roads leading from Croydon to Chartwell.

"So, Inspector, are you ready to go back to work?"

"I don't think so, George. I'm too old and rusty since I retired – and just so you remember, I am still ex-Inspector Thompson to you."

"Fine, ex-Inspector. For your information I'm retired too, but 'ere I am, driving a car for the Old Man again. I got a call last week, and quite frankly, with the trouble and strife gone off with another man and children grown up. I'm glad to be back in service."

"Oh George, I'm sorry."

"Nah – it was 3 years ago – but I don't like being on me own. This job suits me just fine."

"Who's paying you?"

"The Old Man – three quid a week from his own pocket. But it wasn't me 'e wanted guarding him.'

"No?"

"No – you know very well what I'm talking about. He knows if has me, he might be able to lure you away from the grocery trade."

Walter let out a small sigh.

"I don't wanna steal the Old Man's thunder, but he's just run back from France. Got a tip-off some of Hitler's agents were planning to knock him off at the Duke of Windsor's place. I've seen the latest intelligence reports. Hitler's far more worried about Churchill than 'e is about the Prime Minister."

"Well, I suppose that's where Hitler and I do agree."

"Remember those famous words last time 'e was voted out?" George lowered his voice in a comical rendition of Churchill's accent. "In the twinkling of an eye, I found myself without an office, without a seat, without a party and without an appendix." George chuckled. "So, d'yer care enough about the Old Man to come back, ex-Inspector?"

"Well, he's sharp and critical but it's all a façade. I'd like to try and help him, but I think I've done my bit. I'm the only man left in our little family, and I've been acting as an honorary father to both Stella and Bernie. I have to admit, I quite like the quiet life. And now there's the possibility of our new garage to get under way."

"Well, good for you, ex-Inspector. I, on the other hand, am a loyal guard dog." George let out a long, low howl. Walter laughed and patted him on the head.

George brought the car to an abrupt halt on the short gravel drive in front of Churchill's country home. The large, red brick-gabled house was quite ugly, but Churchill had been captivated by the grounds from the moment he set eyes on the valley. It was sheltered by tall, beech woods to the south, and commanded sweeping views over the Weald of Kent. By far the house's best feature was the terrace, which was set high up, with a magnificent view over the rolling hills.

Before Churchill bought this extravagant house, Walter had accompanied him on several long walks to survey the land. *New hedges in here, Thompson. We can divert this channel, dig out this little bog, and put in a pool.*

Walter felt a twinge in his back as he looked over at the swimming pool. He remembered excavating it by hand with Churchill by his side, giving commands and helping by emptying the wheelbarrow.

He surveyed the huge expanses of grass. *I want several acres of perfect lawn, Thompson – please get up early and see to it.*

Walter had groaned at the time, but in truth he had enjoyed the hard work and exercise that kept his body in good shape. He glanced over to the trees in front of the house and shook his head as he recalled one of his many arguments with Churchill about security. *I just can't protect you here, sir, from any sniper from the south – the hill and the trees provide excellent cover for anyone breaching security. Surely there are many other fine houses that would at least give me a fair chance of keeping you in one piece.*

He walked around the side of the house and entered the property through the door into the walled garden. He glanced at the familiar low garden wall Churchill had attempted to build. Churchill had claimed the wall as his own, but Walter had instructed the masons to demolish the precarious structure and re-build it straight and even. Walter smiled as he pictured the bricklayers loitering, smoking, and striking up conversations about nothing, in an attempt to look innocent.

***

Churchill waved from the French windows: "Thompson. Thompson."

"I think I'll go and find a cup o' tea," mumbled George, and disappeared through the back door of the house.

"Come on up to my study," Churchill commanded.

Walter followed him into the house and up the wide, oak staircase to the office. Churchill stood behind his desk and leaned forward with both palms on his blotter. "I've tried to warn the world that the Germans are building a mighty army. It's so big it could only be used for one purpose – invasion – war, Thompson. I was on my way to visit the Duke of Windsor, but I was warned there was a trap awaiting me, so I returned home. I have arranged for you to have a full briefing." Churchill paused to stare at Walter for a moment, "No one's listening to me – it's only 21 years since the last war and people don't want to think there could be another one. The only person who has listened to my warnings is Adolf Hitler and now he's trying to kill me. I need your help Thompson. I can look after myself in the daytime, but will you protect me at night?"

Walter stared at the high, wooden, vaulted ceiling, searching for an answer.

Churchill babbled on. "I know you have retired and returned to your wife, and I wouldn't ask – but it's just I can't cope with having to have someone new at my age. You know my peculiar ways – and we get on well, don't we, Thompson?"

"Of course, sir."

"Fine. Five pounds a week, then."

"But…."

"Look, could you just help me out at night? It won't interfere with your shop business."

"Sir, I can help you just for a couple of weeks, until you can find someone younger you like. George will have to cover for me on the weekend. My little sister is getting married and I hope Kate and I will be moving to Brighton. I'm too old and too slow to be of any real use to you."

"Fine – fine. You'd better go and see my secretary for my Colt 45."

Walter looked Churchill in the eye then shook his hand.

15

"Good man. No need to start until tomorrow."

Walter found his way to a tiny office on the ground floor. As he opened the door, he recognised the young attractive woman who had been on the plane with Churchill.

She pulled a sheet of paper from her typewriter. "Can I help you?"

"Mr Churchill says you're holding a gun for me."

"And you are…?"

"I am ex-Inspector Walter Thompson."

"Well, if you are Inspector Thompson, you must have the telegram I sent to you."

Walter produced the telegram but held onto it as she attempted to take it from him. "And you are…?"

"I am Miss Shearburn, Inspector Thompson but everyone calls me Bunny." She retrieved the gun from her drawer and handed it to him. "And your friends call you…?"

"Every time they need me – Miss Shearburn."

"A Mr Downwood is waiting in the dining room for you," she called after him.

Walter entered the dining room without knocking and extended his hand to the pint size Downwood. "Hello there, Mr Churchill said you would be giving me a full briefing." He placed his hand on a chair to sit down.

"Is that how you address a senior officer? Stand to attention, Mr Thompson." Downwood opened a file and began to read aloud:

Thompson, Walter Henry, born Brixton, London 1890, son of an insurance agent, one of 13 children. Father – Presbyterian. Mother…

"…whatever was written here has been removed. Do you want to elaborate, Thompson?"

"No thank you."

Downwood gave Walter a long hard stare and continued to read aloud.

"Your formal schooling ended at age 14; when you worked as a post-office messenger boy. Awarded a silver watch for bravery in 1908 and joined the police force."

He paused and looked up at Walter. "Bit handy with your fists, eh Thompson? Saved a police constable from some thugs. Chased

16

around some suffragettes in 1913. Somehow you managed to get yourself into Special Branch. How did someone of your lowly background achieve that?"

Walter put on his rigid face. He had been here before – bullied by people who thought they were superior. "Will that be all, sir?"

"No, it will not. I see you caught a few spies in the Great War – then was assigned personal protection duty, first to Lloyd George and then to Winston Spencer Churchill. Retired in 1935."

Downwood paused and closed Walter's file. "Well, the Old Man might want you, but I for one can see little benefit in having someone of your background on the team. I will pass any information I have on to Mr Churchill. It will be his decision if he wants to keep the other ranks informed."

Walter studied the tiny man. *Good grief, if this is the best they can send to protect Churchill – I'd better take the job.* He leaned forward and took Downwood's hand. "Thank you. I'll start straight away."

Downwood snatched his hand away. "I haven't finished…"

Walter laughed. "Oh, you're finished – I'll let Mr Churchill know." He left the room to find George.

George was outside the blonde secretary's office. "Well, he didn't bring everyone out of retirement." George nudged Walter and pointed at the door. "Mrs Hall, the old battle-axe, has been replaced by a newer, younger and far more attractive model."

"Yes, we've met. I must say, it was a bit of a shock. I was expecting Mrs Hall. And that's a bit unkind of you, George – Mrs Hall was a treasure."

"A national treasure – should 'ave been in a museum."

"I've just had a run in with an irritating little man called Downwood."

"Oh, you've accepted the job then?" George heaved a sigh.

"No, I've been cornered into two weeks' night-guard duty – that's all."

"Ha ha. Well, take no notice of Downwood. He's an upper-class twit. It put his toffee nose right out of joint when the Old Man insisted on 'aving you. He wanted to look after the Old Man himself. Don't worry 'e's got on everyone's nerves – I've stuck some eye wash in his tea – he'll be shitting through the eye of a needle by lunch time."

***

6 and 7 July – Chartwell and Norwood

For the next two nights, after the grocery business had closed for the day, Walter was assigned to Chartwell, where he met George at the gate to take over the duty.

George handed him the gun. "Glad to see you… I'm bored brainless 'ere."

Walter inspected the firearm to make sure it was in working order and slipped it into the holster of his double-breasted jacket.

"What's up? I 'aven't seen a boat race like that since the Old Man said goodbye to you back in '35."

"Oh… George…."

"Best get it off yer chest you know."

Walter sighed. "It's Kate … the poor woman has waited for me to come home to her for almost 20 years, and now here I am again, playing amateur detective – how bloody stupid." He straightened the line of his jacket, smoothing down the bulge of the holster. "Oh, and by the way – you'll have to cover for me this weekend. Stella's getting married…in Brighton."

"Your little skin and blister, Stella, blimey, 'ow old is she now?"

"She's 24 and quite a stunner."

George smiled. "Sure, I'll cover for yer. I'd rather come to the wedding, though. Give me a chance to drink all yer booze."

"Not my booze, George. Stella's marrying into a wealthy family and they insist on paying for everything. It's going to be some big affair. I feel a bit sad I could've only provided a modest wedding for her but her new family seem really nice. It's them who've invited us to open the garage."

"I see. Well, just remember to bring your old mate a bit o' cake."

"I should have told the Old Man 'no' in the first place…." Walter patted the gun in the holster again and turned to leave.

"You just did your best, ol' chap…."

His words were lost as Walter stomped off around the grounds.

***

It was a humid August evening. Walter pulled at his tie, but his stiff white collar kept his body heat simmering inside the shirt. He gazed out over the Weald, watching as the dim blueness of the landscape glistened in the twilight on the lake's surface.

An aircraft buzzed over Chartwell, heading for Croydon. Walter took in the whole view. *If there's a war, Chartwell will be far too conspicuous from the air.*

He roamed the grounds, staring up at the ponderous mansion with its tile-hung gables, pokey windows and creepers covering the walls. It could be climbed by almost anyone – an assailant would have no trouble accessing Churchill's bedroom via the shrubbery. What was worse, the hillside was overrun by purple rhododendron, providing wonderful cover for any would-be assassin with a rifle.

Walter remembered the long days he had previously spent protecting the Old Man. He visualised the faces of the people who had tried to kill Churchill in the past. He had an exceptional photographic memory and never forgot a face or where he had seen the person. Special Branch had accepted him because of his extraordinary ability to recognise a possible assailant. He made a study of everyone's ears, noticing no two people shared the same pattern of indents and curves. He pictured the face and ears of Michael Collins's IRA assassin, the Terrorists in Egypt, an Asian gunman in Chicago, and an Italian taxi driver who had run Churchill down in New York.

Walter laughed at himself when he awoke from his daydream and saw he was pointing Churchill's gun at the Weald of Kent.

At 04:00 am, George came back to relieve him. Walter returned to the shop at dawn and slept until eleven.

Kate stopped her work and gave Walter the *look* as he came through the door. "What exactly are you doing at Chartwell?" She stood at the counter mixing water, yeast, and flour into dough.

Walter gave her a little smile. "Just for the minute, I'm Churchill's unofficial armed bodyguard, patrolling round the quiet Kentish countryside, ready to pounce on any would-be Nazi murderer." His smile widened. "Or an armed hedgehog, if the need arises."

"Oh, well, if it helps him prevent a war and it makes you happy, dear," Kate pummelled the dough on the marble counter.

"Look, Kate, I'm sorry…."

Kate smudged flour on her cheek as she wiped away a tear. "I know."

"It's just for a few more days…."

"But you are supposed to be retired."

"I'll tell Churchill I'm resigning tomorrow, if that's what you want."

"And then what? You'll feel guilty for not doing your duty, for not fulfilling your promise."

"It's just until Thursday and then he'll find someone else." Walter pulled her close to him and his immaculate suit was dusted in flour. "Churchill's not an important political figure anymore. But he's frightened, and I can give him a bit of comfort by being around."

"I know. I just want you to be the bobby on the beat that I first married." She slammed the dough on the counter. "He only wants you, you know, because he knows you'll step in front of the bullet that's meant for him."

Walter stiffened and held her away from him. "Darling, I'm far too slow to get there in time. Besides, the Germans may have been able to try something in France, but they are hardly likely to turn up in Kent."

CHAPTER 2
Stella - A Rolls Royce and Transport for Evacuees

8 July – Abraham Gold's Brighton townhouse

Abraham Gold paced around the room in a series of small circles. He took out a large handkerchief from underneath his frock coat and wiped perspiration from his forehead. "Martin, my wonderful grandson, come in, come in."

Martin Gold caught his reflection in the large mirror over the 17th century fireplace. He smoothed the jacket of his Savile Row morning suit preparing himself for what could be a difficult conversation on the eve of his wedding.

Abraham halted and picked up the fire tongs. "May I take a few minutes, Martin, firstly to offer you my blessings for your marriage? Stella has studied hard and Rabbi Silverthorne is content with her conversion to our religion."

"Well, thank you, Grandfather, your approval means the world to us both." Martin sat down on one of the high-backed fireside chairs. "We'll be making a fresh start in Paris with The South Downs Bus Company. I'm really honoured to have a part of the business to run."

"We Jews consider the wedding day the happiest and holiest day of one's life – for on this day all past mistakes are forgiven as the bride and groom merge together as one soul. Paris is a beautiful city – a city for lovers. But I have some concerns."

Martin wiped an imaginary bead of sweat from his brow while he waited for Abraham to continue.

His grandfather began to pace again. "I'm just not sure if now's the right time for you to go to Paris. My old bones tell me something's not right. Look, Martin, things happened to our family in Lithuania years ago. We had to get out. And now look how our relatives are suffering in Berlin. Cousin Silverman's London home is full of people who just got on the first boat out.

Ačiū Dievui – thanks be to God; we are safe in England. I'm just not sure Paris will be so safe for you. Jews are being murdered in Germany. And Germany is only next door."

"I've read the papers, Grandfather. But I'll be in Paris, not Berlin – and it's not as if Stella and I couldn't take one of our coaches to a port and come home if necessary."

"I love you, Martin; I'm only concerned for your safety." Grandfather Gold raised his palms to the ceiling. "God give me wisdom." The old man looked at Martin's face, so eager and determined. "Please can you just promise me, if there's trouble, you will come home?"

"Grandfather, we'll be back in a flash, at the first sign of danger – you have my assurance."

They embraced. "May God love you and always protect you, my dear Martin, my only grandson."

***

The wedding service was held at sundown, beginning with the Jewish ritual of Havdalah to mark the end of the Sabbath.

The wedding reception was held the next day in The Grand Hotel on Brighton seafront. Stella wore a white silk couture-wedding gown, cascading to the floor.

Before they sat down at the top table, Martin held her at arms' length and took a long look at her. Her shoulder-length brown hair framed her perfect features. He took in the gentle curves of her slim figure, accentuated by her fitted dress. Martin kissed her hand. "Mrs Gold you are my very own film star."

Stella blushed and took a little curtsy.

Walter walked across the room and smiled. "Mother and Father would be overwhelmed with joy if they could see you today. Your happiness is shining on all of us."

Stella kissed Walter on the cheek and folded back the sleeve of her dress to reveal a patch of white lace she had sown there from their mother's wedding gown.

Martin took in a deep breath as the Master of Ceremonies called the chattering wedding party to silence. He fished in his pocket for the piece of paper he had scribbled some notes on for his speech. *I should have talked this speech through with Stella's family first. What if they're cross with me? But how could Stella not love Paris? And how could Paris not love her?*

Stella whispered. "Anything you say will be just fine. I love you dearly." She fiddled with her linen serviette she had folded into a swan. Martin's mother had frowned when she had seen her earlier undertaking the task in place of the staff. Stella explained the swans gave the wedding her personal touch – her mother had taught her how to fold them – and it was a pleasure to make each one.

"My darling – My *Neshama...*" Martin began his speech thanking everyone and revealing his plans to open a continental travel business run from Paris.

Stella twisted her hands together in her lap. She looked across the room and studied each one of her family. Walter looked stunned. Kate was gripping Walter's hand. Bernie mouthed "No." Bernie's mother, Emily, dropped her head in her hands.

The wedding guests cheered, and Walter jumped to his feet to show support. He held out his hand for Kate, who rose as if in a trance.

Sid Millward and his band struck up *Someday Sweetheart*. Stella walked with Martin to the dance floor and the guests applauded. She pulled in close to him and tried to lose herself in his arms as they danced. She felt dizzy as the room moved in slow motion – thoughts swirled around in her mind. Her passion for Martin and her love for her family seemed to be on opposite sides of the room and her eyes moistened as she had no idea how to bring the two together. *Perhaps I should have broken this to them earlier. But then I would have had a week of Kate and Emily sobbing and Walter and Bernie slamming doors.*

Walter touched Kate's hand, which was shaking as she drank her champagne. He leaned forward and kissed her on the cheek. He noticed Emily was drying her eyes and Bernie had vanished. He walked over to Emily and held out his hand for her. She rose slowly and clung to him as they danced. "So, my dearest sister, when will you be free for a trip to Paris? How about we give them a month?"

"Oh, Walter that would be wonderful. But how will we afford it?" She held a strong resemblance to her brother and younger sister but was a little overweight – being an excellent cook and having a hungry boy to bring up on her own had seen to that.

"Now don't worry – we'll have a big sale and sell off all the old stock from the shop."

The band struck up the new Glenn Miller number, *In the Mood*. Martin embraced Stella and they danced a quickstep. Walter kissed Emily's hand as she sat down and offered his other hand to Kate. *This is going to be a busy night if I'm going to keep both these ladies happy and the waterworks at bay.*

As he danced with his wife, his eyes took in the description of every face in the room. *Old habits die hard – I should switch off.*

Meanwhile, in the downstairs hotel bar, Bernie gave a half wave to the barman. He hated to think of his Aunt Stella going further away – after all, she was like his sister – or no, more than that – his best friend.

He forced a smile as a weary-looking bartender took his money and gave him a tall pint without questioning his age. Bernie stood by the bar, keeping one eye open for his uncle. When he thought the coast was clear he turned to find a bar stool, slopping his beer over a young man in a bad suit.

Bernie began to sputter apologies. "Sorry, mate. I'm Bernie, the bride's nephew… I don't want to upset the new in-laws… let me get you a drink."

"Johnny Smith," said the boy, shaking Bernie's hand with a sparkle in his eyes. "No bloody relative at all – I'm a mate of a mate of a mate of the groom. Oh, and don't worry about me ol' dad's suit. Mum'll have it pawned again by Monday night."

Johnny was a good four inches smaller than Bernie, but muscular and athletic, with a handsome angular face, bright-blue eyes, and fair hair.

"Here, let me get you a pint then." Bernie checked his own suit over for beer stains.

"Are you sure yer old enough to get served?"

"Well, no – but just now I waited for the old boy there to come over. His eyesight's not so good. What's your poison?"

Johnny flashed a smile. "I'll have a beer please, mate – same as yours is fine."

Bernie gave the barman another wave. "A pint of your best bitter, please."

A wedding guest pushed open the door to the bar, shouting to the young men who had escaped the formality of the banqueting suite. "Come on, everyone, the bride and groom are leaving."

"Where d'yer think they're off to then?"

"Didn't you listen? They're going to Paris, and probably not damn well coming back." Bernie slammed his pint down on an empty table and stormed off.

"I only bloody asked." Johnny took a large gulp of the free drink he had artfully acquired and moved Bernie's unfinished pint to rest in front of him on the bar.

Bernie walked alone along the seafront, kicking stones. He kicked a large one and bent down to rub his throbbing foot.

Martin and Stella left in their hired Rolls Royce for the next ferry to France. Everywhere people were weeping and applauding, shouting, "Good luck. *Mazel tov. L'chaim.* To Life."

Walter held Kate on one arm and Emily on the other. "Good luck and good fortune my little sister. We all love you." *We love you enough to let you go.*

Kate and Emily were sobbing.

Walter produced a clean white handkerchief for each one. "Come on now. If the new business turns out well, we'll be taking a trip to Paris before you know…."

Bernie walked for an hour along the beach. The moon reflected in the surf and he took large gulps of salt air and fought back his waterworks.

***

1 August – 4th floor apartment, Rue Séguier, Paris, France

Stella and Martin rolled on the thick living-room rug, entwined together.

From the street, Pierre could see shadows through steamy windows. The moonlight streamed in from the large oval skylight. He waited.

The curtains moved, letting in a cooling breeze that stroked their naked bodies as they lay on the floor. Martin kissed her lips, face and hair, consumed by her beauty and the warmth of her skin. He caressed her breasts. His touch was sensual, and he was patient. The stimulation became more intimate and Stella's desire was burning.

She turned over and sat astride his toned abdomen. She arched her back and her body tingled as she reached a plateau. Martin stopped moving below her and she pulsed with her need for him. She took on the work, rising and falling with determination. She rode him until her nipples became erect and crinkled with the intensity of her orgasm. She allowed the luxurious sensations to sweep over her body.

Martin let go – his body kicked up in spasm. They held each other until their raised pulses ticked to a regular beat.

A sharp knock at the door made them both jump up. Martin moved first, throwing Stella his shirt while struggling to put on his trousers. He opened the door a few inches.

"Pardon, Monsieur." A Catholic priest stood at the door. "May I come in?"

"It's a bit late Father." Martin looked round to check that Stella had gone to the bedroom.

The priest, glanced from side to side, concerned that someone from a neighbouring apartment might overhear. "*C'est une question de grande urgence, Monsieur.* A matter of great urgency."

Martin checked again inside the room. Stella had left. "All right, come in."

"It's about your auto-coaches."

"Oh, well, if it's about transport, I have an office on the Rue du Lattre. Please make an appointment any time between 8 am and 6 pm." Martin started ushering the priest back towards the door.

"Oh *monsieur*, please, may I speak with you now. It is very urgent. It's a life or death matter and I have no-one else to ask."

Stella appeared dressed in a beige silk robe. "Hello, can we offer you some refreshment, father?"

"That is very kind. I am rather partial to your scotch whiskey if you have any."

"Well you're in luck, we had a bottle of single malt as a wedding present and since we don't drink spirits, it would be lovely if a whiskey drinker was to sample it." Stella retrieved the bottle from the sideboard and looked over to Martin. He shook his head, so Stella poured a generous measure for Pierre.

Pierre sipped his drink and took a moment to enjoy the taste. "I'm afraid this is not a mere social call." The priest sat on the sofa, holding the glass with two hands. He had been told the man was of Jewish origin, and expected him to be sympathetic, but he was unsure of the woman. Both were well spoken and appeared to be very English, and perhaps a bit naïve about world affairs. "My name is Father Pierre Picard; I work for a French society that co-operates with a Jewish organisation to help Jews who are trying to leave Germany. I have come to appeal for your help with arranging travel for the Jews during this terrible time of persecution against our people." He paused.

Stella topped up Pierre's glass.

Whether she was a Jew or not, he knew he had grasped her attention with his initial statement.

Martin's frown lines deepened.

Stella slunk into a chair beside Martin. He reached for Stella's hand.

The priest looked nervous. "You may be aware that during the last year, thousands of Jews have fled from Germany. Many of them have come to France, even to Paris. Well… there are now some German children who are trapped at the border."

"Germans? I thought we were discussing Jews?"

"*Monsieur*, these are children and their parents - German Jewish children. I have reports of about 500, stuck at the border – which is now closed. We need to get them out. Every night, a few slip through, and it is my responsibility to arrange their transport to a safe location."

"Is it really so bad in Germany that they need to evacuate their children to France?" Stella tucked her knees up on the chair.

The priest drained his glass. "Let me explain. Where shall I start? Hitler, the man the Germans call Führer, is determined to persecute the Jews. But many of his own people don't agree with him. His tactic is to stir up hatred against the Jews. After Kristallnacht last year, when Jewish shop owners had their windows and bones broken, those Jews who still had money and somewhere to go, ran. But it was becoming very difficult for them to get into other countries. Others had more to lose; Germany was their home. I am here because I need to hire your coaches to help transport these refugees away from Germany and to safety in a neutral country. We have been helping them get to Switzerland and Spain, but the numbers have increased, and we need more transport. It is very urgent we do this now."

"Father Picard, we are new here ourselves – and we are trying to set up a business for a profit, not run a charity. Why not seek help from your church? This is a very dangerous mission you're asking us to get involved in. Besides, the company is not just my own; it also belongs to my family back in England." Martin looked at Stella for support. But Stella squeezed his hand and gave him an appealing look.

The priest sighed. "I am not associated with the Catholic Church. I am a Jew, just like you. I'm actually a schoolteacher, not a priest. But these robes allow me to access many people, as well as providing a disguise." Pierre stood up and to the amazement of both Martin and Stella, did a theatrical twirl to emphasise his point. "My own family were the first I helped. My cousins lived just across the border in Rœschwoog. I helped them leave, and they are staying with friends at Haguenau. I think I've grown fond of dressing up – but lately, *Monsieur*, it's become a serious job. It was your cousin, Ludis Silverman in London, who said you would be reliable."

"So, cousin Ludis is a secret agent?" Martin had suspected his cousin must have been involved in something clandestine. His home was full of *relatives* Martin had never heard of.

Pierre grinned and shrugged.

Stella squeezed Martin's hand. "I know Haguenau, it's lovely. I remember the forest – I went through there once with my brother, Walter when I was a child."

Pierre leaned forward to explain, "Fortunately, my family left the Bas-Rhin area when there was still time, when you could still at least take a few possessions. Now people are leaving with very little. We can pay you, *Madame et Monsieur*, but we don't have much money. By the way, you must keep my true identity a secret – no one in Paris knows I am Jewish or even my name. The real Pierre has given up the cloth, married a former nun and started a new life in America. He was a friend and it has done us both a favour to swap identities because I plan to stay here as long as I can to help my fellow Jews when the Germans invade."

Martin stood up. "Germans? Invade Paris?"

"The Germans have plans to control all of Europe, and it will not be long before they attack France like they have done to other neighbouring countries. They are stronger and more determined than our forces. They could even invade Paris within the year. Well, that's my prediction anyway, and I will feel safer in future if people say, *there goes Pierre the priest rather than, there goes Pierre the Jew*, when just a few hundred kilometres away, Jews are being broken and destroyed by a cruel German regime."

"Well, I hope your predictions are wrong, Monsieur Picard." Martin looked at Stella, expecting her to be nodding her head in agreement with him, but instead found her studying the Frenchman.

Pierre was young, about 25, with light-brown hair and a thin beard. He had high cheekbones and a fine, aquiline nose, with dark lashes that hooded deep-set green eyes. Stella mused to herself that if Pierre ever shaved off his beard, he would look quite attractive – and perhaps could be mistaken for a girl, if he ever needed to find an alternative disguise.

Martin touched Stella's hand, and she responded by giving her husband an earnest, pleading look. He knew that look – she wanted him to approve Pierre's request.

With a sigh, Martin nodded. "Yes, Pierre, I – I mean we – will help you. But I would prefer to discuss this with you as a business proposition in my office tomorrow. Can you come back then? Whatever time in working hours suits you best." He got up and opened the door for Pierre. "Don't worry about anyone overhearing us – I assure you; my office is very private."

Pierre could see that it was useless to attempt any further discussion and rose to leave. He turned to address each of them, bowing his head as he said, "Thank you for your hospitality, *Madame*. And until tomorrow, *Monsieur*."

Martin closed the door behind him. "Hmmm, Hitler invade Paris? Surely not. He only wants land in the East, what he calls *Lebensraum* – living space for his expanding population."

Stella was already working out in her head the logistics of transporting 500 people from the border, the number of busses needed, and the fuel required. She followed Martin to bed with a fierce look of determination on her face.

CHAPTER 3
Walter – WAR

1 September – Norwood

Kate stared unblinking at the words written in chalk on the newspaper stand: *State of Emergency Declared.* She stood rigid on the pavement. A blackbird chirruped from the cherry tree outside the shop. She remembered reading these same words 25 years earlier and the following day – the headline *WAR*.

Walter came up behind her and held her waist. "I'll have to report to the superintendent. When I retired, I signed an agreement saying I'd become a part time reserve policeman – if ever there was a national emergency. I hope they'll let me report to the Brighton station."

A tear trickled down Kate's cheek.

Walter led her back into the shop and turned the sign to *CLOSED*. "I'll probably have to go back in uniform. You always did like me in uniform…." He held her in his arms and let her sob until the ringing of the telephone disturbed them. Kate reached out and picked up the receiver. She listened to the operator and passed it to Walter.

"This is Walter Thompson."

"I am trying to connect you with Mr Churchill, sir," said the operator.

Churchill's voice boomed down the line: "Where have you been Thompson? I've been trying to reach you."

"In Brighton, sir, organising my new business, but I have to report for part-time uniform duty. I've sent you a brief note to explain."

"You don't need to bother about that. I've been through to the Commissioner. You now work for me, officially. I don't want anyone else. They've sent me all sorts of rubbish these past few weeks. I'm too long in the tooth to have new people around me. No need to report until tomorrow – you can choose your own staff."

Walter pulled Kate closer.

Kate's body began to shake with her tears. She sniffed them back. "There's going to be a war, isn't there?"

"I'm afraid you're probably right, old girl."

"Then I shan't be any worse off than any other wife whose husband goes off to fight then, shall I? Except most men your age would be on home front duty and I would know you'd be home for your supper at six." She jerked away from him and stood straight. "I just wish that blasted man would leave us alone."

***

3 September – Churchill's London apartments

The morning sun streamed through the Victorian sash window to Churchill's study. The polished wooden floors in his large Westminster flat were decorated with exquisite Turkish carpets, and paintings adorned every room.

Walter and George stood listening to the soothing *tick-tock* of Churchill's ponderous grandfather clock.

The staff were tiptoeing around and talking in whispers, waiting for news from Germany. Britain had sent Hitler an ultimatum at 9:00 am:

Get out of Poland or we will be at war.

Walter watched Churchill work.

At 11:00 am, just as the ultimatum was due to expire, Churchill jumped up and switched on the radio to listen to the news. There was absolute silence for Prime Minister, Neville Chamberlain's broadcast. He told a British nation on tenterhooks no answer had been received from the German government to Britain's demands. He ended with the words: "This country is now at war with Germany. We are ready."

"Ready? Are we, hell." mumbled George. He knew from overheard conversations in Churchill's office, Britain only had a small professional army, an out-of-date navy and an almost non-existent air force. *We are certainly not ready and not bloody able.* George stomped off to find a cup of tea and a slice of cake.

Churchill marched to the entrance of the flat and stared up into the sky like a warhorse scenting battle. Walter joined him, and together they listened to the deafening screech of an air-raid warning.

Walter covered his ears.

Churchill was transfixed. "You have to hand it to Hitler. The war is less than a half-hour old, and already he has bombers over London."

"We ought to proceed to the air raid shelter." Walter held open Churchill's coat for him.

Churchill grunted, but did not move.

Walter felt his pulse rising "If only to set an example to others, sir."

Churchill marched back inside the flat, picked up a bottle of brandy, and summoned his wife and staff.

Walter found himself face to face with Miss Shearburn. He moved to the left to let her pass and she moved in the same direction. He shuffled to the right and she stumbled into him.

Churchill marched on the spot, irritated his party had come to a halt. "Come along, now, Miss Shearburn, the Inspector wants us to set an example."

Walter took Miss Shearburn's elbow to lead her out. They caught up with Churchill, who was quick marching along the street to the underground bomb shelter set up for the local residents.

Down in the cellar, everyone huddled in silence and Churchill paced up and down. Miss Shearburn sat on a chair opposite Walter. He noticed her tense, elegant posture. But her face betrayed her fear: her pale green eyes were wide and unblinking.

Walter ground a small pebble stuck in his shoe into his foot as he worried. *Where are you Kate? Did you get to the shelter in good time?* He opened his leather wallet and slid out her photograph tucked behind his warrant card. *Stella you better be on your way back here. I don't want you in Paris with all this going on....*

"Damn it." Walter was completely alone. His boss and all the staff had left after the false alarm. Walter took the steps two at a time and ran down the street after him. *I'm too old for this job.*

As he dashed into the hall, the maid saw him and pointed up the stairs. Walter ran up three floors and found Churchill on the roof, scanning the sky for aircraft.

"Right then, Thompson – House of Commons, I think." Churchill pushed past his bodyguard and headed downstairs to get into the waiting car. Walter followed him, checking both rear doors were shut before taking his place next to George.

In the Common's chamber the session was about to begin. Churchill waited a few minutes as the Members took their seats. He rose to explain why the government had been unsuccessful in persuading the Germans to withdraw from their invasion of Poland. He praised the work British ministers had done to try to avoid a war. "In this solemn hour, it is a consolation to recall and to dwell upon our repeated efforts for peace. All have been ill-starred, but all have been faithful and sincere."

Outside in the car park, George and the other detectives exchanged the usual inconsequential chatter of those who spend most of their working days waiting for orders. When Walter emerged with Churchill, they dropped their half-smoked cigarettes onto the gravel and straightened up. Walter's position as Churchill's right-hand man kept him apart from his colleagues. But he held their unwavering respect for his professionalism and total recall. It was known that Walter could remember every day of his career in the police force and every criminal. He never forgot a face.

The guards stiffened in their boxes beside the front gate as the heavy iron grilles of Westminster Palace swung open.

George started the engine and turned to look at Churchill for instructions.

"10 Downing Street, George, please."

George waited in the car outside the residence of the Prime Minister for Churchill and Walter. *What job is the Old Man gonna get, I wonder?*

Churchill emerged from behind the black door with Walter and a gleam in his eye: "It's the Admiralty," adding with a chuckle, "a lot better than I thought. Oh, and Thompson – you are remaining with me permanently. I have arranged it with your Commissioner."

"What's that?" muttered George under his breath to Walter. "So, the Old Man's been put in charge of the navy yet again. Well, God help us all... people still blame 'im for all the lives lost at Gallipoli when he was in charge of the Admiralty during the last war. And as for you... so much for you going 'ome to the Missus."

Walter said nothing. *How will I explain this to Kate?*

Back in Churchill's apartment, Miss Shearburn was busy typing an announcement to all the national newspapers. She read it back to herself aloud, aware Walter was listening: "Inspector Walter Thompson has been reappointed as Mr Churchill's private bodyguard. No reference to this appointment must be made in the press. No photographs showing Inspector Thompson with Mr Churchill are to be published. Furthermore, Mr Churchill is not to be photographed where the pictures show any recognisable landmarks. Strictly forbidden areas are his homes, the House of Commons, Admiralty House and Downing Street..."

Walter gave Bunny a half smile and headed for the kitchen.

The cook noticed Walter was looking glum and handed him a large cup of steaming hot brew. "There, a nice cup of tea, Inspector?"

Walter nodded and sat down at the kitchen table; his thoughts were elsewhere as he took large gulps.

"That one didn't touch the sides, did it, lovey? Here, let me pour you another."

Walter smiled and took the tea. He lingered over the second cup. He got up, rubbed his face in his hands, and went off walking. The fresh air helped him quiet his thoughts. Once he had calmed himself, he decided to look for Churchill.

He found him in his study, also in a foul mood. "They've sunk the *Athenia*, Thompson - an unarmed passenger vessel on its way from Liverpool to Montreal... over 100 souls lost." He tore into his paperwork, as if to avenge the dead.

Walter stood in silence.

After about an hour, Churchill leapt up and announced, "I'm off for a bath."

Walter knew the routine. Churchill often took two baths a day, and would spend at least an hour soaking, and reading the daily newspapers as he reclined in the tub.

Walter rested on the bed in his room in the attic. The scream of the air-raid warning made him jump up. Sweat ran down his back as he took the stairs two at a time and flung open the door to Churchill's bathroom.

"I won't have my bath disturbed by Mr Hitler." Churchill slid under the water.

"Sir we have to leave the apartment to go into the underground bomb shelter." Walter grabbed the chain and pulled the plug out of the bath.

The Old Man splashed water at him.

Walter laughed and splashed Churchill back.

Churchill feigned shock, and then, like a child at the seaside, began to splash his bodyguard until all the bath water had run out.

In the middle of their fight, Walter caught his reflection in the bathroom mirror. He was laughing and a warm glow filled his chest. In that instant, Walter recognised, in reality, he had two families – his loving one – Kate, Stella, Emily, and Bernie – and this other strange family that was him, Churchill and George.

Churchill had taken the place of his own father in much the same way he had become a father to Bernie and Stella. And George was like the brother he had never had. Walter swallowed hard and stared at Churchill realising, this second family life was far more stimulating and dangerous than anything he had experienced with his own flesh-and-blood. And he hated himself for feeling torn between the two.

Walter held out a large fluffy towel to Churchill, who hesitated, looking like a baby hippo sitting in a shallow pool. "Well, it will never do, will it – if we fight amongst ourselves."

Churchill grinned, stood up and accepted the towel, giving Walter an affectionate slap on the shoulder as he clambered out of the bath.

"Come on, I'm not having you killed yet." Walter urged, feeling a stab of guilt at the force of his affections for the man they all called *Father*. "We need you to see the war out. I wouldn't want to get up tomorrow and read a headline in The Express:

Winston Churchill, victim of the first air raid found naked in his bath.

Churchill threw the damp towel at Walter then marched into his bedroom, humming *Land of Hope and Glory*.

***

4 September – Himmler's office in Berlin

Schellenberg stood to attention as he handed Himmler a photograph of Walter. "This is the retired police officer brought back into service to guard Churchill. Inspector Walter Henry Thompson, Special Branch, Scotland Yard."

"I see. How good is he?" Himmler was sprinkling fertiliser on a large houseplant. He removed his gloves and took the photograph.

"He's still pretty fit and is apparently an excellent shot."

Himmler lifted his steel-rimmed glasses to examine the photograph of Walter. "What do you know about him?"

"There is a full report here, sir." Schellenberg, clicked his heels, eager to leave the office. He had heard rumours that Himmler used the ashes of Jews to feed his plants. He didn't want to breathe in any of the dust his boss was sprinkling around.

"Oh, indulge me and give me the potted history." Himmler opened another bag of ash and the powder puffed into his face.

Schellenberg tried to ignore that Himmler had a smear of dust on his cheek. "Inspector Thompson was appointed as bodyguard for *Herr* Churchill in 1921. His first assignment was to Egypt. They would have been killed by an angry mob if it hadn't been for Lieutenant Colonel T. E. Lawrence, the man the British called Lawrence of Arabia, who stepped in and saved Churchill by calming the rabble. Thompson appears to have never forgiven himself."

"Churchill was attacked by Irish gunmen in London the same year, but this time the bodyguard saved his life. He allowed Churchill out of his sight in America in 1932, when Churchill was run down by a taxi in Chicago. Again, he doubts his competence, but he is devoted to Churchill. It's for this reason I think he's a good bodyguard. He's got something to prove. I am sure he'd step in front of one of my snipers for the man."

Himmler took off his gloves and picked up a damp cloth. He began to polish the big green leaves of his favorite Aspidistra displayed on top of a marble Roman column. "Can't the Inspector be persuaded to think along the lines of the Duke of Windsor?"

"It's highly unlikely. But we've got some information coming out of London again now, and we are checking to see if he's got any skeletons in the cupboard." Schellenberg gave a stiff-arm Nazi salute and waited to be dismissed.

Himmler reclined in his chair, making Schellenberg wait for permission to leave. "Sometimes, war hangs on the drive and energy of just a few men. I think we could shorten the war for Germany if we eliminate Winston Churchill. Make me a plan...."

"Sir, he is going to be most vulnerable when he travels. But he doesn't seem to be going anywhere much at present. He's developed a pattern of visiting his home at Chartwell most weekends. It's a clear target from the sky. I think an air raid might prove effective."

Himmler nodded and replaced his glasses. "Then organise an extra trip for the Luftwaffe. I will leave the matter in your capable hands."

Schellenberg waited to be dismissed.

"Do you have plants *Sturmbannführer*? My storm troopers bring me this excellent fertiliser – would you like a bag?"

***

9 September – Chartwell

Sawyers, the butler, rubbed his aching hip as he climbed the steep stairs to the secretary's bedroom and knocked on the door. Miss Shearburn sat up in her bed and called for him to come in.

"Sorry Miss, I haven't brought any breakfast, it's just Mr Churchill is asking for you."

"Oh. What time is it?"

"It's 8:00 am, Miss. I thought you'd be up by now."

"I might have been, but I finished at 4:00 am last night and was told I didn't need to report until midday."

"If you'd like to follow me, I can show you a quick route down. I'll wait outside while you dress."

She looked at her clothes, which were still strewn across the chair where she'd left them the night before.

Sawyers puffed as he led her down a secret stairway and through a concealed door into the room where Churchill was waiting with Walter. She sat at the table and opened her notepad.

Walter began to dictate. "To the commissioner of police."

Miss Shearburn raised an eyebrow but continued to take down the dictation.

"Mr Churchill has requested the police are no longer to be routinely informed of his movements. He is happy for his security to remain my sole responsibility. With fewer people knowing Mr Churchill's timetable or whereabouts, the risk of a security leak to the enemy is lessened." Walter turned to Churchill. "Sir, should I mention the rumour of a German para-troop attack on Chartwell?"

"No, no, it's not necessary at this stage to reveal what we know or how we know it. Carry on, you two," Churchill said as he waved them away. "Oh, by the way, Thompson, I've arranged for an old chum of yours to take the message to Scotland Yard."

Miss Shearburn typed the memorandum with nimble manicured fingers.

Walter stood by her side. He breathed in her scent. His pulse intensified.

She handed him the note to read.

Walter fumbled as he signed it and passed it back. "Thank you, Miss Shearburn." Walter took the envelope and went to find the courier. He smiled to himself as he handed the note to Anthony Downwood, who was to act as a messenger boy.

Downwood's intelligence reports were always addressed Mr Churchill - *in strictest confidence* as an intentional affront to Walter. Churchill ignored this direction and passed them on to his bodyguard unopened.

The intelligence reports came from a secret location called Station X, where the British Secret Service had broken the

German codes. Walter received a report every time Churchill's name was mentioned – the pile on his desk every morning was overwhelming, and it wasn't fan mail – it was death threats.

It was a chilly evening, autumn was on its way and Walter made his customary round of the old house, checking doors and windows. He looked up at the sky and was relieved to see there was no moon. Cloud cover hid Chartwell from the air.

A sentry saluted him as he approached. "Everything's in order, sir."

Walter paused and his fingertips traced the shape of his gun in its holster. He was beginning to feel more in control now he was officially in charge. "I'm going to do one more round of the buildings, and then I'll lock everyone inside. No one will be in the grounds after midnight – unless they are a sentry or a German agent. The latter you will do what with?"

"Shoot on sight, sir!" The sentry shouted.

"Thank you, Corporal. Goodnight." Walter walked off around the grounds and heard a distinct rustle in the shrubbery. He reached for his gun. A pulse beat hard in his neck. A small brown bird flew out of a bush. His hands were shaking as he put the gun back in its holster. *Who am I kidding? A younger man should be doing this job.* He stood straight and continued on his round, signalling to each sentry as he passed. He returned to the house where he locked the door behind him. He walked up to Churchill's bedroom and sat down on a hard chair, guarding the room with his gun drawn and ready.

Churchill emerged wearing a bright coloured dressing gown and smoking a large cigar. "I won't need a good copy of that until 8:00 am tomorrow," he called to Miss Shearburn. "I think I'll take a stroll in the grounds."

Walter held out his hand, barring Churchill's path. "I've changed the security arrangements, Sir. The sentries have been ordered to shoot on sight."

"Well, is there a password?"

"Yes, but Sir…."

"Well then, you can go first, and say the password." Churchill marched downstairs to a side door and unlocked it. "Go on then."

He laughed and pushed Walter ahead of him. "I don't want to be shot. But security officers have to take their chances."

A plane buzzed overhead as they walked around the grounds giving the password to each sentry. A momentary gap in the clouds revealed the silhouette of an aircraft.

Churchill withdrew a white handkerchief and wiped his forehead. "I didn't recognise that one…"

"It wasn't one of ours." Walter took Churchill's arm and manoeuvred him towards the door. It was becoming foggy. "Can we go inside now, sir?" Walter peered at the sky. "The British weather may be on our side today.

1940
Fleeing Frenchmen, rescuing refugees and Hitler's metal rainstorm

CHAPTER 4
Walter – Irritations

2 February - The Rose & Crown public house, London SW1

Anthony Downwood settled at a small round table in the corner of *The Rose & Crown* to read the latest edition of the *Daily Express*. He slammed the paper down and stared at the printed silhouette of Walter Thompson accompanying the lead article.

WINSTON FINDS HIS 'SHADOW' AGAIN
.... Inspector W. H. Thompson of the Special Branch of Scotland Yard.
In future, wherever Mr Churchill goes – by air, ship or car – he will be accompanied by this, clean-shaven tower of a man.
A handsome young man joined him at his table. "Good morning, sir."

"Bad morning, Bullock. It simply won't do. The unfairness of it all. See this?" He waved the paper at Bullock who strained to see anything at all. "Thompson – a low class 'oik' is preferred over me – an educated man from the right class. Don't sit down. Go away and find something on Thompson, something to force him from Churchill's good graces for good.

"Thompson, sir?"

"Churchill's blasted bodyguard…"

"Yes, sir, I'll do what I can sir." Bullock marched out of the pub.

"Damn him." Downwood gathered up his paper and knocked over his sherry.

The barmaid mopped up the mess and gave Downwood a hard look as he scuttled away.

***

2 February - Thompson's Grocers, Norwood

Kate was in the garden busy removing the stiff, frozen clothes from the washing line.

Bernie wore his uncle's long white apron and handed a customer her ration book. "I'm really sorry, Mrs Spencer but you've used all your butter allowance – I can let you have some margarine."

"Oh, I can't get used to these ration book coupons and my Alf spreads it so thick on his toast. He'll have to have margarine tomorrow and serve him right."

Bernie handed the woman her change. "Thank you, see you tomorrow."

The shop was empty, so Bernie wandered into the parlour. He picked up a tea towel and began to dry cups and saucers left on the draining board. He looked through the door into the shop and surveyed the counter display and all shelves he had stocked this morning. He was approaching seventeen and his boyish features were beginning to sharpen. He was the man around Thompson's Grocer's, no longer just the delivery boy and he was determined to make a good job of it.

The phone began to ring. "Hello, Thompson's Grocers, may I help you?" He listened to the voice at the other end. "Cripes – hang on please...." He opened the back door and called to Kate. "Quick, quick, Auntie – it's the operator for you. It's long distance – France."

Kate dropped the basket of washing and ran inside to pick up the receiver. "Hello? Hello?"

"Hello Kate. It's Stella."

"Oh, my love. How are you?" Kate cupped her hand over the receiver and whispered to Bernie, who was jumping up and down in front of her. "It's Stella."

43

Stella's voice was tinny over the poor line. "We're both fine, thanks, Kate. Is Walter at home?"

"No, I'm afraid not – he's taken up his old job again with you-know-who. I'm not supposed to talk about it." Kate tucked her left hand under her right arm to warm her fingers.

"Well, I guessed that might have happened. I'll have to be quick. But first I need to know something – do you think anyone listens in on this line?"

Kate swallowed. "I think Walter would have mentioned it if the Germans had got round to that already. I can't call him on the telephone, but I believe there are plans to go to the country you are in – on Wednesday."

"Oh, that's just super... listen, Kate, can you ask Walter if he could meet me? Do you know where he'll be?"

"Maybe, I shouldn't say this on the telephone, but do you remember the first hotel we stopped at on the way to Switzerland?"

"Would that be the hotel we visited on a family holiday when I was about 16?"

"You know your brother, he likes to have advance knowledge of the lay of the land... but Stella, Walter wants you to come home now. He thinks things will get worse for Jews in France, and you could both be in danger soon... besides we miss you ... please come back ...."

"I will, I will – but first I have something important to do. Can you ask Walter to meet me at the hotel at mid-day? There are people relying on me and I can't let them down. Dear Kate, please kiss Bernie and Emily for me – I love you all – take care...."

"Yes, we love you too, I'll tell Walter but come home, Stella. Come home – Stella? Stella?" The connection was lost, and Kate replaced the receiver and turned to her nephew. "If you overheard anything, young Bernie, then just forget it."

"Zip," said Bernie, pretending to fasten his lips.

"You're a good lad, and don't worry... she'll be home soon – you'll see." Kate reached up and ruffled his hair. "Be an angel and take a note to your uncle? I'm pretty sure he won't be able to get home tonight – even if he has got any petrol left from his ration in that old bike of his. If you hand the envelope in at the

Admiralty and tell them it is for Inspector Thompson, the policeman at the gate will make sure he gets it."

"Would it be all right if I took the train?" Bernie was already taking off his uncle's apron.

"Yes, of course – here's your fare. But you don't need to go right now. Stella didn't say it was urgent. You can take tomorrow off – don't worry about getting back to work in the shop. Drop off a note for your uncle up there and enjoy yourself a bit. Maybe stop at a fancy cake shop and have a bun with your tea – it's not on ration in cafés."

"Thanks, Aunt Kate." Bernie stared at the money she had thrust into his hand. "But Aunt Kate – that's a pound note."

"You're a very hard-working young man, Bernie, and you deserve it. I don't know what I'd do without you. Now, you go home and have a nice time tomorrow."

Bernie was already thinking about getting some iced French fancies. He knew to buy chocolate for his mum, lemon for Auntie Kate and pink ones for Stella – their favourites. He looked at the one-pound note in his hand. "Auntie, you're too kind. I love working with you in the shop, you don't need to pay me. But can you at least tell me something about what's going on?"

"Well, I can't telephone your uncle anymore – so I've written him this note to ask if he can meet with Stella in France. She wants to ask him something and I'm pretty sure he's going to have something to say to her – like get on the next boat back here."

CHAPTER 5
Bernie - Whistle a Happy Tune

3 February - Westminster, London

The London Underground train squealed to a halt at Westminster station. On the platform was a chocolate machine. *I wonder*? Bernie searched his pockets, found a thruppenny bit and inserted it in the slot. He pulled out the drawer and there was a bar of chocolate – a rare treat.

In the hall, a busker leant on a wooden crutch, with his back supported by the curved wall and played the bagpipes. Bernie recognised the tartan of the Argyll and Sutherland Highlanders, his dad's old regiment. There was a row of medals from the last war on the man's chest. He dropped a sixpence into the piper's beret and picked up his tune with a cheerful whistle.

Bernie jogged up the steps from Westminster Underground station and emerged opposite the Houses of Parliament. He stopped and admired the imposing, gothic architecture of Westminster Palace, looming over the river Thames. The tall St Stephens tower cast a long shadow in the weak winter sun and the bell, known as *Big Ben,* chimed a single bong to indicate 10:15 am. He stood and stared at Parliament Square, so different from when he had been here with his uncle two years ago. Sandbags surrounded the entrance of every building and every statue. Tape was stuck across all the windows of the once striking buildings adjacent to the square. The stained-glass windows of Westminster Abbey were boarded up. People were hurrying along in uniform, carrying identical small round cardboard boxes containing their gas mask.

He walked along the pavement in Parliament Street. The brutal landscape was a daunting reminder that London was getting ready for a ruthless attack from the Germans. The preparations were unsettling for the lad, so he whistled the piper's tune, *Scotland the Brave* and tapped a drum accompaniment on his gas mask box.

The policeman at The Admiralty Building, stood outside the huge, iron gates and stared in his direction.

Bernie looked up at the ornate pillars either side of the entrance. *Very grand, Uncle Walter*. He approached the officer and held out the envelope. "Could you please give this note to my uncle? He's Inspector Thompson."

The policeman noted the young lad's physical resemblance to Churchill's bodyguard, and without turning, reached behind him and pushed open the gate. "Guess who we have here? The Inspector's nephew."

"Come in, young man," said a second policeman. "What's all this about?"

"Could you give this note to my uncle, sir? My aunt asked me to leave it with you."

"You'd better give that to the secretary, I think. Come on, this way please."

Bernie followed the policeman to Bunny's office, gawping at the huge oil paintings of old sea battles lining the walls.

The policeman opened the office door and ushered Bernie through. "Here's a young man with a message for the Inspector, Miss Shearburn. Can you assist him?"

"Certainly, officer." Bunny's quick fingers were hitting the typewriter keys with a rhythmical click. She returned the platen with a ting and tore a piece of paper from the machine.

Bernie watched her dexterity open mouthed. "Uh... hello miss, I'm Bernie – Inspector Thompson's nephew. I've an important note for him from my aunt."

Bunny smiled. "Of course. I'll see he receives it as soon as he gets back." She started writing on a slip of paper. "Here's my sister's telephone number. I stay with her quite a lot, and she works nearby. Please ask your aunt to leave any future messages for the Inspector with my sister and I'll make sure your uncle gets them."

Bernie thanked her and both police officers as he was ushered out of the building. He walked back along Whitehall towards the Houses of Parliament, with his hands in his pockets, whistling *Brown Bear*.

To his surprise, he saw his Uncle Walter just ahead of him, walking towards him with a small, round man.

The Old Man turned to Bernie and shouted, "Stop that blasted whistling!"

Walter raised his eyebrows. *Oh Lord, Bernie – is everything alright at home? I must get Churchill off the street. Bernie. Why are you here?*

Bernie ran over, making a point of whistling louder as he approached.

"Is everyone safe and sound?" Walter began to hurry Churchill along towards Admiralty House and Bernie kept in step.

"Yes, we're all fine, uncle. And great news, we've had a telephone call from Stella. Auntie's put it all in a note. I've left it with a secretary called, Miss Shearburn." He turned to Churchill. "Don't like my whistling eh? I can whistle *your* favourite tune if you like."

"No, I don't like it – it's a horrible noise," growled Churchill.

Walter's eyes widened. He knew Bernie meant no harm, but he was afraid the Old Man might not see it the same way. They walked three abreast along the wide pavement. Walter surveyed the area. "Please take care of your aunt Kate and give her and your mum a big hug from me." He waggled Bernie's right ear. "So, are you going to have a look around?"

"Yes, I want to get some cakes and chocolates for Mum and Auntie. I'm even going to buy something for Stella – in the hope she'll be home soon."

"Well, they deserve it. Why not walk up to Maison Lyons at Marble Arch. It's on the corner, with a sign in gold lettering. They sell everything. Here take some money, have a cup of tea and get them something nice from me."

Bernie's face reddened. "Oh no need for money, Auntie has already made me take far too much."

"You know the way?"

"Yes uncle."

"Well off you go and have a nice time. I'll see Miss Shearburn for the note." Walter held open the gate for Churchill and took one more scour of the street.

CHAPTER 6
Walter and Stella - Missing Each Other

5 February: The English Channel

Churchill paced the foredeck of the destroyer *Codrington*, a ship chosen for its speed and accommodation. The huge, grey vessel was taking Churchill and Prime Minister, Neville Chamberlain for a secret meeting in France.

Churchill raised his arm when he spotted another cylindrical floating mine.

The gunner was already on it. A splash of chilled water hit the deck as it exploded away from the ship on the port side.

The sailors cheered with a "hip hip hoorah," each time the gunner destroyed a mine.

"Bloody mines look like German sausages – only problem is they blow up in yer face." George took a small white paper bag of sherbet lemons from his pocket. His face puckered as he popped the sour boiled sweet in his mouth and offered one to Walter.

"Thanks," said Walter. "At least we can see the mines. The German's used to leave them on the seabed, loaded with strong magnets and they would attach themselves to any passing ship."

Churchill kept watch as the ship moved at slow speed ahead through the deep, green waters of the English Channel.

Bunny came up on deck to get some air. She squealed, as a little water sprayed on her from the next mine dispatched by the gunner. Her dress billowed in the wind and she was soon surrounded by admiring sailors.

Walter stood on the bridge and hated himself for not being able to draw his eyes away from her.

Bunny glanced up at Walter and smiled.

Walter felt as if she had read his thoughts and raised his hand in a half wave. He took the stairs to the lower deck and tapped Churchill on the shoulder.

Churchill turned while still looking through his binoculars. "Ah Thompson, we've got six of the blighters so far."

Walter shouted to be heard above the deep rumble of the ship's engines and the constant boom of the gun. "Sir, we're heading to safer waters. It's beginning to get dark. I've arranged a cabin for you. We'll dock at 05:00 am and then we've got a long ride by car to Metz. It might be advisable to have dinner and try to get some rest."

"Thank you, Thompson. Yes, I'm going to need all my strength if I'm going to persuade the French to keep fighting and not to surrender to the Germans."

A blustery swell greeted them as they sailed towards the alabaster, ocean carved cliffs of the Normandy coastline.

The ship sailed through the mouth of the River Seine in the early hours of the morning and into the port of Le Havre. A fishing vessel made way for them, allowing them to moor in the deep-water dock. Churchill took Bunny's hand to help her disembark along the riding gangplank.

George looked around at the fishing boats. "Where's the French navy then?"

Churchill smiled. "All in North Africa, fighting Germans, I hope."

Four cars with engines running, each with a police bike outrider, waited to meet them on the high, concrete dock.

Walter spoke in perfect French to the drivers and handed each one a map with instructions. His eyes flickered up and down the road at the elegant four storey town houses lining the quay. "Where's the bloody armoured car I ordered? None of these vehicles have bullet proof glass."

This was the first time Churchill had left Britain since the start of the war and was a perilous journey into unknown territory.

Walter stood rigid, his eyes sweeping around the dock, searching for danger. When he satisfied himself nothing was amiss, he took his place in the front of the second car, drew his gun and left it lying in his lap.

George – who wasn't used to driving a left-hand vehicle – sat in the back with Churchill. "The French countryside looks the same as England. I thought it'd be different...." He offered Churchill a sherbet lemon and the Old Man winked and took one.

George put the bag back in his coat pocket and took out his gun. "I'm quite enjoying my 'oliday in the comfortable back of the car."

Churchill smiled and patted George's arm. He opened his papers and began to work.

Frost covered every tree and mist collected in the fields and valleys as the convoy sped towards Metz.

Walter gave clear hand signals from one car to another. He maintained a constant survey of the roads, studying each person and vehicle they passed along the way. He checked and re-checked his maps to make sure the French driver of the first car did not deviate from the agreed route.

Walter touched the message from Kate in his jacket pocket and stared at the road. *How will I get away to meet Stella without putting the Old Man at risk?* He glanced behind at Churchill who looked relaxed, reading his papers.

***

Stella's unruffled confidence was being tested. The police had closed all the major roads around Metz, and she was forced to leave the bus and go on foot the rest of the way. She knew time was against her. She began running, but the long road seemed never ending. She spotted one of her favourite cafés, *Les Moulins*, and knew she still had six or seven hundred yards to go. She forced her legs to push harder and the fog caused her lungs to burn. Just when she thought she could not go on, she saw the 17th century *Hôtel de la Cathédrale* in the distance across the vast *Place de Chambre*.

***

"Ralentissez ici, en face de l'hôtel, s'il vous plaît conducteur." Walter instructed the driver to slow up as they passed the hotel to see if he could spot her at the window.

Stella was in the next street still dashing towards the square.

Walter shifted in the car seat. They were meeting the French government at the town hall and not at the hotel, which would have been Walter's choice. There were so many people loitering – anyone could be an assassin. *If only I can get Churchill to a secure location – I can leave George in charge and go and check if Stella's at the hotel.*

Stella stopped running when she saw the last of the official cars speed past the hotel and bump over the uneven cobbles in the huge square. She bent forward and touched her toes, to ease the stitch in the side. She looked towards the hotel, tugging at the collar on her coat to keep out the freezing fog. *Why aren't the cars stopping?* "STOP. STOP." Her words were snatched by an icy blast.

The cars drew up outside the Town Hall and a French intelligence officer pulled Walter aside. "Inspector Thompson – the news is not good. There are communist activists in the area and a possible anti-war demonstration."

"Do we have any idea who we are looking for?"

"I'm sorry, Inspector, any of these people here could be a communist or a German. We must be vigilant."

Stella ran across the square in front of the gothic cathedral. *They must be meeting in the Town Hall. Best I wait here – that was the arrangement.*

Churchill was determined to keep the French fighting and was relentless with his oratory. He made speech after speech to their government ministers, their chiefs of staff – anyone who would listen – all strangers to Walter and everyone capable of murder.

Walter dared not leave the Old Man's side. The hours wasted away, and Walter felt his head banging. *I have to get to Stella. Wait for me, Stella darling.*

Stella sat in the hotel lounge staring at the empty pot of tea. It had been cold for hours and still Walter had not come. She played with her paper serviette and folded it into a swan – just like the ones she had made for each guest on her wedding day. She jumped up when a group of men opened the hotel door, allowing the cold wind from the square to whip around her legs. The men ordered drinks at the bar and Stella understood from their conversation, they had been at the conference.

"Well goodbye, *Monsieur* Churchill – go back to England and fight with the Germans if you wish – but why should we sacrifice our young men to yet another war?" A stocky Frenchman poured water into his Ricard. His colleagues grunted in agreement.

"Excuse me, gentlemen," said Stella walking towards the group. "Did you say Mr Churchill had left?"

"Yes, thank the Lord...." The stocky man saluted Stella with his glass. She was back out in the square before he could engage her in conversation. She looked left and right. More people were crossing the square towards the hotel, but not Walter. I'll walk to the Town Hall. The police were taking down the barriers blocking the roads.

Walter organised the cars outside the building. He slipped into the back seat of the second car with Churchill. "Sir, I know this is a bit unusual, but my sister is waiting for me at the hotel across the square, could we give her a lift back to England?"

"My dear Thompson, your family seem to pop up in the most unlikely places. Certainly, she must come with us. This is no place for her. So long as she doesn't want to whistle me a tune."

The official cars drew to a halt outside the hotel, just as Stella disappeared from sight across the square. Walter tore through the hotel doors and looked about. He approached the man at the desk. "Have you seen an English woman? I was supposed to meet her here."

"I'm sorry, *Monsieur* I have just come on shift and I haven't noticed anyone waiting."

Walter dashed into the lounge. There at a table by the window was a single cup and saucer, with a teapot, milk jug and sugar bowl and a paper serviette folded into a swan. He picked up the serviette and held it to his face. *She was here.*

He rushed outside and cast his eyes over the square. He opened the passenger side of the car and George read his intention and got in the back. He leaned over to Churchill. "Sir, I seem to have missed my sister, but think she might be close by."

"Why then we must...."

The Agent from the French Intelligence Service jogged up to the car. "*Pardon*, Inspector, you must leave immediately – there are thousands of anti-war demonstrators headed for the square. The police can't hold them back – they're throwing missiles and shouting slogans against *Monsieur* Churchill."

"Thank you. Drive on please driver." Walter scanned the streets as they left in fast convoy.

Churchill observed his side of the street from the back of the car. "Is that her, Thompson?" He pointed to a lone dark-haired young woman wearing a raincoat.

"No, she's fair and petite. But thank you sir." Churchill leaned forward and placed his hand on Walter's shoulder.

Stella trudged back to the bus, avoiding the streets where she could see a hoard of protestors – she was several hours away from home, and it was already late in the day. A single tear trickled on to her cheek as she imagined the refugees waiting at the border for a ceasefire. She began to run. She screamed at the empty street. "Damn you Walter – where the hell are you?"

***

It was after midnight when Stella turned the key in the door to their apartment. She threw herself down on the thick rug by the fireplace. The warm embers revived her spirit. Martin came and sat beside her. He held her hand and waited for an explanation. None was forthcoming, so he laced her arm around his neck and carried her to bed. She was asleep in an instant and did not stir until the arrival of the crisp dawn. Martin rose early to make a pot of strong tea and brought it to her bedside on his grandmother's tray with two porcelain cups and saucers.

"Oh, Martin, you're such a dear." Stella sat up in bed and savoured the heady aroma of the fresh-brewed English tea. "I expect you're wondering what I've been up to...."

"*Neshama*, when one's wife does not appear until very late in the evening, snivels all over you, and falls asleep, one does wonder."

She crumbled into his arms. "Oh, Martin, my darling, I'm so sorry – I ... I borrowed the small bus and went to try to meet Walter. I saw the fleet of cars, but I couldn't get near and we really need his help."

His fingers stroked her nose and her eyes closed as lines appeared on her face. "*Neshama*, take a breath – I've got all morning. I suppose the *we* means Pierre Picard and the others?"

"Pierre says there are women and children – trapped on the French–German border – in the woods trying to escape the Nazis. I was hoping Walter could talk to Churchill to organise a cease fire and get the soldiers to turn their backs while the refugees came into France."

"God, you're asking a lot."

"Well, yes ...."

Martin turned the situation over in his mind: "Well, I guess we'd better see what we can do to help." He poured them both another cup of tea.

Stella almost knocked the cup out of his hand as she flung her arms around him. "I'm so frightened about what the Germans might do to these people. Pierre is convinced Hitler plans to invade Paris. The whole group is worried the French military are going to surrender."

"*Neshama*, we're in this together. Since listening to Pierre, I've taken some early precautions concerning our own identity papers." He leaned forward and pecked her on the lips – swept up the tea tray, placing it on a side table and hopped back into bed with her. She giggled with delight.

Their passionate embrace was interrupted by a loud, abrupt knock. Martin got up and opened the door, smiling as he let their robed visitor in. "It's secret agent Father Picard."

Pierre scuttled in, looking back at the door, willing Martin to close it behind him.

Stella fastened her robe around her. "Oh, Pierre, I'm so sorry, but I didn't manage to talk to my brother after all. I sent him a message asking him to meet me at the hotel we once visited in Metz, but if he was there – I missed him…."

Pierre held up his hand to stop her in mid-flow. "It's done, *mes amis*, do not worry – I have made a connection within the French army, and we have worked out a plan." He produced a road map from under his long, black robe and laid it open at a marked page. "We will meet our people here." He indicated a place marked with a cross on the map. "We do have a slight problem, though."

Stella and Martin chimed together, "Yes?"

"Numbers. There could be more than 2,000 people trying to escape through this route, and the ceasefire will last for two hours, which is barely enough time to allow them all through."

"Aha, all those bus fares." Martin nudged Stella and she rolled her eyes.

Pierre opened a note pad. "We're going to need about 30 of the large buses that seat 70 people each. Here's the plan. Our Catholic friends in Strasbourg will organise a festival on the day for their local saint. They'll try to sort out lots of local publicity so if the Germans do notice increased traffic on the roads from their reconnaissance planes on the border, there'll be a logical explanation. The coaches need to be there at one o'clock in the morning to collect the refugees. We'll shroud the lights to avoid recognition from the air. Some coaches will go to Switzerland, but the majority are to head to the Pas-de-Calais. We've organised coastal fishing boats to take them to Northern Spain. These refugees are the ones for whom we have been able to get the identity documents from the Spanish consul. They'll go on to Portugal – a neutral country – and be helped by an American-Jewish organisation to reach the United States or South America.

"You've obviously spent a great deal of time planning this." Stella studied Pierre. His beard had grown, and he carried a godly air – just like a real priest.

Martin put a tray of hot drinks on the table. "Ah, well, when you put together a plan like that – how could a chap refuse to help? What can we do?"

"How many coaches can you let us have?"

Martin poured the tea. "At present, I've got 12 coaches that are serviceable, and one small bus."

Pierre accepted the cup and saucer Martin held out to him. "Could we use them all?"

Martin considered for a moment. "Well, that wouldn't be easy. Four of them provide a regular service around Paris, so it would be a bit difficult to take them off the route. But I could reschedule the other eight. Hang on, what date are we talking about?"

"The plan is for May the eleventh. Our intelligence sources believe Hitler's generals are planning an attack sometime later this month, so we have to get as many out as possible before then."

"Oh, well, that's no problem. I've got five new buses on order, and they'll all be ready by then. I'll schedule them in for the religious festival. What's it called, by the way?"

"We're working on it." Pierre sipped from the cup. "Ugh – tea, can't you English make a decent cup of coffee?"

***

9 May – Himmler's office, Berlin

There were two people Himmler trusted during the war – one was his masseuse, who relieved him of stomach pains, and the other was standing in front of him, *SS Brigadeführer* Walther Schellenberg. "Hand me the watering can, Walther. This plant is

57

really dry. And so, you have considered the problem and formulated a plan?"

"Yes, sir. We don't know where *Herr* Churchill will go next. So, I have put together an operation to cover all eventualities. I have searched the *SS* for officers who are foreign nationals. All these people can pass for citizens in their own countries. They all speak the local language without any foreign accent. They are undergoing training as an assassination squad."

Himmler put down the watering can and took the report from Schellenberg. "So, wherever Churchill might travel, we can parachute in people who know the country and the language, and who are trained assassins?"

"Yes, sir. We've even released some Russian murderers from a camp and recruited them – all expendable, of course. I have called it *Operation Long Jump*."

"Criminals, foreigners and dogs." Himmler flicked through the report and read aloud. "*SS 501* – Germans brought up in other countries who understand the culture and the colloquialisms. Excellent. There is an old barracks next to Lake Quentz that you can use. It's just by the Sachenhausen camp. Some of the inmates there might prove useful."

"To add to the squad, sir?"

"No, for target practice."

***

10 May - The House of Commons

Sweat poured down George's face and he stopped for a while, leaning against the stone banister. He took two long breaths and climbed the last few steps to Strangers' Gallery. He threw himself down on one of the empty hard wooden benches, provided for the general public. He glanced through the stone archway to a packed floor in the green-hued House of Commons below. "...got an urgent message. It's from the Secret Service."

Walter opened it, while George took gulps of air.

MOST SECRET: GERMAN COMMANDOS TRAINING AT LAKE QUENTZ, GERMAN HIGH COMMAND SCHOOL. ABWEHR SOURCES STATE THE OBJECTIVE IS THE ASSASSINATION OF CHURCHILL. PROCEED WITH VIGILANCE.

Walter screwed up the note and shoved it in his trouser pocket. "It's another cryptic decode of a German military message from Station X at Bletchley Park, mentioning Churchill. Unless they give us more detailed information, what are we supposed to do?"

"Blimey, Inspector you're in a foul mood. When's the last time you got 'ome?"

"Not for weeks, George and frankly the Old Man's incessant demands are trying my patience."

"He's struggling a bit, Inspector – just give 'im a bit of elbow room." George waved towards the Members of Parliament shouting at each other in the chamber below. "What's all this commotion?"

"There's been a terrible blunder over Norway – Gerries invaded a few days before we'd planned to land there ourselves – caught us on the hop."

"So, Inspector, d'yer reckon they'll chuck out Chamberlain as Prime Minister and give the Old Man the job?"

"Oh, I'm sure of it George. That's why we're off to Buckingham Palace when this has finished." Walter glanced down at Churchill, who was showing no emotion.

Later that evening, after his audience with the King at Buckingham Palace, Churchill was solemn. "Do you know why I've been to the Palace, Thompson?" They strode towards the Admiralty together.

"Yes, sir. Congratulations. I'm very pleased you've at last become Prime Minister, but I wish the position had come your way in better times – you've taken on an enormous task."

Tears welled in Churchill's eyes, as he started up the steps. "God alone knows how great. All I hope is that it's not too late. I'm very much afraid it is."

George searched his pockets for his sherbet lemons. "The Old Man certainly 'as an air for the dramatic – even when it's just us 'e's talking to."

Churchill stopped halfway. "God, Thompson, I have nothing to offer them but blood, toil, tears and sweat."

"Then you must tell them that, sir."

Churchill looked up and nodded. "Yes, I will tell them that. "

Walter took one of Churchill's cigars from his breast pocket and unwrapped it. "Here, you often do your best thinking when relaxing with a cigar."

Churchill sighed. "Yes, you're right, now I'm in the driving seat, I must take stock of everything and see what's to be done. What would I do without you Thompson?"

Walter smiled and offered Churchill his arm.

***

Later that day: 10 Downing Street

Bunny was installed in her new office at the Prime Minister's residence. She was busy typing a report entitled *Government White Paper* that announced:

A collection of reports from an unimpeachable authority has been put together by our British diplomats in Germany over the past few years concerning Nazi concentration camps.

The treatment of inmates is reminiscent of the darkest ages in the history of man.

Hitler is said to have ordered the flogging of Jews. Barbarous and systematic tortures are inflicted daily, by guards aged 17 to 20 in the Dachau and Buchenwald camps. Some prisoners go mad, others feign escape attempts in order to be shot and be relieved from the agony of living.

Bunny was so engrossed in the typing she didn't hear Walter come in.

Intelligence sources tell us that the SS are proposing that all Jews will be made to wear a yellow Star of David.

Walter began to read the report over Bunny's shoulder. He flopped down on the wooden chair beside her and massaged his temples. "Excuse me, Miss Shearburn, I know this is a bit irregular, but do you think you can try and get a call through for me to my sister in Paris?" Walter picked up a pen and wrote the number on her pad.

"Anything I can do to help?" Bunny pulled the finished report out of her typewriter and tidied her desk. She pulled down the blackout blind over the window. "There, the office is all yours. I'll wait outside and make sure no one comes in." She moved just a little too close to him as she made for the door.

"Thank you, Miss Shearburn." Walter picked up the receiver.

George opened the door. "The Old Man's asking for you, Inspector."

"Can you cover for me for ten minutes, George? I need to try and make a phone call."

"Oh right, mum's the word – I'll keep 'im occupied. Bunny, you guard the door."

They left and Walter took out his handkerchief and dabbed the perspiration on his forehead while he waited for the operator to make the connection.

"I'm sorry sir. The lines seem to be engaged or down," she said.

"Can you try another number?"

"Is it Paris again?"

"Yes, it's a business number – Montmartre 347."

"I'll try it for you. Sorry sir, I am unable to make the connection."

Walter replaced the receiver. He moved to leave at the very second Downwood pushed his way through the door, with Bunny following behind protesting. Walter stood his ground and put his hands in his pockets.

Downwood glared at Walter. He knew the Inspector had been up to something – if only he could discover what that might be.

Their showdown was interrupted as Churchill marched in, wearing his multi-coloured dressing gown. "Just that last bit of dictation," he called out. "Oh, hello Downwood – Thompson – everything all right?"

"Just looking for a pencil sharpener," said Walter, as he opened the top drawer of Bunny's desk with one hand while breaking the point of the pencil in his pocket with the other. "Ah here we are..." He produced the broken pencil and the sharpener and ground the graphite. He put back the items and touched the folded paper serviette in his trouser pocket. "Do you mind if I take an hour off, sir?"

"Oh, right, yes of course – I'm probably working you a bit hard."

"None of us has quite your stamina." Walter eyes flashed at Downwood.

Downwood looked at the floor.

Churchill tapped him on the shoulder. "And what can I do for you, Downwood?"

"Oh, sorry sir – I'm to be the new Secret Service liaison for Downing Street. I was trying to find my office." Downwood's voice was an octave higher than he would have liked.

"Well come into my study and explain, will you?" Churchill held the door open.

Downwood smirked as he followed Churchill and shut the door behind him.

CHAPTER 7
Stella - Jeopardies and Refugees

11 May – A secret location near Strasbourg, France

At the French–German border outside Strasbourg, Stella's little gold bus with its new black and orange cloth seats waited in the shadow of the mountains, which were silhouetted against the purple sky. She sat on the step and breathed in the spicy fragrance of the cedar trees swaying in the fresh mountain breeze.

She stood and examined her reflection in the wing mirror of the bus and almost did not recognise the woman who looked back. She was wearing black, cotton trousers and a loose white shirt and her hair had been cut short in a French-style bob.

In the destination panel above the windscreen, Stella had rolled the sign around to read: *Pas en Service*. An ironic message as today the bus would be doing a great service for a group of discarded and desperate people.

As the children emerged from the gloom of the forest, Stella ran over to greet them. She took the first little boy by the hand and led him to the bus, and the others followed. She lifted the raggedy little bodies one by one to a tall, thin man called, Luc.

A small, dark eyed boy wrapped his arms around her neck. His short trousers were torn at the pocket and he wore odd shoes.

His older brother stepped up on to the bus on his own, his glasses broken on one side and held together with a sticking plaster. Two thin, dark haired girls came next, Erica 19 and Charlotte 16. Their coats revealed a dark mark and stitch holes where a yellow Star of David had been sewn on the breast pocket. Their parents, Jacob and Regina followed, wearing felt hats and wool coats with the tell-tale stitch marks of the star and carrying a small leather suitcase… all their worldly possessions.

Regina thanked them. *"Danke, danke! Sie sind so freundlich, uns zu helfen."* Her left hand revealed a white mark on her third finger where she had worn a wedding ring for 21 years.

Many of the weary travellers were too tired to speak. They just smiled, lowering their eyes as they climbed aboard. They all wore shabby clothes and had dirty worn-out shoes.

One small boy with big green eyes took Luc's hand as he climbed the step. "Herbert Glass," he announced with a smile. Others following thought they should give their names.

"Evelyn Aber." A small, dark haired woman with a tatty headscarf.

"Renate Aber." Fifteen with thick dark curls, wearing a man's coat.

"Gisela Levy." A stick thin woman with scruffy grey hair.

"Lotte Levy." Wearing a frayed school uniform with the Star of David sewn on the chest.

"Paul Levy." Limping, in a pair of oversized army boots with no laces.

They each whispered words of thanks as they came aboard. They were followed by a group of children from an orphanage, Bertha, Alfred, Emma, Rosy, Edith, Helene, Eva, Alice, Leo, Willy, Julie, Bella and Miriam.

The light was fading, and Martin had already left half an hour earlier with a full coach, heading for the Swiss border. Other coaches shut their doors and started their engines. Pierre fiddled with his rosary. "What is the hold up? Where are the rest? We need to get going to Boulogne. We can't be late – the Spanish boats won't wait."

"Just give them a little longer?" Stella looked down the aisle. The bus was not yet full. Twenty children, eight women and five men were slumped on the seats. She looked towards the woods. Nothing moved in the gloom.

Pierre shoved the rosary in his pocket. "Have you heard the news? The Germans have broken through into Holland and Belgium. We think they're about to cross into France. This will be our last run. God help any Jews still left in Germany. The Nazis have made laws to make their lives impossible. They fired any Jew holding a government job, then Jewish lawyers were not allowed to practice and those with businesses were made to sell them to Germans at below market price. They expelled all Jewish children from schools and universities and in February, Jews were told to surrender all gold, silver and diamonds without compensation. But it's not just the Nazis – hundreds of petty officials in local authorities all over Germany have made up their own harsh, local laws to make life unbearable for anyone with a drop of Jewish blood."

A squat man with a beret, dark clothing and a rifle tied with string, appeared from the woods, holding a child's hand. A band of nine bedraggled refugees followed him.

"Oh, here are the rest, thank God. Let's get going." Pierre lifted the small girl up the steps. "*Wie ist dein Name, Kleines?* What's your name, little one?"

"Betty Blum."

"Edith Stein." A middle-aged woman with flabby cheeks – once round and rosy.

"Rudolf Stein." Her husband, wearing broken spectacles and a resigned look on his face.

"Ruth and Wilfred Muller." A middle-aged couple wearing matted fur coats and all the jewellery they owned.

"Ludovic and Estelle Wiseman." He helped her up the steps as she was in the latter stage of pregnancy. "Thank you. These are our twins, Rachael and Esther."

"We are six today," said the two bright eyed girls with tight dark curls and Cupid's bow lips.

"Then we shall sing *Joyeux anniversaire* to you as we drive along." Stella gave both girls a hug. "*Alles Gute zum Geburtstag.* Happy birthday."

Luc passed each passenger a baguette with a slab of pork and pointed to the churn filled with fresh water and the metal mug in the back of the coach. He winked at one man who looked orthodox, with dark curls hanging from under his black hat, "Chicken sandwich, sir...."

The man smiled. "Thank you – we Jews haven't been allowed to slaughter our own animals since 1933 but I thank you for your thoughtfulness and respect. I will enjoy this *chicken* sandwich."

Stella squinted as she forced herself to concentrate on the dimly lit road. After about an hour she caught up with the end of the line of coaches heading towards the coast. It was dry and clear, but progress was slow, since they used the back roads and the headlights had to be shrouded to keep their presence hidden.

Several of the younger children on Stella's bus were crying. She longed to stop to tend to them. She turned to Luc: "God knows how many miles these children have walked to escape the Nazis. They smell terrible; they can't have been able to wash properly for weeks. I wish I'd bought them some soap and towels. What am I thinking – they are exhausted." She glanced in her rear-view mirror and noticed most of her passengers had fallen asleep.

The journey took them through a series of tiny hamlets with stone houses and steep pitched slate roofs. Stella yawned and rubbed her eyes with her fists.

***

12 May – Boulogne

The sea was black against a grey night sky, showing the first yellow tinge of the anticipated dawn. Stella's bus was third in the queue. She watched Pierre – still dressed as a priest in his flowing robes, gesticulating to the guards at the entrance to the port.

"I think he really likes that outfit." Luc Moreau joined Stella at the front of the bus.

"What do you mean?" Stella assessed the tall, wiry, young man seated opposite, cleaning a long rifle.

"Pierre – he likes dressing up in that priest's garb." There was a glint of humour in his grey eyes.

"Is he very religious?"

"No, not at all – it's just that… well, you know, he does not like… ahem… women."

"I wouldn't say that."

"Oh, he likes women – he especially likes you. It's… oh well, just forget it."

"Do you mean he's homosexual?"

"Ah well, there you are – you said it, not me."

"And you?" Stella had a hint of a smile on her lips.

"*Mon Dieu*. Certainly not. I love to be with women – whenever and wherever I can."

"So, what are you doing helping with these refugees? You don't look like a Jew."

"I'm not, I'm a friend of Pierre's. I was a farrier before the war. No horses to shoe, so here I am helping my best friend."

Stella could see Pierre's back. At first, his stance was easy, as he held his arms open with his palms facing upwards towards the heavens. As the discussions wore on, Stella could read things were getting tricky. The guards looked hostile and Pierre began to raise his arms in the air.

Betty Blum tugged at Stella's sleeve. "Can I please go to the toilet?"

"Oh, ah… well, I don't know where we might find one. Let me take you off the bus and behind the wall and you can squat there. Come on, little one." Stella jumped down from the bus and lifted the child off the top step. She was light as a croissant. "When did you last eat?"

"I'm not sure. I think it was Thursday."

"But today's Sunday. How old are you?"

"I'm 12." Her face was small and dirty, and the lack of food had drawn her cheeks in, so she looked much younger.

"You poor soul, I thought you were about eight."

"My sister was eight." The little girl sobbed but was dehydrated and no tears ran down her grime-stained cheeks.

"Was eight?"

"Yes, we had to leave her behind with the angels." The girl clutched her hands to her chest in an imaginary hug.

"Oh, my poor, sweet child. What horrible things you have endured."

The little girl went to relieve herself behind the wall. She experienced the sensation of needing to go but she could not. When she returned, Stella bent down and hugged her. They walked to the bus in silence.

There were raised voices in the distance, but Stella was unable to make out what was being said. Pierre had arranged for the passengers to board small boats, which would take them around the coast to Spain. It was taking so long; the refugees were growing restless. But first this little girl needed some water. Stella fed it to her in small sips from a spoon and checked all her passengers had drunk some water and eaten their sandwich.

Stella got back in the driver's seat and yawned. Her eyes became heavy and her head dropped forward as she succumbed to sleep. She fell forward on to the steering column, sounding the horn. She sat up in shock from her few seconds of sleep "Oh no – what have I done?"

The two men at the gate strode towards her bus, leaving Pierre alone in the road, waving his arms around.

The tall French officer poked his head through the driver's window. "So, you're in a hurry with your unlawful cargo. Oh, look who the priest has recruited to his secret army – a woman. And isn't she quite lovely."

Stella smiled. "I am so sorry, Officer, about sounding the horn – it... it was an accident."

"I see – you think we're taking too long to let you through, eh?"

"Oh, I wouldn't dream of criticising at all. I expect you've a lot of very important paperwork to attend to."

"Indeed."

"You see… it's just they're all exhausted …."

The officers looked at each other.

Stella gave them an appealing smile.

The taller of the two men scratched his head while the tubby one waited for the other's lead.

Stella gripped the steering wheel to stop her hands shaking.

"Oh, how could we refuse a lovely young lady such a polite request? Our business with the priest is done. We will raise the barrier for you, *Mademoiselle*, and we shall look forward to meeting you again on your return journey." The officers joked and quarrelled about which one of them would be her boyfriend as they returned to their guard's hut. They waved Pierre back to his coach, reappeared and opened the barrier. All eight coaches started up their engines.

Stella smiled and waved at the officers as her little bus passed their hut. They blew her kisses in return. She drove past two French 75mm guns aimed at the English Channel and two motorised 25mm anti-tank guns. One had broken down and

French army engineers were trying to repair it. The coaches crawled onto the dock and parked alongside the tall black cranes.

The aroma of hot vegetable soup and the yeasty fragrance of warm bread drifted around the bus and revived the passengers. It was set up on rough trestle tables prepared by local supporters.

Stella looked at Pierre and raised an eyebrow. "Do we still need to call you Father Picard while we are here?"

"Of course, my child, I'm looking forward to hearing your full confession later."

The passengers were tired and queued in silence for a little soup. They sat on boxes on the quay, awaiting the dawn and high tide. At 07:00, the officials arrived to check the papers Pierre had acquired for them, and the *verboten* people passed through the customs post. Stella felt drained of energy. She sat down with Betty and cuddled her as she slept.

After an hour or so, the boats were almost boarded. "Hey, what about this little one?" Stella rocked Betty on her lap and the child stretched and sat up.

Pierre consulted his clip board. "She has no money or papers."

"She could have come with us." Regina Gottschalk called out from the deck of the first boat. "We used to know her parents and she could use the papers of our youngest daughter." She brushed a tear from her face. "We lost her to an illness on the way – appendicitis. But we have no money left."

"Oh, my Lord, how much is it?"

"The cost is 200 francs for children." Pierre did not need to consult his paperwork.

"Wait, wait – I'll get the money." Stella counted the money in her purse. "I have 160 francs. Turn out your pockets, Pierre …."

Pierre reached deep into his robe and examined a few coins before handing them over.

Stella counted the money. "Nine francs. Is that it?" She gazed up at the passengers and crew on the deck of the boat and waved at the men working on the dockside. She cupped her hands around her mouth and shouted out: "This little girl is 12 years old. She has no money. I need 31 francs so she can go on the boat with the others. Those who can spare it – please throw me a *sou*."

There was silence. Stella lowered her head. Without warning she was showered with coins.

"Thank you, God. Thank you, everyone." She waved at the sailors and the dockworkers on the quayside who had thrown her the coins. "Oh, it's too much. I've got too much money."

Pierre picked up a few stray coins. "Save it for another deserving case or you can give me my nine francs back."

Stella gave him a sideways look.

The refugees stood on the deck of the first boat with their few possessions and waved farewell to Pierre and his helpers. Stella picked out Betty standing next to the rail and blew her a kiss. The child pretended to catch it, holding it against her heart.

Regina held Betty's hand and called out to Stella. "Don't worry – Jacob and I will see she is loved and looked after."

Stella sent them off with wave. She watched as the three fishing boats headed West. The glass of the wheelhouses reflected the rising sun as the boats took the refugees to safer waters. She returned to the bus and slumped on the driver's seat, closed her eyes and let the weak sun fall on her cheeks while she uttered a short prayer for the safe arrival in Spain of her precious cargo.

***

"The Belgian armed forces on the orders of their King surrendered to the Germans today in the early hours of the morning," announced the BBC newsreader over the radio in the parlour. "By this action, they have created a gap in the front through which Germany's armoured divisions are pouring in to threaten Anglo-French troops."

Kate and Bernie sat together on the sofa in the small back room where they had been waiting for the news announcement. Kate gripped Bernie's hand, "Oh no. Please God, let our army hold them back…"

"Is there any news of Stella?" Bernie rubbed his hand.

"Not a word. Your uncle's been back and forth to France with Churchill several times now, but he's not seen her. Oh Bernie, I'm so frightened – I can't imagine what must be happening in France. Just think of it – Germans – invading. Your uncle will have a devil of a job locating her and Martin. If only he'd found her in Metz. He's very upset. He thinks he let her down."

Bernie looked at the floor.

Kate stroked his head. "It's just that when she spoke to me, she sounded so jolly – not at all as if she was in any danger. I know it's my fault, too – my letter to your uncle contained all my news – and I never would have included something like that if I thought poor Stella was in any trouble." Kate stood up and opened the ironing table with a thwack and plugged in her electric iron.

Bernie handed her a pile of Walter's shirts.

Across the Channel, Stella was celebrating. The Resistance were opening bottles of wine in the farmhouse belonging to Pierre's aunt. Stella was enjoying a shot of adrenalin. She was determined to carry on with her secret work and was oblivious to the dangers that lay ahead.

***

4 June – Thompson's Grocers, Norwood

A month passed with no news of Stella and Martin. Instead, Kate received a cryptic message in her weekly letter from Walter to listen to today's news announcement and let him know if she noticed anything unusual.

He need not have asked. Kate and Bernie had established a routine of sitting together by the radio each day to listen to the six o'clock news.

With food rationing in full flow, the shop had become very busy with customers looking for supplies off ration. So as soon as she could, Kate rushed from the shop into the small parlour, unfastening her apron as she walked. She turned up the volume on the radio to hear the last lines of dreary organ music broadcast by the BBC.

Bernie poured tea from a blue ceramic teapot into china cups and handed one to Kate. She sat down on the sofa.

Bernie sat next to her. "What's all this about?"

Kate blew on her tea. "Your uncle can be so mysterious sometimes. Oh, it's starting."

At the BBC radio studio in London, Norman Shelley leaned into the microphone and began to speak slowly, doing his best to mimic Churchill's distinctive voice. He ended the speech with the famous words:

"We shall defend our island, whatever the cost may be. We shall fight on the beaches, we shall fight on the landing grounds, we shall fight in the fields and in the streets, and we shall fight in the hills: we shall NEVER surrender."

All over the country, people gathered around radio sets in their living rooms. They were anxious to hear the voice of their Prime Minister – and as far as they knew, the voice they heard was Churchill's. Norman fooled everyone and Walter was delighted because the trick could be used to make the enemy think Churchill was in London when he could be elsewhere.

In the back room of the shop, Kate put her arm around Bernie. "Well did you notice anything I should report to your uncle?" She had no idea the broadcast was not from Churchill.

"That bloke hates whistling. I don't know really; it was a good speech but we need to tell uncle to get Mr Churchill to end this war before May 1941."

"May 1941?"

"Yes, I'll be 18 and expected to fight."

  "Oh, my love, NO. NO, that is NOT happening."

CHAPTER 8
Walter and Stella - Lost Government

13 June – Somewhere over France

Churchill and Walter sat together in a small plane headed for France, accompanied by the usual entourage of secretaries and service chiefs.

Churchill slapped his papers down on his lap. "Well? Are we going to land?"

The pilot anticipated Walter's question, as he approached the cockpit. "We're still flying blind, waiting for instructions."

Walter looked at Churchill and shook his head.

Churchill leaned across the aisle to Bunny. "And here we have the Prime Minister of Great Britain, thousands of feet up in the air, trying to discover the whereabouts of the leaders of our principal ally."

Bunny smiled and shrugged her shoulders.

The co-pilot twisted round and called out. "It's to be the city of Tours."

"About time," muttered George.

Once on the ground, they found the roads were choked with refugees. Walter sat in front of the first car, his eyes darting left and right – examining every face. The convoy made slow progress towards the police station in the centre of the town. The procession halted while Walter jumped out and went inside.

Bunny looked bemused. "I've heard about enquiring about a lost purse or a lost dog at a police station, but not a lost government."

Walter tapped on Churchill's window. "I've been informed we can see the French government after lunch. I'm trying to find somewhere for us to eat. The refugees have almost cleared the town of food. The police have suggested a restaurant."

Walter stood guard by the door of the *Brasserie du Ville*, a smart restaurant with curved glass windows leading to a double glass door, with gleaming brass handles. The six waiters with long white starched aprons had polished the silver cutlery and lead crystal glasses on every table, in honour of their private guests. The restaurant was putting on a good show, despite the food shortages and the war.

Churchill's party ate in silence while groups of bedraggled refugees trudged by and stared through the window.

George sat next to Bunny. Having finished his own plate, he watched her as she pushed her food around, glancing now and again through the restaurant window at the forlorn refugees outside.

Bunny put her knife and fork together. "Look at those poor things. What can we do to help them?"

"Win the war, Miss Bunny." George reached over, about to stab a potato on Bunny's plate, but she put her hand in the way.

Walter touched his gun as he studied each face in the crowd for would-be assassins. He drew it from the holster when a thin man banged on the restaurant door.

The man almost toppled backward, knocking into a pale young boy at his side.

Bunny stood and addressed the male diners. "Please don't get up gentlemen." She took her plate over to where Walter was standing by the door. "Please can we let them have it?"

Walter lowered his weapon and assessed the man. He looked over towards Churchill.

"You're the security officer – you decide..." The Prime Minister continued his lunch.

Walter unlocked the door and let the man and the child enter.

Bunny set her plate in front of them.

Walter waved his hand at the plate that had been put aside for him. "Give the boy my lunch – poor lad looks starving."

"*Bonjour, Mesdames et Messieurs. Merci, madame. Vous êtes très gentil.* The man and boy began to eat with their fingers before a waiter could arrive with cutlery.

Bunny studied Walter's lined face. She wished she knew what was troubling him and how she could help.

Meanwhile, a few streets away Stella was herding a party of small children along the pavement, led by Pierre. She was wearing a calf-length brown dress with small pink flowers and talking with a small boy whose hand she held in hers. A nun held the door open for them at the church hall and looked up and down the street at who might be observing. Everyone was too busy hurrying away from the advancing war to take any notice.

Stella counted the children as they entered. "Now, we'll rest here a while... Look, Father Picard has arranged for some soup for lunch."

The children sat down in a group on a mat with crossed legs like they were attending a school assembly. They had been walking for two hours after the little bus had broken down.

"Come on *ma petit*, sip some of this soup for me – it's lovely and tasty." Stella fed a little dark-haired boy on her lap.

The refugees had previously been found temporary homes, but as the war advanced, many French families were headed south away from the battle zone and Pierre was forced to take responsibility for them once again.

Pierre stood to talk to a nun. He returned to Stella smiling. "We can stay here until tomorrow. Luc will have reached Paris by now on his motorcycle and will arrange for another coach."

"What happened?" A nun ladled more chicken *consommé* into Pierre's bowl.

"We have to take these 12 little ones into Spain, where there are good people who will take care of them."

"They look tired, poor little mites." The nun put her arm around a small, curly-haired boy. We'll feed them for you and see they get a good rest. You can sleep in the room next door – we've prepared some mattresses for you."

He followed the nun to the room, leading Stella by the hand, while another sister took over feeding the toddler Stella had been cradling on her lap.

Stella fell asleep in the back room. She dreamed of England, of Martin, Walter, Kate and Bernie. She dreamed of long peaceful days, picnics on Brighton beach, walks along the pier, family dinners and laughter. She shut out thoughts of the ever-advancing Nazi war machine.

14 June – Calais aerodrome and Churchill's plane

Walter stood guard over two boxes of official papers while Churchill strode around the departure lounge talking to colleagues from Whitehall.

A stranger studied the group through the far window. Walter pulled out his Colt 45 from under his jacket. The man disappeared through the main gate and Walter returned his gun to its holster with a shaking hand. "I'm getting trigger happy, George. I see assassins everywhere…."

"No one'll be 'appier than me, Inspector to get back to Blighty." George winked at Walter. "Problem is, we get a lot of nosey parkers now the Old Man's Prime Minister. It's 'ard to tell who's a bad un."

"It's always in their eyes, George and the pull of their mouth."

As the pilot awaited permission to take off, Walter noticed the porter loading the baggage. He strained to see if the official boxes had been put on the plane. He walked along the narrow isle to the steward, who was busy buckling himself into his seat. "Did the official boxes get put on board?"

The plane taxied to the runway.

"I'm pretty sure I saw them coming on," said the steward. "Please sit down, sir, we are about to take off."

Walter leaned over to where Churchill was sitting. "I'm going to ask the pilot to return to the departure building, sir. I am not sure the official boxes are aboard." He crouched in the aisle as the plane sped down the runway.

"Sit down, Thompson. You can get on the radio to Calais as soon as we are safely in the air." Churchill flipped open a file on his lap.

Walter returned from the cockpit. "The French customs office – the *Douanes* at Calais have them in safekeeping," Walter's face reddened at his mistake. "They're sending them with a courier on the next plane."

Churchill frowned. "You know what danger there might have been if those boxes had got into the wrong hands."

"I'm very sorry, sir."

"It was really my responsibility," interrupted Bunny. "It's entirely my fault."

Walter held up his palms. "No, I should have put them on the plane. I'm to blame."

Churchill grinned and waved them away. "You had both better be more careful in future."

In the narrow aisle, Walter turned to Bunny. "Thank you for your support there, Miss Shearburn."

"Inspector, would you do something for me?" She looked up at him.

"Yes, of course." Walter leaned in towards her so he could hear her over the noise of the engines.

"We work together every day. Would you please remember to call me Bunny? Everybody else does, including your colleague, Sergeant George. Frankly, your stiff formality towards me is becoming – well, a bit irritating."

Walter nodded and gave a half smile. He resumed his seat next to Churchill, loosening his collar and wiping his hands on his handkerchief. He peered out of the window. Even in the half-light of the early morning, he could see cars on the road below. His eyes were drawn to a bus trying to push through on the crowded highway below. He turned to Churchill, "Sir, may I ask you a question concerning my family?"

Churchill smiled and nodded.

"I'm worried about my sister. She's married to a Jewish man and they were living in Paris, but I've lost all contact with them. Are we able to do anything to help?"

Churchill took out a cigar. "I'm afraid it's not good news Thompson, especially if the Nazis pay your sister some unwanted attention, just for being considered a Jew. Our information is that Hitler has ordered the construction of a new concentration camp at Auschwitz, near Krakow in Poland. There are other camps too, and we have reports it's not just Jews he's interning, but Slavs, gypsies, homosexuals – even the mentally ill."

"But sir, how would I be able to find my sister and her husband if they were interned?"

The Prime Minister's face looked grim. "I don't know Thompson – I'll give the matter some thought."

Walter wiped perspiration from his forehead and peered out of the window. The English Channel was covered in storm clouds. It was so black it was as if night had already fallen.

Churchill began to doze as the plane left the coast. He had exhausted himself in his talks with the French government. His arguments had been strong, and he had delivered them with force and sincerity. There were many French supporters who agreed with him, but he knew he had failed to convince them not to surrender to the Nazis.

All at once, the aircraft plummeted below the cloud cover. The passengers screamed. A diminutive general was thrown from his seat. He slid backwards down the aisle. George caught him and pulled him into the empty space beside him. Briefcases and papers flew about the cabin.

Walter caught a glimpse of a German plane, a *Heinkel 111* bomber, probably lost and looking for a target before returning to Germany. He buckled Churchill into his seat. "Hold on, sir, we have trouble."

The pilot manoeuvred the plane ahead of the *Heinkel*. He put the plane into another steep nose-dive. The passengers gripped the arms of their seats, their yells masked by the scream of the plane's engine. The *Heinkel* attempted to track their steep descent. Machine gun fire left red and white hot trails flying past Churchill's plane. A few feet above the water, the sea mist cleared. There was a French fishing boat ahead.

The pilot and co-pilot wrestled with the controls.

The fishermen looked up open mouthed as the passenger plane almost clipped their mast. They dived for cover when they saw the *Heinkel* in pursuit.

"Thompson, give me my Colt." Churchill shouted above the shriek of the engines. "One never knows... I do not intend to be taken alive."

As both planes levelled out, the Heinkel let go a burst of gunfire at the French boat and vanished out of sight in the fog.

The young co-pilot sat rigid - his face drained of blood.

The pilot gave Walter a wide smile. "I've never had to do that before in a passenger plane. Quite frankly I didn't think it would come up – I thought we'd had it. Damn good luck I've been reading Jane's *All the World's Aircraft*, I only noted yesterday that *Heinkel's* cannot dive at such a steep angle compared to this little beauty of a plane."

Walter patted the co-pilot on the shoulder. "Well done both of you."

Churchill had a fierce gleam in his eyes, but Bunny was pale and shaking. Walter moved into the empty seat beside her and squeezed her hand. "It's all over, Miss… Bunny. Come on now, it's all right."

Bunny took in the warmth of his touch and the smell of his skin. She found herself staring at a tiny bead of sweat on his temple.

"Breathe in and breathe out." Walter patted her arm and got up to assist the rest of the party in picking up all the belongings and papers.

George walked up the aisle, placing his comforting hand on shoulders and checking seat belts. "Okay are we sir? Yes, that's right keep buckled up. Alright are we sir?" He reached the front of the plane and sat next to Bunny. "Boiled sweet?"

"Thank you, George."

He took her hand. "That was a bit of excitement – some German pilot'll never know 'ow near 'e was to winning an Iron Cross – first-class."

Churchill turned and looked over his half glasses. "If I get hold of him, he'll hang. It's against the Geneva convention to shoot at an unarmed civilian plane."

***

1–14 October – The War Cabinet, and the bombsites of London

George joined Walter in the War Cabinet room at 10 Downing Street. "What's this meeting going to be about then?"

Walter studied the damaged buildings opposite before he closed the steel shutters over the window. "The Chancellor is proposing raising taxes by three per cent to cover the cost of reconstructing the homes destroyed by the bombing. And the country's running short of food."

George closed the next shutter. The noise of the demolition gang making the buildings safe on the opposite side of the street was silenced. "Oh, and I overheard some bright spark says we've only got six weeks of food left and they're thinking of fishing for plankton in Scottish lochs – to feed us all. The spirit of the British people is beginning to dwindle – that's what the Old Man said yesterday. He told the Cabinet, only 22 miles of sea separates us from enslavement by the Germans. The bombing's taking its toll. Now the Froggies 'ave waved the white flag – we're alone, Inspector – a bunch of amateurs up against the might of a professional German army. If I was a betting man – I wouldn't be giving good odds on us."

Walter put his hands in his pockets. "I know, it feels like we're taking the brunt of it. Everyone seems to be down. I passed a damn hospital that had been blown to bits yesterday."

After the meeting, a pitiful group of Ministers filed out of the long Cabinet Room, picking up their papers from the polished kidney shaped table as they left. Churchill stood up and stretched. He walked along the chequered passageway and stood next to Walter in the doorway of Number 10. They watched the bursts of light from the anti-aircraft shells fired at German planes in the distance and the searchlights making giant crosses in the sky.

An ear-splitting whistling sound made them screw up their faces.

Walter's flung his arms around Churchill's middle and swung him inside, behind the safety of the heavy door.

In the same second, a bomb hit the railings of the building opposite and exploded, showering Walter with shrapnel and dust. He lay on the soft, squashy body of Churchill. From behind the protection of the door, Walter saw everything go by in slow motion and without sound.

Churchill began to wriggle and went blood red in the face, fighting to shove Walter off. "Don't do that, ever again," he shouted.

Walter could only lip read as he got to his feet. He offered the Old Man his hand, checked him over and moved him aside to check on the others.

George was lying face down in the hall.

Walter squatted beside him and lifted his head into the crook of his arm. "Get this man some help. George, George...? Walter's voice was unusually high as he could not hear.

Churchill leaned over George. "Don't let those buggers get you, too."

Walter held his handkerchief on George's bleeding head. "George... hang on, hang on, the ambulance is coming. Will someone get a blanket?" He began checking George for wounds and mouthing in a strange voice: "I think the bastards missed you, old pal. You just seem to have struck your head. Can you sit up a little?"

The *tring tring* of the ambulance could be heard pulling up outside. Walter helped the stretcher-bearers to lift George inside the vehicle. A little of his hearing returned but the high pitch of tinnitus rang in his ears.

Churchill patted George on the shoulder. "You'll live, Sergeant, but you'd better hurry back. You'll find the food's awful in hospital." He brushed himself down and returned to his office.

The bombing continued in a relentless siege, stretching on into the evening. Bunny met Walter in the corridor. His back was completely covered in dust. "I'll watch the Old Man, Inspector. He's having dinner downstairs in the Garden Rooms and I've run a bath for you."

Walter opened his mouth to protest.

Bunny put her index finger across his lips. "Unless you want me to call an ambulance for you too."

Walter retrieved some clean clothes from his room and grinned when he saw Bunny had added bubble bath. He stepped in and slipped his whole body under the warm water. It seemed to help the ringing in his ears and when he swallowed, he found he could hear again.

Churchill was dining in a basement room with three guests. The bombing was getting close again and little chips of plaster

82

dropped on to the table. "Damn them." Churchill coughed and kept eating.

Walter, fresh in a clean suit, opened the dining room door. "To the shelter, gentlemen. This place is a death trap."

Churchill's guests jumped up and dashed for the door, followed by the staff.

A shrill whistling noise signalled another bomb. Dust and smoke filled the corridor as it crashed down between the Treasury and Number 10, wrecking the kitchen.

A cloud of toxic dust followed the escaping staff out into the street. Each person was coughing and trying to spit the taste of damp mortar from their mouths. Walter counted every person present and checked to see if they were injured before directing them to the air-raid shelter. "Where's Miss Shearburn?"

Downwood scurried past, choking and spluttering.

Walter put his arm out to halt the small man's progress. "Mr Downwood, please escort The Prime Minister to the shelter. Miss Shearburn is missing."

Walter jogged back to the entrance of 10 Downing Street. The door was open, and sitting on the bottom step of the stairs, wearing her gas mask and with no shoes, was Bunny. She rubbed her ankle.

Walter lifted her into his arms. "Let me help you. We'll get to the shelter and see if you need a hospital for that ankle." He carried her to where everyone was waiting and set her down on a blanket. He took off his jacket, wrapped it around her shoulders. She was still wearing the mask, her long hair tangled in the straps. He took care not to snag her curls as he removed the goggles from her face. "Now let's take a look at your foot." He knelt down and examined her ankle.

"I fell down the last few stairs. Bit stupid really – I couldn't see properly with the mask, but I was so frightened there would be gas, so I kept it on."

"Well I think you've got a nasty sprain, but I don't think anything's broken. Can you wiggle your toes again for me?"

Bunny moved her toes and her foot felt comforted in his warm hands. "Thank you for coming back for me."

Fires blazed all around them, illuminating the night sky, while they sat on the freezing concrete floor of the shelter waiting for the siren signalling all clear. Walter handed Churchill his handkerchief and the Old Man wiped the dust from his face.

Winston tapped Walter on the arm and passed him his own handkerchief with a sly grin.

***

The next evening, the air-raid warning sounded as soon as it was dark. "Sir, we must leave for the shelter." Walter stood behind Churchill's chair.

"Yes, yes, Thompson." Churchill nodded but did not look up from his papers.

The building shook and echoed with the reverberations of the anti-aircraft guns. Walter picked up the cap to Churchill's fountain pen and held it over the paper where he was still writing notes. "Sir…?"

Churchill pushed his hand aside and continued.

"Sir, do I need to repeat myself?"

Churchill looked up above his half-rimmed glasses at his bodyguard.

"If we don't go now, we'll have no need to go at all in a few minutes time… because we'll all be blown to bits – I insist." He held the back of Churchill's chair, ready to pull it out.

Churchill got up in slow motion and marched to the Number 10 Annexe by St James's Park. A few seconds after entering the building, they held their chests with the pain of burning as oxygen was snatched from their lungs. They were lifted from their feet and slammed against the wall. The whole street shook, sending roof tiles and a chimney crashing into the road as a 1,000-pound bomb dropped on the corner. The Old Man wheezed and gasped for air.

Walter took great gulps into his body. "I've found you a better headquarters, sir, if you will permit me. It's the disused Down Street Underground station in Mayfair."

Churchill looked down at his trembling legs and took Walter's arm to steady himself. "Yes, Thompson, a good idea, it would be foolish to get blown up."

From then on, Churchill's new routine was to work and sleep in the railway company's offices, often holding meetings while German bombs dropped above them. Walter was on hand throughout the air raids, ready with Churchill's steel helmet and gas mask slung over his shoulder.

As the Blitz stormed its way to the doorsteps of millions of Londoners, Churchill worked hard to uphold their spirits. He made regular radio broadcasts to try to bolster morale. The Old Man carried on his normal work every day, Blitz or no Blitz.

Homes were destroyed, schools and churches burned out by explosive and incendiary bombs, and people got up in the mornings to find their workplaces gone, or returned from nightshifts not knowing if their homes would still be there. During the chaos, Churchill was determined to stay in the thick of it and support the people.

***

The next day they toured London to inspect the damage. George was driving. He had a large sticky plaster on his forehead and a bandage on his wrist.

"Stop here, George, I'd like to see for myself." Churchill stepped out of the car in a bombed-out street.

Walter scrutinised each face. A crowd had gathered to form a human line to uncover a school, brick by brick.

"Good Lord, it's only the Prime Minister, himself. Hello, Sir – come to help out, have you?" The dust covered man held out his hand for Churchill.

Churchill took it. "The children?"

"All evacuated to the countryside, sir."

A cheer went up from the determined rescuers. "We can take it, sir – but give it to 'em back."

"We will give it back tenfold, but first we must make more tanks and planes." Churchill shook more dirt covered hands. "Give us a little more time, and I promise the Germans will get repayment for what they've done – repayment with compound interest."

"Three cheers for the Prime Minister." The first man called to the crowd. "Hip hip…"

Walter looked at the faces of the people, and saw their eyes told it all. Despite the cheers, London had taken about all it could stand.

***

That evening, as Walter was waiting by the Prime Minister's car, he glanced at his newspaper. The headline urged Londoners to *KEEP CALM AND CARRY ON* in the face of the Blitz.

Despite Hitler's constant terrifying metal rain storming over London, people still smile. Jokes are still cracked in the pubs; laughter is still heard coming from the bombed homes of humble families. Everyone still finds his or her bright spots in life. Ordinary people who are sticking it out, discover little sparks of happiness and joy: a new love, a new baby or extra rations from the black market. In these days of hardship and passions, when we all walk on the edge of a sword, a simple pleasure like a few ounces of butter can bring endless joy to a simple soul. These tiny delights brighten days and give hope. Life is still worth living. The British keep smiling through.

Churchill was working in the new reinforced War Rooms, deep under the Treasury Building, protected by fourteen feet of concrete. Old age and the relentless onslaught of the bombing was making him ever more irritable. "Where's my damned papers?" he called to Walter.

Walter picked up a pile of newspapers and handed them to him.

"Not that bloody rubbish – I've read those. Where's *The Express*?"

"I'm not sure sir; I'll go and ask Miss Shearburn."

"Well hurry up about it."

"You're looking a bit glum," said Bunny as Walter entered her office.

"I just got another rocket from the Old Man for no purpose at all. He's depressed and for good reason – we're losing the war and unless he gets us some help…." Walter checked the window. "Have you seen *The Express*?"

"Oh sorry, I have it here," said a General, looking up from reading the paper in the corner of the office. "Profuse apologies – I thought the Old Man had finished with it. By the way, I get it just the same, you know. But if it relieves his overtaxed mind, I suppose we'll just have to put up with it. You're not getting enough sleep, old boy." The General put his pen to his temple. "In my estimation, you only sleep about four hours a night." He handed Walter the paper and left.

Bunny touched Walter's hand. "He's shouting a lot today…"

Walter took his hand away. "I'm used to it. But the tough part is putting up with this constant yelling and scolding from someone I care about. It's time to hand in my resignation and go and look after my wife and my family. I'm 50, too old to really be any use. I can serve out the war a whole lot better as a beat police officer in Brighton. Enough is enough."

Bunny looked after Walter as he left the office with a soft sadness in her eyes.

***

1 November – Churchill's apartments

While Churchill was taking his bath, Walter went to find George. He was in the kitchen, tucking into a large, slice of apple pie and washing it down with a cup of hot tea.

"I'm really sorry, Inspector, but Mrs Churchill says I am no longer allowed to provide food for you or your sergeant." The cook laughed at George with his mouth full and his face covered in crumbs. "But your sergeant asked me not to tell you until he had finished his pie."

"Oh, that's quite understandable, Cook. We're only here because Downing Street is still under repair. Would it be all right if we used your kitchen as an office for fifteen minutes? It's a bit cramped in my room."

"You help yourself, lovey. I was going to nip out and see if the butcher has made any sausages anyhow." She turned to the kitchen maid. "Come along, you. You can take your nose out of whatever these officers need to discuss and come with me to the butcher."

The maid took her coat from the peg and lingered while she gave Walter an appreciative look.

George helped himself to another piece of pie. "She resents you; you know – 'is wife, Clemmie. He talks things through with you to get the common man's view, and she gets cut out of the discussion. She's 'is wife, but she thinks you take her role away from 'er. She likes me all right, though – can't imagine why she'd have any problem with feeding me." He wiped the crumbs from his face, trying to decide whether to risk a third piece of pie. "You see, I never rock the boat. I don't spend hours and hours discussing the war with the Old Man like you do."

"Common man …? Well, Mrs Churchill can stop worrying, because I'm going to see the commissioner and ask him to put me back on uniform duty."

George opened his mouth to protest, but Walter held up his hand. "I'm too old for this, and my mind is not focused on the job. We've been together too long – he and I. I'm getting on his nerves, and he is not doing mine any good either."

Walter handed George a memo. "Oh, and this came through today. It's the latest report from Station X about another possible planned attempt on the Old Man. You're going to have to double the guard on the apartment, the War Rooms, Number 10 and the House of Commons. It's useless of course, except that we now know the Germans have a name for their campaign to kill him – it's called *Operation Long Jump*."

George pulled a face. "So, what now? You mean you're going to abandon me?" He stood up. "Hello everyone – I'm the officer in charge of *Operation Longshot* a bloody hopeless mission to keep the Old Man alive."

"Look, you'll be all right here – so long as you can herd him along to the bomb shelter when the sirens sound. Your main problem will be when he decides to travel. But if the Germans have got a slick operation planned, your gun is going to be as good as mine. His instructions still stand. The last bullet will be for him – he won't be taken alive."

"I'm not going to bloody shoot 'im, Inspector."

"You won't need to. He has courage enough to do it himself."

"Oh, God, I'm going to miss you, my old mate – but I understand your decision. I'd do the same thing in your shoes." George wiped his mouth. "That annoying creep Downwood, introduced me to an interesting fellow the other day, 'e's been tasked with finding doubles for you and the Old Man. He's found an actor, codenamed Larry Lamb. He looks just like the Old Man – in the right light, if you could just see 'im with a homburg and a large cigar. He won't need someone for you now, which is a relief because he swore you were a one off – no one comes close. So, he'll have to find someone for me. Who d'yer think? John Wayne?"

"Oliver Hardy." Walter ducked to avoid the thump he anticipated from George.

"What that fat old bloke? You cheeky basket."

1941
Risks and Retribution

CHAPTER 9
Stella - A Fraternisation

20 January – The Hotel Majestic, Paris

Martin's caution, back in 1939, was proved justified. With their Jewish origins concealed from the victors, and the acquisition of French passports, Europe Express was now registered as a French company in the name of Martin Thibault. Even with this rebirth, the need to do business did not free them from the danger of having to make face to face contact with the Nazis who had swarmed into Paris and seized its most luxurious hotel for their headquarters – the *Hotel Majestic*.

January 20th was a big day, for Martin and Stella – their first meeting with the most powerful and high-ranking German officer in France.

Stella put a hand on the banister to steady herself.

Martin bent down to untangle the train of her dress from her heel. He brushed her neck with his lips and whispered in her ear. "Stunning *Neshama.*"

Her hand shook as she held Martin's arm. They continued to climb the sweeping staircase, with marble lions either side, guarding the den of the men convinced they were a master race.

"I'll be alright, just give me a minute. Tell me his name again."

Martin squeezed her hand. "Otto von Stülpnagel, the Military Commander in France, *Militärbefehlshaber in Frankreich.*"

"Can I call him Otto?"

Captain Scheben met them at the door. Martin had been sweet-talking the handsome young Captain for months and he was here in person to make the formal introduction.

Von Stülpnagel's eyes widened when he saw Stella. He clicked his heels and kissed the back of her hand, while all the time staring at her necklace of real pearls.

The hairs were raised on the back of Stella's neck and goose bumps crept up her spine, but she held the German's gaze.

Captain Scheben saluted and withdrew.

The ballroom sparkled from six huge crystal chandeliers and polished silver cutlery reflecting the cut glass.

Martin looked dapper in his dinner jacket and his high-collared shirt with a white bow tie.

Things had changed in Paris since France had surrendered to the Germans. The French citizens were paying a high price for peace. It was warm in the ballroom, but 20 days of freezing snow had taken its toll on the people who were short of heating, fuel and food. The French were feeding and entertaining the 300,000 strong German army of occupation who were billeted to the *Zone Occupée* – The Occupied Zone, in the North.

France had been cut in two and marked by a curved line from the border near Geneva to Biarritz on the Atlantic coast. Eight million panic-stricken civilians, those fortunate enough to have somewhere to go in the South, had fled with all they could carry. This area was called the *Zone Libre* – the Free Zone still administered by the French from a spa town – Vichy. Here the people prayed they would escape curfews, forced labour and starvation.

Otto looked like he could be Hitler's thinner, older brother, with his neat moustache, combed-over hair and small mouth. He kept his eyes on Stella. He took a bottle of champagne proffered by the waiter and poured some into Stella's glass. He smiled at her revealing yellowed uneven teeth.

Stella could feel his eyes on her, but kept her own on the elegant singer, *Mademoiselle* Leo Marjane who was singing, *Seule ce soir*. Stella applauded and turned to the high-ranking German as if surprised. "Oh, thank you, Otto." She sipped a little champagne and smiled, remembering the sparkling taste from the toasts at her wedding.

"She's rather good, isn't she?" said Martin.

"But not the loveliest woman here," said Von Stülpnagel, his eyes still on Stella. "Now, you had a proposition to make."

"Well, yes, sir. We run a regular coach service around Paris. These are difficult times, but Parisians must still get to work, for our own sakes and for the German Reich. I have read your information handbook for the German officers. If Paris is to be a *vacation paradise* for your troops – you need our help to provide comfortable transport for troops coming in and out of Paris."

"Yes, *Monsieur* Thibault. You come highly recommended by the Captain. My officers do deserve to travel in comfort."

Martin toasted his host. "I hope that after the war, Europe Express may be a symbol of co-operation between our nations."

Von Stülpnagel, smiled. "Well said. And so, I will authorise Captain Scheben to assist you in winning a contract."

"Sir, you are very generous." Martin forced a wide smile.

"That's a most beautiful necklace, my dear." Von Stülpnagel fingered Stella's pearls. "It's my wife's birthday in three days – I expect to be able to give her one just like it."

Stella constricted her abhorrence within her rigid back. She finished her meal and was just about to place her knife and fork together at 06:30, as the English are taught to do.

Martin's eyes flashed and he touched her foot under the table. "I'm sure I can find something to please your wife."

Stella's hand shook as she left her cutlery strewn at an angle on her plate, as is the French custom, and she began folding her serviette into the shape of a swan.

When more German officers approached the table, Martin recognised their audience with Otto was at an end. He stood to be excused and performed a half Nazi salute. He paused behind Stella's chair and pulled it out as she rose. Their host got up and caressed her hand, held it for longer than was comfortable and kissed it.

Martin gritted his teeth. The transaction was completed. He would deliver the necklace to Von Stülpnagel, tomorrow and go and see Captain Scheben for the permits and the contract. Von Stülpnagel had been taken in by their apparent Nazi sympathies but Martin and Stella were playing a nerve wracking, dangerous game.

Europe Express now owned twenty coaches. Stella designed a new livery for the company – all the buses were painted gold with black sign writing. So well-known had the golden coaches become during the past year, none of the German contacts had thought to ask for Martin's personal papers or look into his background. So far, their luck had held.

They made their way to the cloakroom and strode out of the lions' den, through the sparkling glass revolving door.

Stella's breath puffed white with the frost. "Yesterday, someone in the street called me a traitor and a Nazi lover – me."

Martin steadied Stella as she stepped on the icy pavement. He opened the passenger door of their new *Citroën Advant.* He lifted the train on her dress and helped her into the car.

They drove away from the streets, bustling with German troops. Martin straightened the permit on the windscreen. "Well, it might appear we are collaborators to the outside world, but *we* know what side we're on, so don't worry. As long as the Germans think we are sympathetic and keep dishing out contracts and fuel, we can help Pierre. We need to be cunning if we are to survive this occupation."

CHAPTER 10
Walter - Tragedy and a Secret Meeting at Sea

19 March – Norwood 20:00

Walter stirred in the dark. His face was masked in dust – his tongue was swollen and his teeth ground grit. He used grime covered hands to move muck from his eyes and stared at the rubble surrounding him.

Memories of a few hours ago, sharp pictures began to appear in Walter's head. The Old Man at the window. Riding away from 10 Downing Street on the motorcycle. The air-raid warning, the searchlights, the line of people heading for the shelter, the bus, Kate, the good news for Kate. The bomb. Kate's hand slipping from his grip as the air was ripped from his lungs. "Kate … KATE…!"

Walter pushed loose plaster from his chest and turned his head to look around the parlour. "Kate. Kate. Where are you?" Tears trickled down his dirty cheeks. "Kate, Kate…"

***

Bernie helped his mother, Emily up the steps of the Anderson air raid shelter, in their back garden.

The hand digging of the shelter had been hard work for the council workers as their two-storey red brick Victorian terraced house was built on London clay. Emily had covered the earth floor with the old linoleum from their kitchen and they had installed bunk beds, two deck chairs and a side table with a large primus lamp. A big spider had made a web in the corner and Emily and Bernie called it *Fred*.

Bernie shone his torch over to their house. Dust particles danced in the beam. "Well at least our house didn't get hit. Come on mum let's go indoors, now the *all clear* has sounded."

Emily had a chamber pot in her hand. "Right Bern, I'll just water the rhubarb." She poured the contents on the deep mound of earth covering the shelter, where she had planted a small vegetable garden. "Oh... can you just pop along and make sure Kate's alright and I'll put the kettle on?"

Bernie ran out into the street and stopped short. He screwed up his face and seized hold of his head at the sight of the carnage. It looked like the aftermath of an erupted volcano – black soot and burning embers as far as the eye could see. And the continual ringing of fire engines echoing around London.

He darted towards *Thompson's Grocers* when he saw smoke coming from the end of the terrace. Tears welled in his eyes as he shone his flashlight at the rubble which was once the parlour. "Auntie! Auntie, where are you? Aunt Kate?"

Walter could see Bernie but not hear him. "Bernie – Kate was over there – beside the kitchen sink."

"Oh heavens. Uncle I didn't know you were here."

In the poor light, Walter looked as though he were a part of the rubble pile. "Please look over there Bernie...."

Bernie stared at the indistinct shapes of the wreckage and scrambled over to where he could see broken pieces of the white butler sink. "Auntie Kate! Auntie Kate!" There was no response. "Uncle, I can't see her, and I can't move this lot myself, I'll have to go and get help."

A fire engine appeared through the murky dark. Bernie stood in the road and waved his arms, pointing to the shop. A fireman from the Auxiliary Fire Service, wearing wellington boots and a tin helmet jumped down from the cab. They ran together into the front part of the building, which was intact. It was Kate's parlour at the back that had shared a partial impact with the shop next door.

Bernie tugged the fireman's sleeve. "Over here – my aunt and uncle need help."

The fireman spotted Walter and began to dig him from the ruins.

"No, leave me," Walter pleaded, coughing dust. "Please, please find my wife."

Walter could only watch from where he was wedged as his strapping nephew, with bloodied hands, moved huge timbers and blocks of rubble, to free his uncle's legs.

"Aunt Kate! Aunt Kate!" Bernie called out as he worked.

A senior fire officer arrived with more men. "Right, we need to tunnel into this rubble. The first few yards are always the worst, and are likely to cave in. But first we must know where to start, so what I'd like us all to do is to keep quiet for one minute to see if we can hear her. What's her name?"

"Kate Thompson," Bernie said, streaking dirt on his face as he wiped away a tear.

"Mrs Thompson, Mrs Thompson. Can you hear me?"

They waited in silence.

"There." Bernie pointed to a pile at the back. "Over there…I heard a groan."

"Right lads, we'll trust these young ears and start on the rubble here – and be careful, we don't know what's under there. We don't want to cause any more damage. You two, help to free her husband."

The firemen began to move the debris from the broken dining table pinning Walter's legs. Other local people, including Bernie's mother, Emily, the undertaker and his wife, the greengrocer and his son started to help the firemen. The air smelled of freshly exposed mortar and damp bricks.

Bernie joined in the chain gang passing rubble and buckets of debris from one person to another. They worked with a determined rapid tempo to free Walter. He checked his head. A large bruise was throbbing on his crown. He massaged his leg and was able to pull himself up.

An air-raid warden checked him over. "Well, you're badly bruised, but I don't think there's anything broken. I'm going to fetch an ambulance for your wife."

The dust began to settle in the street, and Bernie could see the houses opposite, had their windows blown out. It was as if a finger from God had crushed the tobacconist's and bruised the shops on either side. The undertaker and greengrocer shops were undamaged. The Fire-fighters, assisted by local men and women, searched through the other wrecked buildings. No fires were alight; the work was illuminated from the flickering of torches.

An ambulance pulled into the street and the Warden flagged it down. "This way, we've got trapped woman."

The rescue team were still digging. "I can see her." Bernie was on his knees in the debris. "Auntie Kate, it's me – Bernie. We'll have you out in a jiffy."

Kate's face was grey.

The Senior Fire Warden examined the tunnel. "Lucky. The bomb's blown her underneath the ironing board, made an air pocket and some protection for her head."

Bernie stood back and let the professionals complete the task of freeing his aunt. The ambulance men waited with a stretcher.

When she was free, Walter limped over to her. "Kate, my love...."

Kate managed a half smile.

The ambulance driver took Kate's pulse. "I can't see anything broken, but she may have internal injuries. Her breathing is a bit laboured, but her heart is beating well. My assistant will put a splint on her wrist, and we'll check out the rest at the Cottage hospital. What a bloody night. We heard over the radio it's the worst night of bombing so far – even Buckingham Palace and the Houses of Parliament have been hit. Are you coming to the hospital with us, sir?"

Walter had tinnitus ringing in his ears. "I... I..." Walter faltered. "Yes, but I must go via Downing Street.... Check everyone's okay there...."

Emily brushed dust from her hands. "I'll go with Kate for now – you catch us up when you've checked on your boss." She ducked as she climbed in the back of the ambulance.

"I'll go too," said Bernie.

"Sorry lad, I can only take one relative." The driver closed the back doors.

Bernie dusted off his hands. "Don't worry I'll follow on the shop bike if it's still in one piece."

Walter stood motionless and watched Kate go. He stared at the shop. The front window was smashed, and cans, packets and boxes lay strewn. The back bedroom and the roof had collapsed, burying Kate's pretty parlour.

It was a miracle, the motorbike survived the blast. Walter eased himself on the saddle to kick-start the motor. His body jolted and he shot in the air. "Agh… FUUUCKKK." He rolled up his trouser leg, revealing a long ugly graze trickling with blood.

"Can I do that for you?" Bernie trotted round the bike and kicked started the engine.

"Thank you, Bernie. I'll see you at the hospital." Walter blew his nose and some of his hearing was restored. He rode off into the night and had been going for several miles before he squinted and realised his headlight had been smashed in the blast – the red glow of London burning was lighting his way.

When Walter reached Churchill's war rooms, he stopped outside and called to the policeman on the door. "Is everything alright? The Old Man? I heard the Palace and the West End has been badly hit." He sat on the idling bike reluctant to get off.

"We've taken no hits here, Inspector – all's well."

"I'll be off then. My wife's been injured in the air raid." He stretched his leg out. "Agh…."

Churchill emerged from the building smoking a cigar. "Gracious, are you alright Thompson? What's this about your wife? Where have they taken her?"

"She's en route to Norwood Cottage Hospital, sir.

"I will have my personal physician, see to her."

"Thank you, sir."

"Off you go, Thompson. I'll send a car for him myself, right away." Churchill waved Walter on and marched back into the building.

When he arrived at the hospital, Walter parked his motorbike next to the Bernie's delivery bicycle. He limped up the steps.

Bernie and Emily were in the waiting room. Emily hugged him and kissed his cheek. "They haven't let us see her yet. They're just transferring her from the Emergency department to Nightingale Ward."

Walter nodded and squeezed their hands before hobbling up the stairs to the ward.

The sister stood by Kate's side holding the blood pressure gauge. "I'm afraid visiting time is over." She caught the pain in Walter's face. She smiled. "Five minutes."

Walter nodded and took Kate's hand. "Darling, what a pickle this is, eh?"

Kate nodded.

Emily put her head around the curtain. "I've sneaked in." She moved to the bedside. "Here's a big kiss from me and Bernie and we'll take care of Walter until you're up and around. Goodnight my love, I'll sort out some washing things and a clean nighty of your own for you to put on tomorrow." She planted a big wet kiss on Kate's cheek and slipped back out through the curtain.

Walter took Kate's hand again. "You will have the very best of care. Churchill is sending his personal doctor."

She beckoned him forward and brushed her lips against his.

Walter held her. "Oh, my love…."

The nurse drew back the curtain. "Mr Thompson? I am afraid sister says you have to go now."

Walter stood up and beckoned the nurse away from the bed. "May I ask if my wife has been given any pain medication?"

"Well, not yet, sir. We've been informed she is waiting for her personal doctor, and we have to wait and see what he prescribes. Please come back and see her tomorrow. Visiting hours are between two and four in the afternoon. I am sure she'll be feeling a lot better – she'll probably be sitting up in bed with a cup of tea."

Walter nodded. He returned to Kate's side and hugged her. "I'm sure the doctor will be along any minute. I love you. Have a good night's rest and I'll be back tomorrow."

She held his hand for a few seconds, let it slip from hers, lay back and closed her eyes. "I love you too…."

Emily was waiting for him by the entrance. "Come on back to our house, I've got some stew I can heat up."

Emily walked over to the bike and started it. Walter stood on the steps and made a face.

"Don't worry I'll get on the back," she said.

When they reached home, they ate dinner in silence. Even Bernie had little appetite.

Walter took the spare room hoping to fall into a deep sleep. But his feet hung over the end of the single bed, while he tossed and turned.

When he woke, there was a cup of tea on the chair by the side of his bed. He sat up to drink it and found a hot water bottle under his calf. He stretched and grimaced with the pain in his leg. In the bathroom he poured the lukewarm water from the rubber bottle into the basin. He stripped naked and washed all over, checking himself for injuries. Bruises were turning blue and yellow on his leg. On the chair in the corner was a set of Bernie's clothes. Walter breathed in as he did up the fly of Bernie's trousers.

When he arrived downstairs, carrying the empty cup and hot water bottle, there was a breakfast waiting of eggs, sausage and bacon.

Emily raised a hand. "Don't dare ask where I got this from – you're a policeman and I wouldn't want to get in any trouble. I just thought we all needed a bit of a boost this morning."

Walter smiled and placed the cup on the drainer. "Thanks for the hot water bottle and the cup of tea."

"I'm off to the shop," said Bernie. "I'm going to take the wheelbarrow and get all the tins and stuff before some blighter steals it."

"I'll be along shortly, as soon as I have finished this feast." Walter put some mustard on his sausage. "I'll go and see what personal things I can recover – I've got time to kill before I'm allowed to visit Kate."

"Yes, pop back here before you go. I'm going to put together some washing things and a nighty for you to take. And Bernie's got her two lemon French fancies – her favourite. I'll find a little tin for them." Emily smiled and busied herself searching the kitchen cupboards.

***

20 March – Norwood and District Cottage Hospital

Having washed again but still looking bedraggled, Walter

hobbled into the hospital, ten minutes before visiting hours. He paced the corridor, holding the bag Emily had given him. In his other hand he held Kate's only childhood toy, her one-eyed teddy bear – rescued from the rubble.

A fat, balding man in a white coat called out to him. "Inspector Thompson? Would you like to come into this little office and sit down for a moment?"

Walter extended his hand. "Yes of course. Thank you so much for caring for my wife."

The doctor stared at the desk and took a deep breath, "I am very sorry, Inspector…."

"Sorry?" Walter dropped the bag.

"Please accept my deepest sympathy. Mrs Thompson did not make it through the night."

Walter ran out of the office and into the ward, where the curtains were drawn around Kate's bed.

The sister came out from behind the reception desk. "Inspector Thompson, I am very sorry for your loss. Would you like to see your wife now?"

His hands trembled as he pulled back the curtain.

Kate looked serene – pale and beautiful. Her hair had been brushed and she wore a pure-white gown. Walter scooped her up in his arms and held her.

George took the staircase to the ward. He held a dozen daffodils in full bloom. He almost bashed into a man hurrying in the other direction. "Doctor?"

The doctor did not reply, and George stopped and looked after him. His pulse beat double time and he dashed upstairs, passing the empty doctor's office. He halted and backed up to the office. There was a bag tipped over on the floor and a single sheet of paper on the desk – Kate's death certificate – cause, pneumonia.

The staff nurse challenged George as he walked in the ward. He flashed his warrant card and handed her the flowers. "Could you give these to one of your patients? I've come for Mrs Thompson."

"Oh, thank goodness. Her husband's in there. I'm afraid …"

"I know, I've just found this." George held up the death certificate. "He won't put the body down."

"Leave it all to me. Can I suppose that as the certificate 'as been signed, we can take Mrs Thompson to a chapel of rest?"

"Yes, of course."

"Well then I'll call, Dickie Bird, the undertaker, he's a good friend and local."

George waited outside the curtain. He watched the shadow of Walter holding Kate in his arms.

Dickie, whose funeral parlour was situated on the same parade as Thompson's Grocers, arrived. He shook George's hand and whispered. "Heavens above. I never thought I'd be burying Kate."

The curtain opened and Walter emerged with Kate in his arms, draped in the white sheet.

George touched his shoulder. "I'm so sorry, Walter…"

Walter nodded and went to walk away. "I'm taking her home, George."

"Yes, of course, but let's take her the back way, cos Dickie's brought his ambulance.

Dickie bowed his head. "We'll take the very best care of her, Walter. I promise you."

George picked up Kate's teddy bear from the bed and used its arm to dab his eyes. He opened the back door for Walter so he could carry Kate through. Dickie did have an old ambulance, rather than a hearse waiting outside. Walter got in the back and rested Kate on the stretcher.

George returned to the sister to let her know what had happened. As he passed the empty doctor's office, he noticed the bag tipped on its side and a small round tin on the floor. In the waste-paper bin was an empty bottle of brandy.

***

12 April – West Norwood Cemetery

Low grey clouds darkened the sky above the cemetery. Walter stood by Kate's grave surrounded by a mist so dense, it was not unlike fine rain. The other mourners had already left under a sea of black umbrellas. Bernie tugged Walter's soaking sleeve, but he did not move.

Two gravediggers sheltered under a large oak. An older man rested on his shovel. "This chap's not going anywhere any time soon."

"Cup of tea then, dad? Give him a bit of time – can't fill in the hole with him standing there like that. She had a good turnout, that nice lady from the shop. Haven't seen that many people for a funeral in a long time. Everyone came to their front garden gate with their hats off to show their respects. There were so many people they all couldn't get in the chapel. She was a lovely woman – generous to a fault – even with the rationing. What a flamin' shame."

George instructed the driver of Churchill's private car to take Emily and Bernie to the wake and then come back for him and Walter. As he waited, he wrestled in his head with the information the driver had reported about the doctor. Churchill had sent him to collect the doctor at his club last Saturday, but the doctor was drunk and had to be taken home. The driver told George he had suggested the doctor call a colleague to attend to Mrs Thompson, but he had dismissed him. The doctor had not arrived at the cottage hospital until 10:00 am the next morning.

George looked at the open grave and mumbled. "One day, I'll have to tell 'im about this, but not today."

***

George unloaded Walter's gun and put the bullets in his jacket pocket. He slipped the gun back into Walter's holster, where it hung on the hook on the back of the door.

Walter appeared from his bathroom wearing a towel. His features were lined with grief. He glanced in the mirror, picked up hand towel resting on the bed and rubbed his face.

George pulled the towel away from him. "Come on Inspector. The Old Man'll be ready in 15 minutes – they're all having to meet in the Lords today."

The House of Commons Chamber had been destroyed in a bombing raid shortly after the one that had led to Kate's death. Walter and George stood by the great door while, Members of Parliament debated the progress of the war in the House of Lords.

George played with the loose bullets in his pocket. He remained close by Walter's side. He covered shifts for him and unloaded the gun when he thought Walter was in danger of turning it on himself in his darkest hours. He gabbled on to fill the strained silence with Walter, who would sometimes reward him by nodding in recognition of something he said. "So, some good news at last. The Russians are going to fight on our side."

Walter put his hand on George's arm to stop him talking.

Churchill stood and placed his notes on the table of the House of Lords. "We have promised Russia whatever help we can; we have offered any technical or economic assistance in our power. We are resolved to destroy Hitler …."

George nudged Walter. "I wonder how many men they've got – the Russians? It's a big country – gotta be more than us. If only the Americans would take our side."

Churchill raised the level of his voice over the cries of "hear, hear" from the members. "As I speak, German tanks are smashing into Russia. Minsk, which is over halfway to Moscow, has fallen. We are hoping the Russians can hold on until the snow comes – when German soldiers and equipment, who are unsuited to the intense cold, will, I believe, run into difficulties."

Walter was not listening. He glanced at a communiqué from the Secret Service. It read: *Operation Long Jump: Latest information. Germans train crack troops of different nationalities at their spy school – Lake Quentz, near Berlin. Recruits are undergoing parachute training.* He folded the paper and handed it to George.

George read the message two or three times trying to make some sense of it. "What are we supposed to do? Station X tells us an attempt on the Old Man's life is coming, but not enough bloody intelligence to do anything about it. If it's to be a sniper with a rifle, the Old Man can only rely on us to put ourselves between 'im and the bullet. I hear they're testing some new body armour, but it's very cumbersome." George turned the paper over in his hand as if there might be a clue on the reverse.

Walter looked up. "If it slows me up and if I don't get to him in time, then what's the use? Besides, a bullet would be a blessed relief."

George folded the note. "I think I might give it a go."

***

6 July – Chequers, the official country house of the Prime Minister

In the Great Hall of the Tudor house, 41 miles from Downing Street, Churchill was having a crisis. Resting on the table next to the gramophone was a file marked *TOP SECRET.*

Walter slipped in the room and glanced at the document. The heading explained Churchill's despair. *Convoy sunk in the Atlantic. Britain has six weeks of food left before the population begins to starve.*

Churchill ignored Walter and continued to parade up and down in his underpants. The Old man's eyes were small red dots and his chubby pink face looked swollen.

From a scratchy gramophone record, Harry Lauder echoed around the hall.

Keep right on to the end of the road, keep right on to the end....

"Right turn." Churchill marched to the far end of the hall, his pants beginning to slip down.

Walter sat on a chair by the door and looked at the floor.

"Halt. Order arms." Churchill lifted an imaginary rifle from his shoulder. "Attention." He stamped his feet and stood straight.

Lauder sang on: *Keep right on to the end of the road...*

"Quick march." The Old Man stepped up the pace. "By the left, left... left... left, left, left, left." A drip of water hung from his nose. He stomped past Walter – halted at the wall and did a smart about-turn. The record stopped. Winston sang. *"Keep right on to the end of the road, keep right on to the end."*

Walter put the stylus back on the spinning gramophone record, opened the door and stood on guard outside.

George joined him. "Bloody hell, what's up? The mad Old Man's marching again, isn't he? Is it one of his *black dog* depressions?"

"Yes, George. You go off duty, I'll see to him." Walter waited outside the door, preventing anyone entering for an hour, until the frenzy subsided. He found the Old Man slumped in a chair. He summoned all his strength to carry him to his room and put him to bed.

***

31 July – Berlin

In Berlin, the Germans were busy formulating plans to exterminate a whole race of people. The orders came from an evil man with poison in his heart. They were bland and did not mention murder or gassing but the words total solution meant death for six million innocents.

Order from Hermann Göring:

I hereby charge you to carry out preparations .... for a 'total solution' of the Jewish question in all the territories of Europe under German occupation....

Submit to me as soon as possible a general plan ... for carrying out the desired 'final solution'.

***

106

2–8 August – A secret sea voyage from Chequers, England to Newfoundland an independent island off the East coast of America

A month had passed since Churchill's depression. "Come in, come in Thompson, I have news…." He beckoned Walter close, put his arm around his neck and whispered, "You were right. President Roosevelt won't meet me publicly, but he will meet me in secret. We're going to meet him – at sea."

They sat together and planned the trip. It was the first time in weeks Churchill had smiled.

George waited outside.

Walter appeared after an hour holding his notebook, full of plans for the clandestine meeting.

George fell into step. "Got a plan, Inspector? Are we going to see the Yanks?"

Walter tapped his notebook and smiled.

"Well let's pray we get some help. We were not ready for war. We're short of food, and still haven't turned out sufficient guns, tanks or planes to take on the Nazis in Europe. If our American friends don't muck in, we'll all be speaking German this time next year…."

The next day, Walter cracked opened the heavy oak door of the Great Hall. Loud music from the gramophone hurt his ears.

Churchill gave Walter one of his bewitching smiles: "Morning Thompson." He executed a smart about turn, fully dressed this time. "left, left, left…"

Walter sat on a wooden chair by the door and watched the Old Man on parade. Churchill shouted orders to himself and carried them out with military precision. He no longer seemed like a man marching alone – Walter felt the presence of a huge army at the Prime Minister's back.

"Is everything ready?"

Walter nodded.

"What time do we start?"

"In about a half an hour, sir."

107

"Oh, for God's sake – he's going to march all the bloody way." George announced in a voice too loud for Walter's comfort. "Mad. It's a damn good job no one else can see this nonsense. Has 'e got any pants on?" George went to find his coat.

At 1pm, Churchill appeared by the door, wearing his coat and hat. "Thompson, is everything ready?"

"Yes, of course, sir. We leave in about a quarter of an hour."

In less than five minutes, Churchill bounded out of the building and jumped into the car: "The station, George, please."

George pulled out of the drive. "Everyone's so excited. D' yer really think the Americans will help us?"

Churchill, cleared his throat: "I have much to ask, George…."

As the train sped north through Scotland, Churchill turned to his scientific adviser, Lord Cherwell. "You're a brilliant mathematician – answer me this: how many pints of champagne do you think I have drunk in the last 24 years at a rate of one pint a day?"

Cherwell smiled. "I suppose around 8,760."

Churchill chuckled. "And how many coaches, like the one we're sitting in, would be required to carry that amount of champagne?"

"Well, it would take up part of one coach."

Churchill feigned a boyish sulk. "That's disappointing. I had hoped it would take up several coaches."

George held open an umbrella for Churchill at Thurso station.

Winston smiled and quick marched along the platform – the pouring rain unable to dampen his spirit.

Walter paused to survey the area.

"Come along Thompson – next stage of our journey awaits – our destroyer to join the battleship HMS *Prince of Wales* at Scapa Flow – pick up the pace will you man."

Walter nodded but his face remained neutral.

Naval ratings whistled Churchill aboard the *Prince of Wales*. Admiral Tovey performed a perfect salute. "Welcome aboard, sir, President Roosevelt's advisor, Mr Harry Hopkins is waiting in the mess, where we have some rum to warm you."

"Lead on, Admiral, please lead on…."

On the bridge, Captain Philips was on edge. "I want minute-by-minute reports from the radio room. We have a precious cargo aboard. Inspector Thompson assures us that German intelligence has not got wind of this, but there has been a great deal of U-boat activity."

"Ay, ay, sir," replied his number-one.

The officers were aware of the significance of their mission, yet no one but the Admiral, the Captain, Churchill and Walter knew their final destination. The seas were pleasant, and the sky was clearing.

Walter retired to his cabin. He had already vetted the whole ship's company in advance, so there was nothing left for him to do. He sat at the small desk staring through the porthole. An hour passed until he picked up a pen and played with it. He took a photograph of Kate out of his breast pocket and stood it up on the desk against the inkwell. His chest tightened and he suppressed the need to howl like a dog – he knew he teetered on the edge between sanity and madness.

After another two hours, he took the pen and paper and began to line them up in front of him. After another hour, he began to write.

There was a tap on the door. George popped his head in: "Come on Inspector, we're all waiting for you in the canteen – your dinner is on the table."

Walter put the pen down and stood to leave. "Would you think me crazy George, if I told you I was trying to write a letter to Kate?"

"No Inspector, you might even find it therapeutic."

After dinner, Walter paced the deck. He had three tight knots in his stomach. Fear for Stella, anxiety for Churchill, and guilt about Kate.

George was always close by. "Slow up, old chum – you can't walk across the Atlantic, you know."

Walter gave him a half smile.

"Hey, is that my old mate in there? May I accompany you around the boat?" George fell into step. They set off together in silence and halted outside Churchill's cabin.

Churchill looked up at his porthole and gave a wave to his bodyguards outside on deck. The Old Man was reclining on his bunk, reading C. S. Forester's *Captain Hornblower, RN.*

George stopped by the rail. "Big ocean and a big man we're going to beg a favour of."

Walter nodded and stared at the white froth as the ship cut through the sea.

"He's a good man, Roosevelt, I hear, letting us borrow supplies an' all to fight the Germans."

As they passed Churchill's cabin again, he put down his book, stretched and yawned before wiggling to his feet. He stepped out on deck and joined them in a stroll around the ship.

"Attention!" signalled an officer as they approached a group of sailors.

Churchill raised his hand. "No, no, carry on. I want to walk about without interfering. Allow the men to be at ease so I can have some personal contact with them."

Later that evening, Churchill was dressing for dinner. He was comforted by the presence of his silent bodyguard. "I need to ask so much of the Americans. I think Mr Roosevelt will help. I believe Britain and the United States have…" Churchill paused to look to Walter for assistance with his tie "…a special friendship. I pray this trip will be the first of many to visit our friends in America. I love this ship, you know, I feel as though it's *my* ship."

***

9 August – Placentia Bay, Newfoundland

The captain ordered a rehearsal of the parade of the ship's company, as HMS *Prince of Wales* neared her destination. Walter and George stood near the bow watching the men emerge from all parts of the ship in their everyday uniforms, looking more like a shipwrecked crew.

George grinned. "Don't worry, Inspector, when the parade itself takes place, they'll all be immaculate."

The mist lifted with the arrival of dawn in Newfoundland's Placentia Bay. Churchill hopped from foot to foot as they saw the jagged grey outline of the US destroyers come into view. The USS *Augusta*, the Presidential flagship was anchored with several other ships, but Churchill's ship steered away from the bay and put out to sea again.

The Prime Minister was furious and marched to the bridge. "Get me an audience with Admiral Tovey."

The Admiral gave Churchill a smart salute. "Sorry sir, I've been asked by the Americans to take a trip around the bay to rendezvous at the correct time. We are an hour and a half early."

Churchill stamped along the deck.

George gave Walter a cheeky wink. "Shall I go and find 'is marching music?"

Churchill took out a cigar. "We mustn't be early for our first date, must we, George?"

An hour and a half later, as the HMS *Prince of Wales* approached once more and passed between the American ships, the band struck up an invigorating version of *The Stars and Stripes*. The *Augusta* replied with *God Save the King*.

When the *Prince of Wales* came to anchor, senior officers from both ships visited each other to exchange formal greetings. At last, Churchill, Walter and George boarded the *Augusta*. George beamed and shook everyone's hand as he climbed the gangplank.

Roosevelt stood by the rail, supported by his son, Elliott, admiring the long, sleek, pale grey *HMS Prince of Wales* at anchor.

The ships band played the two national anthems. There was silence. The ship's company waited. Churchill moved forward and greeted Roosevelt with a firm, warm handshake. He looked into the movie cameras and handed Roosevelt a written greeting from the King. The words were lost, as the sound camera did not work. A second attempt at recording was made, but the equipment failed.

"Mr Roosevelt, we *really* need your 'elp," whispered George. "We British can't even make a sound recorder work."

Once the formal introductions were concluded, Churchill's party returned to the *Prince of Wales* to change for lunch.

A shout went up from the sailors. Several small boats, manned by American Marines, wearing their dress blues uniform and white caps, had come alongside. The boats contained hundreds of cardboard boxes and the Marines began to pile them on to the deck. Each one contained 200 cigarettes, two apples, an orange and half a pound of cheese. There was a message:

The Commander-in-Chief, United States Navy, sends his compliments and best wishes – Franklin D. Roosevelt, President of the United States, August 9th, 1941.

Walter returned to his cabin. He picked up the bookmark Churchill had dropped. Printed in bold was: *Ask and it shall be given. Seek and you shall find.*

***

10 August – Placentia Bay, Newfoundland

The sun's rays burned through the early mist on the bay, illuminating the ships anchored in the harbour. Roosevelt joined Churchill aboard the *Prince of Wales* for a joint service of thanksgiving. Churchill had selected well-known hymns he and all the sailors knew. It was a simple service, conducted by a British naval chaplain who stood at a rostrum draped with the British and American flags. When prayers were said, Walter shut his eyes and asked God to protect Bernie and Emily, Stella and Martin, and to love Kate in heaven.

Later, over lunch, George stared at his plate. He touched Walter's foot under the table. "You can see we need your help, Mr President, we can't even afford a decent spread for you and your sailors. Most of this food looks like it came out of an old tin. Let's 'ope you take pity on us and send us some supplies."

As Churchill waved farewell to Roosevelt, a black-and-white cat, the ship's mascot, wound itself around Churchill's legs. "Hello, puss." He picked up the cat and stroked it while Roosevelt returned his salute by waving his hat. The crews gave a cheer.

Churchill panted as he strode around the deck. He stopped at Walter's cabin and looked round the door. "I've decided to go ashore – give me something to do while the President thinks about my proposals."

"Sir, can you give me five minutes to check the security arrangements with the American Secret Service?"

Churchill and Walter stepped on to the jetty and thanked the Marine Officer for taking them to shore. Walter took stock of the port and Churchill walked towards the hill behind the harbour. The sun warmed their backs as they began the climb.

The Old Man-made schoolboy jokes, nudging Walter every other step. He stopped, looked Walter in the eye and started to jog, attempting to race Walter to the top. Walter let him stay ahead and a few yards from the summit, took the lead. At the top, they sat breathless on the grass, admiring the sight of the ships in the calm waters below.

Without warning it began to shower, even though the sun was still shining. Churchill and Walter half-ran – half-slid back down the hill. By the time they reached the ship, they were soaked. They stood together and admired the huge rainbow over the harbour.

"Good sign," said Churchill. "I've come for that pot of gold."

Back on the *Augusta,* Walter strolled the deck while Churchill resumed talks with the President. Walter recognised the stance of another policeman ahead of him. He called out: "Mike Reilly?"

The United States Special Agent turned and smiled at Walter, "Inspector Thompson, Scotland Yard. Nice to meet you buddy in person. But where are all your men?"

Walter laughed, "It's only George and I for Winston."

"Ha I have 25 men guarding the President and still I feel it's not enough."

"I could imagine his face if I asked for another 23 men. He likes his freedom and wouldn't allow it – he'd rather take the risks."

Churchill appeared along the gangway and stopped in front of the two men. Walter stepped forward, "Sir, this is my opposite number, Special Agent Mike Reilly. We talk all the time on the scrambler phone. He has offered to introduce me to the President."

Churchill took out a cigar and offered one to Mike. "I hear good reports of you, Agent Reilly. Keep up the good work but Thompson, I will introduce you to the President."

President Roosevelt was sitting at his desk in his cabin when they entered. Churchill puffed white smoke as he said "Inspector Thompson has guarded me faithfully for a period of nearly 20 years. It gives me great pleasure to present him to you."

The President replied, "Inspector Thompson of Scotland Yard, Mike Reilly thinks very highly of you and your attention to detail."

Churchill and Mike Reilly withdrew from the room.

The President leaned over his desk. "How is he standing up under the pressure, Thompson? How is he really coping?"

Walter paused for a second, searching for a diplomatic answer. "He has a marvellous reserve of energy and good working habits, including the habit of periodic rest."

The President smiled: "Is he hard to handle?"

Walter took a step back. "Yes, sir," he admitted. "He's reckless and self-willed. He can't bear any kind of restraint being placed on him."

"Look after him."

"Of course I will, it's my job."

"Your Mr Churchill is one of the greatest men alive – you have a very important job, Inspector."

Back aboard the *HMS Prince of Wales,* Walter picked up a document everyone was calling, *The Atlantic Charter*. The first page read: *A joint declaration of war and peace aims of the United States of America and Britain.*

George put his head into Churchill's cabin. "The Old Man is not confident the Americans will fight with us. They'll certainly help us in the Atlantic by attacking U-boats. But American public opinion is strongly in favour of staying OUT of the war. It will take something pretty spectacular to change their minds. Where is he by the way?"

Walter looked towards the heads. "Bathing."

***

Walter stood with George on deck enjoying the salty sea air. Gazing into the distance, he noticed the spikey black silhouette of a city on the horizon. He screwed up his eyes to get a better look. "Reykjavik, George?

The ship slowed, and as the *Prince of Wales* cut through the water, the *city* divided itself into the individual shapes of a huge convoy of American ships. Walter's eyes were moist.

George did a little dance on the spot. "Thank God. Just look at that lot. The President must have sent the convoy to help us even before the talks were over."

Each ship was crammed with boxes, crates, aircraft, tanks and trucks lashed to their decks.

As the *Prince of Wales* drew close to the American convoy, a narrow corridor unzipped itself through the centre to allow the British ships to sail through. The American crews lined the sides to watch them pass. The naval ratings aboard the *Prince of Wales* were summoned on deck to view the magnificent sight. When the British ships reached the centre of the convoy, every American vessel let off its foghorn. Walter put his fingers in his ears and a single tear trickled down his cheek.

George shouted above the noise. "If Adolf could see this lot – he'd be so mad – he'd go into a blind rage. Thank you, Mr President, the British people thank you from the bottom of our hearts."

Churchill looked out of his porthole and took a long draw of his cigar. He played the *Colonel Bogey March* on the gramophone. He saluted the porthole, tightened the cord on his pyjama trousers and began quick marching in his cabin.

CHAPTER 11
Stella - Smugglers and Forgers

16 August – Paris

Victoire was chalked on the wall opposite Stella and Martin's apartment. Despite Martin's assurances to his grandfather, they were still in Paris.

Stella cuddled up to Martin on the sofa to listen to the BBC World Service. *We urge our listeners in occupied France to go out during darkness and chalk the 'V' sign on doors, walls and pavements in order to disturb the morale of the Germans.*

"We need more than words." Martin shouted at the radio set. "We need troops and tanks to stand up to the damn Germans."

Stella pulled him close and kissed him on the lips. "They'll come, my love. In the meantime, we're needed here. Pierre had the last coach fitted with a secret compartment yesterday. It looks like a fuel tank and is long enough to fit a man. I got in, just to try it out. We need to put a blanket inside, so any poor soul hidden there doesn't crash around."

Stella got up and opened the window. A cooling breeze swept aside the long voile curtains. "Look, darling the *V* sign is chalked on the wall opposite – the French are going to fight back."

***

17 August – London

Churchill decided to make the *V* sign his own. All over Britain, his impish grin and his raised two fingers, would greet the people.

It was hot. Churchill fanned his face with his hat as he bounded from his open topped car. There were cheers from the staff at the London Hospital as he waved and climbed the front steps to address the crowd.

Walter searched every facial expression in the gathering. He saw weariness, exhaustion and hope, but not one threatening face.

Churchill put up his two fingers to the crowd. "The *V* sign is the symbol of the unconquerable will of the occupied territories resisting Nazi tyranny".

The sign never failed to evoke a shout wherever he went.

George wasn't fooled. "We all know that sign means – fuck off Mr Hitler"

***

20 September – South West France

Martin and Stella were expecting to come across a roadblock as soon as they returned to the main road outside Bordeaux. A long line of traffic crawled towards the makeshift barrier. Martin chewed his lip and edged the big coach forward. The last group of people had been left with their Spanish friends, and the coach was empty, apart from its cargo of 10 rifles and 2,000 rounds of ammunition hidden in the secret compartment.

A bead of sweat ran down Martin's forehead. "We never should have driven our own coach."

Stella patted him on the hand. "Just think, darling, we've got another forty-three people to safety. Out of reach of the Nazis."

It took 30 minutes to reach the sentry post. Stella touched her neck – she could feel her pulse beating. "The Germans seem to be paying more attention to those who are travelling away from Paris than people like us who are driving north."

Martin watched a car at the front of the line. The soldiers made all the occupants get out with all their possessions. "It's going to get tricky now, if our permits are going to be checked regularly, we won't be able to transport very many refugees – or our people in the Resistance. This last lot of refugees must be our final cargo. How can a respectable business couple like us explain why we are driving our own coaches? Okay, it's us next – are you ready?"

"Yes, my love." Stella hid the gun Pierre had given her under the seat.

The coach drew forward.

"*Ausweispapiere.*" The guard held out his hand for their identity papers.

Martin passed them through the window.

It was five minutes before the guard re-appeared. "*Où allez-vous? Monsieur* Thibault?" The guard wanted to know where they were going.

A sudden bloom of heat spread across Martin's face. "We... err... err..."

Stella leaned over to the window. "We're going to deliver this coach to the bus station by the *Gare du Nord* for the use of the German Reich," she said in German. "But we're late. Are we going to get stopped at *every* roadblock? Some vehicles seem to be going straight through." She gave the guard a wide smile.

The soldier smiled back. "For that privilege, since last Monday you need a special card to display on your windscreen."

Stella let out a sigh. "Oh, you would have thought Otto – *Kommandantur* – von Stülpnagel would have told us," she said in German to Martin. "What a nuisance."

"You know *Oberbefehls-haber* – the Military commander of France?"

Stella pointed to the paper. "Please check the signature, it's signed Captain Wilhelm Scheben on the orders of Otto von Stülpnagel."

The soldier studied the papers. "Wait here."

After five minutes of waiting, Martin began to grind his back teeth. Stella took hold of his hand. The German soldier returned and without a word, handed Stella the card and waved them on.

Martin started the engine. "You're an absolute marvel, that card is worth a fortune to us. We'll have to find out the rules for the issue and put them on every vehicle we use."

Stella looked behind her, as soon as the roadblock was out of sight she sat behind her husband and flung her arms around his neck.

Martin turned his head and brushed a kiss on her cheek. "You saved the day – I just went to pieces. Lord, if the Germans catch me, I won't last five minutes before I tell them everything. But this is not a game, *Neshama*. We need to keep a lower profile. Over 3,000 Jews were arrested in Paris in May, and although the

Nazis ordered it, the French police carried it out. And no one knows where they've been taken. Some say there's a camp on the edge of Paris, and that's where they are now. But if we get arrested, we'll not be able to help Pierre's unit, or anyone else."

Stella nodded. "But my love, we are at war and I want to do everything I can. But now I'm more worried about you. There's a letter at home saying every French male between the ages of 18 to 43 must register at their local police station."

Martin smiled. "I know – I've already spoken to Otto. I will have to register but I'm exempt from the *Service du travail obligatoire.*"

"Pierre says men are being taken to Germany against their will as slave labour. I don't like you being recorded in their system. Things are getting worse – the hostages, the murder and their idea that one German is worth at least three Frenchmen. They're closing in on us."

"Yes, you're right. Perhaps we should think about getting back to England."

"I know – it's crazy but I really miss going to the picture house with Bernie."

"You're so right my sweet. All we get here is German made propaganda films to try to brainwash us into thinking it's a good idea for them to run France and the world."

***

21 September – Moulin de Lonceux, Garnet, France

Martin drove the *Citroën Traction Avant* to the watermill at Garnet, a small village south of Paris, where a local miller and his wife were hiding local boys from being deported to German work camps.

It was just after dawn when Luc directed them into the cobbled courtyard, bordered by the flint stone mill house and several barns. White ducks flew up from the mill pond, when the car came to a halt. Luc was the tall thin Frenchman who had helped Stella with the refugees, over a year ago.

Pierre appeared and watched as Martin reversed the car into the barn, alongside Pierre's bicycle and Luc's motorbike.

"You're late," said Luc. "How did it go?"

Martin opened the heavy mill house door. "All as planned. We would've been later if it were not for this little silver-tongued darling." He gave Stella a kiss on the cheek. "Won't the young miller and his wife be in big trouble if the Germans find out what's going on here?"

"No, the couple have gone. We took them to the coast last night. They're trying to join the Free French. They've seen too many of their friends get into the back of German trucks, never to be heard of again."

"*Vive* General de Gaulle." Luc removed his long rifle from his shoulder and performed a sloppy salute.

"We're looking after the mill for them. The young men hiding from the Germans are being guarded on a rota basis." Pierre sat down on a three-legged stool next to the huge mill stone, stroked his thin beard and put his head in his hands.

Stella laid her arm on his shoulder. "Whatever is the matter?"

"It's my contacts in Lyons, they've been arrested – for having false papers." Pierre produced a gun from under his robes and began to put bullets into the chamber. "They'd been to a secret meeting with some old friends who have formed a group in the south. On their way out of the city, the police stopped them. They took them back into Lyon and said their papers were false – *putain.*"

Stella sat on a stool next to Pierre and gazed up at the vaulted ceiling. "But we all have the same forged papers, and they've been accepted here by the Germans."

"It's the police in the southern Free Zone. The government is more vigilant than the Germans. After all, most of the German soldiers aren't bothered about what the French are doing, as long as we leave them alone. Apparently, the forgeries weren't good enough for the police in Lyon. An ordinary German soldier might not notice the mistakes, but these policemen seemed to know just what to look for." Pierre snapped his gun chamber shut. "We have to take this seriously because we're planning to join some of the operations in the south. We want you to come with us. But first, there's some terrible news – Captain Scheben, the officer who signs your permits, has been assassinated – shot at the Gare de l'Est. What's more, it's rumoured your Otto is becoming unpopular with Hitler."

Martin kicked a sack of flour in the corner marked *MOULURE FINE.* "Oh, dear God, all those months of courting that nasty piece of work – down the drain. What use can we be to you now?"

Pierre waved away flour dust with a map in his hand. "Come with us and help us in the South of France. Quite frankly, you've been protected by Otto. I am sorry but I think your business will be seized by any greedy German that takes over from him."

"But for what reason?" Martin kicked the sack again.

Luc leaned his rifle against a large wooden cog. "Just because it is profitable, and they want it. And stop kicking that sack – it's all the flour we have left. The bastards only need to send a troop of *SS* to inspect your buses. If they find the secret compartments ...." Luc drew his hand across his throat.

Stella selected a bottle of red wine from the rack in the corner and passed it to Pierre. "So, we go south. I have always enjoyed the sun anyway."

Pierre looked about for where he'd left the bottle opener. "It's no holiday, Pétain's people are hunting out foreign Jews and putting them into camps. Now there's talk French Jews will soon be arrested and interned."

Martin passed on the wine. "But will my travel permits be accepted in the south?"

Pierre swilled the wine around his glass. "No, not there and we'll all need new identity papers if the forgeries can be detected so easily."

Stella raised her glass to Luc. "Have you registered with the police?"

"Hell, no. I roam around like Pierre. I go where he goes."

"Yes, Luc got me papers, as Pierre Picard, a Christian, and not under my real Jewish name. Otherwise, I would be wearing the yellow star by now." Pierre sipped his wine.

"...The least I could do," muttered Luc.

Pierre stood. "We will all need new forged papers if we are to carry on our Resistance work."

Stella finished her glass. "Pierre, do you know anyone could do it?"

"I've been making some enquiries. The best man seems to be someone called Henri Leclerc. He can make his own equipment and execute the forgery. He can copy a signature so well, even the person he's copied can't tell. But it's hopeless. First, he's in prison, and second, he's a nasty piece of work who wouldn't help anyone except himself." Pierre picked up another pistol and began to strip it apart. "Most people who could do the job are afraid to have anything to do with Resistance groups. Others have gone missing since the occupation."

"Well, at least we know where Henri is – so let's go get him." Stella gave Martin a playful look.

"But how? It's hopeless." Martin opened a box of ammunition and filled his revolver.

"I'm sure my cousin could help – he is a guard at the prison." Everyone turned and stared at Luc. "He's talked to me about Henri – because he can't stand the toad."

Stella stood up. "Terrific, can he get me into the prison as a relative to meet him?"

"But what about your papers? How will you get past the guard? They'd surely be more suspicious in a prison." Martin's eyes signalled his disapproval.

"Luc's cousin will have to be the person to inspect my papers." Stella was getting that buzz again.

Martin touched her arm. "But no one could ensure that."

Luc finished his wine. "It's not impossible, it's worth considering. And in the meantime, we can make enquiries among our other contacts in the criminal world to see if there are any other master forgers who could help us."

"I'm sure you'll come up with someone else." Martin gave Luc a sideways look and a shake of the head.

***

22 September – Moulin de Lonceux, Garnet, France

All day, Pierre had been cycling around the rolling green countryside, visiting local resistance supporters to warn them. He returned with heavy eyes to the mill house at Garnet.

Stella poured him a glass of cold water. "Do we have a plan?"

Pierre untied his cassock he had raised up, so as not to get caught in the bicycle chain. "Most people agree, there are more effective resistance groups in the South. I have decided to leave. It's too dangerous here. Try as hard as they like, the Germans cannot instil an ideological hatred of Jews in all the French people." Pierre drank the water. "The *Gestapo* are beginning to operate in France. They are growing increasingly efficient in hunting down any one vaguely Jewish."

Gertrude Meyer, an elderly, grey haired, Jewish woman sat at the kitchen table. She had been taken ill during the journey across France and had stayed behind to cook for the resistance members. She gazed at Stella and dabbed her misty eyes. "What will you do with those of us who are old and useless?"

Stella put her arm around *Frau* Meyer. "If Jewish children can be adopted, so can grandparents. In fact, I'd like to adopt you myself, because I never knew my own grandmother."

123

The old lady's face glowed.

Over dinner, Stella whispered to Pierre, "What are we going to do about dear old Gertie? I told her I wanted to adopt her as my grandmother, but she would probably be in greater danger with me and my forged papers than if she were walking the street."

"Oh, I'm glad you've mentioned papers. Luc has contacted his cousin, and he says we can get inside the prison to visit Henri."

"The forger?"

"Yes – and the team agreed, if anyone could convince him to escape and help us, it would be you. He has two loves. One is painting pictures, the other is pretty women."

"Is there no one else we could use – someone who's not in prison?"

"We've contacted other forgers, but they are afraid their skills are not up to the task. Unfortunately, Henri is the best, and before he got arrested, he had a marvellous collection of counterfeiting apparatus. Once we get him out, we can find out where he's hidden all his equipment. If he runs, we can blow the whistle on him."

"Or kill him." Luc added.

"When do I go?" Stella set the table for lunch.

"On Tuesday, at midday. Luc will drive you to within one mile of the prison, and you will walk in with the other visitors. Here's a pass – you might as well take it now. Luc's cousin, Philippe, will be the guard who inspects your papers; he's on duty then, and it's all arranged. You'll know him by his red hair. He also has a reddish birthmark on his chin, here." Pierre pointed to the end of his own hairy chin. "Tomorrow we'll discuss what you'll say to Henri."

CHAPTER 12
Bernie - Raw Recruits

21 September – Norwood

Bernie swept up the newspaper and letters from the doormat, almost knocking over the coat stand as he turned. He laughed as he righted it, but stood rigid when he saw the brown envelope addressed to him. He slumped down on the stairs and tore it open. His mother came and sat next to him. He read aloud the first few words: "You are requested to report to…. Colchester Barracks"

He handed the letter to his mother, who hugged him hard and kissed him. "So, I'm going to lose my baby boy." Emily wiped her eyes with her apron. "Well, your granddad was a major in the Great War – it'll take more than a few Nazis to destroy us."

"I knew it was coming, Mum, once you're 18, you get a letter from the Ministry of Labour, and you're conscripted – made to fight whether you want to or not. I suppose we all have to do our bit. At least I won't be too far away. Hopefully, I'll get home for some of your wonderful cooking. I'm just not happy about you being on your own."

"You just let me know, son when you're given leave, and I'll get all I can from the black market to feed you well. Is that another letter in your hand? Oh Lord, it's from Stella. Look it's got an English stamp. Oh, Bern, she must be back. Thank goodness." She ripped it open and her face fell. "She's still in France" Someone is smuggling her letters out and posting them from…" she paused as she studied the postmark, "aha, Southampton."

"She says she and Martin are fine but are moving to the South of France into the Free Zone - everything's a bit more normal there. That's hard to believe. If it was normal, I could write or telephone her. I wish she and Martin would come home. What *does* she think she's doing?"

She handed the letter to Bernie who tried to read between the lines. "Oh Stella, what could possibly keep you in France when we need you here? I need you, and now I am going away, mum needs you too."

***

Same day – Brighton

Seventeen-year-old, Johnny Smith sat on the stairs in the hallway of his parents' small council house awaiting the postman. There was a clank as the box was opened and a *whoosh* as letters landed on the mat. He rushed forward and picked out the brown envelope addressed to him with *On His Majesty's Service* printed in bold black letters on the front.

He examined each one of the words on the envelope and slid his finger beneath the seal, almost tearing the letter inside. *You are requested to report to Colchester Barracks....*

He ran into the kitchen, thrust the envelope into his mother's hand and before she could say anything, he left the house and ran to the end of the road to Tommy Farr's Long Bar.

Once inside, he sat down by himself and ordered a tea, which they served early in the day. Three empty cups were on the table by the time his older brother, Owen sat down opposite him. "Dad wants a word with you. What did yer go and sign up for?"

Johnny followed his brother back home.

"What have you done now, you soppy little bugger?" Johnny's dad looked up from the anvil, where he was repairing shoes.

"I've joined up, Dad – I volunteered ter go an' fight the Gerries."

His father looked at him long and hard. "But you're only 17."

"I know, dad – I lied about me age."

"Well, you'd better come back down the Long Bar with me, son, for a pint of beer."

"But I'm not old enough ter drink."

"If you're old enough to join the army, son, yer old enough ter drink." His dad stood up and put on his coat.

***

One thousand eighteen-year-old boys undressed in silence in the huge gymnasium, their actions reflected in the large oval windows. They stood in their hand-me-down pants and vests waiting for their uniforms to be issued. They had arrived on coaches from all over England – *cannon fodder* from poor families.

The Corporal in charge opened the door and gripped his nose. The acrid smell of nervous teenage body odour permeated the room like a noxious gas. "Right then. Put on your uniforms boys," he shouted showing appalling teeth. The recruits called him Corporal Blue Gums. "Now listen very carefully. All listening now, are we? That's better. Now put all those garments you just removed into that suitcase you brought with you. Yes, son, that's the one – the large oblong box-like thing with a handle."

Each boy placed all his clothes in his suitcase.

"Now, I want you each to take one of those large white sticky labels and write your name and address on it – and that's the address that you have just come from, F-R-O-M – from." Corporal Blue Gums took out a large handkerchief and blew his nose.

The boys obeyed and addressed their cases.

"Listen carefully, now. You stick the label on the case – and guess what we do?"

Johnny stood next to Bernie in the second row. "Store it for us, Corp?"

The Corporal swaggered to where Johnny was standing and put his face so close that their noses touched, and Johnny could smell his breath. "No, you little runt, we send it back home to your dear old mum. For those of you horrible boys who have got mothers, that is."

Bernie removed a pack of cards and a small tin of sweets from his suitcase. He'd guessed he would not see it for some time. Now he would not have any clothes to wear apart from the uncomfortable army issue.

The Corporal formed the boys into a line and trooped them off past the high red brick permanent barracks, towards hundreds of wooden huts erected for the recruits. Johnny drew attention to himself again by marching out of time.

"There's always one." The Corporal gave Johnny a long hard look.

When they were alone in their hut. Johnny feigned a punch at Bernie. "It's rude to stare, you know."

"Oh, I was just wondering where I've seen you before."

Johnny grinned. "Give yer a clue. I come from Brighton. On the booze at that wedding reception – I sneaked in. They 'ave weddings every week. It was my regular haunt for free beer."

"Oh, that's it. I knew you weren't invited."

"How d' yer know? Bit of a detective, are you?"

"No but my uncle is, and you didn't know the groom's name, for a start. And no one hires a suit as bad as yours."

"Who's yer uncle?"

"Sorry, mate – top secret." Bernie punched Johnny in the arm.

"Ahh, me injections." Johnny squared up to Bernie.

Bernie stood up to his full 6'3" and looked down at Johnny.

"All right, all right. I'm not going to take on the biggest recruit in the barracks". Johnny held out his hand. "Let's call it evens."

Bernie took his hand. "Evens." He looked down the long narrow room. It had wooden walls and a highly polished wooden floor. "I'll bet I know who puts the shine on that floor."

They cleaned the barracks with the pain of smallpox, typhoid and cholera serum in their arms. The boys were given regular inoculations. Many days were spent dusting and sweeping before the new recruits were given useful employment.

There were 22 straw-filled mattresses in the room, each with two thin blankets folded on top. The boys placed their kit next to their beds. It comprised a big pack, a small pack, webbing and a belt, gaiters, a ground sheet – which, doubled as an all-weather raincoat, a kit bag, a helmet and spare boots.

At the end of the sleeping area were the washing facilities: 12 basins and six cold water showers with no curtains, a cold linoleum floor and clinical white tiles.

"Attention!" Corporal Blue Gums was back.

The boys jumped to attention. Johnny put his hat on and then took it off.

The Corporal glared at him. "At 05:30 hours, you will wash, put on your singlet, shorts and plimsolls, and be ready for physical training at 06:00 hours. You will press your uniform every night under your mattresses. You will shine those boots until you can see your ugly face in them. You will polish your buttons and you will Blanco everything white that needs bleedin' Blancoing. Is that understood?"

"Yes, Corp," came a half-hearted reply.

"Yes, Corporal, sir!" screamed the Corporal.

"Yes, Corporal, sir!" shouted back his conscripts.

Bernie caught a glimpse of himself reflected in the window opposite. He almost did not recognise the figure. The army uniform made him look older, like someone else – like someone who would go and fight a war.

He wandered along to the showers and studied himself in the mirror. He stroked his hair, the boyish sandy colour had mellowed to a dark gold, his freckles had faded, and he was even taller than his Uncle Walter.

"Hey, Johnny, it's quite an art placing a uniform under your mattress so it can be recovered the next morning looking pressed." Bernie flopped the mattress down on his jacket and trousers.

Johnny was struggling with the heavy mattress and folding his trousers with a crease. "Bern, I'd do better mate if I just sleep in mine."

"Right you hold it up and I'll fold them for you. Now Johnny, just let the mattress go…."

"Thanks, Bernie you always look so immaculate."

"It's just a natural way of life for me, I was brought up by my Uncle Walter, who was – well still is, a policeman and always well turned out for his duties. He told me for a fact to keep smart. If you want to do well, stay up with me after lights out and do an extra bit of polishing and cleaning – trust me it'll pay off later."

The 06:00 am physical training was followed by a cold shower and an unappetising breakfast. The days were divided into drilling or testing. This meant the boys were either marched up and down the huge gravel parade ground or subjected to examinations to determine their aptitude for different jobs in the army.

Bernie gave Johnny a wide grin. He was given ball bearings, a hub and an axle to assemble. "I spent most of my childhood building and stripping Thompson's Grocer's bike." He put the completed task on the desk and watched Johnny finish at the same time.

"I used to get old bikes from the dump and mend 'em and sell 'em," said Johnny as they left the test room. "What do you think we've got for lunch?"

Bernie rubbed his stomach. "Floppy cabbage, black potatoes and lumps of grey meat swimming in gravy. Oh, and rough-cut bread. I can't tell you how much I miss mum's cooking."

"Same food as yesterday." The boys made their way to the mess.

"Two prunes in yellow water for dessert – all washed down with a lovely cup of bromide tea." Bernie opened the door of the NAAFI for Johnny.

"Bloody awful, the food here." Johnny held the door for Bernie.

"Never mind, Johnny, me old mate. It's Sunday tomorrow and I know where there's going to be some good nosh."

"Oh, tell me more…."

"Well, we must give thanks to the Lord."

"Gawd 'elp us." Johnny took a tray.

After lunch, there was a lesson in Morse code. Johnny and Bernie finished together again. "How did yer know all that Morse, Bern?"

"I was going to join the air force, and I thought it would help if I learnt Morse. My mum knows a neighbour who's in the RAF, so I was going to volunteer to be a gunner. But when he heard about it, he begged me not to volunteer. He said, 'We're burying two a week… Bern, please don't do it.' So, I waited to be called up, and here I am – and you?"

"Me older brother taught me, we used to tap out messages on the wall between our bedrooms – mum and dad never did get to know what we was saying."

***

Bernie could hear singing from the Presbyterian chapel while he and Johnny played the slot machines in the amusement arcade.

"In about another five minutes follow me – full pelt across the park." Bernie dropped another penny in a machine. When the time was up, they ran a 100-yard sprint to the church. A Church elder held the door for them.

"Sorry we're late," Bernie panted and joined in the last few lines of the final hymn.

"Now, if everyone would like to retire to the church hall for afternoon tea…" said the Minister. "Please feel welcome."

There were plates stacked with a variety of sandwiches, sumptuous cakes and pots of tea.

Bernie looked at Johnny. "Tea?"

Johnny nodded. "Thank you, so kind."

"Milk?"

"Yes, please."

"Sugar?"

"Two lumps and hold the bromide."

"Best meal of the week." Bernie filled his plate with as much as he could eat.

***

The boys were not sorry when their testing was completed. The Corporal ordered them to get up half an hour earlier than normal and lined up the new soldiers outside the barracks.

Bernie screwed his hands into fists behind his back.

The Corporal read from a clip board. "Right then, Whitby, Yorkshire. One step forward Private 0212 and Private 0246."

Bernie and Johnny took a step forward and stood to attention.

"I wonder if there are Presbyterians in Whitby?" Johnny asked with a twinkle as the soldiers marched out of the barracks in their new groups.

They accepted their train passes from the Corporal and prayed they would never meet him again.

An old man at the gate watched them leave. He stood to attention and saluted them – each one. Bernie noticed the Distinguished Service Cross from the Great War on the jacket and he returned the salute. "Eyes right," he called out to his pals and they replied with a smart turn of their heads to honour the veteran soldier.

By the time they arrived in Whitby on the Yorkshire coast, Bernie was four pounds and ten shillings up at cards. But he was not a cheat – he had a keen eye and a sharp memory. Perhaps this was why he expected he would live a charmed life.

CHAPTER 13
Stella - Youthful Courage

1 October – Fresnes prison, Centre penitentiaire de Fresnes, Val-de-Marne, south of Paris

The grey stone prison loomed over the valley. The high damp perimeter walls were covered in dark green slime. It looked forbidding in the cold October half-light.

Luc's cousin, the Prison Officer, Philippe Moreau, paced up and down in the courtyard. He jingled his heavy keys and thought about Stella's illegal visit at midday. *Should I tell horrible Henri, the forger he has a visitor?* The old man was grumpy when he had spoken to him earlier, so Philippe said nothing.

It was 11:30 am, and Philippe was sweating.

"Sergeant Moreau." A senior officer walked towards him.

"Shit," mumbled Philippe. "Now what?"

"The prisoners in the hole are making a lot of noise. Please take a few of your men and quieten them. I'll take over your duty at the gate for now."

"Yes, sir." Philippe was supposed to be at the gate checking all the passes to allow Stella through without question. He could not leave the senior officer in charge. He ran over to where a few prison guards were drinking coffee. "You, you and you, come with me now. Leave the damn drinks."

His subordinates looked at each other – picked up their rifles and meandered down the steps towards the area known as *the hole.* This was where the most dangerous and difficult prisoners were held. The bored inmates were shouting and banging on the doors of their cells.

The guards aimed their rifle butts through the bars at any prisoner foolish enough to stand within range. After 15 minutes, the prisoners were enjoying the fun and making even more noise. Philippe did not want to remove any of them for punishment because it would have entailed spending half an hour with a more senior officer and he would miss Stella.

Stella was early. She allowed a number of women in the queue to go ahead of her so she could arrive at the gate at noon. She could see a ginger-haired officer ahead. When it was her turn to show her identity papers, she looked the guard in the eye and raised an eyebrow in recognition.

The officer's eyes widened. Her sparkle was a marked contrast to the miserable people filing into the dismal building. He just glanced at her papers.

Stella entered the courtyard to see a red-haired guard running up the stairs from the *hole*. He stopped and they stared at each other. Stella's eyes focused on the birthmark on Philippe's chin.

Stella felt a sharp pain in her chest.

Philippe took her aside. "I am so sorry. I had some trouble to sort out. Let me show you where to go."

Henri Leclerc was painting in his cell. He was a short middle-aged man with thinning grey hair and a scraggy beard. Each week he exchanged some of his rations for paint and paper, and when he ran out of paper, he painted the walls.

"He's an extraordinary artist," remarked Philippe. "But he's an aggressive little man. He didn't get caught by the police, you know – he's far too good for that. No, no, he fell out with his underworld boss and one of his associates gave him up – probably because he'd gone too far, and they couldn't stand him any longer. Wait here. I'll fetch him."

Philippe ushered Stella into a windowless room, which contained a metal table and two chairs.

Henri did not like to be interrupted when he was painting, so Philippe gave the lightest of taps on his cell door. "Henri, good news, you have a visitor."

"Not me. Three years in here, and I've never had a visitor – go away and try someone else, *con*."

"But you do have a visitor."

"Tell them to fuck off, *con*." Henri continued painting.

"You will see the visitor, or I will confiscate those brushes."

Henri growled. "What bastard comes to see me now?"

Stella held her trembling hands together as she sat in the visitors' room. Philippe led Henri to her table and withdrew to the corner.

"Who the hell are you, *con*?" Henri slumped on a metal chair.

"My name is Stella. I work with some people who need your skills. I want to help you to escape."

"With remission, I've only 18 months to serve. Why the hell would I want to escape now?"

"We desperately need your help to forge papers for us. Our people risk being arrested because we can't get their papers one hundred per cent correct."

"I don't give a shit about your people. If I escape and they catch me, they'll put me away for another ten years. Goodbye."

"Please, Henri, sit down."

Henri hesitated.

"Please." Stella indicated to the other chair and he sat down again. "Look, Henri, you may not care about us, but it is our people and others like us who are fighting the Germans on French soil."

"It's not my war. I was in here before it started, and it'll be finished when I come out." Henri stood up.

Philippe moved forward. "Well, *Mademoiselle,* no point in you bothering to visit us again. I might be out of a job soon."

"Out of a job?" Stella began to put her coat on.

"The German military are taking over the prison."

"That's all I need – *putain* Germans guarding me," growled Henri.

"Oh no, they won't be guarding you. It's rumoured the place will be just for political prisoners." Philippe began to usher Stella towards the door.

"I'll be going home then. Well, goodbye, young lady."

Philippe winked at Stella. "I shouldn't think so. I'm pretty sure I heard one of the senior officers talking with a German lieutenant about transporting prisoners from here to German labour camps. Anyhow, I'm sure you'll be fine – you've 18 months left to serve. It's the poor buggers in the *hole* I feel sorry for. The Germans have decided to execute all the murderers."

Stella used his cue. "What will it take to get you to help us? Name it."

Henri's eyes flickered. "What – anything?"

"We'll give you what you want if you work for us, until the Germans have been driven out of France."

"Mm mm…" Henri looked at the ceiling. "I want a full pardon and 20,000 francs."

"Well..." began Stella.

Henri interrupted. "A house with a studio to work in… and err… someone to cook and clean and a pretty girl, just like you, to attend to my *other* needs."

"We have a mill house where you can live, and we can arrange some domestic help for you," said Stella.

Henri leered at her, revealing brown tobacco stained teeth. "So how do you get me released? You blow up the guard house?"

Stella smiled – she had him. "If we get the information, can you forge your own release papers?"

"Get me a copy of Pétain's signature and one of the stamps for his personal seal. Give me paper and a pen – I'll make a list."

"But why Marshal Pétain, when we're in the occupied zone?"

"Several prisoners have been released to Vichy on Pétain's request. It seems they have rich French relatives, with influence. The prison governor and the guards here have been asked to co-operate. Probably to keep the peace."

"But how can we get hold of one of Marshal Pétain's stamps for you?"

"I think that's your problem …."

Stella fished in her pockets and produced a small notebook and pencil. Henri began to write a list.

She approached Philippe and whispered: "Will you bring him what he needs? I know it is a huge risk for you."

"Surely Luc told you I'm with the Resistance – with the *Confrérie Notre Dame.*"

"No, we never discuss individuals, for security reasons. Each of us is told only what we need to know in case anyone gets captured and interrogated." Stella smiled at Philippe. "Anyway, thank goodness you can help. We'll be very grateful."

136

Henri finished his list and handed it to Stella. "Now get lost – I was in the middle of putting the finishing touches to my latest work." He got up and walked to the door, he turned and gave Stella a sardonic smile before heading back to his cell.

Stella plunged her hands in her pockets as she walked out of the prison. "How are we going to get a stamp used by Marshal Pétain?"

Philippe escorted her as far as the bridge by the gate. "I think you'll have to consult your group. It's not going to be easy. He's the Prime Minister of Vichy France in the Free Zone.

CHAPTER 14
Walter - Secrets and Rescue

7 December – The War Rooms, London

It was quiet in the War Rooms apart from the low buzz of the bare light bulbs illuminating the stark corridors. The evening shift was on duty, and crept around the underground rooms, sensitive to their day colleagues' need for rest. Fourteen feet of concrete protected the sleeping personnel from the nightly bombing over London.

Churchill sat up from his armchair with a start. It was 02:00 am and he had been dozing. His half-smoked cigar extinguished in the ashtray next to him. A deep crease lined his forehead as he opened his hand and smoothed out the note from Station X, he had held for the past two hours.

Walter stood in the corner of the room.

Churchill massaged his chest and pulled a face. He switched on the table lamp beside him and read aloud the words. "From Bletchley Park: *The Japanese Admiralty Code, JN25….*"

He stared at the telephone connecting London to the White House, but it was silent. His hand shook as he laid the note from his code breakers on the desk and reached for his cigar.

Walter leaned closer and moved his thumb over the wheel of his Zippo. The flame shot in the air. "What does it mean, Sir…?" Walter lowered the flame to meet the cigar.

Churchill looked up at him and reached forward for the note. "The Japanese Fleet left Tokyo and refuelled… since there has been no reconnaissance from Malaya, our only conclusion is… the destination is Hawaii."

He concentrated on inhaling for a few moments. His eyes closed and he abandoned the smouldering cigar.

Walter turned off the lamp and stood in the semi-dark, staring at the smoke curling up from the ashtray. He read the note over again. "What's in Hawaii apart from beaches and hula-hula girls?"

Churchill began to snore.

Walter reached in the wastepaper basket and pulled out an earlier note from the code breakers at Bletchley Park. "Oh God, the American fleet. The Japanese are en route to attack them. Shouldn't we be alerting President Roosevelt? But if we do that – we reveal to the Japanese, we can decipher their codes…. You're letting it happen. Because it will take an atrocity to get the Americans to join the war on our side – a war they think has nothing to do with them. Wake up, Sir you have to call the President."

Churchill opened one eye. "I can't Thompson…."

***

7 December – Pearl Harbor, Hawaii, Pacific Ocean

Six aircraft carriers flying the Japanese flag hid in the fog as they crossed the Pacific. Admiral Yamamoto asked for complete silence as a Russian cargo ship passed them during the night.

The fog lifted and the sun rose in an angry red sky 270 miles north of Hawaii, silhouetting the six Japanese ships on the horizon. Aboard the carrier, *Shōkaku,* the radio operator tuned in to the soft sounds from the American radio station *KGMB*, broadcasting from Honolulu.

On the deck, Mitsuo Fuchida started the engine of his *Nakajuma* torpedo bomber with a roar. He smiled at the red of the dawn and touched his chest in salute to the large red circle painted on the wing of the plane. His heart began to beat in time to the steady throb of the engine of his bomber.

Admiral Yamamoto had spent weeks organising a surprise attack to wipe out the American fleet, which was resting in Hawaii. The Japanese Prime Minister, Tojo had elaborate plans to control the whole of the Far East. Once the American navy was destroyed, Japan could invade any country, without challenge.

Fuchida closed his cockpit cover, strapped himself in and waved to the deck crew before his plane was catapulted from the ship.

The American sailors moored in Hawaii at the port nicknamed, Battleship Row were listening to the same radio station over the ship's loudspeaker. On board the USS *West Virginia*, a *Colorado*-class battleship moored outboard of the *Tennessee*, Marine Corps bugler, Jonesy Jones stood up in the mess. A roar of laughter went up behind him. "Give us a tune on your bugle, Jonesy."

"Nah, you'll hear me tomorrow morning, pal, as usual, when you want to stay dreaming in your hammock." Jonesy headed up to the deck to take his usual morning walk.

He screwed his fist into a pretend bugle and toot-tooted out the tune of The Andrews Sisters' *Boogie-Woogie Bugle Boy* to a delighted crowd of sailors who were enjoying their breakfast out on the open deck.

He took a bow as the men sung the chorus along with the broadcast: *He's the boogie-woogie bugle boy of Company B....*

Above him, Fuchida also tuned his radio as ordered to KGMB, just in time to hear The Andrews Sisters singing the last line: *The boogie-woogie bugle boy of Company B.....*

Flying in formation, he led his countrymen against Japan's sworn enemy.

He headed the first wave of 183 bombers and fighters. When they neared Oahu, the Japanese planes split off to their chosen targets. Fuchida's squadron flew south to the port, Pearl Harbor. *Tenkai* he commanded and fired a green flare. "Take the attack position."

Approaching Battleship Row, Fuchida fired a single torpedo and it moved as if in slow motion, pushing through the clear water, followed by a white, foamy wake. The USS *Arizona* exploded as the torpedo pierced her forward ammunition store. A burst of red flares showered white hot metal pellets and burning embers on screaming sailors. Fire reached up in yellow plumes and men ablaze, leapt into the water. A warning claxon screeched but it was too late. Explosives were launched into the air and crashed into the sea with a high-pitched wail. There was a final ear-splitting blast before the ship listed and was sucked to the bottom. It created a tidal wave, surfed by oil covered dead seamen.

Fuchida felt his bomber shake to the machine-gun fire he aimed at the drowning sailors.

Jonesy was dead before the *West Virginia* sank.

Fuchida had enough ammunition left for his secondary target. He banked the plane towards Pearl City Peninsula to strafe the American sailors ashore and opened fire as he flew low over the rooftops.

He slid back the canopy on the cockpit and saw women and children fleeing for their lives. The sweet smell of pineapple and coconut from the port was replaced with the acrid stench of cordite and burning flesh. Fuchida swallowed hard. *Women and children. What dishonour. Now Americans will surely attack and kill Japanese civilians in retaliation.*

Fuchida banked the plane and fired his remaining rounds at the battleships, spewing thick black smoke. He checked his compass and steered a course back towards the carrier *Shōkaku*.

The Japanese would later regret not sending a third wave of bombers to finish the job. The billowing black and grey smoke masked ships that would later be repaired and engage the Japanese again in the Pacific Ocean.

***

10 December – House of Commons

George stood by the great wooden door and studied the men in suits, lining the wooden benches. "My God, I've never seen the Old Man so down. Whatever 'as made him so depressed? The Americans are surely going to join us – help us out with troops and all that – after Pearl Harbor."

"Don't count your chickens – it's not yet official. There was a shouting match with the service chiefs this morning about air defence in the Far East. It seems the Old Man's being blamed for the Japanese being able to destroy our ships from the air." Walter touched his chest where a heavy stone lay – the rock that was the island of Hawaii.

141

Churchill felt in his trouser pocket. The crumpled message about Pearl Harbor was still there. He withdrew his fingers as if he had just touched a burning coal and stood up in the House of Commons. He still had not heard from President Roosevelt.

Churchill's voice wavered, his announcement had none of the drama or zest of his usual oratory. "I have bad news for the House, which I think I should pass on to them at the earliest moment. A report has been received from Singapore, HMS *Prince of Wales* and HMS *Repulse* have both been sunk while carrying out operations against the Japanese in their attack on Malaya. No details are yet available, except those contained within the official communiqué, which claims both ships were sunk by air attack."

"He's acting like a man bereaved." George unwrapped a humbug.

"It's Pearl Harbor. He's taken it very personally. Lots of sailors were lost, and now there is the sinking of the *Prince of Wales*, including the Captain and the Admiral. He loved that ship, you know, George. He told me he can't imagine us fighting the war without her, and he can't really believe Admiral Phillips is dead. He feels as though he's lost one of his family."

George sucked on the boiled sweet. "I know how he feels… yes, the Old Man's down, but he's not out – not yet. But he's ruthless, and I think he was wrong."

"You know?"

"Walter, you always think you're the only bloody detective round 'ere."

***

11 December – Outside the War Rooms, London

Walter stood outside Churchill's quarters, stiff and unmoving. The messenger from the communications room arrived breathless.

"Is it?" Walter raised an eyebrow.

"Yes, yes." The messenger handed Walter the note.

"I'll take it to him." Walter opened the door and Churchill looked up from his desk. Walter handed the envelope to the Old Man. "It's official. The Secret Service report was correct."

Churchill feigned a frown at his bodyguard's advanced knowledge. He opened the envelope, took out a small piece of paper, and read aloud: "Hitler and Mussolini have declared war on the United States of America. In return, the US have declared war on…" He paused and stood up. "…Italy and Germany."

Walter swallowed. Under different circumstances, he would have danced around the room, but he knew a terrible price had been paid to bring America into the war in Europe. But it would be salvation for the British who were only weeks from defeat.

"I did it, didn't I?" Churchill reached for a cigar.

Walter nodded but remained silent.

***

20 December – London to Washington and Ottawa

"Yes, Mr Churchill will be delighted to spend Christmas at the White House. Thank you for your help with the arrangements, Mike." Walter replaced the receiver to the special telephone connected to the White House.

He returned to his station outside Churchill's office door. He picked up a wrapped, potted-meat sandwich left on his chair.

Bunny sat at her desk and typed Churchill's travel itinerary.

Walter came up behind her and read the schedule.

Bunny breathed in his scent. Her hand shook for a second as she withdrew the paper from the machine. "I've made three copies, Inspector, will that suffice?"

Walter looked into her pale green eyes. "Perfect, Miss…. Bunny."

She touched his hand. "Please come back safely. If the Japanese can destroy the American fleet in Hawaii and sink the *Prince of Wales*, I'm so afraid of what might lie ahead as you cross the Atlantic."

He gave her hand a little squeeze. "Don't worry. We'll all be back – as far as I can tell the Germans don't know we're travelling to America again."

The HMS *Duke of York* left Scotland in a thunderstorm. The destroyers escorting the battleship ran into difficulties in the rough weather, and by the time the convoy had left the dangerous waters off the west coast of Ireland, they were far behind Walter's schedule.

The captain of the *Duke of York* shouted above the rumble of thunder and the crash of the waves. "May I suggest, sir we sail at full speed without escort for two days until we can meet up with US Destroyers?"

Churchill stood firm on the bridge with his legs astride and his hands on his hips, despite the dip and yaw of the ship. "The *Duke of York* is a new battleship; she can sprint across the ocean. We don't want to be late for our special meeting, do we, Captain?"

Churchill retired to his cabin and got into his bunk. The crew went about their duties in virtual silence. Once in a while, George would take a detour from his route around the ship, so he passed the radio room. As he crept past the open door, he would strain to hear if there were any reports of U-boats. The ship's mess was silent, everyone was listening for German submarines – the *wolf pack*. A few of the crew played cards but no one was in the mood for fun. Most returned to their posts or retired early to their bunks.

The sailors cheered when US destroyers came into view and escorted them to Chesapeake Bay.

***

26 December – The White House, Washington, DC

Churchill was singing *White Christmas* while taking a bath in his suite. Walter looked out of the window and paced the room. George joined him. "Washington looked like fairyland from the plane. There's no blackout here. Did you see this city lit up at night? So nice of President Roosevelt to come to the airfield to

144

meet us. But did you see his entourage – ten armoured cars and more men than I could count, all bristling with guns."

On Christmas Eve, they all went to the grounds of the White House. A huge crowd was waiting. Walter's eyes flickered everywhere, surveying all the faces – but all were friendly and singing carols. The President threw a switch and a thousand lights were illuminated on a tall Christmas tree.

On Christmas Day, a maid came to Walter's post and handed him a package. Inside, there was a blue silk necktie and a small white envelope enclosing a message that read: *Christmas 1941 – a Merry Christmas from the President and Mrs Roosevelt.*

Churchill opened the door and put his hand on Walter's shoulder. He was dressed and ready to go out. George met them at the main door, a noisy crowd had gathered outside the Capital building. Walter looked about for danger.

Churchill gave the waiting people a broad smile and walked towards where the police were holding them back. Secret Service agents rushed across and blocked his path.

Churchill pushed them away. "It's nearly always the unexpected that comes off – they have all been waiting to see me."

Walter assessed the area, searching for blind spots where snipers could be hiding. He stood close to Churchill, with his right hand on the gun in his pocket.

Churchill waved his hat and made the *V* sign, to loud cheers from the crowd.

That evening, back at the suite in the White House, Walter checked the windows.

Churchill yawned and dropped ice into a glass. "It's uncommonly hot in here, Thompson."

There was a tap on the door. Walter looked through the peephole. President Roosevelt was waiting outside in the corridor in his wheelchair, alone and unaided. Walter opened the door wide for the President. Churchill was standing in the centre of the room, naked, with a drink in one hand and a cigar in the other.

The president turned his chair to leave.

"Come on in, Franklin," Churchill called out. "We're quite alone. It's just a bit hot in here – I was off for a cool bath."

Roosevelt hesitated, shrugged his shoulders and wheeled his chair into the room.

Churchill stood in front of him and beamed. "You see, Mr President – I have nothing to hide."

Walter threw him a towel.

The Old Man strolled about the room, happy and talkative, sipping from his glass and pouring drinks for the President.

Walter stood by the door and studied his boss. Churchill looked like a Roman senator at the baths. But did the President know about Pearl Harbor?

***

30 December – Ottawa, Canada

Churchill could not cross the Atlantic without also visiting the Canadians and thanking them for their support. When they arrived in Ottawa, it was bitter cold. Walter shivered and looked with envy at the warm fur hat worn by Churchill. It was a present from the Canadian Prime Minister. Churchill took pleasure in wearing it at every opportunity throughout the two days they spent there, except, of course, when he addressed the Canadian House of Commons.

George had somehow acquired a similar fur hat to keep the biting wind from burning his ears.

At the Canadian training airfield, the ground was icy. Walter kept close to Churchill, so he could reach out to support his arm if he slipped.

To his complete surprise, Walter fell, knocking over Churchill. George stepped forward and pulled both men to their feet. Walter scrambled up; his left side covered in powdered snow.

Churchill took a large cigar out of his case and a number of people rushed forward to light it, but he waved them away and turned towards his bodyguard. Walter produced his *Zippo* and lit the cigar. Churchill looked at Walter, patted him on the shoulder and chuckled.

***

31 December – The Reichstag, Berlin and Lake Quentz

Hitler stood to make his New Year's Eve prophecy. "This year will bring the final decision and will mean the salvation of our people."

Himmler made no announcements; he left the *Reichstag* to find Walther Schellenberg, the man he had left in charge of *Operation Long Jump.* He had the assassination of Churchill on his mind. "So, tell me Walther, about the progress of the training."

Schellenberg was taken by surprise by this unannounced visit. "Sir, good evening. Well the British know about our spy-training facility here at Lake Quentz."

"It's time to move the agents to our targeted locations," said Himmler.

Schellenberg clicked his heels in salute. "Each man is fluent in the local language, as many are natives of the target areas. On your orders, the first batch will be parachuted into Turkey, Algiers and Tehran. The second group will concentrate on Lisbon and the Spanish mainland."

"Excellent. Keep me informed of progress. How are the new grenades developing?" They walked together inspecting the squad.

"We've done some testing, and they will mould to almost anything. I'm having a problem with the *Commandant* at Sachenshausen – he just won't give me fit men. It's too simple for my trained killers to hunt down the worn-out skeletons he sends me."

"Leave it with me. You'll get whatever you need." Himmler raised his arm to dismiss his man. Schellenberg returned the salute.

Himmler smiled. "The next time that little bald British man goes anywhere, we will have a local assassination team waiting for him. This will shorten the war – and save thousands of German lives."

1942
Sacrifice and Capture

CHAPTER 15
Walter – Allies

New Year – Ottawa to Washington, DC

Walter sat in the dining car, listening to the rhythmic *cuckedy-cuck cuckedy-cuck* of the train moving over the rails. He kept Churchill in his peripheral vision and looked out of the window and scoured the snow-covered fields for trouble.

Churchill switched on the light. The smoke from his cigar drifted towards the partially open window.

Walter shut the blind, leaving the vent open to clear the carriage of the fug of smoke. "Sir, always the blind first – there could be snipers in those fields.*"*

"Ha, Thompson, you see assassins everywhere."

Walter smiled. "George, I'm going to do the rounds." He slid open the door to the carriage and walked the length of the private train, taking in every face. He closed the blinds to each car as he passed and checked every washroom. When he returned, Churchill was dozing in his chair.

Walter sat opposite him. He took out his pen and turned it over in his hand. It was the one from the ship, the fated *Prince of Wales*.

Churchill began to snore.

Walter watched the gentle rise and fall of the Old Man's chest. He switched off the light in the carriage, re-opened the blind and stared out of the window at the flashing shapes of the countryside as the train sped through the night.

Secret Service Agent, Mike Reilly met them at Washington Station. He handed Walter a note from Bletchley Park. "I don't know what your intelligence says, Wally, but ours says there's a pack of German submarines out there in the Atlantic, waiting for your boss."

George chuckled. "What we gonna do – *Wally*?"

Walter gave George a sideways look. He turned to Mike. "The Old Man's tired – a short break at one of your sea-side resorts might just be the ticket. With any luck the Germans will get short of fuel and go home.

***

4 January – Palm Beach, Florida

Churchill was happy after the Washington conference and even happier when he woke up in his bunk to find himself in the Florida resort of Palm Beach.

Walter lifted Churchill's cases down from the luggage rack. "Sir, the intelligence from the code breakers at Station X indicated an attack was planned for our return journey across the Atlantic. This little secret holiday by the beach might just work to confuse the German spies – if nothing else, it will be unexpected."

Mike Reilly drove them to a private residence on the beach.

Churchill nodded in appreciation at the Spanish style villa. He stretched and strode towards the veranda overlooking the ocean.

Walter held up some swim wear. "What kind of swimsuit would you like, Sir?"

Churchill began to undress. "I don't think I need one. It's entirely private here. Nobody knows I am staying in this place, and I have only to step out of the back door into the sea."

"You could be seen through glasses, Sir."

"If they are that much interested, it's their own fault what they see." Churchill walked out of the villa on to the beach, wearing a large towel. He strode towards the water, threw the towel at Walter and plunged naked into the ocean.

Walter stood by with the towel over his arm and his hand on his gun. He was unsure of the lay of the land and could feel himself sweating as he scanned up and down the beach.

Churchill was enjoying the freedom of swimming naked in the warm Atlantic and he turned with his arms stretched out in backstroke.

Mike Reilly bounded down the beach from the villa. "Sir," he called, "you really should get out of the water – the coast guard has spotted a rather large shark nearby."

"It's probably nothing," said Downwood, who was following Reilly along the water's edge.

Walter prickled. "What on earth is Downwood doing here?" He waded out to hand Churchill the towel. Churchill stood up in the foam: "I want to inspect that shark's credentials before I take any unnecessary risks." He accepted the towel and grinned at Walter's soaked trousers and shoes.

CHAPTER 16
Bernie - An Evacuation Plan

Bernie opened the door to the parlour and a shock of cold air followed him. He rubbed his hands together in front of the fire while his mother, Emily used the bellows on the dwindling, uncertain flames. The coals glowed into life, in the small arched red brick fireplace, warming them both on a chilly afternoon.

Emily picked up her best Royal Albert tea pot and poured him a cup of steaming strong tea. "Tell me about Whitby."

Bernie was wearing his regimental battledress and home on leave for the first time. "Oh, there's not much there, it's an empty town of old seaside boarding houses. We occupied a large one – a cold old one too, but we made the most of it. Our meals were provided in the swimming pool, no less – I mean the café at the swimming pool, not the pool itself. The cliff-top wind blows so hard, when we go out on drill, we have to lean against the wind and each other. To lift everyone's spirits, I got a daft song going: *Tarantara, Tarantara.* It was shouted more than sang, but it kept us cheerful."

Emily smiled. "You must have remembered the song from *The Pirates of Penzance.* Goodness you were only nine when I took you to see it. So, you're a radio operator?"

"Yes, mum – we started our radio lessons in style in the Grand Hotel on Whitby Cliff. I've learned Morse code. And I've had lessons in a workshop to learn vehicle repairs – which should be very handy at the end of the war for the garage in Brighton, if we are all still planning on doing that – are we?

Emily picked up her handkerchief. "I really hope so, Bernie. Losing Kate was devastating, and I've heard nothing more from Stella. As for your Uncle Walter, he's not been home since the funeral. But his nice sergeant has popped in now and again to see if I'm managing. It's just so awful here alone with everyone gone."

Bernie stood up and held his mother while she sobbed in his strong arms. When the tears subsided, Bernie kissed her on the cheek. "Mum, I want you to leave – it's too dangerous for you here. I want you to come up North with me. I've saved up for the fare and you'll be proud to know I've passed my driving test. If we had a car and petrol, I could drive you."

Emily took a frayed handkerchief from her apron pocket and dabbed her eyes. "But where would I stay?"

"It's all been arranged. I've been posted to Haltwhistle – it's near Hadrian's Wall on the rail link between Newcastle and Carlisle. There's not a lot there, but they have a grand dance once a month in a beautiful dance hall in the middle of a paint factory, no less. The dance floor has been taken out of an old ocean liner and reassembled. There seem to be plenty of girls about, and not all were spoken for by the time me and me mates got there. I'm even becoming a pretty good dancer – thanks to Iris."

"Iris?" Emily clutched Bernie's arm.

"You know me with girls – a bit shy. But my sergeant picked me for the unit boxing team, trained by a man who is famous in the boxing world – Jack London. I'm still with my old mate Johnny, but he didn't get chosen. Most Fridays we go to Scarborough in our physical training gear and trot down to the beach half a mile away to do our exercises on the seashore – much to the delight of the girls from the local chocolate factory."

Emily picked up the teapot and topped up the cups. "Where did you meet girls, Bernie?"

"We met a lot of them in the dance halls and cinemas, and I got friendly with Iris. She's lost her dad too, and lives with her mum. They can offer you a room and a job in the chocolate factory – but only if you want."

"Oh, it sounds wonderful. But what if you get moved on?"

"Mum, let's cross that bridge if and when it comes. If there's a will there's a way – isn't that what you always say? Can you believe it? I am billeted at the regimental headquarters at a manor house. It's an imposing-looking house with a round tower – and it's haunted, if you believe our lads, by anything from a grey lady to Captain Hook. And I've actually got a real bed – I think my

Captain fancies my chances in the next fight, and so is doing his best to make me comfortable."

"I don't think I can stand the thought of you fighting."

"Don't worry, mum – I've got the very best trainer, and I'm very quick on my feet. The last bloke I took on didn't even land a decent punch. What's more, I put ten bob on myself and won 20 quid. Would you like me to treat you up the West End tonight?" Bernie emptied his pockets on the table to show Emily the money.

Emily looked at all the notes and stroked her son's head. "That's a wonderful offer, but I'm going to get packed up here. Oh Bernie – you're such a good boy, Dad would've been so proud of you. Oh gosh, I'll have to get the windows boarded up and the gas cut off. No, no – you go off to London and have a nice time. I'll be all ready on Saturday to come up North with you."

**

Bernie strolled along Beulah Hill. It was an early dusk at 15:30 pm, and it was so cold, he blew white smoke. He was wearing his uniform, which displayed the tartan of his regiment – the Argyll and Sutherland Highlanders. He walked at a pace to keep the cold air out but pulled up short when he came to the bombed-out site that was once Thompson's Grocers. A well-built man with white-blond hair and a pale complexion was sifting through the rubble at the back of the shop. "Hey, what the hell, do you think yer doing." Bernie ran towards the man.

The man took one look at Bernie and shot off.

Bernie stared after the man. "Blasted cheek."

He resolved to go past 10 Downing Street and let his Uncle know.

**

Same time the same day – The War Room, London

Bunny walked past the door of the communications room and

153

stopped as she overheard the telephone operator repeating the message: "The enemy expects PM to return on the *Duke of York*. The enemy is also watching Inspector Thompson. Suggest decoy action. Please respond."

Bunny stood frozen. "What does *suggest decoy action* mean? What can I do?" she whispered to herself.

***

Later the same day – Horseguards Parade, London

Bernie's nose crinkled as he stepped on to the platform at Westminster Underground Station and tried not to breathe in the stench. This end of the platform was up wind of the arriving trains. Frightened people, sheltering from the bombs, were forced to relieve themselves here every night.

He picked his way through piles of blankets, rolled up mattresses and camp beds.

An old lady, seated on the station's wooden bench, waved him over. Her two walking sticks were strewn across four reserved camp beds in front of her. "Has it stopped raining, lovey?"

Bernie put out his arm for her as she struggled to stand. "Yes, it stopped raining when I got on the train – but I can't be sure if it's stopped here 'till I get up top. It's a bit nippy though."

The old woman stretched. "Oh, I think I'll stay here then. Time I get home – the sirens will probably start again." She called to two little girls playing tag around the bedding. "June, Joan, don't go too near the edge, if you fall down there, you'll be toast."

"Yes, grandma," they called and continued their game away from the edge.

Bernie helped the old lady take her seat again. "I'll be coming back this way later. Can I get you anything?"

"That's nice of you lovey but my daughter will be down with my tea at six."

Bernie dodged the little girls and made his way into to the tunnel to find the escalator. He climbed the steps to street level and pulled up sharp at the sight of the devastation. As he walked

154

along the street, he whistled a half-hearted tune and remembered the day he had first met Churchill. The bombing made the city ugly. He took the long way and his route took him past depressing damage. Admiralty Arch had been reduced to a pile of stone and The Mall and Whitehall were full of craters.

As he neared the Cabinet War Rooms, he spotted the pretty blonde secretary who worked for Churchill, walking towards the tube station at Westminster. "Hullo. Miss Shearburn."

She stopped with a start and looked almost angry, but her face softened when she recognised him. "Hello… its Bernie, isn't it? Inspector Thompson's nephew?"

"Yes, miss. Is my uncle around?"

"No… no, he's not…." She faltered for a moment and burst into tears.

Bernie searched his pockets for a handkerchief. "Whatever's wrong?"

The secretary waved her hands in front of her face.

Bernie took her arm. "Come on, Miss." He guided her towards Westminster underground station. "There's a tea stand near the ticket office. If in doubt, brew up, my mum always says. But you'll have to stop that howling – it echoes something terrible down there."

Bunny sniffed and patted her eyes. Bernie held out a wooden chair for her and purchased two mugs of strong tea.

It brought a half smile to Bunny's face. "I'm so, so sorry. I didn't mean to embarrass you."

"Not at all. I'm sorry if I startled you by calling out your name. I was just looking for my uncle. Any idea when he might be back?"

"I haven't, I'm sorry." *But that's the problem – I don't even know if he is coming back. I suspect – your uncle is being used as a decoy.*

Bernie relayed the story of how he had chased away a suspicious-looking man from the bombed-out shop and told Bunny about his plans to take his mother to Haltwhistle. He ended with, "I've even made it into the regimental boxing team – heavyweight."

"I'll let the Inspector know all your news, would you like

155

another?" Bunny picked up the empty mugs. "This one's on me."

CHAPTER 17
Walter - Decoys and Deceit

16 January – Colgate Creek, Baltimore, Municipal Airport, USA

After his holiday in Palm Beach and five days of secret talks in Washington, Churchill was on his way back to Britain. On the previous night, he sped across America in an unmarked train, travelling for hours with the blinds drawn until it reached Colgate Creek at Baltimore Municipal Airport. A flying boat awaited Churchill's party at the end of a long wooden quay, in front a timber faced hangar.

A man sat on the jetty, hidden by a pile of wooden boxes. He checked his gun again – a *Browning* semi-automatic – seven rounds in the detachable clip. He muttered to himself. "I'm going to get that fucking Churchill. I'm going to kill him." He jumped up and pointed his gun at one of the flying boat technicians as he passed.

The technician sank to his knees and ducked behind a box. He crawled on his belly away from the man with the gun. At what he estimated to be a safe distance he stood to run – into the arms of Mike Reilly. "Gun, gun – man with a gun – there at the end of the quay."

"Calm down pal. Where did you say?"

"There, there, behind those boxes. A man with a gun – talking to himself. Saying he's going to kill Churchill."

"Right – go to the control room and ask them to radio the flying boat to warn them. But tell them to shut the door and stay on board. I'm Secret Service. I'll deal with the shooter."

The technician nodded and jogged towards the huge hangar.

Churchill's car pulled up and Walter got out.

Mike jogged up to the car. "We've got a situation, Wally. A gunman behind the boxes at the end."

"Pincer movement?"

"Yes, two of us will take him easier than one."

"George, guard the Old Man."

George drew his firearm and stood in front of Churchill's car. Downwood got out of the car behind. "What's going on?"

George kept his eyes on the quay. "Have yer got a gun?"

"No sergeant."

"Well get in the back of the car with the Old Man and keep 'im calm. If someone shoots me, fall on the Old Man and protect 'im…." George opened the car door for Downwood.

The blood drained from Downwood's face. "G-good morning, sir. I'm going to sit with you for a bit…"

Walter held his gun at his side and edged along the quay.

Mike took position.

The man stood up and pointed his gun at Walter.

Mike charged him from behind. He gripped the man's arm, the gun held out at right angles. "C-could do with a bit of help here, Wally."

Walter kicked the gun from the man's hand. "How's that Michael?"

Mike's eyes opened wide at Walter's agility. "Wonderful, if you could just reach my back pocket for my handcuffs. And only my pop calls me Michael – when he's angry."

"Here you are." Walter handed Mike the cuffs and put his knee in the man's back to keep him there while Mike wrestled his arms into the restraints. "And just so you know how much I like you Mike, my brother only got away with calling me *Wally* – once."

Mike put his foot on the man's back. "Sorry pal. No offence."

Walter picked up the man's gun. "And none taken, Mike. None taken."

The Baltimore police arrived and charged along the quay. "Lay down your weapons."

Mike showed his gun and placed it on the floor. "Agent Reilly, Secret Service and this here is Inspector Thompson, Scotland Yard. He poked the man with his foot. This is the man you want – says he wants to kill, Mr Churchill."

The police inspected Mike's badge and Walter's warrant card. They dragged the man along the quay. He regained his consciousness and began to shout profanities. A police officer punched him and threw him into the back of a waiting van.

Mike checked everywhere along the quay and then knocked on the door of the flying boat. "All clear, Captain. Would you like me to send down your passengers?"

Walter returned to Churchill and opened the car door when he saw Mike wave the *all clear*.

Downwood dived on Churchill and the document he had been studying flew in the air.

George chuckled.

"Get off me." Churchill pushed Downwood aside and stepped onto the quay. "Pick up those reports and put them back in order." He smiled at Walter. "Bit of trouble?"

"All clear sir, thanks to Mike Reilly."

"Well done, Agent Reilly," said Churchill as he stepped aboard the plane.

"Just look at the size and accommodation on this beast." George climbed the ladder. "There are sleeping berths that convert into armchairs and a proper dining room for 12 people. We're travelling back to *Blighty* in style."

"I'd like to try the controls," said Churchill, sitting next to pilot and lighting a large cigar.

"Yes, sir," replied the pilot waving away the heavy reek of cigar smoke.

Just before they were about land in Bermuda, the pilot called out to Walter. "I have a Mike Reilly on the radio, Inspector."

"Hello, Walter – the man's been questioned – just wanted to say that he was not part of any master German assassination plan, but just a crackpot.

"Thanks Mike. Lucky he wasn't a skilled assassin, I'd never got away with that kick."

"That was quite some acrobatics. You'll have to teach me that one. Often these nut jobs are more dangerous though, because they care little about their getaway, and will often sacrifice themselves to achieve their objectives."

"Sounds like you've got the situation under control, Mike. Thanks for your help. Keep me posted."

"Will do, *Walter*. Over and out."

They flew over the sea-horse rock formation of Bermuda's islands and banked low over the lagoon, fringed with white sand beaches and angled palms.

As they circled to land, Walter could see the familiar sight of the *Duke of York* in the pale turquoise waters of the harbour.

At Government House, Churchill arrived at the door the same time as an American Secret Service messenger. "Can I help you?" Churchill barked.

"I have a communiqué – for Inspector Thompson."

"Give it here then, young man."

The Secret Service official handed it over, unsure of his situation.

Churchill looked at the note, screwed it up and put it in his pocket. "Ah, Thompson, I have decided to take the flying boat for my return to Britain. It can only carry a small party, so you'll have to be left behind."

Walter flashed his eyes up and down the parade ground in front of the building as the Governor's official car drew up. "Sir, I must protest. Just think of the risk of taking such important people together with you on a plane."

Churchill turned to Lord Knollys, Governor of Bermuda. "The Inspector is very sore because he is not coming with me."

Walter held the door open for the two men. He caught Churchill's arm. "Sir, I still think it's foolish to have all your eggs in one basket."

Churchill patted his hand: "We shall be all right. And you'll have a well-earned rest on board ship."

"So, Winston," said the Governor, "I've had more protests from the Duke of Windsor. It was all I could do to stop him flying over here. He wants to know when he and the Duchess are going to be allowed to come home from what he refers to as a third-class British colony."

"I hear he is doing a wonderful job there calming some civil unrest over low wages. A plum job in the Bahamas, pah. Most people would give their right arm...."

"Wallis is driving the Duke mad – away from her society friends."

"Well, let's hope it's not too long before we win the war. Now we have the Americans with us, and the Russians have changed sides our chances are looking much more promising, don't you think?"

The next morning Churchill re-boarded the flying boat. He said his goodbyes to the Governor and his staff, in a closed hangar, in secret.

Churchill offered Walter his hand. He looked him in the eye. "God speed, Inspector. I hope to see you again very soon."

***

16 January – Berlin, the Reichstag

Schellenberg sat in his wood panelled chambers in the German parliament building. He was dubious about waking Himmler at this early hour. The telephone at Himmler's home rang for five minutes, before anyone answered. Schellenberg had received reliable information that Churchill was about to leave Bermuda on the *Duke of York*, accompanied by his bodyguard.

However, in order to proceed with his plans for the attack, Schellenberg knew he first needed permission from his superior to contact Admiral Canaris. Only Canaris could activate the *Wolf Pack* – the German submarines waiting in the Atlantic to sink Allied shipping. The plan was to involve all the submarines in the area working together as a team to block the ship's path and sink the *Duke of York*.

Himmler was delighted to hear the news, and so granted Schellenberg immediate permission to wake up the Admiral.

***

16 January – Bermuda

The flying boat taxied away from the quay. George's large face filled a window. He shrugged his shoulders and Walter gave him a wave from the quayside. The 106-foot-long craft made a

161

ponderous lift off, just clearing the reef and the low hills. It was predicted to be a perilous flight – 3,300 miles at 190 miles per hour. One of the furthest distances ever attempted by air.

Churchill retired to his bunk and the aircraft rumbled on through the dark, cloudy night. When they reached the English Channel, the plane was hundreds of miles off course. Instead of viewing the Isles of Scilly below, the plane was just six miles south of Brest, one of the most heavily defended towns in France.

A claxon was sounded at the aerodrome and the *Luftwaffe* scrambled their *Junkers* and *Heinkels.*

Aboard the Flying Boat, the captain realised his error and turned sharp left, North for Plymouth.

Radar at Plymouth picked up a large aircraft approaching from the south. Air-raid sirens sounded, and British pilots scrambled. Twelve fighter planes took off in minutes and flew in a deadly formation to hunt Churchill's plane.

The *Berwick* droned on over the English Channel, the passengers oblivious to the frantic search playing out in thick clouds by the opposing air forces.

The flying boat broke cloud cover over Plymouth and landed with three small bumps at Plymouth Sound.

Captain Kelly shook Churchill's hand as he disembarked. "Did you know they scrambled *Hurricanes* – they thought we were a German raider?"

Churchill took out a cigar. "Fortunately, Captain, they failed in their mission."

***

17 January – Bermuda

The *Duke of York* was not allowed to sail until the flying boat's arrival in Britain. Walter boarded the ship with Larry, who was sweating like a boiled ham in the heat. He was wearing Churchill's coat and homburg. He puffed at one of Churchill's cigars and almost choked. A small crowd had assembled to send *Churchill* off. Larry waved and gave them Churchill's

162

characteristic *V* sign. "Oh look there's Mr Downwood on the quay. What a lovely man. He spotted me at *The Lyric* you know. I was in some ghastly review with Tarquin Barclay, which bombed – all Tarquin's fault – such an old queen."

"So how is Mr Downwood getting home?"

"Oh, I know the answer to that one, Inspector. Mr Churchill's sending the flying boat back for him in a few days."

"Ah look it's the Governor, what a handsome man. Pity we're not in the Bahamas, I'd have loved to have met the Duchess, isn't she quite divine? How wonderful of Lord Knollys to come and see me off."

"Come on Larry, don't overdo it."

Larry glared at Walter. "I'm a pro. I've spent hours watching him on film and practicing with Mr Downwood. I've been hired to impersonate Mr Churchill, and I'd like you to trust me to get things right."

"Well, you'd better stop taking curtain calls."

"Come on now, Inspector Thompson. Would you give me any less attention than you normally give your real master?"

"You're right, Larry, I'm sorry. I just don't want you to overdo it. Come on, old fellow, just one last wave and we'll go to the mess."

"Oh well, if you put it that way." Larry beamed and gave the *V* sign once more from the deck to the cheering crowd.

Walter gave Downwood a hard look. He patted Larry on the back. "The architect of my demise. If the Old Man had just let me in on this, I would have been happy to help. He didn't need to hide you, Larry – I'd have willingly been his decoy. Ha. I don't suppose you'd like to come aboard, Mr Downwood?"

***

24 January – The War Rooms, London

Churchill paced the green linoleum in the long corridor, lit by a line of bare bulbs. He stuck out his bottom lip and held the bridge of his nose as studied the floor. He had arrived back a week ago

163

and made daily passes of the communications room, even though he knew the *Duke of York* would maintain radio silence.

Bunny could not bear to look at him. For the past six nights she had not slept, and there was still no news. As she typed Churchill's dictations, she struggled to keep her feelings in check – anger at Churchill and fear for Walter.

In the middle of a memo where he was dictating instructions for more troops to be sent to reinforce Singapore, Bunny put down her pencil on the desk. She blew her nose. Churchill stared at her and offered her a clean cotton handkerchief, but instead she brushed him aside as she got up and ran to her room. She slammed the door behind her, fell on to her bed and sobbed herself to sleep.

Churchill continued working in his study. George opened the door. "A messenger's outside, sir. Say's it's urgent."

"Bring him in then." Churchill took the message and read it to himself. "Thank you, there will be no reply."

The man left. George was about to close the door.

"Come in, Sergeant." Churchill put his fingers on his temple. "The Japanese have driven almost all our British Commonwealth troops out of Malaya and are poised to invade Singapore. Good God, less than four weeks ago in Ottawa, I told the Canadians that Singapore was impregnable. The War Cabinet wants me to send orders that senior officers should die at their posts rather than give up. What shall I do?"

George shuffled on the spot. He was relieved to see the door open and Walter enter. "Perhaps the Inspector is better to help you with that one…" He retreated back outside the door.

"My dear Thompson." Churchill jumped up and shook Walter's hand. "So, you've arrived back safely. Good man. Have you heard the terrible news from the Far East? Do you realise why I had to return with all speed?"

"Yes sir, I think so."

"You see, Thompson, I am surrounded by critics who want to lay the blame for every setback at my door. I keep telling them we've never had the power to fight Germany, Italy and Japan single-handed at the same time."

"What will you do, sir?"

164

"I have forced a vote of confidence. There will be a debate in the Commons next Tuesday." Churchill paused and reached for a cigar. "Oh, Thompson, there seems to be something amiss with Miss Shearburn."

"Would you like me to go and see if she's all right?"

"Yes, do so – please. Thank God you're back."

Walter knocked on the door to Bunny's bedroom and waited a few moments, but there was no answer. "Miss … Bunny…"

Within seconds, the door was flung open. Bunny threw her arms around his neck. "Where have you been? No one would tell me anything."

"I have been on a lovely cruise on one of our very best ships." He peeled her away from him.

"And you weren't attacked by the Germans?"

"Well, we had a few adventures along the way. The *Duke of York* is a very fast ship, but the Captain steered a circuitous route around all the places he thought the German submarines might lay a trap."

"Oh Walter, Walter. I thought…."

"Come on, you know what thinking does."

Downwood was spying on Walter from the corridor. He choked and gasped for breath. He kicked and struggled.

George's thick forearm tightened around his throat. He let up the pressure a little and whispered: "Go away, Downwood – this is not your domain. And if I 'ear you have spoken of this to anyone, you'll be very sorry."

"How dare you." squeaked Downwood, as George's arm constricted his gullet.

George spoke through gritted teeth: "I won't say this again. Get out and mind your own business." He shoved Downwood away.

Downwood rubbed his neck. He was about to speak, but George raised a finger and the small angry Secret Service agent scuttled off.

Bunny wiped tears from her cheeks with the sleeve of her blouse. "I thought you were being sacrificed for the Old Man. I… I… I'm so sorry."

Walter's heart raced as he looked at her imploring face. He fought with his feelings for her – what were they? A mixture of surprise, bemusement, fascination… and guilt.

"Oh, and your nephew…"

"Bernie?"

"Yes, Bernie, came to see you – I couldn't tell him where you were. I promised to let you know, he has taken his mother – to Haltwhistle – he's the regiment's heavyweight boxing hopeful. Your sister is staying with Bernie's girlfriend, Iris, in the town. And a suspicious-looking man was examining the wreckage of your grocers shop. Bernie was worried." Bunny stopped talking and took a breath.

"Bernie – a girlfriend? Haltwhistle? Boxing, eh? Suspicious-looking men? Okay, Miss Bunny, thank you for the news. Are you all right?" He took her hands in his and gave them a gentle squeeze before walking back to his post.

Bunny stood in the hallway. A suggestion of Walter's *Aqua Velva* shaving cream lingered, and she breathed it in.

***

15 February – The BBC, London

Churchill stared straight ahead. He touched the top of his head with light fingers as if reading braille. His voice was low as he leaned into the microphone to broadcast to the nation. "The loss of Singapore is a heavy and far-reaching military defeat. Here is the moment to display that calm and poise, combined with grim determination, which not so long ago brought us out of the very jaws of death."

George nudged Walter. "The Old Man's very downcast. We can't defend our empire – we can't protect those countries who depend on us. The Japanese have a mighty army and it's aimed at all our territories in Asia. I suppose the fall of Singapore is the last straw."

Walter stared at the Old Man through the glass of the control room. "He's overtired and not sleeping well. I don't know how to help him. Singapore was a symbol of the British Empire in South

166

East Asia. The Old Man thought its large gun emplacements facing the sea were impregnable."

George looked at the crumpled figure of Churchill sitting at the microphone. "Poor Old Man thinks it's 'is fault. Although you'd think someone might have noticed we were poorly defended from the land – the Japanese just avoided our guns by going around our fortifications and coming in through the back door."

Walter flicked through a pile of news reports on the desk – all bad news for Britain. "The Old Man's sinking into one of his deep *black dog* depressions. All I can think of is to get him out to visit some military establishments."

"Good idea. Let's get the lovely Miss Shearburn to make some phone calls. I could do with getting out of London for a bit. You think she'll come too?"

CHAPTER 18
Stella - A Carnival

30 March – South of France

An icy wind heralded the arrival of *Satan* to Paris in early 1942. His name was Carl-Heinrich von Stülpnagel. He left behind him an ugly trail of evil from his last posting in the Ukraine – thousands brutally murdered, including women and children… their only *crime* – being Jewish.

Carl-Heinrich was Otto von Stülpnagel's vicious cousin. Otto was re-called to Berlin, for being too accommodating towards the French. Carl-Heinrich began his regime by hunting down the Resistance. Ordinary people lived in fear, while his troops banged on doors, threw suspects and their families into the streets and executed them in front of their neighbours.

Martin's three and a half years of hard work on behalf of the Resistance were about to be lost. The new, harsh administration meant danger for Europe Express.

Martin had become rich with lucrative German contracts. He donated his wealth to Pierre's Resistance group, financing their fight against the Nazis. He was allowed extra rations of petrol and diesel, which enabled him to maintain the fleet of buses and his *Citroën* car.

Pierre's requests for coaches had almost dried up. The borders were closed, and the only people they transported were those young men escaping forced labour.

The Resistance movement was growing all over France – involving opposition to the Germans and to the despised French puppet government, run from Vichy.

France was split in two. The North was run from Paris by the Germans. But the South was governed by Frenchmen who were, in effect, Nazis. This government was officially neutral, but it collaborated in secret with the Germans.

Charles de Gaulle, Leader of the Free French Forces was waiting in London for the invasion. He described Vichy as *an illegal government run by traitors*.

Pierre had called a meeting at the Mill to discuss their forged papers.

Martin strode around the kitchen. "The Resistance can get this forger out themselves. I don't want my wife involved."

Pierre held up his hands. "Within the *Zone Occupée*, your coaches are a familiar sight. The soldiers wave them through without checking papers. They display the correct permits. But how long will you be safe now Otto's been replaced? He's probably facing a firing squad right now. We have to move South, and we need fool proof documents. We need Henri."

"He says he can't get out of jail unless we get him Pétain's seal and a recent copy of his signature," said Luc. "My cousin Philippe assures me Henri is willing to cooperate if we can get him the right tools to forge his own parole or pardon. However…" He paused and looked at Stella, "We've had to make him a few additional promises we know we won't be able to keep."

Stella shrugged her shoulders. "If what Pierre says is true, and all those Jews held at the camp at Drancy have been shipped to Germany, who will be next? We'll all be needing new papers soon. We have to go to Vichy and steal a recent copy of Marshal Pétain's signature and a stamp." Stella put her arms around Martin's neck and pecked him on the cheek. "I don't want you to get shipped off with the other men as slave labour. You've not registered, and you're not protected by Otto anymore. We need new identities and we have to go South."

"I'll go." Luc wiped a cloth over his rifle.

Martin sighed and hugged his wife. "We'll take the little bus because I have the special travel permits for it. It will be easy until we get to Nevers, that's the furthest the bus normally travels from Paris. The tricky part will be passing between the two zones."

Luc spent the next two nights scouting the route on his motorbike, inspecting every road and every checkpoint within range. He plotted the final section leading to the town of Vichy so they would only be stopped twice.

The first checkpoint was at a railway crossing. It was not always manned as very little traffic used the route.

They set out at sunset and Luc helped Martin to navigate along the winding lanes. No vehicles passed them. No one was in sight. The only signs of life were the shadows of cows sitting in the open fields. At two in the morning, Martin drew the bus to a halt just before the frontier post

"Do you think there's anyone in the sentry box?" Martin cut the engine.

"Wait here – I'll take a look." Luc laid his rifle down under the seat, dropped off the bus and edged alongside the hedge in the shadows. It was quiet.

Luc couldn't see anyone in the box as he approached, so he continued towards the barrier, until he heard the nervous high-pitched voice of a young guard.

"Halt! Who goes there?" The sentry had been relieving himself against a tree. He approached Luc from behind and Luc put his hands in the air.

Martin leapt from the bus. Having raised the bonnet, he ran down the road shouting, "Luc, it still won't start." He arrived breathless at the sentry box. "Sorry," he said to the guard in German. "We've broken down just back along the road. We need some help."

Luc smiled, keeping his hands raised in the air.

"Oh, please ignore him. He's a bit simple."

"Put up your hands. Where are your papers?" The guard seemed more frightened than the two men he threatened.

Martin glanced upwards and gave an exaggerated sigh. "I can't very well give you my papers and put my hands up at the same time, can I? Look, let me take my hands down and then I can give you my papers. I'm Martin Thibault. I'm delivering this bus to Vichy on the *Kommandantur,* von Stülpnagel's authority. Look, here's his official letter. Now, do you know anything at all about diesel engines?"

Martin prayed the recruit would not know the difference between the deposed and the newly appointed von Stülpnagels, since the former had signed his documents. He flashed his travel papers at the guard. The corner of his right eye twitched and Martin forced a smile, while the guard read the official letter.

170

"I know a bit about diesel engines, yes." The guard lowered his rifle. "My father owns a garage."

"Well, come on." Martin put his arm round the young man's shoulder and started to lead him towards the bus.

"I can't leave my post."

"What if we push our bus forward, roll it downhill to your sentry box?"

"Well… all right."

Martin tugged Luc's arm and they walked back to the bus.

Luc pulled a face: "Simple, eh? Yes, yes I know enough German to recognise that word."

"Simple in that you can't spot a guard in your path. The von Stülpnagel letter worked a treat, though. If I'd have known it was that good, I'd have driven right up to the box."

"But there's nothing wrong with the bus. What if he's some junior super-mechanic?"

"He's not going to look at the bus." Martin shut the bonnet and climbed on board. "Stella, we're not stopping at the barrier. Get down under the seat. Luc, get out again and push the bus – there's a slight hill."

Stella did not question.

Luc's veins bulged in his neck as he summoned all his strength. The bus did not move. There was not enough gradient on the hill.

Martin cocked his head to one side. "Listen… A train. Luc, Luc, get in."

The sound of the train grew louder. When Martin considered it was loud enough, he started the engine. The train was on the level crossing, puffing out steam.

Martin let the bus move forward in second gear. As he approached the barrier, he shouted to the guard. "Hey, hey. Open the barrier, open the barrier. Come on, you've seen our papers, open the damn barrier. If I stop this thing, it'll conk out again and we'll never get to Vichy on time."

The sentry looked around.

"Come on." Martin waved. "Open the barrier. We've got it started and we can't stop again."

The sentry ran towards the barrier and lifted it just in time for the little bus to carry on through.

Martin accelerated the bus away.

Luc reached under his seat and lifted out his rifle; checking the action and polishing the barrel with a cloth he pulled from his pocket.

Stella put her head up. "Can I come out?"

"Whoops. Sorry, forgot you were still under there."

She climbed up to the seat behind Martin. "Where's the next roadblock?"

"About 100 miles down this road. Just on the outskirts of Vichy. We'll have to take our chances." Martin put his hand on the Walther inside his jacket for comfort. As they reached the brow of a hill, he noticed a succession of lights.

Luc spotted them at the same time. *"Merde."*

"What, now?" Stella leaned forward from the seat behind.

"German army convoy. I'll pull into these trees and we'll hide while they pass." Martin steered the bus off the main road.

Stella reached down for the gun she had left under her seat. "Germans? I didn't think there were German troops in Vichy France. I thought they were only in the occupied zone."

"Not the army of the occupation," said Luc. "They're supply trucks, passing through with equipment for the German war effort. The Germans are free to travel in and out of the south."

"So why can't we just keep going?" Stella played with the gun in her hand.

Martin bounced in his seat as the bus bumped over the rough track. "It's too risky. We're registered in Paris. Someone might get curious; think he can show how clever he is."

"But we've got von Stülpnagel's letter." Stella picked up a bullet she dropped in the isle.

"Yes, but the wrong von Stülpnagel." Martin drove the bus up a muddy trail into some woods. "Let's just try to avoid having to show any papers." He parked in the thick of the trees and killed the engine.

He and Luc jumped out.

Luc hacked off part of a branch from a tree with his knife and they attempted to cover the tyre tracks.

After a few moments, they realised the track was waterlogged. They looked at each other and shrugged.

172

Martin threw his branch into a bush. "Too late to worry about it now. Let's tackle one problem at a time."

They returned to the bus. "Where's Stella gone?" Martin stood on the step. Stella popped her head up from under a seat. "I don't think we'd better hide in here, *Neshama*. Just in case the Germans do find the bus. We'll hide in the woods, so if we're discovered we'll have a chance to run."

Stella scrambled out from her hiding place. The flickering covered lights of the convoy was getting nearer.

Martin pointed up the hill. "Come on, let's look for the highest point in the woods to hide. Then we can choose the best exit."

They climbed up the track into the woods until they found a clump of bushes and thick undergrowth that appeared to offer a suitable hiding place. Luc shinnied up a nearby oak tree and concealed his thin frame like a stick insect behind the trunk. He watched the slow convoy wind its way up the hill until it disappeared. They waited. Martin looked up at Luc in the tree, and Luc shook his hand to indicate there was nothing in sight.

Stella began to get fidgety and cold. Martin took off his coat and gave it to her, which she took, her face frowning in silent protest.

Martin rubbed his hands together. "I think I'll go take a look." He crept off to find out what was going on. Halfway down the track, Martin pulled up sharp when he realised the convoy had stopped in a clearing, blocking his access to the bus. He lay flat to the ground in the bushes at the side of the track and counted ten German army supply trucks. They were not heavily guarded; there were two soldiers assigned to each truck and six motorcycle outriders with machine guns. The soldiers seemed to have stopped for a break. They were busy lighting small Primus stoves, and he could smell the aroma of fresh coffee brewing as it wafted across from the clearing.

Pain stabbed through Martin's hand as a German took a step back to avoid a puddle and trod on his fingers. He gritted his teeth and didn't dare make a sound.

The sentry was smoking with his back to him. After a final slow inhalation on his cigarette, he moved off.

Martin retracted his throbbing hand and crawled away from the camp to rejoin Stella and Luc high up in the woods. "There are between 20 and 30 German soldiers camping in the clearing. The bus is on the other side. They must have driven past it. They haven't seen it – yet." He winced as he nursed his hand.

Stella touched Martin's arm. "What happened?"

"A damn Gerry stood on it."

"Let me look. Can you move your fingers?"

Martin stretched out his fingers.

"Well, it doesn't look as if it's broken – it's just bruised." Stella opened her bag and produced a scarf. She wrapped it around Martin's throbbing fingers.

"Thank God for the soft ground." Martin kissed Stella.

Luc slid down the tree. "Now what do we do *mes amis*?"

Martin nursed his hand. "Well, we'll have to wait until they go and then get the bus. I think they are just taking a break."

They waited for an hour. Stella shivered and cuddled up to Martin. Luc stripped and cleaned the same parts of his rifle over and over. A faint glimmer of light began to appear in the sky.

Luc stood up. "I'll go and take a look again, *n'est pas*?"

Martin nodded.

He rested his rifle at the foot of the oak and climbed up to his viewpoint in the tree to scour the camp. "They seem to be making themselves comfortable. I can't see any signs of them moving on yet."

"I'm sorry, old girl." Martin used his clipped upper-class English accent, hoping a touch of humour would help to cheer her up. "We'll just have to go and get our bus and continue on our way. We could try to push it down the hill and start the engine when we get to the bottom."

Stella pulled up the collar of Martin's coat against the cold wind. "But why don't we just play safe and wait until they go?"

"Because, my love, if we drive into Vichy before daylight, there will be far fewer police around who might stop and question us."

They kept to the trees and dense undergrowth at the side of the track. They stopped and stood rigid each time one of them broke a twig or crunched some leaves as they crept passed the Germans' camp.

Martin found the bus first. "Stella, you jump in and steer while Luc and I push."

Stella climbed into the driver's seat, released the brake and waited. The bus did not move. Martin's head appeared at the window. "It's bogged down in the mud. You'll have to get out and help us push."

Stella wondered how she could help as she went to the back of the vehicle.

Martin lodged a branch between the seat and the steering wheel to keep the wheel straight.

Luc cut branches with his knife and laid them in front of the wheels to help the tyres gain some grip in the slippery mud. "We'll all have to push, *un, deux, trois*."

They heaved together, but still the bus did not move.

"Come on, one more time." Stella's face flushed red as she strained hard, willing the bus to budge, but it stayed where it was. She slid down the back of the vehicle and onto the muddy ground.

A roar from the hill made her jump. The Germans were starting their trucks.

"Quick, get back on the bus – they won't hear us." Martin hauled Stella to her feet.

Stella sprang back to life and hopped into the driver's seat. She turned over the old diesel engine and slipped it into gear. The wheels spun in the mud.

"*Attend.*" Luc jumped off the bus and rearranged the branches under the wheels. "Right, take it slowly."

Stella let out the clutch and the tyres gripped the branches. She backed out of the track and turned onto the main road while the German convoy went on its way up the road and over the other side of the hill.

Martin unfolded the map. "I fear the daylight will catch up with us and we'll have to go back."

"No," said Stella. "We must go on."

"I'm worried about the next checkpoint." Martin peered at the map.

Luc pointed to a village he had marked. "Couldn't we go around it? When I did my reconnaissance, I noticed we can cut out the checkpoint, if we crossed fields at Creuzier-le-Vieux. That is, if we don't get stuck in any more mud. *Que penzez vous?*"

"Go around." Stella took the bus to its top speed. "Please let's keep going." She pushed the bus to its limits, staring hard at the dark empty road for several hours. She stopped the bus when they reached the little track marked on Martin's map.

"You must be tired. Let me take her across the fields," offered Martin.

Stella nodded, and took a double seat.

The track was bumpy and the ride uncomfortable until they joined the road about two miles south of the checkpoint.

Dawn was breaking as they entered the town of Vichy. The faded grandeur of Napoleon III's spa town greeted the travelers with an interesting skyline of minarets and domes. The French government had installed themselves in the *Hotel du Parc*. It faced the *Parc du Source* with its elegant wrought iron and timber covered walkway, leading to the charming opera house, built at the turn of the century. The addition of the Paris officials meant the town's casinos, upmarket restaurants and brothels thrived. And there was the spa water to take, should they suffer a hangover from their excesses.

"We're almost there." Martin, drove through the quiet streets. "Where do we go?"

"Turn left here," said Luc. "The garage is right opposite the little church – can you see it?"

Martin manoeuvred the little bus into the side street. "Look, there's Nicole."

A petite, dark-haired woman, dressed in men's trousers and a hand-knitted pullover, nodded at two men who opened the heavy wooden doors of a large garage.

Martin drove the bus into the safe, dark space. "What's that terrible smell?"

Luc put his handkerchief over his nose. "It's the sulphuric water from the volcano. It fills the town with the smell of bad eggs when the wind comes from the south. People come for miles to sit in baths of the stinking stuff."

The two men closed the huge doors to conceal the bus, which, according to the paperwork, was supposed to be delivered to the Vichy bus depot.

"Bonjour, mes amis," said Nicole, kissing each of them on both cheeks. *"Tout est prêt."* She handed them hot coffee and uncovered a basket of fresh baked rolls on the table. She was Pierre's liaison with the *Réseau Brutus*, a Resistance group with its headquarters in Lyon.

Nicole's team drank coffee and talked in low voices while the three travellers snatched some sleep on old mattresses, at the back of the garage. The volunteers cleaned their weapons and played cards until the newcomers were awake.

Nicole gave Stella a large, bowl of warm water to wash in.

Stella splashed the water on her face behind a makeshift screen. She brushed her hair and joined the others gathered around the wood burning stove.

Nicole stepped forward. "You want to break into Pétain's headquarters in the *Hotel du Parc*. You know, it's very well-guarded. We'll need a distraction. There's a café next door – many Germans and French collaborators eat there in the evenings. A bomb in there would give you time to enter the building."

Martin rubbed his hands together in the heat from the stove. "Brilliant idea. Let's destroy a few of those bastards and steal the papers."

"There's always a price to pay." Nicole's folded her arms. "100 innocent French were taken hostage in reprisal for the last Paris café bombing. Many were shot."

Stella cozied up to Martin. "Ah. Let's try another distraction – something that won't endanger lives."

Nicole put a pot of coffee on the stove. "We've been trying to think of something that would take the guards away from their posts, but we haven't come up with anything suitable yet."

"What about women?" Luc winked at Nicole and nodded towards Stella.

Nicole poured the coffee. "It's an idea – we could try it. But the problem is while we can distract the guard on the door, what about the ones inside?"

Martin accepted a small black coffee from Nicole and held it to his nose. "It's a pity it's not Bastille Day. You French go berserk, and everyone's either drunk or mad – it would be a perfect cover."

"Can't wait until July, *trop longtemps*," said Luc.

"What about Easter, next Sunday or Monday?" Martin sipped his coffee and sat at the makeshift table made from an old door, raised on piles of bricks.

"We used to have a carnival – with music and dancing," Nicole recalled. "But we haven't put it on for three years."

Stella sat down next to Martin. "Couldn't we ask permission to have a celebration?"

"Yes, but it takes months to make all the costumes, let alone rehearse all the songs and dances." Nicole put the coffee pot back on the stove.

"What happened to the old costumes?" Stella cupped her hands around her demitasse.

"I'm not sure… I'll go and ask my sister – she used to be the carnival organiser. Meanwhile, have some bread and more coffee to refresh yourselves while I'm out. I won't be long." Nicole tucked a revolver into her belt and buttoned her coat around her, then slipped out of a side door and into the street.

Stella, Martin and Luc joined the others in a hearty lunch of bread, goat's cheese and salad. They sat around the table and Luc tucked a wedge of wood under the bricks at his corner to stop it rocking.

Nicole returned after they had finished the meal. "The costumes are tatty, but my sister says she and her friends would be willing to work on them this week to make them presentable. My uncle says the bands will sound terrible from lack of practice. I said we don't care, so long as they are a distraction. He said they'll certainly be a distraction."

"How do we get permission to hold a carnival?" asked Luc.

"My sister will speak to her doctor. He's the most respected man in town as he used to be the mayor. He will ask permission."

"I'll go with him if I can," said Luc. "I want to get an idea of the layout of the building, *d'accord*."

***

31 March – Vichy

The doctor kissed Luc on both cheeks when he heard the plan the next morning. He and Luc walked together, past the impressive 19th century town hall, with a dome and intricate stonework. In the *Parc du Source*, patients in wheelchairs were being promenaded by nurses wearing starched white uniforms from the *Source d'hopital*. The doctor stopped in the middle of the park. "Are you sure you want to walk into the wolf's lair?"

Luc smoothed back his hair and checked his borrowed suit of clothes. "Think like you've got nothing to hide and it will show in your face."

The guard at the front recognised the doctor and let the two men pass without question. Once inside, they approached the police officer at the desk.

"Good morning. I'd like to make an appointment with Marshal Pétain. My name is Doctor…."

"I know your name, doctor," snapped the police officer. "Marshal Pétain is very busy – I don't think he has time for local doctors. What's your business?"

"Actually, I probably don't need to see the Marshal at all. I just need your permission."

"Permission? Permission for what?"

Luc was busy looking around, scouting out the details of the building. He noticed a high window left open at the top of the stairs. Through the window, he could see a roof. *C'est parfait.*

"It will be Marshal Pétain's 86th birthday on 24th April. The local townspeople would like to use this opportunity to celebrate his achievements with a carnival dedicated to him and his success. He was our hero at Verdun with his outstanding military leadership, and he is our hero here, too." The doctor swallowed as he lied.

"Ah, well, I think you had better go up and see Marshal Pétain's personal secretary." The police officer pointed up the stairs. "Turn right at the top. Follow the corridor to the end."

179

Luc observed everything on the way, taking a long look at the high window at the top of the stairs. He noticed the catch was broken and wondered if he was thin enough to squeeze through. However, if a policeman were on duty at the desk, any noise would draw his attention. He also noted the 12-foot drop to the floor. He caught hold of the doctor's arm as they walked along the corridor, directing him. "Slow down. Go in this office. I want to take a look at the roof out there, *d'accord*."

The doctor tapped on the office door and entered.

"May I help you?" asked a clerk.

The Doctor smiled. "I'm looking for Marshal Pétain's secretary."

"He's in the office at the end of the corridor." The clerk waved his hand in the direction of Pétain's office.

Luc studied the roof through the window. It looked old and weak. Would it be able to take his weight? Perhaps someone small and slim, like Stella would be better?

"Thank you." The doctor steered Luc out. "Should I go into the next office as well?"

"No, I've seen enough. Let's get permission for the carnival."

Pétain's personal secretary, a small, grey-haired man with a huge moustache, beamed. "It sounds like a marvellous idea. I'll tell Marshal Pétain the town would like to hold a celebration in his honour. However, his birthday is not until the 24th, and I know for certain he has an engagement elsewhere on that day."

"That's no problem," the doctor assured him. "We would really prefer to hold the festivities earlier, to make the whole of April a special month."

"In that case please return tomorrow, and I'll try to have an answer for you."

They left the building and walked back to the garage to meet the others. "We'll know the answer tomorrow, *mes amis*." Luc took off his coat.

"Can you break in?" asked Martin.

"There's a window with a broken catch. It's very high up, but I used to go climbing in the Alps before the war, so I'm not bothered about that. But I don't think I can squeeze through. I could lower someone who was *petite* down to the floor...." Luc looked at Stella.

"Oh no." Martin stood in front of his wife. "Not Stella."

"Why not?" Stella stood up.

Luc laid his hand on Martin's shoulder. "Sorry, Martin, but she's our only hope of getting in and out undetected."

***

1 April – The Resistance HQ, Vichy

Martin read a newspaper, Luc cleaned his rifle and Stella mended clothes for the carnival she hoped for, while they waited for the doctor.

He arrived breathless. "I'm afraid we can't have the carnival for Easter. However, we can have *Marshal Pétain Day* the week after next, on Thursday the 16th."

Luc stood to attention. "Hooray for Marshal Pétain."

***

The news of the carnival travelled fast, not only among Resistance fighters and their supporters, but to the population around Vichy. For two weeks, eager participants prepared for the celebration with speed and vigour. Women mended old carnival costumes. Bands rehearsed and trucks were decorated with displays. One group of people made a papier-mâché statue of Marshal Pétain, complete with moustache and military peaked cap. He looked very stern and unpleasant, which Luc said was fitting.

On the day of the carnival, Stella could feel that buzz again as she washed and dressed.

The sound of people practising their musical instruments echoed all over town. Delivery trucks and tractors were taken out of service and dressed into carnival floats. The smell of *La potée auvergnate,* Auvergne hotpot, of country vegetables and pork permeated the town and drifted into the garage where the group waited.

The procession was planned to begin at midday. The team put on their costumes.

Martin said he felt ridiculous dressed as a white rabbit, but Luc insisted he wear the costume.

"You need to be covered up – you look too much like a Jew." Nicole explained. "I've no idea how you get away with it in Paris."

"But I am a Jew, and I do get away with it. Why do I have to look ridiculous?"

Nicole placed a hand on his shoulder. "No one will see your face in that outfit. You'll be safe."

Stella put on her black cat costume, which accentuated her slim figure. "*Miaow*," she said, adjusting the cat's head. "I'm a pussycat."

"My little cat burglar." Martin gave Stella a squeeze.

Luc was dressed as a cat too, his lean muscular body concealed by the baggy, dark-brown costume, which also hid a rope and small harness. "Come on kitten, we have a job to do, *chaton*."

The three carnival animals slipped into the noisy, colourful procession, blending in with the crowd as it marched along behind the floats and six brass bands. Thousands of people had made costumes or mended old ones so they could join in the carnival. Here and there the *V* sign was sewn into sequins on the dresses of some of the dancers, chalked on walls along the route and painted on the insides of trucks in the parade.

When the procession reached the road behind the Vichy government headquarters, the three of them slipped into an alleyway and removed their animal heads.

"You'd better put your costume head back on," Luc tapped Martin on the head. "If anyone comes, blow this trumpet and dance about so we can hear you. Stand next to the old woman, frying cabbage and bacon – she's one of us."

Martin blew into the trumpet to test its sound. "It's one o'clock. I expect you both to be back in half an hour." He put on the rabbit's head.

"We'll be back in twenty minutes." Luc touched the gun, harness, and rope concealed inside his costume.

Luc and Stella left their cats' heads and tails in a doorway and Luc helped Stella climb the wall to the roof. Stella stretched up and clung to some old metal guttering. Her fingers slipped, sending small pieces of cement scattering down to the street. Luc put his shoulder under her, and she scrabbled up on to the precarious little roof.

Martin stood on the corner, helping the old lady serve hungry revellers with steaming hotpot. He glanced left and right every few seconds, keeping watch for the police. He could hear the sound of the bands getting closer. He prayed Stella and Luc had enough time to break in, before the procession turned the corner and passed the *Hotel du Parc*.

Stella knew they must be in position in time. She crawled across the old roof. A sharp tile cut her costume and grazed her knee. She gritted her teeth.

Luc climbed up behind her and pressed the sleeve of his suit over her knee for a few seconds until the bleeding stopped. "Okay, let's do the difficult bit. Oh no, we've done that – let's do the easy bit then. See the small window over there?"

"Yes."

"You're going to cross this roof and climb through the window. Nicole assures me the staff have been given the day off – but the policemen in the hallway will be able to see you if you make any noise."

"See me?"

"Well, they're not going to see you, because they'll be watching the parade. You'll be behind them at the top of the stairs. Remember, when you get in, go to the end of the corridor to your left. Marshal Pétain's name is on the door – the outer office belongs to his secretary. There are filing cabinets in there. Let's hope you get lucky and find the special stamp he uses. And take any documents you find with his signature, *bonne chance, chaton*." The procession was approaching, led by one of the bands. Luc lifted Stella so she could reach the small window. She wriggled through. She had not anticipated the 12-foot drop. Luc felt the rope run between his hands and stopped it when the ribbon marking 12 feet met his palms. Stella slipped down the wall headfirst. Her eyes opened wide when her face stopped short of the hard marble floor. She twisted upright, undid the straps and left the rope hanging from the window. She tucked the torn flap of material back in the costume. Her knee stung as the soft cotton touched the drying graze. She tiptoed along to the last office, as Luc had instructed and opened the door. She froze. There, in front of her, standing on the corner stone balcony, surrounded by his staff, was Marshal Pétain watching the parade. Stella shook her head to bring life back to her paralysed body. She slipped out of the office and into the corridor before Pétain or any of the other people with him could spot her.

The rope hung from the window in full view. She peeped down the stairs at the policemen in the entrance hall. They were absorbed by the distraction of the procession. One of the bands was just marching past, sending a tremendous blast of sound through the open door.

Don't turn around or we're done for.

She crept along the opposite corridor trying each door. They were all locked. The last door was the men's cloakroom. She went in, sat in a cubicle, and put her head in her hands. There was a noise from someone in the next stall and she looked under the partition to see a pair of large, black boots. She opened her door a crack and saw a policemen's jacket hanging on the back of the main door. She sneaked out of her cubicle, felt in the pockets and found keys.

"Jean-Paul, is that you?"

"Oui," answered Stella in her deepest voice.

"Pass me the newspaper. I think I might be in here for some time."

Stella spotted the newspaper on the hand basin and slid it under the door to the guard.

"Merci."

She crept out and her hands were damp with perspiration as she tried each of the keys in the door to the first office. She gave a long exhalation when she found one that fitted. It creaked as it opened but the carnival was masking any sounds. Once inside, she opened the first filing cabinet and took out some official-looking papers with signatures. She posted the papers down the front of her costume. She searched the drawers of the desk and her eyes widened when she discovered a wooden stamp.

She opened the door and peeped out into the corridor. *Empty.* She fumbled with the keys. In the end she decided to leave the door open. She tiptoed away to return the keys to the policeman's jacket in the men's cloakroom.

The guard heard the keys rattle. "I'll be with you in a minute, Jean-Paul."

Back beneath the window, she stepped into the harness and tugged the rope.

Luc began to haul Stella up. He bit his lip as the rope slid through his bloodied palms, but he held on until Stella found the narrow ledge. She gripped it with her hands, pulling herself towards the small window. Luc's muscles bulged and burnt with the effort, but he would not let go. At last, Stella hauled herself through as the music of the bands was receding into the distance.

"Did you get it?"

"I don't think so. Did anyone know Pétain would watch the carnival parade from his terrace?"

"Nicole came to tell Martin as soon as she spotted him, but it was too late – you were already in the building."

"Well, let's get out of here – Martin will be worried. We've been much longer than we said."

Just after Stella had disappeared through the window, the police officer in the hall looked up the stairs, thinking he had heard a noise. He relaxed when he saw his colleague coming out of the men's toilet.

"Here's your newspaper, Jean-Paul," called the guard from the top of the stairs.

***

Back in the garage, Martin pulled Stella towards him. "*Neshama* you've torn your costume – oh you've cut your knee."

"It's nothing. "Don't fuss. I must get some clean water for Luc – his hands are bleeding."

"I was so worried. Pétain was in his office, but it was too late – you were already there. I tried to warn you by blowing the trumpet, but one of the bands marching past, drowned us out."

Martin started to remove his costume.

Stella tapped her chest, bulging with her haul and removed the documents and the wooden stamp. She laid them all out on the table. "I hope these papers will be worth it."

"What do we have here?" Nicole began to examine each document. "Look at this, it's a letter of pardon… but it's signed by Pierre Laval."

"Magnifique. We can use that to free our forger." Stella went behind the screen to take off her cat costume.

Nicole laid it to one side. "Unfortunately, not. Pétain had Laval removed from office 18 months ago. He didn't trust him because he started negotiating with Germany on his own initiative. I thank Pétain for that. Laval's a nasty piece of work. They say he's close to Hitler." She resumed scanning the papers. "Well, they're all useful, but none of them have Pétain's stamp. Never mind, there are plenty of documents signed by Pétain, so we do have his signature, but what we really need is the stamp."

"I did pick up a stamp." Stella retrieved it from under some documents and handed it to Nicole. "It's Laval's."

Nicole lifted a cloth, and an aroma of warm ham and fresh herbs infused the garage. "It's a *pounti* – a meat loaf, stuffed with herbs and prunes. My mother made them to sell at the carnival and she's made this one for you." She cut a slice and handed it to Stella.

Stella took her time savouring the blend of flavours. "It's delicious, come and try some, Martin."

Martin finished bandaging Luc's hand and sat down with Stella to enjoy the feast.

After eating Martin fetched fresh water in a bowl. "Sit down here *Neshama* and let me bathe your wound. You don't want to get an infection." He dipped a sponge in to some warm water and salt and washed Stella's knee.

"Ouch, that stings."

"Then it must be doing some good, my darling. Oh well, we'll just have to think of another way of freeing our forger."

"Let's sleep on it," said Nicole. "I have to go and talk with my men. It's not safe for them here – they have to return to our hideout in the Montagne Bourbonnaise. I've left you my first-aid kit so you can tend to your cuts and bruises."

Lively music echoed around the garage as Nicole opened the heavy door. People danced past in bright costumes, singing and playing musical instruments.

"It was all for nothing…." Stella fastened the buttons on her shirt.

"We'll think of something else." Luc sat down on a mattress and lit a cigarette.

"Come on, old girl, I think you deserve to be awarded the honourable order of the SC for your brave effort." Martin pulled Stella down to the mattress.

"SC?"

"Special Care, my darling – which only a devoted husband can administer."

Luc looked over. "*Zut.* I'm going to join in the drinking. *Alors, bonsoir, mes amis.*" Luc tucked his rifle behind a steel tool cabinet at the back of the garage and left.

Stella kissed Martin on the lips. "I love you".

"I know. I suppose we've been pretty stupid trying to take on the Germans. I think we should consider our own escape. If we can't get good forged papers – we'll have to run." Martin massaged her aching muscles and held her close until she fell asleep.

***

17 April – Vichy

The rattle of the garage door woke Martin. Nicole walked over to the makeshift bed, where Stella was still fast asleep.

"What time is it?" whispered Martin.

"It's 10 o'clock." Nicole touched Stella's arm. "Wake up, Stella. Laval has been reinstated. They are going to swear him in as the new head of government."

Stella shrieked and hugged Nicole, then Martin, then both of them.

Nicole tuned in the radio set, which was concealed in the far corner of the garage. The reception was bad, but they could still hear an old speech by Laval being broadcast.

"France can be strong again if we work together with Germany."

Nicole spat on the floor in disgust. "What a pig that man is."

Stella laughed. "What a stroke of luck. Now we can use Laval's stamp to free Henri."

CHAPTER 19
Walter - The Human Decoy

30 July – Tehran

The Iranian watched as the canisters dropped one by one from the sky, landing with a thud in the desert. Three of his robed helpers lifted the German supplies into the back of two waiting trucks.

He was one of Oberg's *SS501,* trained at Lake Quentz and parachuted into Tehran for *Operation Long Jump.* Guns and ammunition were in the consignment, but one canister burst open and when the men went to retrieve the cargo, the sniper rifles inside were strewn across the rocks. The Iranian swore as he waved to his men to gather up what they could. He would need to contact Berlin and let them know, but he was wary of Oberg, who had struck him as a dangerous and unstable man. He hoped he would be left alone to complete the operation.

***

1 August – London to the coast of Spain, off Gibraltar

Walter and Churchill sat together planning their next trip to North Africa. Churchill put down his pen and closed his eyes for a few seconds. "I'm sorry Thompson – Downwood was quite convincing that only three people should know I was on that flying boat."

Walter held out his hand to Churchill. Churchill grasped it and held on to it.

Walter placed his other hand over Churchill's. "If someone is watching Croydon and sending information to Berlin, we need to flush them out. But they just won't believe it's you unless they see me – after all, any small round man with a homburg and a cigar could pass for you, but I suppose I'm unique."

"You'll risk your life and travel with Larry again?"

"Of course, if it flushes out the spy." Walter patted Churchill's hand and he released his grip.

Two planes, flying along different flight paths from separate airfields, took off in the middle of the night. Churchill boarded his plane with George, in a closed hangar, at North Weald aerodrome.

Larry was once more playing the role of Churchill and he waved and smoked a big cigar in full view of all the airport staff at Croydon, while Walter scanned the airport for threats. There was no moon, which made England look very dark.

As they approached the English Channel, the constant fire from the anti-aircraft guns on the cliffs ceased. The men at the gun sites looked up at the sky. They could not see the small planes passing over – but they could hear them.

"Someone important is leaving," said the number-one gunner to his mate.

"Let's hope 'e's gone to get reinforcements and more ammo." replied the other.

After a few minutes, they got the order to begin firing again.

Walter peered out of the plane at the coast of France below. As the blackout was not in operation for most non-military targets, he could see thousands of tiny lights winking at him along the coast. He let his thoughts drift. First to mind was Stella. Where are you? Are you safe? I must find a way of getting you and Martin out of France.

"You look worried, Inspector. Do you expect trouble?" Larry lit a cigarette and offered one to Walter.

Walter refused the cigarette and rubbed his temples. "Sometimes a photographic memory is a curse."

"Oh, what I'd give for that," said Larry. "You don't know how hard it is to learn lines. So, what is it you have on your mind? I find it's helpful to say things aloud when their going round and round in my head."

"It's a paper I read – a report from Adolf Hitler."

"Oh do share, please…."

"We must be ruthless! Only thus shall we purge our people of their softness. We have no time for fine sentiments. I don't want the concentration camps transformed into penitentiary institutions. Terror is the most effective instrument. I shall not permit myself to be robbed of it simply because a lot of stupid, bourgeois molly-coddlers choose to be offended by it."

"Gracious. What an awful man."

Dawn approached. Without warning, the pilot banked the plane. Walter looked out the window and saw the white-hot streak of bullets from three enemy fighters. The plane dived as the next round of machine-gun fire missed them. Walter stood up and slid down the aisle of the diving plane towards the cockpit.

"*Heinkels!*" shouted the pilot over the din of the engine, straining to keep the plane level.

A round of machine-gun fire smashed through the cockpit window, killing the co-pilot and hitting Walter in the leg. Walter cried out.

The pilot summoned every last resource to swerve to escape the attackers.

Walter whipped two white cotton handkerchiefs from his pocket into a makeshift tourniquet. He screwed up his face as he fastened them around his thigh and pulled them tight.

"I can't hold her!" screamed the pilot. "Help me!"

Walter leaned across the bloodied co-pilot's body to grab the joystick. The small plane was still diving as the two men wrestled with the controls.

"We're losing fuel and the landing gear's gone. She's coming up, I'm going to try to bring her down on the sea. Look – we can see Gibraltar. Go strap yourself and Larry in tight."

Walter crawled back to his seat to find Larry looking white and shaking. "Inspector... your leg...."

"We're going to have to make an emergency landing on the sea. Get your life jacket ready."

"Thanks, I can manage, Inspector," said Larry.

The plane was billowing smoke from the right engine and was flying at an awkward angle, descending towards the growing shape of the rock of Gibraltar. The pilot was aiming for the bay, where the waters were calmer than in the open Mediterranean. The enemy fighters backed off, circling high so they could watch the plane crash into the sea.

As the plane swerved towards the water, Walter pushed his body down hard on Larry and they braced themselves for the impact. The tip of the wing skimmed the surface, creating a white wall of froth. It slowed the plane but spun it full circle, throwing up a shield of sea water. The pilot sat upright in his seat. Walter hobbled towards him and touched his shoulder, but the man slumped forward, his head at an impossible angle. Walter grappled with the cabin door, but it was stuck. He could feel the plane sinking as water flowed over his shoes.

Behind him Larry was groaning.

"Come on, Larry, we have to get out of here. Come on, Larry, the pilot's dead – it's just us two." Larry did not move. Walter dragged him towards the cockpit. "We're going to have to get through the broken window somehow."

The plane heaved and a loud creak echoed around the cabin. Walter picked up a fire extinguisher and smashed away the glass windshield in the cockpit. He summoned all his strength to haul Larry through the window.

At first Larry's body floated on the surface, but as Walter pushed the life raft and life jackets through the opening, Larry disappeared below the swell.

"Wait, Larry. Wait!" Walter threw himself through the window, dived down, caught Larry by the collar and pulled him to the surface.

The life raft inflated with a *thwack* and Walter clutched its side. He spat salt as he tried to drag Larry onto the raft. He could not climb aboard as well as keep hold of the man in his care, so he seized hold of Larry's life jacket and tucked it under his arms, tying the straps around his chest. "That will have to do Larry. I'll keep your head up." He let go of the life raft.

Walter nursed Larry's head in the crook of one arm as he began to kick away from the plane. The sea opened, hissing and fizzing as the hot engines filled with water and the plane was sucked down, taking the empty life raft with it.

Walter coughed sea water as he dragged Larry towards the Spanish shore. "Perhaps they saw the crash from Gibraltar and will send us a boat?" The beach was further away than he imagined. "Lucky it's not winter, we'd be dead from the cold…"

Larry responded with a continued moan.

Walter counted his strokes, all the while trying to talk to Larry, his small whale, in tow. After an hour, they washed up on the beach. Walter dragged Larry away from the surf, laid him in the recovery position and collapsed beside him.

***

2 August – Spain

When Walter woke, a yellow light was showing in the sky from the east. He turned to rouse his companion. "Larry, wake up. We need to get moving. We're in Spain but look – the rock of Gibraltar isn't far." He shook Larry, but the man who had served as Churchill's double did not move.

"Larry. Larry. Oh please, Larry." Walter felt for a pulse. There was none. He listened for a heartbeat. He heard nothing except his own blood rushing through his head. He tried to move Larry's arms and legs, shifting him so that his belly was flat on the ground. He tugged at his arms. He smiled as he saw water appearing from Larry's mouth. "That's it, Larry, take some breaths. Why won't you wake? Why can't I save you? You could have been the Old Man, and I failed to protect you. I failed you, Larry, and I would have failed Churchill." He pounded Larry's chest over and over, sinking towards the same dark place he had lived in after Kate's death.

He sat on the beach and dropped his head towards the sand. A single tear hung from the end of his nose. "I'm so sorry Larry." He reached over and closed Larry's eyes.

He ripped open his trousers to inspect his leg and saw the bullet had passed straight through the flesh of his thigh. The makeshift bandage had helped to quell the blood seeping from the wound. He felt for his gun and checked through his pockets. He found his Zippo lighter, three rounds of bullets, his Special Branch card, a photograph of Kate and his passport, a penknife, a pocket watch, some soggy cigarettes and two wrapped boiled sweets. *Bless you*

George. He opened one of the sweets and started sucking on it to get some energy for the walk up the beach.

After a few feet he halted – there could be mines. He headed back to the water's edge and began to limp towards the grey rock. The yellow sky was turning to light blue.

He could see the outline of La Linea off to the left. To his right, Algeciras shimmered across the bay. He crouched by the water and noticed to his right – skirting the edge of the Bay, a small fleet of fishing boats returning to the beach with their catch. He walked towards the group of men, trying not to limp. He put his hand on his gun and slipped off the safety catch, not sure if it would fire.

The men were busy with their chores.

Walter chose the largest and most influential-looking fisherman to address.

"Gibraltar, *por favor.*" He waved his silver pocket watch at the man and indicated towards the boat and the sea.

"Madre de Dios! Creo que es un Inglés ahogado!" The large fisherman marvelled at the sight of the soaking wet Englishman who stood before them.

"Gibraltar, *por favour.*" Walter waved the watch again.

The fisherman caught hold of the watch by its chain. *"Plata."* He admired the gleaming silver and his friends discussed what to do with the man.

Walter knew a small amount of Spanish and soon gathered they were debating whether to take him to someone named Miguel or turn him over to the police and steal his watch.

The big man beckoned to Walter. "Gibraltar." He pocketed the watch and began to push one of the brightly painted boats out to sea. Another man tried to get in the boat.

Walter stopped him. "Just him and me, *gracias.*"

The man attempted to push past Walter.

"I said, him and me – *solo dos.*" Walter shouted and shoved the man into the surf.

"No te preocupes," said the wiry fisherman, urging him not to worry. "Is okay – Luis take care of things." As soon as they got out into the bay, the fisherman tried to steer away from Gibraltar.

194

Walter kept his eyes on the man. He had heard the treachery in the voices on the beach.

In an instant, Luis picked up a wrench and came at Walter.

Walter let him advance and used his bulk to unbalance him and throw him over the side.

"No señor – No me dejes aqui. You no leave me here."

Ignoring the plea, Walter pointed his gun at the man. "Give me my watch."

Luis reached into his pocket and threw Walter the watch. He extended his hand to Walter, who turned his back and began to row towards the rocky point.

Walter pulled hard on the oars. He winced with the burn in his biceps. "Blasted Gerries – my bloody leg…"

Something bobbing in the water, drew his gaze. He steered away from the object, which looked like a mine. He felt his leg. His trousers were soaked in blood and his head began to spin.

As he drew close to the port, Walter saw a British naval launch cutting through the water. He waved at the patrol boat and shouted, "Over here. I'm British. British."

The vessel drew alongside. "Who are you?" asked the Royal Naval petty officer. "Do you have any identification?"

"I'm Inspector Thompson, Scotland Yard." Walter put away his gun and fished inside his pocket for his identity papers. He found his soggy Special Branch card.

"What are you doing out here, you bloody lunatic? That water you have just navigated is mined."

"Well, officer, I didn't have a choice. Did you not see the plane crash this morning?"

"Good God, man, so that was you. Any other survivors?"

"No, Petty Officer, the other three are dead."

"Right then, we'll take you to the naval hospital and sort out your story with the military police."

***

3 August – Gibraltar to Cairo

Churchill descended the metal steps of the aircraft and looked to George for a cigar. General Smuts, a South African and a member of Churchill's war council gave a smart salute.

George looked around the airfield for the other aircraft, carrying Walter and Larry, but it was nowhere to be seen. He approached the pilot. "What happened to the other plane?"

"Apparently, they had a small fire on board," said the pilot. "I'm not sure of the cause, and we have not heard from them since. I am trying to get further information."

George brooded while Churchill inspected the guard of honour.

***

4-8 August – Gibraltar to Cairo, Egypt

Two days after his arrival in Gibraltar, Walter discharged himself from the hospital. He stood on the deck of the Royal Naval patrol boat. A tender with six marines drew alongside and lifted Larry's body up to the boat. Walter swore under his breath when he realised Larry's watch and ring were missing. He looked over to where the same fisherman were tending to their nets on the shore. He nodded to the Petty Officer, "I'd like to fire one of your rockets over there."

The Petty Officer saw the marks where Larry's watch and ring should have been. "Be my guest, Inspector, but it might start a war with another country – and we've got enough damned trouble with the Spanish over Gib."

"Can you arrange for Larry to be shipped back to Britain with a recommendation for full military honours?"

"It's the least I can do, Inspector."

"I need the Royal Air Force to fly me to Egypt. Who do I see?"

"Well the services don't usually mix, but on Gib we're all packed in and we're friendlier. I've a half-brother who's a Captain in the RAF. Can we get a signal to your boss to authorise it?"

A naval Chaplain covered Larry's body with a sheet, and he was taken below.

A driver was waiting for Walter when he landed at Cairo airport. Walter shook the RAF Captain's hand, "Could I introduce you to the Old Man, Captain James?"

"I have to refuel and get back, Inspector. Can I look you up back in England one day?"

"Be a pleasure."

The road into town was chaotic and military police were trying to control the traffic. A policeman waved them to the side of the road. "You'll have to pull over and wait here."

Walter stuck his head out of the car window. "What's this all about?"

"General Montgomery has been put in charge here. We've got a parade on tomorrow. There's 20,000 men coming down this road any minute to rehearse."

Walter flashed his warrant card. "Mind if we turn around?"

"Go on, Inspector, make it quick." The policeman stopped the traffic coming from the other direction.

"I know another way round," said the driver.

"Thanks." Walter pulled at his shirt collar. The heat suffocated the town. As soon as the car slowed, there was no air to breathe.

The alternative route was over rough tracks. Walter squinted and scanned the area when they reached Churchill's base.

The driver opened the door for him. "Did you have a bag, sir?"

"No, no bag. Thank you...." Walter found himself being spun around before he could finish his sentence.

"Inspector, is that really you? What the *Henry Neville* 'appened to you?" George beamed.

"I'm fine. How's the Old Man?"

"Concerned – very concerned. We all were."

"You heard about Larry?"

"Yes. Lawd above, poor Larry. I liked him."

"George, it could have been The Old Man. The Gerries really mean business, don't they? And they seem to have good knowledge of our travel plans. We're going to have to look sharp. Did you have any trouble with your plane?"

"Nah, nuffin'. We took off from RAF North Weald. It was very quiet all the way."

"They're definitely watching Croydon Aerodrome. They knew exactly where we would be and found us. What's the latest intelligence?"

"They're on the move. Enemy agents 'ave been dropped by parachute all over North Africa. There's nuffin' specific – the information is patchy, but we're pretty sure it's for *Operation Long Jump*."

Walter began his survey of the area for signs of weakness in the security. George tugged his arm. "Come on, Inspector, the Old Man wants to see you – you'll 'ave plenty of time to do your reconnaissance later. Oh my God, you're limping. What the…?"

"It's nothing – just a nick – bullet passed right through. Healing up nicely." Walter rubbed his leg.

"You fool, Walter. Why didn't yer fly 'ome?"

"It's my job, George. Shall we go and find the Old Man?"

"He's in 'ere resting." They approached the door to Churchill's room.

Walter knocked and entered before waiting for a reply.

Churchill was standing by the window in a bright coloured dressing gown. "Good Lord. Thompson."

"Sir…."

"Whatever happened? Are you all right?"

"Well, we've established our information is infiltrating to the highest level of German command, sir. Intelligence picked up a signal sent in a rush from London to Berlin, and like clockwork, the *Luftwaffe* was there in person.

Churchill scratched his head. "We need to decide whether to catch and hang the blighter or leave him be and feed him false information."

"Perhaps if we get Scotland Yard to find out who he is, where he lives and what else he's up to, we'll be better informed to make that decision."

"Yes, good idea, Thompson – let's not be hasty. Can you let the Commissioner know? Congratulations, Thompson, you've done an excellent job on a mission of the highest importance. I must say, though, I was very sorry to hear about Larry. He served his country well." Churchill heaved a long sigh. "Well, you'd better find me my dinner suit. We're dining with General Montgomery in two hours."

"Yes, sir, that's if...."

"Yes, what is it?"

"If you don't want my immediate resignation, sir."

"Resignation? Whatever are you blathering on about?"

Walter dropped his head. "Well, I lost Larry, sir."

"Yes, a good man. Where's my valet?"

"I'll find him for you, sir. Sir, should I resign?"

"Don't be so damn stupid, Thompson. I authorised transport for you myself, you know. Now, go and give my valet a jolly along."

"Thank you, sir."

***

After dinner, they returned to England without incident. George found Walter in the kitchen in the War Rooms nursing a cup of tea. "What's up, Inspector?"

"We're off again, George. Moscow – I've really no idea about Russia. And I've got no opposite number to talk to about security – like I have when we go to America."

"Come on chin up, Inspector. At least we can feed our German spies some misleading information. Let's leak we're off to Portugal – I hear it's nice there this time of year."

CHAPTER 20
Stella – Deception

12 October – Garnet, France

"It's time we all went to join the *Maquis* in the South." Eight members of the unit were gathered at the mill house, sitting around the large oak kitchen table. Pierre opened a map. "From observations of troop movements, we think the Germans are planning to occupy the zone governed from Vichy, so there'll soon be little difference between the two areas, as the whole of France will be occupied. The Resistance units all need to unite, so we can muster the most powerful force we can against them." Stella placed a water glass in front of each person sitting at the table. "Isn't it still more dangerous to be in Vichy France? I mean, ever since Laval came to power, I've heard reports of things getter hard for people living in the south. Remember that speech he broadcast on the radio last June, when he said he wanted Germany to win the war."

Pierre flattened out the large map. "Agreed – but we're getting word from other comrades that far worse is happening right under our noses."

"What could be worse?" Stella poured water from an earthenware jug.

Pierre pointed to the map. "You already know about the transit camp at Drancy, northeast of Paris? There's a rumour that on two nights last July, the French police – yes, our own police – rounded up thousands of Jews and took them to the Vélodrome d'Hiver, before they were shipped off in cattle trucks to a camp in Poland, called Auschwitz. He sipped from his glass. "Perhaps, it's time for us to try to get you both back to England."

Martin joined them. "Stella and I will soon have our new forged papers. And we'll be safe from arrest. Besides, you are our family. We've come to love you all."

"The Italians are not supporting Hitler in deporting Jews," said Pierre. "We must concentrate on getting as many Jewish families as possible into the Italian-occupied zone."

Stella opened the oven and the smell of her baking drifted around the mill. She placed a basket of warm bread on the table. "Won't the Pope stand up against Hitler?"

Gertrude carried a terrine of soup from the stove.

Pierre lifted the lid and ladled a portion into his bowl. "The Pope is a coward. He won't publicly denounce Hitler for the murder of Roman Catholic priests, so there's no way he'll publicly support Jews. Now, let's eat."

Henri Leclerc was working away under a bright desk lamp in a corner of the farmhouse. Gertrude brought him a bowl of potage. She was proving her worth as an excellent cook. Stella treated her with respect and loved her as if she were her own grandmother.

Thanks to Henri, they all now possessed the *Ausweis*, the travel pass allowing them to enter Vichy France.

"Here you are, my sweet." Gertrude winked at Henri.

Henri ate his soup and wiped his mouth with the serviette provided by his attentive housekeeper. "Pah, I get a fat old woman like you for a housekeeper? When I made my demands, I said someone young and pretty."

"Oh, sweetheart, do you not think me young and pretty?" Gertrude fluffed her hair.

"No, I don't, you old hag. I would strangle you in the night if your cooking wasn't so good." Henri feigned a sulk. "I wanted a pretty girl who could come to my bed. A lovely young girl like Stella."

Stella heard her name, so she walked over to where Henri was working. "Have you finished my documents?"

"Yes, but they will cost you a kiss," Henri jumped up and grabbed Stella around the waist. As she laughed it off, and struggled to get free, he groped her more.

She let out a shriek and slapped him hard on the cheek.

Henri took a step back and went for her. "You little…." He was stopped in mid-sentence by a blow from Martin, striking him in the face.

Luc grabbed hold of Martin's arm before he could hit Henri again. The others helped Henri to his feet and restrained him.

Stella caught Gertrude's wrist just as she was about to strike Henri with the cooking pan.

Gertrude withdrew the weapon with a scowl.

Pierre strolled over to the scene, acting the role of priest. "Come, my children, we have bigger enemies outside this room. Please let's not fight among ourselves."

The tension eased, and everyone resumed their tasks.

Stella glanced at Henri's desk. "Are those my papers?"

Henri rubbed his head. "Take them – they're finished."

"And Martin's?"

"They're not ready." Henri picked up his pen.

Gertrude put a cold compress on his temple.

Stella took her papers and left Henri to finish his work.

Henri stared at Martin's papers and rubbed the bruise turning blue on his face. The papers were ready; he just didn't want to hand them over. Picking up his pen, he made a tiny change to the document – a minute alteration that only an expert would detect. After another hour, he ambled across to where Martin was sitting. "Here *con*," he said, thrusting the documents on the table.

"Now we've all eaten, let me finish my briefing," said Pierre. The group gathered round. "Hitler has sent Klaus Barbie, a particularly nasty sadist, to France as a last resort to round up the rest of the Jews for the Third Reich. His headquarters is the Hotel Terminus in the centre of Lyon. Barbie is a committed Jew-hater. He sees his first task as smashing the Resistance movement."

Stella sat down at the table. "What are we going to do? We're in a bit of a backwater here in Garnet. As far as we know, we're not on any card index yet. But that's only because Martin got away with not having to register."

Martin sat next to her. "That's good. If we're not on their records, they won't be looking for us. And with our new papers, we'll be able to move about with more confidence."

"We need to recruit more people into the Resistance." Pierre smoothed his beard. "We had a good position for our operations here outside Garnet at the mill. But the conscription of French workers means many young men are taking to the hills and joining the guerrilla bands, the *Maquis*."

"Where will we go?" Luc poured himself more coffee.

"My own contact is based in Lyon. De Gaulle is trying to unite the movement. Despite Barbie, I think we should go there. The man is a doctor, and it's possible we could use his house for meetings. He has a nice three-storey villa just outside the town where he also holds his consultations. We could all pretend to be patients if the Germans showed up."

"What about me?" Henri walked over to the table but kept on the opposite side to Martin.

Pierre stood up. "Henri, you've done a great job here. But our work at Garnet is almost complete. We have to head for Lyon, where we're needed most."

"Lyon." Henri spat on the floor.

Pierre pointed to a place on the map. "But we've found you a nice house just outside the city at Saint-Genis, where you can continue your most valuable work."

"*Putain.* What if I won't go?"

Stella poured the coffee. "Come on, Henri, we want you to come with us."

Henri walked towards her, but Martin stood up and blocked his path. The two men glared at each other, and everyone stopped what they were doing.

Henri stood defiant. "Certain promises were made to me that have yet to be fulfilled *con*."

"None of them personally involved my wife," Martin warned. "So you'd better keep away from her, you hear."

Realising he had little support from any of the others, Henri rubbed his face and walked back towards his desk.

"I've been having a bit of trouble with this old injury." Luc rubbed his shoulder. "I really should go and see a doctor – I hear there's a good one in Lyon."

Gertrude massaged her hip. "I should get my arthritis looked at."

"I need my eyes examined for living with you," grumbled Henri.

"You and your lovely housekeeper will stay at the house in Saint-Genis," said Pierre, "The rest of us will meet at the doctor's house in future."

There was a tap at the door, and Pierre stiffened. Luc picked up his rifle and opened the door a crack. Nicole stood there, out of breath.

Luc opened the door wide. "Come in. Come in. What are you doing here?"

"I came personally to warn you. Yesterday I sent one of my men to Europe Express in Paris to arrange transport for himself back to Vichy. He caught lifts home. Europe Express has been taken over by the German military. All your staff were arrested and shipped off in trucks. Martin, there's a warrant out for your arrest – you too, Stella." Nicole sat down at the table.

"What will we do?" Martin poured Nicole some water.

"I couldn't get the full story, but it seems as if one of your staff went free because he showed the Germans the false fuel tanks and told them you worked for the Resistance. Whatever you do, don't be tempted to go back there. They've laid a trap for you."

"Oh, Nicole, how kind you are to come all this way to tell us this." Stella put her arm around her and kissed Nicole's grubby cheek. "How did you get here so quickly?"

"I travelled all night on my motorbike."

"Come along, let's get you a drink and something to eat, and you can clean yourself up." Stella guided Nicole to the kitchen.

"What the devil will we do now?" Martin helped Gertrude to collect the coffee cups.

"I'm sure you can stay with the doctor for a while." Pierre peered at his map at the town marked *Lyon*.

"Will he mind us there?"

"He's on our side, so he'll do what he can to help us." Luc reached for his rifle and cleaned it. He wasn't going to help with what he considered women's chores.

The team began to make preparations for the move. Weeks ago, they had repainted the small bus so they could take it to Vichy, France without attracting attention. Martin and Stella's car had been left in Paris and the little bus was all they had left of their enterprise.

***

3 November – Lyon

The new papers Henri forged were accepted at the checkpoint, and the trip passed without incident. Lyon was a little warmer than Paris and Stella enjoyed the weak winter sun on her face through the window of the house in Saint-Genis. Gertrude cleaned the house and before long it was looking like a home.

Despite the sun, it was a crisp morning. Pierre, Martin and Stella took the bus to Lyon to meet with the head of the local Resistance – the doctor.

Despite Henri's acid tongue, Gertrude had continued to care for him in a way that was above and beyond what was required. She anticipated his requests, and they were fulfilled before he had to ask. Coffee was supplied just when he was feeling thirsty and she seemed able to make a hearty meal from whatever rations they could procure. She admired his painting and complimented him on his forgery. As the days went by, Henri began to warm to her, and now and then he would even pass her a kind remark.

Gertrude looked out of the window. "Walk into town with me today," She could see the frost had melted. "It would be nice to get some fresh air – explore our new surroundings."

"I've got papers to make." Henri waved her away. "People need new identities. I need to get my machinery set up."

"We won't be long – and anyway, a walk will do you good."

Henri shrugged and put down his pen.

Gertrude collected her shopping basket and they left the house. The sweet smell of pine from the forest welcomed them outdoors. The weak midday sun was warm and pleasant, and for a few moments the countryside seemed idyllic.

Two German troop-carrying trucks rumbled past and pulled up outside a school.

Gertrude and Henri ducked behind a hedge.

Four German soldiers, and the vile and merciless, Klaus Barbie, strutted into the school.

His men barked, *Raus, raus* and banged their truncheons on the walls and doors.

A teacher emerged from the first classroom. "What's going on? Stop all this noise."

The young woman was clubbed across the face. She crumpled to the floor. Blood oozed from an ugly gash on her head, her eyes unblinking at the officer.

The children came running out, shrieking and crying. The soldiers caught them and flung them into the back of the trucks as if they were sacks of rubbish.

Henri and Gertrude stood open-mouthed.

An *SS* officer jabbed Henri with his gun. "Get out of here – clear off."

Henri and Gertrude scrambled away. At a safe distance, they hid behind a fence to watch. As the trucks drew away, they could hear the children sobbing. Gertrude got up from her hiding place and walked towards the school, where the Star of David was set over the door.

"Where the hell are you going?" Henri began to walk away.

"I must see if there is anyone left. It's a Jewish school." Gertrude walked up to the entrance and opened the door.

Henri looked around to see if anyone else could see them and followed behind.

Gertrude searched the classrooms and sat at a child's desk and sobbed. "They've all gone."

"Come on, It's none of our business." Henri tugged her sleeve.

"None of our business. How can you say that, you brute? It's everyone's business, and we've got to stop it. We must let the others know what's happened. Come on, we'll go and find Pierre."

The journey by foot and by bus to the other side of Lyon took them nearly an hour. When they arrived, Gertrude cried as she told the story.

"What can we do?" Stella's put her arm around the old lady.

"They'll probably be taken to the railway sidings and put on a train to a transit camp," said Pierre. "Then taken to a labour camp."

"You mean a death camp." Luc stood his rifle against the medicine cabinet.

The doctor pulled down the blind. "It's not one of our military targets, but perhaps we could blow up the railway line?"

Martin paced the room. "Then they'll just repair it, shoot a few railway workers for sabotage, and carry on with the children the next day."

Gertrude yawned and began to nod off in the chair.

Stella kissed her on the forehead. "Come on Gertie. Let me drive you home in the bus."

Pierre stood up and offered Gertrude his arm. "I'll come too."

"Me too," said Henri.

Stella pecked Martin on the cheek.

"We'll rack our brains for a bit," said Martin. "And then the doctor can drive us home in his ambulance."

As Stella was going through the door, Martin pulled her back and kissed her long and deep on the lips.

Luc lit a cigarette and passed one to the doctor. "Oh, to have a love like yours. You kiss like you're not going to see each other again in a few hours. So doctor – perhaps a glass of wine will help us think of a few ideas."

It was beginning to get dark, and the doctor opened a bottle of wine. Martin and Luc sat in the surgery and took a long slow drink. They savoured the oaky smooth taste of a bottle of *Premier cru*.

The doctor toasted them. "Last good bottle I have left."

"There must be something we can do." Martin cupped his hand around his glass, to swirl his wine.

"We're short of ammunition and supplies," said Luc. "The last lot dropped by the Allies got captured by the Germans. And – worse – so did three of our men. I've been worried they will talk –"

Before he could finish his sentence, a fist banged on the door. It was so sudden, they all jumped up, and Martin spilled his wine.

Luc went to grab his gun.

The doctor got to it first and put it in the medicine closet. "Just a moment, the surgery is closed, but I'm seeing emergency patients. I'm coming to open the door to you."

Four *SS* troopers stormed through the door. Not wishing to wait to be asked questions, Luc pushed past the doctor to the consulting room. He opened the window and looked at the drop. They were on the first floor, but there was nothing to break his fall. As he hesitated, an *SS* officer struck him on the back of the head.

"Stop!" protested the doctor. "These are my patients."

He was answered with a punch on the jaw and fell to the ground.

Martin tried to join in the fight but was slammed in the stomach and kicked.

The doctor began to struggle up until an *SS* officer pushed his head hard against the wall. The doctor collapsed on the floor unconscious.

"Where's the rest of your unit?"

Martin tried to speak, but his mouth was full of blood.

"Stand up!"

Martin tried to stand and overbalanced. Two of the Germans grabbed him and pulled him to his feet. Luc saw his chance, stood up and toppled out of the window. The soldiers threw Martin down and drew their guns. When they reached the window, Luc was gone. Furious, they kicked Martin and the doctor until they were both unconscious.

"Take them to headquarters," said the officer in charge.

"I think this one's dead, sir." The *SS* soldier poked the doctor with his foot.

"Well, bring him anyway."

***

4 November – Saint-Genis

Luc hobbled towards the villa in Saint-Genis, wincing as every muscle in his body screamed in pain. He tried to keep to the shadows as his head and shirt were covered in blood. It hurt to move, but his progress was driven by loyalty. He had to warn his friends. The last members of the Resistance who were given an *SS* beating were not able to tell them anything for 24 hours.

It was almost dawn when he arrived at the villa.

Pierre opened the door. "My God." Luc fell in and the Frenchman caught him before he collapsed.

"Luc." Stella opened the front door wider and looked along the gravel path. "Where's Martin?"

"They most likely took him and the doctor to their headquarters," mumbled Luc.

Stella held Luc's shoulders. "NO. What can we do?"

"We must get out of here." Luc slipped out of his jacket.

"But what about Martin?" Stella shouted.

"There's nothing we can do, unless they let him go."

"Oh yes – of course they'll let him go. His papers are in order. He was just visiting the doctor."

Henri said nothing, but started to pack his belongings. Gertrude stared at him.

Stella bathed Luc's wounds and he winced when she dabbed iodine on his cuts. "I think you're just badly bruised from the fall. I don't think you've broken anything, but you might have pulled a tendon in your leg. It's going to be pretty sore for a few days."

"They got a good look at me. I'll put you in danger if I stay with you. They know I have something to hide because I ran. Doubtless they'll find my rifle, too."

"*Putain*. Were you followed? We'll all be caught. I knew I should have stayed in jail. Here, take your emergency papers and get out. Henri tossed Luc's papers on the table.

"Shut your mouth." Pierre shoved Henri away. "You're not in charge here."

Luc looked up at Henri. "You're a miserable little bastard, but I thank you for your excellent papers and for the idea of a double identity for anyone who needed to leave in a hurry. I'll go as soon as I've washed and changed my clothes."

"You will be a *Gestapo* officer – an agent passing into Switzerland," said Pierre. "I have some suitable clothes for you to wear. You will contact my aunt in Lausanne. She will take care of you until it's safe to return. The little toad over there is right.

Martin and the doctor could be telling them about this place even now."

"But they wouldn't," protested Stella.

Luc raised his eyebrows. He felt a good deal better after he ate some of Gertrude's stew and drank half a bottle of wine.

Tears streamed from Stella's eyes. Gertrude put her arm around her neck and pulled Stella to her bosom.

Pierre started to destroy any evidence the Resistance had used the house. He turned to Henri. "Do you want to keep the radio, or shall I destroy that too?"

"No get rid of it. I hear the *putain* Germans are driving around in trucks with special listening equipment. I don't want a reason for them to call at the house."

Pierre threw documents on the fire. "We'd best head to the coast and join up with the rest of the Resistance leaders there. The national leader, Max, is staying with Nicole. He's busy recruiting in the countryside. Stella, your escape papers mean you will be travelling with me as a nun."

"Travel with you? How can I leave without Martin?"

"You must. Henri and Gertrude can stay here and pretend to be local people – brother and sister. I have to move on – why would a priest be living here? And I hardly look like a farm labourer. Look at my hands. Henri, how long will it take you to finish the secondary identity papers for Stella?"

"I just need you to choose your new name."

"I will be Sister Martine," said Stella, wiping the tears from her eyes. "And we'll meet up with Max and think of a way to get Martin back."

***

4 November – Lyon

When Martin regained consciousness, he couldn't remember where he was, or why he was there. He was lying on cold linoleum. There was a tang of vomit in his mouth. He lifted his face, pasted to the floor in a pool of his bile. His head thumped and his eyes were swollen. He found it difficult to breathe and a terrible pain ripped through his chest. He began to remember the beating. He opened his eyes again and the bare bulb burned his pupils. The walls of the cell were moist with damp. He tried to move, but became dizzy and passed out for another few hours.

When he woke, he sat up carefully. There was a metal bucket of water in the corner. He knelt and scooped water to his mouth. He put both hands in the bucket and splashed water on his face. He sat up and checked his pockets. Everything had gone except the spare key to the little bus. It had fallen through his trouser pocket and caught in the lining. He looked around the cell for a hiding place and settled on the hollow leg of the metal bed. Someone was coming, so he resumed a pretend state of unconsciousness on the floor.

Two officers dragged Martin up and along a corridor, then up two flights of stairs and into a large office where they shoved him onto a wooden chair. Martin cried out.

"No need for all that noise," said Klaus Barbie. "We just want a few answers. Then you can go home. Let's start with your name. We know it is not Thibault, because that's a French name, and my friend here thinks you may be a Jew."

A thin, pockmarked German with the steel-rimmed spectacles was sitting in the corner of the room.

"Karl is an expert on Jews – he can sniff them out wherever they are hiding – but you are a gift because your papers are forged."

Martin held his head. His hair was matted with dried blood. *Where was Stella? Where was the doctor? Did Luc escape? How does he know my papers are forged?* He felt numb. But before he could think any further, he fainted.

The guards slapped him until he opened his eyes and sat him back on the chair.

Martin brought the man's face into better focus. He forced himself to concentrate hard on being able to recognise him again in the future. *What was it Walter would say? Oh yes, you can change the colour of your hair or puff out your cheeks, but you can't change the shape of your ears.* Martin studied the man's ears. They were decent specimens, long and rounded with big lobes. They reminded him of Ireland – there was an indentation for Belfast and a funny curve leading to Dublin. *I will remember those ears. But those ears must not hear my story.*

He glanced at the floor, where spatters of blood were drying on the white marble. He could smell disinfectant. *What time was it?* He looked over to the window, where he could see the blind was drawn tight, but he thought he could detect the first glow of dawn at the edges. *Has it been eight hours already?* He knew they needed 24 to be safe.

The man tapped Martin's papers. "Just tell me your name. Then you can go."

Martin squeezed his head to try and combat the throbbing.

The secretary came back in the room and handed the man a key.

"What does this key open? We found it hidden in your cell."

Martin was silent.

The man studied the key. "Actually, it's more like the key to a truck or a delivery van. So where is this vehicle parked?"

Martin didn't look at the key. He concentrated on Klaus Barbie's ears. He said a silent prayer, hoping Stella was several hours away. He had gone over various scenarios of the lies he could tell, but he knew all of them would put the people he loved in grave danger. He said nothing.

The secretary stood in the doorway and turned back. "Sir, the French police are demanding to interview the Jew, and the Italian captain is here to see you."

"How irritating. Come Karl. We will deal with the Italian together."

While Martin was left sitting alone in the room for a few seconds, he wondered whether it would be possible to escape. But before he could work anything out, the two guards returned him to his cell. This time he walked.

***

10 November – Switzerland

When he got to the French–Swiss border, Luc showed his papers at the checkpoint and was saluted by the guard. He would wait until he got word it was safe and then go back to France to join up with the Resistance in the south.

***

28 November – Nice

Sister Martine and Father Pierre headed south. Their new papers and Stella's nun's disguise worked well, and they passed through each checkpoint unchallenged. During the long journey on foot, they stopped off at several villages where the *Maquis* were hiding. They were given food, drink and somewhere to sleep.

A stone grew in Stella's stomach with every mile they moved further away from Martin.

When they arrived in Nice, they discovered Max had his own plans. He was a clean-shaven, handsome man about the same age as Walter. "Do you remember the collaborator, Admiral Darlan?" Max adjusted the scarf around his neck hiding an ugly scar. "He's sailed the ships under his control to British ports. This has placed him in a strong position, and he has declared himself chief of state and the leader of the French Empire in North Africa."

"What's this got to do with rescuing my husband?" Stella sat down on a chair and looked out over the sea.

"Everything and nothing," said Max. "Everything. I have no spare men. And even if I did, I have very little chance of getting your husband away from the clutches of the *Gestapo*. And nothing, because we have to concentrate on the larger issues of the war, and this is a major turning point. The German army is in control of the whole of France. When Darlan went over to the Free French, Hitler used it as an excuse to occupy the Vichy and Italian zones too. I am very sad about your husband, but we all know the risks and we have to accept losses."

Stella was numb to the truth of his words. She looked so beautiful, even dressed in the nun's habit; Max felt a deep sympathy for her. "Do not cry. I will send someone to make enquiries about your husband." He pulled her close to his chest and held her for a few moments until she could compose herself.

"I'm sorry. "It's just…."

"It's your husband. I know… I also lost my wife and family. Come on, *petite,* let's eat together and talk of victory."

Stella could not eat. Nothing in her private world made sense. Everything around her had disintegrated. Martin had disappeared, swallowed up by the Nazis' cruel bureaucracy. Somewhere, his name was on a card in their index file marked with an instruction.

***

29 November – Lake Quentz, Abwehr Oberkommando sabotage school

Forty miles west of Berlin, lay the Nazis' sabotage training school, which had received a direct order from Himmler to train *Kommandos* for *Operation Long Jump.*

The fitness and attack training had long finished. The recruits were bored, so they were being indoctrinated with hatred. This involved identifying targets by their photographs and repeating words of loathing over and over until the assassin believed in the righteousness of their mission. The indoctrination ensured they would kill without hesitation or conscience.

The *Kommandos* sat in the classroom, where they were handed sheets of paper from Himmler's office.

SS Unterstumführer Oberg pulled the nearest recruit so close to his face the conscript could smell sour coffee. "Who are Churchill's advisors?"

The *Kommandos* shouted the list of names, adding after each name the words: *the Jew.* This mantra was recited over and over. The object of their hatred was all who were considered to be enemies of the Third Reich, but in reality, few on the list were actually Jews. The final name on the list was *W. H. Thompson, Inspector, Special Branch – the Jew.*

The next day, inside a handsome lakeside villa in the elegant Berlin suburb of Wannsee, *SS Obergruppenführer Reinhard Heydrich*, chief of the Security Service and second in command to Heinrich Himmler, addressed 15 senior Nazi bureaucrats and *SS* officials on the question of the Jews. "Another possible solution to the problem has now taken the place of emigration, and that is the evacuation of the Jews to the East, provided that the *Führer* gives his approval in advance. 11 million Jews will be involved in the *final solution* of the European Jewish question...."

At six-foot-tall, with a long aquiline nose and straight blond hair, Heydrich looked the perfect Nazi – an Aryan. His words were so dispassionate and matter of fact that his chilling proposals seemed routine – a conventional answer to an everyday problem.

The listening bureaucrats accepted this plan with utter detachment as the assembly nodded assent. They agreed in unison to the annihilation of a whole race – not just the men, but also the women, children, old people and babies. Death to anyone who had a trace of Jewish blood.

And at the training camp, and soon to be repeated all over Germany, the indoctrination of hatred continued, urging individuals to kill their perceived enemies.

It went like this: "Holten-Pflug, you lost your mother in an air raid. Let us respect one minute of silence while we render homage to her memory."

The *Kommandos* bowed their heads and stood in silence.

"Holten-Pflug, what would you like to do with the person who ordered the air raid?"

"Kill them, sir!" replied Holten-Pflug, the tall, blond, blue-eyed assassin with a pock marked face.

"Who is responsible?" demanded Oberg.

"Churchill, sir." Holten-Pflug's neck puffed red with rage.

"What will we do to him, then?" goaded Oberg.

"Kill him, sir! Kill him, sir!"

Six months at Quentz was sufficient for the recruit eager to kill to learn every method of assassination. Oberg knew his men were ready. They just needed to wait for the right information: when and where they should strike.

1943
Falling off a Train and Operation Long Jump

CHAPTER 21
Stella - Martin's Ordeal

31 January – Nice, France

Stella sat in Max's apartment overlooking the town. She put down Max's pen and folded the writing paper into a swan. Three paper birds sat in a line on the dining room table, each holding her scribbled thoughts to Walter, and Martin's grandfather. Her brow was knitted with lines, from weeks of torment.

She stared out of window. *It's all my fault. It was me who wanted to join the Resistance. It was me who wanted to stay in France. Martin's arrest was because of me. I made him break his promise...*

She imagined Martin's face – on their wedding day, when he first called her *Neshama*.

Outside, the pale winter sun illuminated the pinks and creams of the delightful old buildings, but Stella saw none of it. She was numb to the charms surrounding her.

She folded another sheet into a swan and a tear spotted a wing.

Life seemed so unclear – a haze. What could she tell Martin's grandfather? Her eyes flickered with images of Martin. She wanted to keep hold of her picture of them together on their wedding day, but it wouldn't stay still.

Max picked up the last swan, smoothed it out and read it. Later, he handed it to a colleague to forward to England. He liked the plucky, pretty English girl, but her naïveté was dangerous. He hoped if her family received word she was alive, he might be able to get her back home.

***

14 February – A deportation train, Lyon

Martin lay semi-conscious on the floor of a cattle truck with his head cradled in the hands of a small, dark-haired young woman named, Simone. She wiped his brow, thinking of how much he reminded her of her own husband – where was *he* now?

It was dark in the wagon, with not enough room for everyone to sit down. The young stood, while the old squatted on the thin layer of straw. The wagon stunk of urine and faeces, but Simone could smell fear and hostility. The men were angry Martin took up so much space lying on the floor. But he was already in the wagon when they were herded in, so there was nothing they could do about it.

The French police got no response from Martin. And his silence brought him was daily beatings. He drifted in and out of consciousness – oblivious to his location.

Short of their quota of Jews to ship to the east, the police added Martin to the list of deportees on the train. His papers had been forged, making him just one more Jewish scum to be disposed of.

Simone's four-year-old daughters – identical twins, stood next to her, dressed in matching frocks and coats. They were pretty with large brown eyes, pale faces and shiny, brown hair.

Martin's mind swirled in a sea of faces from his past – Stella, Walter and his grandfather, Abraham. Occasionally, Pierre would appear in his dreams, riding his bicycle and waving at him, or Luc, gesturing to him with his rifle. Stella was there constantly: on their wedding day, on the boat train to Paris, in the Paris apartment. She looked like an angel, laughing, reckless and devil-may-care. Then there were the distorted faces of the Germans, punching, kicking, beating and shouting obscenities in their horrible guttural tongue.

"Stop, stop." Martin called out in English.

Simone bent down to soothe him, and to wipe away the congealed blood from great knots in his hair. She wanted her fellow deportees to quieten and so she began reciting the *Shema* in Hebrew, then in English so the man she held in her arms could understand it:

"*Sh'ma Yisrael...* Hear, O Israel. The Lord is our God, the Lord is one...."

An old woman next to her joined in the prayer:

"Blessed be the name of His glorious kingdom for ever and ever."

The air filled with the sound of whispered prayers. A serenity crept over the railway wagon as men and women mouthed the words:

"And you shall love the Lord your God with all your heart and with all your soul and with all your might. I am the Lord your God, who led you from the land of Egypt... *Ani Adonai Elohaychem.* I am the Lord your God."

With a hiss of steam, the train began to move out of the station. An old man, who had once been a cantor in the synagogue, sung from the Psalms.

Simone leaned against the side of the truck and pulled her twins to her. She looked around at the faces huddled near her in the dark, thankful for their prayers for each other and the poor young man collapsed on her lap.

The eldest twin stroked Martin's head. "I miss you, daddy." Tears trickled down her cheeks, "I hope we will see you very soon."

***

22 February – Poland

The train took a long and slow journey to the East. Simone peeped through the slats of the wooden wagon. An old man stood by the track. When he noticed her face, he held his finger up stiff like a knife and drew it across his throat. Simone understood the warning. The Germans were merciless and were going to kill them all. She pulled her beautiful twins close to her chest.

"I'm so thirsty, Mummy."

The other said nothing, but stared into space with large, brown eyes, appealing for answers. Why were they here? What had they done to deserve such treatment?

Soot from the engine drifted into the wagons and the people held scarfs over their faces and coughed. They were given no food and had barely enough water to share, and there were no toilets. The men urinated through the gaps in the wagon and the women had no choice but to squat in the corner. There was a thin layer of straw on the floor, which stunk of ammonia. Not once had they been allowed to get out of the train. The final warning from a man standing by the track served to underline the inevitable.

It was three days before the train came to a halt in a siding. Nothing happened for 10 minutes. The people were silenced by their terrible ordeal. The large sliding door was thrown back with the sound of scraping metal and a *bang* when it hit the stop. The exhausted occupants blinked at the bright sunlight.

"Raus! Raus! Get out, get out!" The *SS* trooper pointed his gun at the shattered, sorry group of people. He poked an old man with his bayonet. The man was stiff and found it difficult to move but desperate enough to force himself to his feet.

Simone tried to wake Martin. He was still breathing, but his pulse was weak, and he made no response.

The men climbed out first. They helped the women and children down from the wagon.

Simone stayed with Martin and her two daughters.

"Get out! The *SS* trooper jumped up into the wagon. Simone looked at his face. He was young, 19 perhaps. "Get out!"

Simone stood up. She was not afraid – she knew she was already dead. She looked him hard in the eyes. She was so beautiful the *SS* trooper dropped his gaze for a second.

An older *SS* trooper struggled up into the wagon. "What is going on here? Get out and join the line."

The young woman took the tiny hands of her daughters and walked towards the door of the wagon. Martin still did not move.

"Get up!" The *SS* officer kicked Martin in the ribs.

He did not move. "Get up, Jew!" Martin was lost in his dreams: dreams of Stella; dreams of England; dreams, swirling dreams.

The young *SS* trooper climbed down from the wagon. Simone handed him one of the twins. He took the child; she was light as a feather, and she smiled at him. He looked away. Simone handed him the other child; she was weak, and her large brown eyes stared straight ahead.

The older *SS* trooper drew his gun. "Get up, or I'll shoot you."

Martin could not respond.

Simone joined the miserable line of 1,000 people. There were 20 guards, each restraining a snarling dog, pulling hard against its leash. She whispered to the Cantor: "We could overpower these guards. Some of us would die in the effort, but we could get the better of them. But where would we run to? Where could we go – a thousand weak and starving people?"

As they were herded through the front gate, Simone looked up and read the inscription: *Arbeit Macht Frei* – she knew enough German to understand it meant, *Work makes you free*.

A shot rang out and Simone turned back to see the older *SS* trooper leaving the goods wagon in which she had travelled. "I didn't even get to know his name. He was a handsome young man. He looked just like my husband. May God look after his dear soul in heaven."

The thousand new arrivals were crammed into barracks, originally designed as stables, with a capacity for 500 people. The doors were locked, and everyone did their best to get comfortable. There was some water in buckets inside the crowded space and they shared it out carefully between them.

***

23 February – Brighton, England

Abraham Gold woke with a start. *Was that a shot being fired?* He thought of Martin and his heart sank. Outside, the night sky was purple like a bruise. He could hear distant waves of the English Channel. He recited every prayer he could remember until he fell asleep again.

When the dawn broke on Abraham Gold's tall, Victorian townhouse, a shaft of light illuminated a letter on the hall mat.

To: Mr A. Gold,
34 Marine Parade,
Brighton, Sussex, England

By hand.

Abraham did not want to read it. He knew what it would say.

He sat on the hallway floor and howled until his throat was sore. He held the unopened letter in his hand and recited the *Kaddish*, the Jewish prayer for mourning.

"Yisgadal v'yiskadash sh'mei rabbaw... May His great name grow exalted and sanctified in the world that He created as He willed... *Oseh shawlom...* He who makes peace in His heights, may He make peace upon us...."

The laments were powerful and reached through the door of his house and into the street. Neighbours stood outside in silent vigil. No one dared knock on the door. The pain in his voice was overwhelming.

***

24 February – Auschwitz-Birkenau

When Simone woke up, she shook her head and opened and closed her eyes. *Am I really here – this living hell?* She rubbed her aching arms and legs. The twins were already awake. One was playing with a two-year-old boy. The other twin stared into space. Simone pulled them towards her and touched their faces and hair. She hugged them tight and steadied her back against the bunk – she worshipped them with kisses. She washed and dressed them as best she could.

The door opened and the block leader, a man wearing the star of David walked into the room. "You will see the doctor now."

The prisoners made a straggly line and dragged themselves outside. The doctor sat in the middle of a muddy courtyard and the thousand new arrivals paraded around the edge. He pointed at each person and indicated whether they should exit to the left or to the right. When it came to the young woman and her twins, the doctor selected the dull-eyed twin for death.

"Where are you taking my little girl?"

An *SS* officer stepped forward. "Perhaps you would like to give the other one up instead? Which one would you like to keep?"

"Both of them." Simone pulled them to her.

"Then you shall all go. Wait a minute – they're identical twins. Doctor, do we still want identical twins?"

The doctor shook his head.

The *SS* trooper pushed them to the left.

Simone walked with dignity with the others chosen to die, past an office block where clerks worked around the clock typing out death reports.

When they were in the chamber, Simone encouraged her beautiful twins to breathe deeply when the gas was poured into the room, so their deaths would be quick. She told the little girls over and over, how she loved them until she could speak no more.

***

The transportation train with its empty goods wagons was shunted into a siding. Two young *SS* soldiers waited with a high-pressure hose as it came to a halt. The relief driver and engineer busied themselves checking gauges and oiling moving parts. Rudi, a young *SS* recruit, climbed aboard the first wagon and waved to his comrade.

"Turn on the water, Fritz."

"Water's coming, Rudi."

Rudi braced himself for the sudden rush of water. He aimed the jet around the wagon. "Dirty, filthy Jews, shitting in the wagon. God, it stinks. Here – come and help."

"Ach, you're right. It's awful. What a job to get – just because we accepted a little jewellery from a Jewish bastard." Fritz coughed. "What a stench." He was a small, dark fragile boy – lucky for him, Rudi had the heavy hose.

"Well, we'd better do a thorough job because we're assigned to return to Paris with this rancid train to collect some more fuel for the ovens." Rudi motioned towards the large chimneys billowing out smoke and ash.

It was a dreadful punishment to have to clean the wagons. Unknown to them, Martin's body lay motionless in one of the trucks towards the centre of the train. The boys were beginning to feel tired when the engineer approached the wagon they were cleaning.

"Hey, boys, would you like a break? We got some wine from Drancy. Fancy a little drink?" The engineer held up two bottles of alcohol.

"Thanks." Fritz put down the shovel.

"We'll get in trouble again," muttered Rudi.

"So, what will they do to us next? Make us clean more wagons?" Fritz jumped down from the train.

"Well, all right, just a quick one, in case a senior officer turns up." Rudi made his way to the tap and turned it off.

The young *SS* men joined the driver and the engineer in their hut. The driver had set out an array of bottles on the table.

"Well lads, we've got this Pernod stuff, brandy and wine. Enough for a party, eh? The driver opened all the bottles.

The driver and engineer, each around 50 years of age, were hardened drinkers, unlike the two young *SS* soldiers. As the older men swapped jokes and roared with laughter, they failed to notice Fritz and Rudi were drunk.

"Oh no. Just look at those two, they've passed out. And we've got to leave in an hour. What shall we do with them?" The engineer prodded Rudi who had fallen on the floor.

The driver shook Fritz and the boy grunted and moaned but would not wake up. "Well, they said they had to return with us. We'll put them in one of the cattle trucks they've already cleaned. They'll have to sober up on the way."

It was dark when the two heavily built railwaymen carried the unconscious boys to the train and put them in the first wagon. They slid shut the doors, making it appear the young men had finished their duties.

They climbed back into the locomotive and the train hissed as it pulled out of the siding towards the main line. The journey would take four days to reach Drancy, near Paris. They would stop at various points to eat and rest and allow military and freight traffic to use the line.

It was midnight by the time they crossed into Belgium.

***

25 February – Belgium

Rudi awoke first as the darkness of the wagon gave way to dawn. He held his stomach as bile rose in his throat. "Fritz wake up. Wake up. The train is moving."

Fritz groaned.

"Fritz, Fritz. We're right in it now."

Fritz got up and almost fell down again as he slipped on the damp, wooden floor of the cattle truck. "Ugh, I feel ill."

The train was slow through the countryside. Rudi slid open the door and gasped as the cold air rushed in. Squinting to see, he gripped the frosted metal ladder on the side of the wagon then climbed forward to the engine.

The driver was loud and cheerful. "Good morning, boys."

"Well," said the engineer. "You got a little drunk, so when it was time to leave, we just put you on the train. Here, have some of this." He poured the steaming liquid from a flask and handed a tin mug to each boy.

"Thanks – but what about our senior officer? Did he notice?" Fritz warmed his hands around the mug.

The engineer checked his gauges. "We didn't see him."

Rudi sipped his drink. "It looks like we've got away with it."

The engineer tapped the glass of a gauge. "Well, yes and no. You didn't finish cleaning the wagons, so we closed them all. You can clean them on the way. We've got three days before we get there." The gauge responded. "Ah there – that's working at last."

"But we don't have a pressurised water hose – any more coffee in there?" Fritz held out his mug.

"If you open all the doors to the wagons to let in some fresh air, they may not be too bad when we arrive." The engineer poured him another cup.

"What about the shit?"

"There's a shovel and broom you can borrow. You might just be able to do a reasonable job before we get to Paris."

By midday the young *SS* officers' strength and spirits had revived with the help of the coffee and food picked up at stations on the way.

The engineer held a flask as he climbed over to the first truck, where the boys were camped. "In five minutes we'll be slowing down. You should be able to clean the rest of the wagons. Here's some more coffee, and bread and ham for later on."

"Thanks." The boys nodded.

They climbed the metal ladder fixed to the side of the wagon and walked along the roofs, leaping across the wide gaps between the wagons. Rudi carried the shovel while Fritz took the broom.

"I think this was the last one we cleaned. We need to climb into the next truck." Rudi stood on the footplate and opened the wagon door. There, lying motionless in the gloom, was Martin.

"*Scheisse* – a dead body." Fritz dropped the broom.

They took small steps towards the lifeless figure, with their hands over their mouths, anticipating a bad smell.

Martin let out a murmur.

"Oh, shit, shit, shit. He's not dead." Fritz backed away as if the injured man was about to leap up and attack him.

"What do we do?" Rudi poked Martin with the shovel.

"Kill him." Fritz drew his revolver and aimed it at Martin's head.

"No, no. What if the driver and the engineer hear the shot? As far as they're aware, the train is empty. We were meant to take dead Jews that get left on the train straight to the ovens."

"So?" Fritz clicked off the safety catch and curled his index finger on the cold metal trigger.

"So, they can get us in enough trouble already if they want to – let's not give them any more ammunition. We're the only ones to know some Jew got left in the train."

"What are we going to do? We can't turn up at Drancy with him."

"No, we can't. But he looks almost dead anyway." Rudi gave Martin a kick.

"Let's throw him off the train. He'll die in a ditch and he'll no longer be our problem."

The two boys got busy with the broom and shovel, cleaning up the wagon as they waited for a section of track where they could drop Martin's body without being seen.

Rudi paced the wagon. "Let's get rid of the Jew and we can make an early start tomorrow."

Fritz leaned the shovel on the side of the truck. "This looks like a good place, nice thick hedges. No one will see the body."

They lifted Martin and dropped him from the train into some bushes.

***

26 February – Eastern Belgium

Marcel no longer enjoyed walking his dog beside the railway line, but he needed to search for his lost lambs. He was a small, neat man of around 55 with a narrow, grey moustache and thinning grey hair. His warm brown eyes matched the kindness of his good heart.

German troop trains were using the line more and more, and a young soldier had taken a pot shot at him for staring at a train yesterday. He saw a train moving away in the distance and saw his chance to search near the track. One of his favourite ewes had lambed early and both offspring had strayed.

Since 1941, he had noticed many trains were carrying people in cattle trucks. He wept when he heard their pitiful moans and appeals to him for water as the train travelled at less than walking speed over the damaged track. Wanting to avoid any further harrowing encounters, he had set off at mid-day because he knew there were fewer trains at that time.

"Come, *Roi*." he called to his black-and-white sheepdog. "*Roi, Roi.*" *Roi* did not move. He was investigating something in the hedge.

"Ah, clever dog – found the lambs, eh?" Marcel pulled back the bushes to reveal a dark-haired man lying still.

Roi licked Martin's face. Martin stirred.

Marcel stepped back. "*Mon Dieu.* Are you alright, *Monsieur?*"

Martin did not respond.

"Oh Lord, you are injured. I'll come back – I'm going to get my wife, she's a nurse and the cart."

He ran back to the little house on their smallholding, followed by his dog. "Madeleine – quick, the first aid kit. There's an injured man by the railway line."

"What?" Madeleine paused from plucking a chicken. She was a small round woman with rosy cheeks.

"A man – he's injured. He's lying by the railway line." Marcel searched a cabinet for the medical kit.

"*Ooo, la la.* Is he bleeding? Does he have a pulse?"

"Er... I didn't look that closely." Marcel packed bandages into a bag.

"Oh, Marcel…."

"Look, I'll leave all that to you. Let's get him back here before the next train comes along." Marcel stroked *Roi*.

Madeline put on her coat. "Oh gracious, there's a train due at one o'clock, and we only have 20 minutes. There could be other military trains as well."

"Come along, then. Let's be quick."

Madeleine took charge of the first-aid box and they puffed hard as they pushed the large, three-wheeled wooden cart towards the track.

Roi led the way back to the railway line, running forward to indicate the direction and then running back, panting and wagging his tail. It was hard work as the field was rough and took longer than they had anticipated. When they reached the spot where Martin lay, his position was unchanged.

Madeline bent down and put her face close to Martin. "*Monsieur, monsieur….*"

He groaned.

She checked his pulse and respiration. "We must get him on the cart and back to the house."

Marcel put his hands under Martin's back to lift him. "Oh, he's in a terrible mess. I wonder what happened. Do you think he's from one of the trains with all the people?"

A whistle sounded from a short distance away.

"A train." Marcel took hold of *Roi's* collar.

They hid in the bushes. The train approached with a squeal of wheels on metal rails. It was carrying tanks and armoured cars, guarded by light artillery. Armed troops sat at the end of every other carriage.

Roi sat down next to the frightened couple.

The train chugged past their hiding place and stopped.

"*Merde.*" Marcel pushed Madeline's head to the ground and lay over her.

Above them two German soldiers sat next to a fixed machine gun and smoked cigarettes. *"Scheisse.* We've stopped again. We're sitting ducks here for any enemy planes." After a final drag, a soldier flicked the butt into the scrub at the side of the track.

Marcel could see the stub still glowing, near to where Martin was laying. The train moved off with a jolt. Marcel and Madeleine lay rigid. *Roi* began to bark, running up and down where the cigarette stub had set the dry grass alight. Marcel stood, removed his coat and began smothering the small fire.

"They'll see you." Madeleine rubbed her aching hip. The train was not yet out of sight.

"What can I do? I came to get a man – not firewood." Marcel put his singed coat back on. "We must get him home. If we don't hurry, he might die here."

They heaved Martin onto the cart, then pushed and pulled it across the field. *Roi* raced backwards and forwards, barking. At last they struggled back to the little house. Chickens scattered and clucked as they shoved the cart up to the back door.

"Where will we put him?" Marcel lifted Martin in his arms.

Madeleine became Nurse Coupé, glad to put her previous nursing experience to good use. "We'll have him on the kitchen table. You boil some hot water, please, and I'll examine him."

She undid Martin's clothes and cut away his shirt. "He's very weak. He may have lost a lot of blood. He has a wound in his head. Mmm… the bullet appears to have entered his skull, but there's no wound for the exit. It's to the side of his head, so we don't know what part of his brain might be damaged."

Marcel shuddered. "A gunshot wound. We're going to be in trouble if we are found with this man. What shall we do? Should I report this to the White Army?"

"Could you put some hot water in a bowl and add some salt?" Madeleine was scrubbing her hands. "He appears to have broken ribs. Goodness only knows how many other broken bones he has."

"What if he's a fugitive, or an escaped criminal? Someone wanted by the *Gestapo*?"

"He's a man who needs my care right at this moment. We'll find out who he is when he comes round – *if* he comes round. Then we'll decide what's to be done. Let's get to work and attend to his wounds because the poor soul will be in pain when he does wake up and I've only got aspirin."

CHAPTER 22
Walter - A Famous Double

28 May – Algiers

Walter and Churchill were in North Africa again, this time for a conference with General Eisenhower, the man the American's called, Ike, the Supreme Commander of the Allied Forces in Europe. Churchill wanted Ike's agreement to set up the French Committee of Liberation. This meeting was to decide who would run France after the war.

Mike Reilly placed his hand on the white twisted column decorating the terrace of the elegant marble house. The American army sentries, patrolling the beach, dripped with perspiration under the fierce mid-day sun.

"Look Inspector, Ike wants him, back in London. Here, he's a target."

Walter was sitting in the shade of the terrace, cleaning his gun. "I understand, but he's not been too well and needs to rest. Here, he's got hot water for a bath, the Admiral's soft bed with a radio alongside, and a nice sunshiny day. What sort of reports are you picking up from the enemy?"

"Lots – they know he's here, and they think he'll use a civilian route to go home again. Their agents are watching Gibraltar and Lisbon."

"Okay, I'll try to sort it out. But don't rely on it. Can you take over for a short while? I'll send my sergeant in to relieve you. I'm going to talk to London on the scrambler." Walter left Mike guarding Churchill while he sought out George and went to the communications room.

***

Later that evening, Walter sat in the corner Churchill's bedroom, listening to his grunts and rapid, hoarse exhalations. He didn't like the look of the old man. He had watched his own father die from pneumonia and recognised the signs of the illness.

He found himself repeating *in… out… in… out…* as he listened to Churchill's breathing.

At 02:00 am, the sound ceased.

Walter rushed to Churchill's side, and put his ear to the old Man's face – nothing. Churchill was not breathing. Walter began resuscitation, rhythmically banging on the Old Man's chest for the count of ten and then breathing into his mouth, while holding his nose. Sweat trickled down Walter's forehead. His thoughts drifted to Larry. "Please, please, breathe… breathe."

Churchill let out a long low rattle.

"At last…" Walter ran out of the room to find Dr Moran.

He bumped into George in the corridor. "Where's Moran? Where's Moran? Stay with the Old Man and make sure he keeps breathing."

"First floor, second door on the right. Is he okay? What do I do if 'e stops breathing?"

Walter was already halfway up the stairs.

George's hand shook as he opened the door to Churchill's room. "Right then… I'll go see to the Old Man."

Moran's door was locked. Walter banged hard with his fist. "Dr Moran… Dr Moran…."

Moran came to the door in his pyjamas.

"His breathing…."

"Right, let's take a look." Moran put on his dressing gown and puffed as he followed Walter down the stairs to Churchill's room.

While Moran was with Churchill, Walter paced up and down in the corridor outside. George found him and offered him a cigarette.

"No, thanks, George."

Moran emerged from Churchill's room: "He is breathing better now. You were quite right to call me. I can trust that you will keep listening?"

"Certainly, sir. Have you given him some penicillin?"

"Oh, I didn't bring any with me… but I'm sure he'll be all right." Moran flushed pink and puffed back upstairs.

"Didn't bring any penicillin! That's like me not bringing my gun. What the hell's the matter with that man?"

George shrugged and kept quiet. He was sure that if he told Walter the awful secret, Walter would kill the incompetent doctor.

Walter went back into Churchill's bedroom to tuck in the bedclothes and adjust the pillows.

Churchill lay back on the pillow. "Thompson, I am tired out in body, soul and spirit."

"No, not in spirit. You're just very tired. It's been a strenuous time. Now the conferences are ended, I hope you'll be able to get a little rest. I'm going to see to things so you can stay a few days longer – take some action to put the Germans off our scent."

Churchill lay there for a few minutes and took Walter's hand: "Yes, I am worn right out. But all is planned and ready."

Walter handed over to George at 04:00 am and George passed him the latest information from Station X at Bletchley Park. "Well there's a sighting of a prominent German agent in Algiers – his orders to assassinate Churchill – and if unsuccessful, 'e is to radio Schellenberg in Berlin who will send the *Luftwaffe* to attack Churchill's plane – the *Liberator*."

Walter tidied Churchill's bedclothes while the Old Man snored. "We need some diversionary action to confuse the buggers. He's safe enough while he is here but the Germans mustn't know we've broken their codes, and at the same time I can't let him fly. There has to be a credible reason the plane won't take off."

George nodded. "There's no better story than a mechanical breakdown or that he may have taken another route."

"Cover for me George, I have to go to the aerodrome at Maison Blanche."

"Right you are, Inspector. Would these come in handy?" George handed Walter a pair of pliers and wire cutters."

"George… how the devil…?

"Let's just say, Inspector, great minds think alike…."

It took Walter an hour to reach the aerodrome at Maison Blanche. His plan relied on absolute secrecy. He needed all the people accompanying Churchill to appear surprised and irritated tomorrow, when his sabotage would cause a technical fault with the plane. The staff at the airport, including the suspected German spies, needed to believe the deception.

He turned off the car headlights and switched off the engine about half a mile from the field. The sky was filled with thousands of stars. He picked up the torch and George's pliers, cut a small hole in the perimeter fence and slipped through.

The guards at the aerodrome were focusing their attention on the main gate. Walter crept up to the plane and undid the right engine cover. It clanked open and Walter stood motionless, willing the guards not to turn around. He stretched to get a view of the engine, but he could not see.

Walter ducked and ran towards a wooden packing case. He tried to lift it, but it was too heavy. He used the pliers to prise it open. It was full of spent shells, ready to be shipped back to England as scrap. He started taking them out of the crate. One rolled across the concrete, clanging so loud Walter felt sure the guards would turn and see him. But they smoked in their hut facing the gate. Once the crate was empty, he returned with it to the plane. He stood on the box and leaned over the engine. *Ah there it is.* He used George's pliers and removed the magneto wire.

He returned the box to the hangar and replaced the shell casings. He was about to recover the one that had rolled onto the tarmac when a jeep pulled up and parked over the runaway shell. Walter slid around the corner of the hangar. He was anxious to return to Churchill. So he crouched and ran in the dark back to his car.

Churchill's plane would not fly tomorrow. Instead, a civilian aircraft would take off from Lisbon airport on 1st June. Aboard would be a man dressed as Churchill, and with Walter's friend, Leslie Howard Steiner, who bore a remarkable resemblance to Walter, posing as Churchill's bodyguard.

Leslie and Walter had known each other since childhood. Walter smiled when he thought of the two of them playing football together in Dulwich Park. In those days, Walter's mother ran the sweet kiosk in front of the football field and Walter was a talented footballer.

Leslie was one of the *posh toffs* from Dulwich College, an expensive private school, and had asked if he and his friends could join in with Walter's football game. Leslie was quick on his feet, and Walter soon wanted him to play for his side. The two boys, near in age, were both sons of mixed Jewish-Christian parents. Walter was amused when he discovered Leslie had changed his surname to *Howard* and had become a famous Hollywood star, acting in many well-known films, including his unforgettable role as, Ashley Wilkes in *Gone With the Wind*.

Walter telephoned Leslie in his Lisbon hotel, on the scrambler phone. "I'm really sorry to wake you up at this early hour."

Leslie yawned. "Walter Thompson, well, well, well. How the devil are you?"

"I'm fine, Leslie – I wouldn't have bothered you but we're in a bit a pickle here in North Africa."

Leslie sat up in bed. "Don't tell me, you need some propaganda films to further the Allied cause?"

"No, I need you to help me with some deception. Churchill is very unwell and his only way of getting back to England is on the long-range *Liberator*. The problem is, the German's are watching the airport. Their assassins are not going to be able to get into the villa and I've got an armoured car to take him to the airport. But the *Luftwaffe* has bases in Italy – and they'll be on us as soon as we're in the air."

"I see – so what do you want me to do, exactly?"

"Can you find someone to impersonate the Prime Minister? I need the Germans to think he has got as far as Lisbon and then be seen boarding a plane on the first of June. I'm hoping the German spies across Lisbon airfield in the *Lufthansa* hangar will think that it's Churchill and his bodyguard, and they've missed their chance to assassinate him while he is in North Africa."

"I see – bit of a problem for you and your boss."

"Yes. We can stay here a few more days until the Old Man has recovered and then fly home safely. It's not without some risk but the Germans are hardly likely to break the Geneva Convention and shoot down an unarmed civilian plane." Walter smiled to himself at the thought of Leslie impersonating him.

"I'm delighted to be of some help. How amusing that my debut role in Portugal will be playing you." Leslie chuckled.

"Leslie you don't know how grateful I am. I still owe you for the time you gave me a pair of your football boots after I put nails in my school shoes"

Leslie laughed and switched on the lamp by the bed to make notes on the hotel stationery. "So, can we meet up when we both get back to London – provided they don't whisk me off to make some damned awful propaganda film?"

"Absolutely. Come along to the War Rooms, and I'll introduce you personally to the Old Man. He's seen all your films. Wait 'till I tell him what your next role will be."

"Do you think I'm good looking enough to play you?"

"Ha – I'm 52, Leslie – you'll need makeup to mask those film star looks of yours, so you seem old and tired. Here's the plan. The Old Man will go to his long-range plane – the *Liberator* – tomorrow and it won't fly. Forty-eight hours later you take off with his double from Lisbon and the Germans might be fooled into thinking he took a short-range plane to Lisbon and then a civilian airliner to England."

"I've got it Walter."

"Thank you Leslie, see you in London."

"My pleasure."

***

29th May – Algiers

Churchill's head glistened with sweat as they travelled in the stifling armoured car. His body was shivering with fever and he pulled a blanket around his shoulders. They were on their way to Maison Blanche aerodrome. Churchill was unwell, but insisted on continuing with the subterfuge now he knew of Walter's plan.

They pulled up at the airport and boarded the *Liberator*, which had a cabin containing a bunk, specially adapted for the Prime Minister.

The plane taxied down the runway and the pilot tested each engine. When the right-hand engine failed to respond, the pilot returned the plane to base.

"What's the problem?" Walter looked at the pilot. "Should we stay on the plane or disembark?"

"You may as well jump off and make yourselves comfortable for a while," replied the pilot.

"Right." Walter helped Churchill from the plane. He settled him inside the Nissan hut, but it was hot and airless. After about ten minutes, Walter walked back to the *Liberator.*

The pilot was peering under the engine housing. "It's the magneto causing the trouble. I'll have to get a part flown in. Might as well take him back."

Walter shouted at the drivers in the armoured cars. "Get over here now. Bloody plane won't fly, we'll have to go back to Algiers." He lifted Churchill into the first car and slammed the door.

Churchill winked.

Dr Moran had taken sleeping pills and could not be roused to get off the plane. George kicked Moran's foot. "Serves you right." He left him dozing on the hot plane.

Walter pulled George aside. "See the jeep over there – well underneath it is a spent shell. Can you recover it without anyone seeing you?"

"I think I can manage that, Inspector."

***

1 June – Portela Airport, Lisbon

Alfred Chenhalls, Leslie Howard's English accountant, chewed on his cigar as he shook hands with the Portuguese dignitaries waiting to see them off. He looked very much like Churchill, dressed in a wool coat with an astrakhan collar.

The British Ambassador smiled and bowed as the Prime Minister passed through the airport.

Leslie wore a grey pinstripe three-piece suit like the one Walter had on, when he appeared in *The Express.* He acted the part, glancing up and down the airfield.

The technicians from *Lufthansa* stood on the far side of the runway and watched through binoculars. Their radio operator was frantic – sending the same message over and over to Berlin:

Churchill and his bodyguard observed departing on civilian flight 777 from Lisbon to London.

The passengers climbed the ladder to the plane. "Mind your head, sir," said flight engineer, Rosevink, just as elderly passenger, Wilfred Israel boarded.

Chenhalls removed his homburg and gave the *V* sign before climbing the ladder, followed by Leslie Howard, who surveyed the airfield one more time.

Rosevink closed the passenger door while Captain Tepas taxied the *Ibis* towards the runway. He revved the engines and pulled back the joystick when the aircraft reached 140 miles per hour.

Leslie smiled at Chenhalls while he watched Lisbon receding into the distance below. "Well done. The Germans definitely saw you waving. I could get you an acting career yet."

"Ha. Well, thank you. I didn't think I'd ever get a role acting alongside you, Leslie." Chenhalls undid his coat.

The Dutch radio operator, Cornelis van Brugge, called Whitchurch control. His cipher message read: *From AGBB to GHK-Flight 777 left Portela 09.40. Thirteen passengers on board.*

***

The same day – Bordeaux-Merignac, Luftwaffe Flight Squadron 40

Eight *Junkers JU 88s* flew in spotter formation. The planes were armed with three 151/20mm guns and three machine guns. Herbert Hintze, the radio operator of the last plane to take off, sat behind the pilot. The planes proceeded along the Bay of Biscay, moving in a chessboard fashion so as not to miss anything. They were searching for Churchill's plane.

The *Ibis* flew at 10 000 feet in a cloudless sky.

Hintze was the first to spot the *Ibis*. "Target at 11 o'clock."

The *Luftwaffe* captain accelerated the plane towards the two-engine grey civilian aircraft flying below. He squeezed the trigger of the machine gun and bursts of white-hot bullets ripped through the air.

The second-round tore through the *Ibis's* port engine. Flames shot out.

"From AGBB to GHK – am attacked by enemy aircraft." Captain Tepas put the *Ibis* into a steep dive. The engines screamed. The cabin vibrated and contorted.

Roosevink dragged himself along the aisle. He pulled canvass bags from a string holdall and threw them to Leslie and Alfred. "Get these on *quick.*" He fought with the cabin door. Air sucked from the plane. The passengers yelled. The door fell away.

Alfred grasped the rail by the door. "I can't do this…."

Leslie helped him buckle the harness to his body. "Hold on to me. It's jump or die…"

Flashing spears of light shredded the engine.

Hintz watched from the German *Junker*, as the aft door of the *Ibis* dropped to the sea and two men wearing parachutes appeared. The men jumped from the burning plane. They were sucked towards the inferno of the burning engine. Their chutes went up like Roman candles. The blazing men plunged into the churning sea.

The smouldering *Ibis* circled. The pilot steered the plane in a wide last curve, smashing into the foam. The plane floated for a few minutes. A great whirlpool of water sucked the craft under the turbulent ocean.

Hintz gripped his seat while his captain banked the *Junker* and strafed the sea with machine-gun fire.

Survivors from the civilian plane were trying to inflate a life raft.

Hintz counted the charred bodies floating on the water – one was a child. He shut his eyes when his captain fired at the bodies one more time before giving the signal to return to base. *We will have to answer for this.* Hintz feared. "God forgive us…"

***

"…the civilian plane was shot down over the Bay of Biscay. And that is the end of the BBC news. Good evening."

"Where's Churchill?" Bunny stopped Downwood in the corridor, her eyes flashing.

"As far as I know, he took off yesterday and was flying back. I can't understand why they're not here." Downwood did not bother to look up from his desk. He had fought his way back into Churchill's good graces by seeking out and training doubles, but he had insisted there was no one who could imitate Walter. *The Inspector will just have to go with anyone I find.* He did not know about Walter's plan with Leslie.

Bunny flopped down on her chair. "He's been shot down."

"What? How?" Downwood jumped up. He ran into the main office, where the whole place was in uproar.

Bunny fanned herself with her hands. She made off towards the ladies' toilets and locked herself in a cubicle.

She sat staring at the door for more than an hour. She looked at her wristwatch – almost 6 o'clock. She got up, washed her hands, splashed water on her face and returned to her room where she switched on the radio to listen to the news.

This is the BBC from London. Enemy aircraft shot down a civilian plane today as it flew over the Bay of Biscay.

On board was the film actor and acclaimed director, Leslie Howard. He will be sadly missed as a great romantic actor and a gentleman. Some of his more memorable performances were as Ashley Wilkes in 'Gone with the Wind' and as Professor Higgins in 'Pygmalion'.'

Bunny wiped tears from her eyes. "Leslie Howard? Leslie Howard? Oh, thank God, not Walter – Leslie Howard. Oh, poor Leslie Howard." She felt a pang of guilt as she recalled a strange conversation with Walter. He had asked her if she had ever seen an actor called, Leslie Howard at the picture house. When she had replied, she had seen all his films, he asked whether he resembled the actor in any way. *"Yes, you are both very alike."*

***

6 June – The War Rooms, London

The next morning at work, Bunny found her colleagues animated and chattering together. "What's going on?"

A clerk squeezed her arm. "We're not meant to know, but there's going to be a big pow-wow – they're calling it The Great Power Conference."

"But they haven't returned from their last trip yet." Bunny put her coat on a peg.

Downwood shut a file on his desk and stood up. "They arrived last night."

"Last night?" Bunny strode out of the office. She stormed to Churchill's bedroom. She clenched her fists together and stood outside.

Walter sensed someone outside and opened the door.

Bunny could see Churchill sitting up in bed in his dressing gown, reading his mail. She shot a glance at Walter and went back to her office. By the time Churchill looked up, she was gone.

Walter stood holding the door open.

He waited until mid-day, when Churchill took his bath, before going to find Bunny. When he opened the door and stepped into the corridor, she was blocking his path.

Walter put out his hand to her. "Hello, how are you Miss Bunny?"

She stood with her hands on her hips, glaring.

"I don't know why you're looking so angry at me. I've just lost one of my oldest friends – shot down in an unarmed, civilian plane."

Bunny's lips tightened.

Walter took her elbow and walked her to her office. He edged her through the door and locked it behind him.

Bunny stood with her chin in the air. "Damn you, Walter, I thought you were dead. Oh, and when I began work this morning, someone informs me you have returned. Not you – someone else informs me. And to put the icing on the cake, I'm told you are off again to some big power conference. Thanks for letting me know…"

Walter sat on her typist chair and put his head in his hands. "I… I…"

"Well?" Bunny's face and neck were red.

"We got back very late last night. I assumed you would be asleep. The Old Man wanted to get an early start, and I suppose I didn't like to wake you. I thought I'd come and find you when he had his bath."

"I wasn't even asleep. I was lying awake worrying about *you*."

"Well, I didn't fancy banging on your door and waking others at that time of night. And to be honest, I was feeling pretty awful after losing a good friend."

"And you're going away again?"

"Yes, but not for a few months. There are a lot of security arrangements to make." Walter paused. "And there'll be another conference first, in August. I'm sorry, I'm the wrong person for you to be angry at right now. I'm angry enough with myself. Please let's not fight like this." Walter turned from her gaze.

She sat next to him in silence for a few minutes. "Oh, there's a private letter for you there in my tray. It came by hand."

Walter picked up the letter, unlocked the door and went to find Churchill. He stood in the corner of the room while the Prime Minister worked.

Walter slit open the letter.

My dear Walter,

I don't know how to begin. Life has changed here in France. The Gestapo brought in a new leader, a man called Klaus Barbie, and he has made things much worse. Martin was arrested at a known Resistance leader's home and now he's disappeared. My friends here in the South are making further enquiries, but they all act as though Martin is dead. I refuse to believe that. Apparently, everyone cracks under interrogation, but the Gestapo haven't visited the farm or the house that was our HQ. If he was alive, I am sure he would tell them what they wanted to know. I just don't know what to think. I won't give up on him. Walter, what can I do?

"Oh dear God…" Walter slumped down on the chair by the door.

Barbie is finding everyone who is remotely Jewish and shipping them off to the East. It's rumoured they're being killed there. I still can't believe it. There's far too many people being shipped, and most of them are women, children and old people.

Walter knew the truth about the shipments.

Dearest Walter, I do miss you so – and when I find Martin, I promise I will return home. Is there any way your friends at Scotland Yard can help to trace Martin? You know I love him so much and I am heartbroken to be apart from him. I have written letters to Grandfather Gold and also to Emily for Bernie – just in case he can help when the invasion comes. I don't know what else to do. I feel so hopeless.

Your loving sister,

Stella xx

Walter let the letter flutter to the floor. He should have intervened earlier and rescued his sister from France. Martin had been missing for….

He picked up the letter again to look at the date. It was almost seven months old. *Oh God, Stella, where are you?*

He shut his eyes.

Churchill looked up. "Thompson …?"

"Sir, may I ask you a very serious question?"

"Depends how serious." Churchill was in a light-hearted mood after his bath.

"It's very serious, sir."

"Then you'd better go ahead and ask."

"What are we going to do about the Nazis shipping the Jews to death camps?"

"Well, let me think. Ah, yes, back in December, all three governments – that is us, the United States and Russia – read out a declaration condemning Nazi atrocities. We told the Germans we know they are following Hitler's instructions to exterminate all the Jews in Europe. We underlined that those responsible for such crimes shall not escape retribution."

"But what are we *doing* about it? I'm sorry, sir…."

He turned, and was about to leave the room, when Churchill asked: "What's this all about, Thompson?"

Walter mopped sweat from his brow. "It's my sister, sir, and my brother-in-law – they're Jewish. They were in Paris, and they had contacts with the Resistance. He's been arrested. Now I've lost touch with both of them."

"I'm sorry to hear that, Thompson. Well, tell the officer in charge of communications you have my permission to contact Major Brown at Special Operations Executive. You never know, he might be able to help. Take some time out immediately. Your family is important to me, Thompson."

"Thank you, sir."

***

6 June – Baker Street, London, Office of the Special Operations Executive, SOE, better known as Britain's spy headquarters

The Marks & Spencer building looked innocent enough. A simple sign indicated the offices of the Inter Services Research Bureau. Walter knew this was the recruitment and operations centre for the Special Operations Executive – otherwise known as the SOE – where Churchill ran his spy operation.

The street door opened to a staircase covered in brown linoleum. A single unshaded bulb lit the way. The corridor at the top of the stairs led to a plain waiting room. A young, athletic, fair-haired woman glanced up as Walter entered, but she did not speak.

Before Walter could sit down, a secretary appeared. "Major Brown will see you now." She led Walter to a drab room where the furniture comprised a small wooden desk and three chairs.

Walter stood by the window, peering through a tiny hole in the blackout blind at people going about their business in Baker Street.

"Inspector Thompson." Major Brown extended his hand to Walter as he entered the room. "Please have a seat." He was a non-descript, mousy-haired man, wearing a checked suit and sporting a brush-like moustache.

Walter took one of the wooden chairs while Major Brown sat opposite.

"We've been asked to make some enquiries about your sister. It seems she may be hiding with the *Maquis* in the South of France."

Walter placed his hands on the desk. "Can we get her out? What about her husband, Martin?"

"Well… I'm not sure if she'll want to come out. Martin Gold, who was using the name Martin Thibault, was arrested. Your sister, Mrs Gold, seems set on his rescue." Brown tapped a file he had placed on the desk.

"What are her chances of finding him and getting him home?"

"You want the truth, Inspector?" Brown folded his arms.

Walter nodded. "Of course."

"Well, old boy, I'm afraid there's no hope at all. I'm sorry to have to say this, but he's probably already dead. The problem is Mrs Gold won't accept this. She's in danger of getting caught herself if she takes silly risks to find out about her husband."

"Can you get her out?"

"Possibly, Inspector… excuse me one moment." Brown stood up and went to the door. "Diana, my dear, would you join us?"

The young woman Walter had noticed earlier, walked in and gave Walter a flashing smile.

"Inspector Thompson, may I introduce Diana. Diana is one of our agents, and she'll be flying to France to meet up with the Resistance quite soon. Do you have a recent photograph of your sister?"

"The most recent one I have was taken on her wedding day, four years ago." Walter handed the photograph to Major Brown, who took a look and passed it to Diana.

Diana studied the photograph. "Oh, she's lovely." She returned it to Walter.

"Don't you need to keep it?"

"Oh no. If I were caught with a photograph of your sister, I would put her life at risk. I have been well trained to recognise people, Inspector Thompson. I never forget the curve of a forehead or the shape of an ear."

"So, what happens now?" Walter replaced the photograph in his wallet.

"Just leave it to us, Inspector. If we can help, we will – if we can't, well…."

Walter turned to Diana. "But when are you going to France?"

Major Brown fielded the question. "I'm sorry, Inspector, we can't give you any more detail. We know how to contact you and we will. Thank you for coming along. Good afternoon to you." He extended his hand and Walter shook it.

Walter held out his hand to Diana. "Thank you for all you're doing. She really does mean so much to me."

"Inspector, I assure you I will do my best." Diana smiled at Walter, appreciating his good looks.

CHAPTER 23
Stella - A Reluctant Rescue

11 October – Sochaux-Montbéliard, France

Robert Peugeot's house was furnished in a lavish way. He was someone who had been wealthy for decades. He welcomed the British Resistance field agent known as Jules with a warm handshake and a glass of Hospices de Beaune, Burgundy Grand Cru 1935.

Jules breathed in the aroma of blackcurrant from the expensive wine. His eyes bulged with pleasure as he swished the wine twice around the glass and took a long, slow drink. "Truly an excellent year."

"I've quite a few bottles, you might like some for your comrades. I'm not letting the damn Nazis get their hands on it."

Jules reached for the bottle. "Well, you can take your chances with the RAF, or you can let us in to do a neat job."

"How can I be sure of your credentials?" Robert appeared calm in view of the fact they were discussing he sabotage his factory. It had been taken over by the German army for the manufacture of tank turrets.

"I can arrange for my credentials to be broadcast over the BBC if you so desire."

"I do, *monsieur*. I do. And if I agree to the sabotage you have planned, will you guarantee an immunity from the bombing?" Robert poured them both another.

"Your answer will come from the BBC. Choose your own code phrase, and I will arrange for it to be broadcast at 19:30 the day after tomorrow...." Jules drained his glass and stood to leave. "Now, how many of these bottles can I take?"

***

13 October – Sochaux-Montbéliard

Robert Peugeot sat in the attic, listening to his illegal radio set through large headphones. *All these years of making cars, now to have to destroy my own factory.* It was 19:29. He grinned as he heard his chosen code phrase. "*Merde.*"

Later that evening, he handed over keys and internal plans of the factory to Jules. "Your contact inside will be Jacques de Wilde. God be with you, *monsieur.*"

Jules returned to the old farmhouse where the Resistance network had its base in Eastern France. Known in London as *Violinist* – his profession before the war – Jules was the code name of an Englishman sent by the SOE to lead a team of French Resistance fighters in the mountains of the Jura, not far from the Swiss border. Among the comrades waiting there was, Stella.

Three months earlier, Max had disappeared, and everyone was sure he had been betrayed to the *Gestapo*. Many believed he was dead. A few weeks ago, one of Max's deputies had sent Stella to Jules's unit to distract her from her worries about Martin. Once she arrived at Montbéliard, she had at last exchanged the nun's habit for a shirt, trousers and boots. Here she gained a reputation for fighting the Germans with a reckless disregard for her own safety.

***

14 October – A field outside Montbéliard

Jules signalled *C* in Morse code with his torch when he heard the rumble of the *Lysander's* engines. A full moon lit the plane's silhouette. Stella crouched against Jules at the edge of the field.

Placed around the field were eight more Resistance fighters. They stepped out of the shadows and pointed their torches towards the *Lysander*, forming the letter *T* to indicate the runway.

Jules tucked the torch in to his back pocket. "When the *Lysander* lands, it will not remain stationary. You must run together with me and help me unload the cargo."

Stella nodded and he squeezed her hand.

As the plane touched down, Stella and Jules ran alongside. Diana opened the door and looked at Jules.

"Is this her?" Jules pulled Stella closer to the moving plane.

"Yes." Diana jumped off.

The co-pilot threw a large canvas bag to Diana. He held out his hand for Stella.

"Get on board, young lady." Jules grasped Stella's wrist.

"What? No. I'm not going anywhere." Stella tried to break from his grip.

Jules drew his gun. "Get on board. Every minute this plane is on the ground, you risk the life of the pilot and all of us. Get on board, now!"

He and Diana bundled Stella into the plane. On the ground, they watched her small face at the window as the plane took off.

Diana extended her hand to Jules. "Hello. I'm Marie. I've brought you some new explosives to try out on your Peugeot factory." She handed Jules a sample of plastic explosive as they walked back towards his car.

Jules handled it with care.

"Oh, it's quite harmless until you pop one of these detonators into it." She waved a small pencil detonator at him.

***

18 October – Baker Street, London

Major Brown studied the report from *Violinist* and smiled.

20:00 – Arrived at the factory. Jacques was not there with the keys. We hung around with a group of factory workers. We played football with the German uniformed guards while we waited.

Franco dropped a homemade Bakelite bomb from his pocket and a German guard handed it back to him.

21:00 – The guard went off duty and Jacques arrived with the key. We have caused extensive and carefully selected damage to the production line in the factory. It is out of operation indefinitely. Your gift with Marie has worked well.

Brown enjoyed the Violinist's reports. They were always lively and undisciplined, using far too many unnecessary words. "A roaring success."

There was a tap on the door.

"Yes?" Brown closed the file in front of him.

"The Inspector is here." The secretary held the door open.

"I'll come and get him." Brown gave the file to his secretary as he passed her in the doorway.

Walter stood with his hands in his pockets. "Any news?"

"Yes, as a matter of fact there is." Brown led Walter along the corridor. He opened a door, revealing a room with a small iron bed and a side table. Laying on the bed was, Stella.

Walter rushed in and swept her up in his arms. "Oh, Stella... my love. How can I thank you, Major Brown?"

Stella sat up. "Walter, Walter, it's so good to see you. You must help me get back to find Martin."

"We've finished our debriefing." Brown indicated towards the small side table, where a plate of food lay untouched. "Perhaps you can encourage her to eat something? Take your time though, we won't need this room until tomorrow." He shut the door and left them alone.

Walter hugged his sister. "Look at you. You're so skinny. Try some of this wonderful beef stew."

"Darling Walter, I can't get over the fact that it's you and I'm back in England. But we must find Martin and get him out too."

"Yes, of course. Come on, eat up, and we'll work out a plan." Walter cut some meat and picked it up with a fork and held it to her mouth.

She turned her head away.

"Come on, you don't want me to have to do *choo-choo*, do you? You remember, I used to have to feed you when you were a baby."

Stella grinned. "Okay, I give in. I'll eat something. Not because I want it – just to save you the embarrassment if Brown comes back in."

"Stella. I need to tell you something – it's Kate…"

Stella's face was red and wet with tears while Walter explained about Kate's death during the Blitz.

He held her in his arms and listened for several hours as Stella explained about her years in France. She ended her story with the capture and disappearance of Martin.

Walter strained to listen as her voice trailed off. They sat together in silence, holding hands.

"Haltwhistle." Walter broke their sorrowful silence. "Emily and Bernie are there together. She's working in a chocolate factory and he's the heavyweight boxing champion for his regiment. Would you like to go and see them?"

Stella smiled. "Chocolate – my favourite. I can't remember the last time I had a bar. Boxing champion – our Bernie?"

"Wait until you see him – he's six foot three."

Stella kissed Walter on the cheek. "I can't wait to see him. Our little Bernie – six foot three?"

CHAPTER 24
Bernie - Boxing Clever

20 October – A bombed-out hotel in Scarborough

"Any more bets?" Johnny called out.

"What's the odds on your mate to win?" A Corporal thumbed a wad of notes.

Johnny consulted his clip board. "Odds are ten to one." He gave the Corporal a wide grin. Johnny was a friend of Tommy Farr, the ex-heavyweight champion of England, and knew him from his Long Bar in Brighton. Johnny had telephoned Tommy a few weeks ago and told him about Bernie's *knock-out* punch. The two of them had worked together to exploit Bernie's top form in a boxing match in Scarborough.

"I'll have ten shillings on your mate to win – he's not the favourite, but I fancy his chances." The Corporal offered Johnny a ten-shilling note.

"Thanks. Go give yer name to Bob, there." Bob was the newest member of Bernie's gang, a bespectacled boy of 19, with big green eyes.

Tommy was desperate for money. He had been in Scarborough for the last week and had found an empty hotel in a nice part of town. He and Johnny transformed the ballroom into a boxing arena. Tommy recommended Scarborough as it was far enough away from Haltwhistle for the locals not to have heard about Bernie's form. Tommy and Johnny were expecting a big payday from the bets they had placed.

At six-foot-tall, with a broken nose and a long reach, Tommy looked imposing as he stood by the door, next to his barmaid, taking five shilling entrance fees from the punters.

Johnny – whom Tommy had nicknamed *Slippery John*, due to the dubious ways he made money around Brighton was offering Tommy a way to settle his financial problems. Despite having had a shot at the world heavyweight title against Joe Louis at the Yankee Stadium in New York in 1937, Tommy was almost bankrupt. He had been delighted when Johnny had proposed he go to meet Jack London, Bernie's enthusiastic trainer, in Scarborough.

"Well, is your boy ready?" Tommy asked London.

London feigned a punch to Tommy's arm. "Put your house on him. He's fit, he's fast and he's hungry."

The ballroom was filling up fast, and Tommy had brought his two barmaids with him to help out.

Emily sat in the front row with Iris, who looked stunning in a fitted dress with small blue flowers, reflecting her bright blue eyes. Her brown curls shone under the hot floodlights. She was by far the prettiest girl in the room.

Emily had made an effort to look smart and wore her best suit, although she had put on a little weight since working at the chocolate factory. She gripped Iris's hand tight. "I don't think I can stay and watch this. I'm so frightened Bernie'll get hurt. And I don't think I can control myself. If the other man hits him hard, I'll be in the ring bashing him with my handbag."

Iris giggled. "Don't worry, it'll be fine. The other chap will be lucky if he manages to land a single punch."

The room was full, and the lights were dimmed. The barmaids made their way to the ring. Tommy Farr introduced the boxers. A cheer went out for Bernie from his friends, but the biggest shouts were for the local hero.

The referee asked Bernie and his opponent for a fair fight, to Marquis of Queensbury rules. The barmaids stood on each side of the ring and held up signs indicating it was *Round 1*. The rivals touched gloves and the timekeeper rang a bell.

Bernie was straight out and on to his opponent, who was sweating like an ox. A fine mist of water flashed across the ring each time Bernie hit the local hero.

His opponent soon countered with an equal number of scoring punches to Bernie's torso, making it clear he wasn't going to be a pushover.

"I can't watch." Emily shouted over the clamour to Iris, although she continued to observe through screwed-up eyes.

At last the three minutes were up, and Bernie returned to his corner.

London dropped a sponge in a bucket of ice-cold water and put it on the back of Bernie's neck. "You're doing great – just fine, Bern. I know he's hit you a few times, but he lacks stamina. Just keep doing what I taught you and he'll tire."

Bernie nodded and jumped up in advance of the bell.

The barmaids left the ring to the sound of wolf whistles and the bell sounded.

The local contender came at Bernie like a train, but Bernie was fast and dodged his telegraphed punches.

The spectators got to their feet, shouting at their champions.

Johnny and Bob walked down the aisles carrying large trays, each holding ten glasses of beer. "Shilling a pint, 'elp yourself from the tray." By the time they reached the ring all the glasses were sold, and they returned to the barmaids for a refill.

The bell rang for the end of the round.

"Well done, boy, you're in the lead on points," said London. "What did I tell you? Just keep at him. He hasn't got a lot left."

The bell sounded for round three and the local man spat blood from his mouth after Bernie hit him on the nose.

The boxer held on to Bernie and growled.

"Break," instructed the referee.

Bernie winked at London; he could feel his opponent's blows getting weaker. He took an inhalation of sweat and stale beer in the ballroom and got himself ready to land his knockout punch.

There was a flash of light across the spectators as the door was opened at the back of the hall and a lone figure walked towards the ring.

Bernie was distracted for a second. As his head hit the canvas. "Stella...."

The crowd got to their feet and cheered for their local hero.

"Oh, what have I done?" Stella's idea had been to surprise Bernie and Emily, not to bring the match to a halt. The referee counted while standing over Bernie.

Emily jumped to her feet. Bernie's girlfriend grasped her arm to stop his mother climbing into the ring.

Stella walked up and tapped Emily on the shoulder. "Hello, dearest sister…"

"Stella. Stella!" She pulled Stella to her and hugged her tight. "This is the best day of my life. Oh Stella…."

The bell rang and Bernie crawled to the corner. The punch had caught Bernie off balance. He took the sponge from London and squeezed the cool water over his head and face. He stood and faced the spectators. "Stella – Stella – give me three minutes…."

"Oh, Bernie, look at you – you're huge… you're a man. I'm so sorry to have startled you."

The bell rang for round four. Bernie walked over to his opponent and socked him hard in his torso.

The local contender dropped his heavy arms. "Arghhhh…"

Bernie teased the man with his left before taking back his right arm – muscles taught like a bow. He released his arm and caught the man's left cheek.

His opponent dropped to the canvas.

Bernie leapt out of the ring before the referee could raise his arm as the match champion. He swept up Stella and Emily, hugging them tight.

"Iris, Iris." Bernie called to his girlfriend. "Come and have a hug too… we're almost a family again, now my aunt is back."

***

Bunny turned on the electric fire next to her desk; the cold October weather permeated deep into the war rooms.

Walter came in and stood by the inadequate fire and rubbed his hands together.

Bunny reached into the tray on her desk and handed Walter a note. "It's from your sister Emily… she telephoned my sister and she wrote it down for you."

"How the devil…?" Walter unfolded the note, which was handwritten.

FOR INSPECTOR WALTER THOMPSON message from Emily.

I am so worried about Stella. She comes home in different military uniforms and disappears for days at a time. She won't tell me anything. Now she's just left with a goodbye that sounded… well… rather like she wasn't coming home again. And she kept talking about Martin as if he was still alive and she was going to see him. Can you please find out where she's gone and talk some sense into her? Love Emily

Walter folded the note. "Oh Lord, I need to go and make some enquiries."

"What is it?" Bunny looked up from her desk. "Can I be of any help?"

"Could you ask George to cover for me for an hour. I've got to nip out to Baker Street."

Outside freezing rain was hitting the pavement. Walter put on his raincoat and waved to a taxi outside the building. He jumped back from the curb to avoid the splash as it pulled up. He was at the SOE building in minutes, where he flung open the street door and bounded up the stairs. The secretary recognised him. "Can I help you, Inspector?"

"Where's Brown?"

"The Major has someone with him at present, Inspector. If you'd just like to…"

Walter marched towards Brown's room. He saw the room was empty. "Brown? BROWN."

Brown emerged from a side room. "Why, Inspector – how nice to see you."

"Where the hell's my little sister?" Walter squared up to Brown.

"Ah yes… well… look, it wasn't my fault. She insisted on going into training for the SOE. She was persistent. And how could I resist, with her fluent French, local knowledge and obvious courage?"

"You bloody fool." Walter thumped Brown in the chest. "Where is she?"

Brown gasped and stumbled before recovering his composure. "Er… it's too late, I'm afraid, Inspector. She left for the SOE training camp in Scotland this evening."

Walter stormed out of the building and Brown shouted after him: "She'll be well trained and in good hands."

When Walter returned to the War Rooms, Bunny handed him a memorandum from the American Secret Service.

To: Inspector W. H. Thompson
From: Special Agent Mike Reilly
Conference
Considered dangerous to travel by boat to Gibraltar and flying on to Cairo. Please suggest alternative.

Walter passed his fingers through his hair and sat down next to Bunny's desk, looking at the floor.

Bunny shut the door to her office and placed her hand on Walter's shoulder. "Can I help? I have security clearance at the highest level."

Walter nodded, his eyes were moist. "My sister is going back to France to fight the Germans… she's just a slip of thing but brave. Her husband's most probably been shipped off to a death camp – he's Jewish – well, so is *she* now; she converted to marry him. I should volunteer and go to France with her but there's to be a meeting of the three Allied leaders, Churchill, President Roosevelt and Stalin. This is where the Germans are sure to execute their plan to kill Churchill – *Operation Long Jump*. I need to keep the Old Man safe."

Bunny pulled Walter to her. "Well is it feasible or possible for you to go to France?"

"No, I suppose not, I would have to get permission and then undergo the training – I just got her back and she's damn well gone again."

Bunny crouched to look Walter in the eyes. "We all have to fight our own war, Inspector. Your job is here... keeping the Old Man safe so he can do his job to get our Allies together to end this war as soon as possible. It seems to me that Mike in America needs your help to come up with a safe route to bring the leaders together in Tehran."

Walter took Bunny's hand and kissed it. "Thank you, Miss Bunny."

Bunny pulled him to his feet. "Come on, let's put our heads together and sort out a safe route. I'll go and find Sergeant George."

George opened the door to the office just as she was about to leave. "Last big pow-wow before we win the war eh? Let's 'ope the three of 'em can find a way to end it quick. It's just a matter of time and strategy. The sheer quantities of enlisted men from America and Russia outnumber the bloody Germans. What?"

Bunny and Walter were smiling. "Nothing," said Bunny. "It's just your political commentary in your cockney accent always sounds amusing."

"You cheeky little basket – don't fink I'd get a job on the BBC eh? Well this meeting is vital – the Old Man's worried about who's going to govern each country – so we get a lasting peace and don't start fighting all over again. There's going to be a signed agreement. Let's 'ope it works."

Walter opened a map on Bunny's desk. "We need to get him there and back for his *Great Power Conference*. But this is where we're going to be most exposed to risk of attack by those fanatical Nazis who still believe in German supremacy."

The three of them worked into the night, with Mike Reilly on the scrambler phone to ensure the safety of all three Allied leaders. Bunny made tea every time she thought Walter was losing focus. His forehead was lined in a deep frown.

Bunny yearned to hold Walter close to her. She could see he found it hard to concentrate because nagging at the back of his mind was his grave concern for Stella.

257

CHAPTER 25
Walter - *Operation Long Jump*

1 November – Berlin

Schellenberg flicked over the three-page report provided by the Spanish Embassy in Washington. The headline read: *Churchill and Roosevelt meeting at the White House.*

It had taken a week before the mistake in the translation was discovered. Churchill and Roosevelt were meeting in *Casablanca* (white house written in Spanish).

He scratched his head and re-read the old radio communication from Lisbon airport. *Lisbon: Churchill boarding KLM flight 777.*

Reports of Churchill being back in London meant the British leader had not been on that ill-fated civilian plane. Schellenberg screwed up the copy of the order he had given to shoot down the aircraft and tossed it in the wastepaper basket.

He was the youngest officer for his rank – 20 years Walter's junior – bright and sharp. But his efforts to eliminate Churchill had come to nothing, and in the eyes of Himmler, Schellenberg was looking incompetent.

As head of the Section IV foreign intelligence unit, Schellenberg could already see the direction the war was going in, but his superiors in the Third Reich did not share his logic. He ran his fingertips over the guns strapped under his desk. He knew he should be trying to persuade Himmler to seek peace with the West. His mobile killing units, the *Einsatzgruppen*, were ready and well trained; all he needed was good intelligence on when and where they should be deployed. But lately he found himself debating *if* they should be deployed.

He reached under the desk and stroked the firing button on the two pistols aimed at the door. *How is this to end? How can I come out of this alive?*

What approach can I make to Herr *Churchill? My only bargaining chip will necessitate saving certain Jewish lives and even halting the* Final Solution *in order to gain some time. I don't really want to have to do that – but I have nothing else to offer them for my liberty.*

He looked at the document he had appended to his *Informationsheft* handbook in 1940. This included a list of all-important Britons who should be rounded up and killed in the event of a successful German invasion, the *Sonderfahndungsliste GB*. He sighed and dropped it in the waste bin. The moment for all that kind of thinking had passed.

What to do now? We should be talking to Roosevelt, Stalin and Churchill, but my orders are to kill them. But someone else will take their place – motivated people, not so weary of war – perhaps not so willing to negotiate. But if Churchill and the others were to die, the confusion that followed might just give Germany a chance.

The secretary knocked on his door and was summoned forward. She handed Schellenberg a note and stood to attention while awaiting a reply.

"So there is to be a conference of the three leaders. One last possibility, to implement *Operation Long Jump*. Once we know exactly when – this is our final chance." He placed the note on his desk. "Send for Oberg, right away."

***

17 November – Malta

Churchill insisted on sailing to the conference, though Walter advised against it.

On Friday 12 November, Churchill left Plymouth on HMS *Renown*. As they approached Gibraltar, the weather worsened.

"What will we do?" George stood on deck and pulled up his borrowed waterproofs against the driving rain.

"Malta." Walter shouted back above the storm. "At least this weather will keep the *Luftwaffe* away."

The sun was shining as they disembarked at Malta's Grand harbour. Walter looked around trying to observe every face – but the crowds were ten deep as they walked down the gangplank. He was on edge. He was awaiting confirmation from Mike Reilly that security in Tehran was satisfactory.

Churchill wanted to tour the island, much to the joy of the population – who welcomed him as if the war was already won. The Old Man was horrified at the bombing that had been inflicted by the Germans – hardly a building stood intact in Valletta.

George walked at Churchill's side and shook hands with person after person. "What wonderful warm-hearted people. They've gone through so much. What a welcome. Look at how they're living." He pointed out the hovels some of the Maltese had improvised.

A crowd was cheering and waving Union Jacks. Behind them their houses had been reduced to rubble. George waved and smiled. "These poor buggers deserve a bloody medal."

A little girl stepped forward with a hand-picked bunch of wild yellow daisies and red campion.

Churchill bent down and accepted the gift. He raised the flowers in the air and the crowd went wild.

George picked up the little girl and placed her on his broad shoulders. She smiled and waved to the crush of people.

***

27 November – Egypt to Tehran

By the front gate if the of the Mena Hotel in Cairo, Walter shook Mike Reilly's hand. He admired the palatial yellow, sandstone building, situated in the shadow of the pyramids at Giza.

Armed guards patrolled the forty acres of verdant, green gardens inside the high walls of the compound. Sentries were posted every twelve feet. Their bayonets glinted in the sun.

Walter took a few seconds to enjoy the sunset over the great pyramid. "I'm really impressed, Mike, you've covered every angle. I couldn't have done better myself. First class – thank you."

Mike lit a cigarette. "The gardeners are causing a bit of a headache. They've been laid off until the conference is over –

with full pay – but they won't go away. They're constantly hanging around by the main gate over there."

"Shall I get my Sergeant to see them off?"

"You can try. My men have had no luck up to now. If they don't go in the next hour, I'll be forced to arrest them and that might start a riot."

George joined them at the main gate. "The Old man's settling in nicely. He's taking a bath." He extended his hand. "Nice to see you again, Agent Reilly."

"And you, George. The Inspector here, seems to think you can help get rid of the gardeners outside the gate."

"Certainly, Mike. Heavy hand or kid gloves?"

"Gloves, George. We don't want to start trouble."

By the time Generalissimo and Madame Chiang Kai-shek arrived from China, the gardeners had gone.

Mike patted George on the shoulder. "Well done – how did you manage it?"

George waved some Egyptian bank notes. "I gave them one of the blue ones each."

Mike chuckled. "Ha – do you realise that's about a month's pay for each man?"

Walter found Churchill stomping around his bedroom, half dressed. Roosevelt was late. "We can't be early for him at sea, but he can be late for us here."

"Come on, sir, we're on the homeward stretch – let's not waste our energies getting cross about a bit of time keeping." Walter helped Churchill fasten his bow tie for dinner. He looked over to the window. "The President may have paused to take in the magnificent sunset tonight."

"You're right as usual, Thompson. I will be gracious."

Walter led Churchill into dinner and went to find Mike. "I'm worried about the next stage of the trip. It's when the Old Man meets Stalin in Tehran. If I were Himmler, this is where I'd make my move. There I'd get all three."

Mike peered at the map of Tehran city on the table in front of him. "You're right. I'm going to fly on ahead and get things in order. I'll see you there in a few days."

The flight from Cairo to Tehran took six hours, and Churchill worked throughout the journey. The Lysander raised dust and sand, when it touched down at the aerodrome.

Walter decided the British Legation would be the safest location for the meeting. He dismissed the chauffeur of the car waiting for them and nodded to George, who took the driver's seat.

"What's up, Inspector?" George eased the car along the crowded street.

Walter took his gun out. "This lot, George. Where are the guards?"

George turned a corner where the street was lined with market stalls. He tooted the horn and people scattered. "Cripes, did anyone tell the Iranians we were coming? Everyone's just going about their everyday business, like nothing important is happening here."

Once at the British Legation, George carried Churchill's luggage to his room.

Walter looked out of the window. "There's far too many people within potting range. We need to tighten up the security arrangements. Mike has installed President Roosevelt at the American Embassy. But it's about a mile away. Can you look after the Old Man for a bit while I walk the route between the two buildings and do some reconnaissance?"

Walter paced the road, taking ten steps forward before turning and looking for all the possible threats from the reverse angle.

When he arrived back at the British Legation, George was waiting for him. "I've got good news and bad news."

Walter frowned. "Yes?"

"The good news is that Roosevelt has accepted Stalin's invitation to stay at the Soviet Embassy."

Walter peered at the plan of Tehran on the table. "Excellent. That's next door and I can get the road shut off. Thank God. There were too many places where a sniper could take position, if he'd stayed at the American Embassy. And the bad news?"

George scratched his head. "German secret agents have parachuted into the area."

Walter walked to the window. "How many? Have they been caught?"

"About six have been rounded up but more are expected. Under some intense interrogation they've revealed their plan is to assassinate one or all of the leaders. This is it, isn't it – *Operation Long Jump* – Aryan super assassins, come to kill the Old Man and 'is chums?"

Walter glanced at the map one more time. "Let's tighten up security as much as we can. If they can't get to him – they can't kill him. Cover for me – I'm going to have a chat with Mike." Walter touched the door to Churchill's bedroom as he went through. "Oh George, could you move his bed – this door is so thin – I could stand outside and fire a shot right through."

George began to push the bed away from the door. "And this is us – *Operation Longshot*… Two old coppers trying to keep the Old Man alive."

***

There was no moon that evening as a second wave of German agents dropped one by one with a thud onto the arid, rubble strewn desert.

The Iranian driving an old truck stopped on the road and switched off the engine. He could smell the musk of camels that had passed by earlier in the day. The hum of a plane was receding into the distance. He peered into the dark – not sure where the parachutists had landed. He flashed the truck's headlights twice.

Rudolf von Holten-Pflug landed first, rolling forward in the dust as soon as his feet hit the ground. His body was hard and fit and his piercing blue eyes searched the rough ground for the others. The practice parachute jumps had paid off – he wasn't even out of breath. He rolled up the chute and headed towards where he had seen the truck flash its lights. He drew his pistol as he approached. "Are you the Iranian?"

"Yes, sir."

"Put the chute in the back of the truck. I'm going to find my men."

"Yes, sir."

Holten-Pflug put his gun in its holster and took out a torch. A half-moon illuminated the coarse outlines of the rocky desert. "Turn off the lights." He stood motionless for a few seconds, to allow his eyes to adjust to night vision.

He found the first man rolling up his chute.

"The truck is over there – take your chute with you, Major Dietrich."

"Yes, sir." Dietrich, a chunky, muscular man caught hold of the billowing silk and packed it into a canvas bag.

He saw the next man untangling himself. "Major Graf, leave nothing behind. Take the chute and head for the truck. Have you seen *Hauptmann* Holz?"

"He landed ahead of me, *Oberst* Holten-Pflug, over there."

Holten-Pflug strode off towards the rocks.

Captain Holz was sitting with the parachute still attached to him and nursing his leg. "I think it's broken, sir."

Holten-Pflug sighed and took out his knife. "I'll cut you free."

"Thank you, Sir."

Holten-Pflug slipped behind his man and drew a breath. In a flash, he gripped the top of the captain's head with one hand and drew the razor-sharp blade across his throat. He had wanted it to be a clean, painless kill. But his men were well trained, and he knew that even when injured, they would put up a fight. Holz turned his head and Holten-Pflug missed the artery. Blood filled the man's throat and he let out a hideous gurgling scream.

The two German agents heard the sound from the truck and rushed towards the noise. Holten-Pflug snapped his man's neck and, in the stillness of the vast silent desert it sounded like a pistol being fired. Holz looked up with unbelieving eyes as his body gave one last contraction and slumped forward.

Holten-Pflug marched to the truck as he shouted to the other two men. "Get shovels from the truck and bury the body."

After a brief glance at each other, both men followed and found shovels in the back of the truck.

Holten-Pflug wiped his bloodied hands. "And be quick, we don't want to be behind schedule." He climbed into the front of the truck, lit a cigarette and waited for his men. "Have you received the latest communications?"

The Iranian handed him an envelope.

Holten-Pflug pulled a thin knife from his boot, slit it open and read the contents to himself.

Churchill at British Legation, Roosevelt at American Embassy. Stalin at the Russian Embassy. Will meet at the Russian Embassy. All vulnerable travelling to aerodrome. Signal the word Helga *for success.*

Holten-Pflug folded the note. "Where are the supplies?"

The Iranian shrugged his shoulders. "They were dropped off target. By the time I got there, a group of desert people had already picked them up."

"You stupid fool."

The Iranian glared. He had a bony face with high cheekbones and a bronze complexion. His dark eyes were set close together, and he wore a constant frown. "I couldn't tackle them. They were seven and I was one. But I have obtained two excellent high-powered rifles for your marksmen."

Holten-Pflug slapped his hand on the dashboard. "I suppose there's a price?"

"Sir, you cannot expect businessmen to give you valuable supplies for free. But the price can be negotiated, and there are clothes for you to wear in the back of the truck."

Holten-Pflug gave him a long hard look and slid out of the cab to inspect the clothes. "These rags are not fit for German officers to wear."

"Do you want to blend in or not?" The Iranian started the truck.

Holten-Pflug shot him a poisonous glance. "The Iranians trained for this mission have all been captured – so it's left to loyal Germans to finish the job. You had better be right about these clothes."

Majors Dietrich and Graf climbed in the back of the truck and brushed the dirt from their hands.

***

265

Churchill's car was stationary in the busy street outside the twelve-foot-high alabaster walls of the Russian Embassy.

Walter wound down the car window. "Get a move on will you? Every minute we sit here in this vehicle, we're a target for a sniper. We don't even have bullet-proof glass."

The Russian guard stood stiff and continued to look at the papers.

Walter ground his back teeth. "Edge forward, George."

The other guard raised the barrier and assumed the papers had been checked,

Walter snatched the documents from the first guard as they passed. "Drive on, George."

No one tried to stop them.

Walter walked behind Churchill into the Russian Embassy. He held a heavy wooden case. It contained a steel sword, which was to be presented to Stalin. It was a gift from King George to the citizens of Stalingrad in recognition of their resistance to the Germans' five-month siege of the city.

Walter grappled with the heavy box while his eyes shot glances around the building for danger. He placed it on a table in the entrance hall and was glad to be rid of it. He stalked around the embassy, looking out of windows and deciding where he would station snipers if he were the enemy.

Churchill was in a good mood: "Let's walk back to the British Legation."

"But sir – we can't." Walter touched the gun in his holster. "Sir, we have information a German attack is imminent. But we have no idea where and when."

"You've had the road blocked off between the two buildings, haven't you, Thompson? And the whole area is sealed by troops?"

"Yes, sir, but –"

"But, nothing. I shall walk." Churchill strolled along the empty street.

George walked backwards and eyed every window and opening. *Crazy old man thinks 'e's immortal.*

Walter watched the front with his gun drawn. Sweat trickled down his temple, even though the air was fresh. "Is this where I'll have to throw myself in front of a bullet, sir? You know these marksmen will be professionals."

Churchill gave Walter a sideways look and took out a cigar.

***

Holten-Pflug had not yet finalised his plan. The three German agents were installed in a back room of the Iranian's house. The single small window was covered with a shutter and a large oil lamp gave the room a flickering yellow light.

The Germans looked around in awe of the ornate interior. It was surrounded by a high wall, which was accessed through a thick wooden door. On the outside, the door was weathered – its paint peeling off, and the plaster on the wall was blistered and cracked. However, the walls were two feet thick and on the inside, they were covered with an exquisite green and gold mosaic. Through the door was a magnificent courtyard, whose central feature was a marble fountain, bubbling clear water into a shallow pool. Rooms led off on each side, screened from the glaring sun by huge curtains hanging over the high doors. Behind one curtain was the sound of chattering women.

When the Iranian lit the lamp, they could see the room was full of luxurious, Persian rugs and huge cushions. A manservant brought in some mint tea, and they were invited to relax and smoke from hookahs.

"This is not a tea party." Holten-Pflug started unpacking the equipment. Dietrich and Graf jumped to attention and began to assist.

The Iranian opened the large, wooden courtyard door. He nodded to a messenger and returned to the Germans. "You've missed your chance of making a hit between the British Legation and the American Embassy. President Roosevelt has moved to the Russian Embassy. Your best chance will be when they return to the aerodrome, unless you can get yourselves invited to

267

Churchill's 69th birthday party tomorrow. He'll receive a number of gifts; one of them could be from us."

Graf nodded and began to check the ordinance.

Dietrich began unpacking the grenades. "Unless he dies of old age in the meantime. He can't have long to live."

"About one more day, by my calculations," said Graf.

Holten-Pflug walked to the door. "Clean those high-powered rifles. I'm making my reconnaissance." He stopped the Iranian in the courtyard. "Take me to the British Embassy."

The men un-packed the rifles the Iranian had obtained. They were of Russian manufacture, and the Germans were unfamiliar with them.

Major Graf lined up the sight with the window. "We'd better give them a good clean and make sure they fire."

Dietrich sniffed his sleeve. "We ought to clean ourselves. I think the last owner of this shirt was a dead donkey and I can't move in it – *verdammt*."

***

30 November – The British Legation

The British Legation was surrounded by a wide, nine-foot-high brick wall. In the darkness, sentries toured the grounds.

Holten-Pflug lay rigid on the thick branch of an old juniper tree at the back of the building. He muttered a curse. He needed to urinate. *Damn that Iranian monkey and his mint tea.* He could see into the compound and the sentries looked alert. He timed their patrols as they moved in pairs, passing his hiding place every two minutes. He would have had Captain Holz along to help, but Holz was dead. Graf was a long-range marksman and Dietrich was a Hitler fanatic who had volunteered to be a suicide bomber. The Iranian waited for him in the shadows of a narrow alleyway close by.

Holten-Pflug's plan was to kill all three heads of state at close quarters. He knew once he fired the first shot, Secret Service agents would surround him. He was prepared for that; he was

268

ready to die for the Fatherland. He touched his pocket where he had two revolvers and four grenades.

An armoured car patrolled the exterior of the compound. Holten-Pflug moulded himself to the tree branch trying to ignore the pain in his abdomen. "*Scheisse!*" Not enough time to scale the wall and now he was trapped.

***

It was cold in Tehran. Walter checked every room to make sure the windows were fastened. He tried all the doors to ensure none of them opened. He descended the stairs to the hall, where Mike's team were waiting. "We must make a continuous systematic search of the building. Start with the cellar. Go in pairs. Check every room. George, come with me."

Inside the kitchen of the grand banqueting hall, the cooks and the waiters were hurrying about, preparing the dinner and carrying huge silver dishes.

The doors of the dining room were flung open to reveal a huge birthday cake with 69 candles. The 34 assembled guests sang *Happy Birthday* and Churchill beamed and accepted his presents.

Walter moved from foot to foot in the corner. "George, stand opposite me in the room. My gut tells me there's an attack coming any minute."

Churchill opened his gift from the Roosevelts – it was a blue-and-white porcelain bowl that looked priceless. Inside, there was a card. Churchill's guests applauded as he read the words aloud: "*For Winston Spencer Churchill on his 69th birthday, at Tehran, Iran, November 30th, 1943. With my affection and may we be together for many years. President and Mrs Roosevelt.*"

George eyed the expensive bowl, wondering how they would get it home in one piece – along with its recipient.

Walter watched each one of the staff as they came and went from the kitchen to the dining room. He remembered every face from the day he arrived, like a falcon scanning the countryside.

The band played *Happy Birthday* again and everyone joined in the song.

Churchill took a deep breath and blew out the candles, then picked up the knife to make a large incision in the cake. "Thank you my friends. I would like all the toasts to be made in Russian style. Anyone who proposes a toast must stand up and go to touch glasses with the person whose health is being drunk."

Walter's eyes flickered from person to person as he tried to scrutinise the room for an intruder as the guests began moving around.

"I sometimes call you Joe," Churchill began by addressing Stalin, Premier of Russia. "And you can call me Winston if you like – and I like to think of you as my very good friend." He raised his glass. "Marshal Stalin – Stalin the Great."

"Stalin the Great." the guests echoed, and the two Leaders clinked glasses.

Stalin replied in Russian: "We want to be friends with Great Britain and America, and if they wish to be friends with us, they can show it by their actions." He touched Churchill's glass. "To my fighting friend." Churchill looked at the translator.

A waiter, carrying a huge ice-cream dessert, tripped as if in slow motion. Everyone in the room froze. Walter took out his gun and held it at his waist. There was a stunned silence.

George watched the dessert fly in the air, separate and fall like pink hail on Stalin's interpreter, the diminutive Pavlov.

Pavlov stood firm and with a shaky voice, finished the translation.

Walter's pulse quickened, checking every face and every hand for a weapon.

A waiter mopped up the mess and everything returned to normal. He nodded to Mike Reilly, who had his gun drawn held by his side.

Churchill raised his glass again, this time toasting President Roosevelt. "We have been friends for many years, but since the outbreak of war, our friendship has been such that I have gained inwardly. I trust that friendship and mutual understanding between our two countries will continue through the ages. The President – and Roosevelt, the man." Churchill touched the President's glass with his own.

270

"Winston has long been my personal friend," replied Roosevelt. "He has been a great man for 69 years – anyway, 60 of them."

The guests laughed as the toasting continued around the banqueting room. Anthony Eden, the British Foreign Secretary, rose to toast his Russian counterpart, Mr Molotov. He looked at his glass in dismay – it was empty. Churchill's butler appeared at once at the table with another two bottles. He poured Eden a glass of wine with a shaking hand. Stalin slapped him on the back and shouted: "To the butler."

***

Holten-Pflug waited outside. Every muscle in his body ached but he did not move. Further soldiers arrived to patrol the grounds. He had been pinned down for an hour when at last he saw his opportunity to escape. He slipped down the tree, without drawing the attention of the troops.

He panted as he darted towards the narrow alleyways.

The Iranian stepped out of the shadows. "This way." He checked behind him several times.

A manservant opened the door to the Iranian's house. Holten-Pflug barged his way inside. He stomped across the courtyard to find his men.

Graf and Dietrich were lying on cushions, holding the high-powered rifles.

Holten Pflug tore back the curtain. "Get up, you imbeciles… and salute an officer."

The men looked at each other and rose to their feet.

"My mission this evening was unsuccessful. Graf, make sure you can fire that rifle accurately. We will need you to shoot Churchill when he is returning to the airfield. Dietrich, you are our last resort if all fails. You will wait for the official cars to pass and throw your Gammon Grenades. If necessary, you will step in front of Churchill's car. Have you checked the grenades?"

"Yes, sir – for the Fatherland, sir." Dietrich gave the stiff-arm salute.

"I want you ready in two hours." Holten-Pflug marched out into the courtyard.

Dietrich checked the Gammon Grenades. He leaned over a bowl and splashed cold water on his face.

Graf shook as he adjusted the sight on his rifle. "Russian rubbish."

When Holten-Pflug returned, his officers snapped their heels to attention. "Now, let's go and test the rifles in the desert."

***

1 December – British Legation, Tehran

Churchill strolled in the garden. He turned to Walter: "Thompson, how much would it take to get you to walk across that pond?"

Walter glanced at the wall surrounding the compound. He stopped when he noticed the juniper tree. He screwed up his eyes to get a better look. "Look – the little twig bent over on that branch; someone was there. I'm sorry, sir, but I can see no reason to get wet."

Churchill looked at Walter with wide appealing eyes.

"Yes, there are still German agents on the loose in the area. I'm very concerned about security on the way back to the aerodrome."

***

Holten-Pflug had a problem. The Iranian's informant in the police force could tell them which roads were to be closed off in the city as Churchill prepared to leave, but they could not be sure of the exact route.

"We will have two chances to get Churchill. First, Graf with the rifle. Second, Dietrich with the Gammon Grenades. Our insignificant deaths will change the course of the war."

"*Heil Hitler.*" They gave the Nazi salute.

Holten-Pflug turned to the Iranian. "We need lookouts to tell us which route they take. If *Herr* Churchill takes another road, we need enough people to cause disturbances in the city to make Churchill take a detour into the path of my sniper."

272

The Iranian beckoned a dark eyed, chubby man forward. "Sir, may I introduce you to Misbah Ebtehaj. He's a wrestler who's respected by all classes in Tehran. In an instant, he can mobilise the beggar army of thieves and idlers. He's a reliable man. He holds the respect of the homeless, who can cause public unrest when ordered. The idea is to cause a riot, which will force the British to shut off certain roads and drive Churchill towards the sights of your marksman."

Holten-Pflug opened a plan of the city. "Excellent. I've chosen the three-storey building at this T junction. It will give Graf a clear line of sight and plenty of time to get his shot off. Ebtehaj, can you place your rabble at the junctions of the other routes he could take – and drive him towards my sniper?"

"Yes, I will get it organised. Where will I meet you?" Ebtehaj bowed.

The Iranian sharpened a long, thin blade. "Come back to the house. The Germans will wait in a cellar close to the chosen building – here." He looked up at the pale-yellow sky. "You better go soon, while it's still dark."

Ebtehaj left and walked to the British Legation to find his British Secret Service contact – the newly promoted, Anthony Downwood. "I've been asked to organise some civil unrest. The German assassins are on their way to hide in a nearby cellar. I need to make this seem real to the Iranian, so I'm going off to talk to the leaders of the beggar army."

Downwood was dressed in Arab clothes. "I need to get some men together – can you trap them in the cellar in the meantime?"

"Yes, there are only three Germans so I'm going to find my brother and my cousin to help me. They think I'm with them, so we should take them by surprise."

Downwood quick marched to Churchill's suite.

George stood outside the door. "He's in there with the President, Mr Downwood – can I help you? Or you'll find the Inspector by the main gate."

"Do you want me, Mr Downwood?" said Walter joining them in the corridor.

Downwood adjusted his Arab headdress. "There are still three German para-troupers on the loose. We know they have explosives, grenades and rifles."

"Thank you for the intelligence." Walter smiled.

George nudged Walter as Downwood swept away. "Where did 'e find that outfit – a bad fancy-dress shop?"

***

2 December, A Cellar in Tehran

The Germans were late. Ebtehaj, with his brother and cousin, sat in silence in the cellar and waited in the dark. A grey light fell on the stairs as the German assassins descended. Ebtehaj stood up and pointed his gun.

The Germans froze.

The brother took advantage of the confusion, darting around each one, relieving them of their weapons. The cousin followed, tying the three Germans by their wrists. He shoved them one by one to the floor and bound their feet. He turned on the light to examine his work. Dust rose in the glimmer from the bare bulb illuminating the filthy cellar.

Holten-Pflug glared at Ebtehaj. "I will kill you for …."

Ebtehaj stuffed a rag in the German's mouth and spat in his face. "Let's go." He switched off the light and shut the door, leaving the Germans writhing on the dirty floor.

The brothers ran together to the British Legation.

Downwood came to the gate.

Ebtehaj was panting. "The three Germans are tied up in the cellar. You can go and get them. And don't forget my five thousand American dollars"

In the cellar, Holten-Pflug writhed on the floor, twisting and winding his body against his bonds. Foam lathered his lips as he cursed himself over and over.

The Iranian waited at his house for news. He paced the courtyard. It had been two hours and Ebtehaj had not returned. He picked up his gun and tucked it into a holster, beneath his robes.

"I'm going to the cellar," he called to his wives.

Ebtehaj's cousin was standing guard. He did not see his executioner.

The Iranian shot him in the head. He kicked the body to one side. He stepped over the pool of crimson blood and opened the door to the cellar. At the foot of the stairs were three shadows.

Graf sat up. "It's the Iranian. Down here!"

The Iranian cut the bonds tying Holten-Pflug, Dietrich and Graf. "Help me – I had to kill a man standing guard outside."

Holten-Pflug nodded to Dietrich. He followed the Iranian into the street. They lifted the dead cousin down the steps.

Holten-Pflug spat dirt from his mouth. "Hide him at the back."

Dietrich touched at the cousin's clothes. "I'm going to take his robes. This outfit I'm wearing stinks and is too tight."

The Iranian uncovered the two high powered rifles hidden at the back of the cellar under sacks. He handed them to Holten-Pflug and Graf. "The only safe place to hide you now will be at a Police Station."

Dietrich began to undress the dead cousin. "I'm going to change my clothes then search the cellar for the grenades."

The Iranian opened the door and peered into the street. "I'll take you first, sir with Graf and come back for Dietrich. All clear – let's go."

The nearest police station was five minutes' walk from the cellar. The duty officer was an enthusiastic supporter of *Hitler-Shah*. The Iranian handed him £5,000 of counterfeit sterling, printed at Sachsenhausen. He left the Germans to rest in open cells guarded by the police, to wait for the announcement the leaders were leaving.

***

Ebtehaj and his brother were wet with sweat when they arrived back at the cellar. "Go get the weapons. Over there – under the sacks at the back of the cellar." Ebtehaj looked around for his cousin. "Where is that stupid boy?"

They opened the cellar door and heard a rustle.

Ebtehaj put his index finger to his lips. He crept down the stairs.

275

Dietrich was alone, busy fixing small bombs inside his jacket.

"Where are the others?" Ebtehaj drew his gun: "*Hände hoch!* Get your hands up!"

Dietrich dropped one of the bombs and it rolled across the floor.

Ebtehaj kicked it back towards the German and kept his gun on him. He called to his brother: "Go and get Downwood. Something's gone wrong here."

The brother nodded and ran off.

Ebtehaj's dead cousin was lying under a pile of old rags in the gloom at the back of the room.

Dietrich's hands were tacky as he fidgeted with the three Gammon Grenades strapped to his chest and he began to work the detonator out of his pocket. If he could just fit it into the grenade.

Downwood met Ebtehaj's brother in the next street. He was, driving a small jeep. "Get in. Where are the others?"

"Ebtehaj's holding a German at gunpoint in the cellar," replied the brother.

Ebtehaj waved his gun at the German to begin walking up the steps. Dietrich smiled. He had almost positioned the detonator into his bomb.

Without warning, the Iranian arrived back at the cellar at the same moment. He had given his gun to Holten-Pflug, but reached into his pocket for a grenade.

Ebtehaj anticipated the man's intention and using his expertise as a wrestler, tripped him and pushed him down the stairs on top of Dietrich. He yanked his brother from the jeep and threw him with the ease of a professional wrestler, across the street and fell on top of him. The cellar door blew out with the explosion. They were showered with rubble, pummelling their heads.

Downwood lay in the gutter covered in blood.

Ebtehaj helped his brother up. They limped over to Downwood. Ebtehaj leaned over his body. "Too late. He's dead …."

***

2 December – The streets of Tehran

At 05:00, the local police guided Holten-Pflug to the spot he had chosen for his marksman. A three-storey building commanded views of a long, straight road. From there, they would be able to get a good head-on view of the cars travelling to the aerodrome. Holten-Pflug noted the British security services must also have decided it was a good spot for a hit. A sentry had been posted in the actual spot Holten-Pflug had chosen to put his marksman.

Holten-Pflug and Graf were dressed in the traditional long, pale-blue robes worn by the mass of immigrant, Arab workers. The clothes skimmed the floor, concealing their German army boots. A white turban covered their hair. They had stained their skin with a strong tea solution provided by the Iranian. Like many of the local men, they wore sunglasses. They sauntered across the road in front of the target building, watched by a British sentry. The sun was already bright.

They stopped at the back of the building, where a tiled staircase led to the first and second floors.

Holten-Pflug withdrew the long blade strapped to his leg. "Start an argument with me. Don't speak in German – make angry noises."

Graf began shouting and pushing Holten-Pflug.

The British soldier on the first floor turned towards the quarrelling men. "Halt. Do not enter the building."

Ignoring him, the *Arabs* continued their dispute as they ascended the staircase, hidden from the view of the other sentries.

"Halt. Do not come any further." The guard raised his gun.

Still, the *Arabs* argued with each other and continued to climb the staircase.

"Halt. Or I will…."

His command was interrupted as Holten-Pflug withdrew the blade and sliced the sentry's throat in one quick, expert motion. He lowered the body to the floor.

"Quick – strip him of his uniform, Graf." Holten-Pflug removed his Arab robes, put on the dead sentry's uniform and took up his post. He waved to the sentries in the buildings on either side.

The British sentries signalled back.

Graf slid forward on his belly to the open window and took up his position as marksman. With little shade, Graf was bathed in sweat.

Holten-Pflug eased the collar of the British uniform from his neck, it was sticky and unpleasant. Blood from the dead sentry had seeped into the collar of the shirt and appeared as a dark stain. As the sun rose higher, he stepped back into the shade. He moved forward again, when he realised the other guards could not see him. Holten-Pflug sniffed the air. "Graf, can you see someone cooking? I can smell garlic – but it could be sulphur mustard gas."

Graf scrutinised the street through his rifle sight. "I can smell a charcoal fire, so I think it's a civilian."

Holten-Pflug turned his head from left to right. "If Churchill's car doesn't arrive soon, the British might change the guard. Keep a look out."

***

Same day: British Legation

Dust rose as the procession of cars rolled into the courtyard. Churchill got into the rear of the last vehicle. The engines idled while the staff loaded the luggage.

Just as the procession was ready to drive off, Walter opened the car door: "Sir, I've had second thoughts about joining the convoy. Would you mind getting out of the car?"

George got out from the passenger seat. "Oh, 'ave you got some more intelligence?"

"No, George – it's just a gut feeling. Walter bent forward to catch Churchill's eye. Sorry, sir, but would you please wait in the building a few moments."

Winston got out of the car. "Very well, Thompson." He trudged up the steps and slumped on a chair in the hall.

Dr Moran waited in the courtyard and wiped sweat from his forehead with a large white handkerchief.

George held out his arm to prevent the doctor taking a seat in the second car. "Here you are, sir – take this vehicle." George, ushered Moran into the very seat Churchill had just vacated. "Would you like a cigar, sir?" George offered Moran one of Churchill's own. "Here, let me light it for you." George closed the car door, tapping the roof twice to indicate that all was ready for the driver to move off.

***

The minutes ticked by for Holten-Pflug and Graf. At the end of the long, narrow road, a group of vehicles shimmered. Graf looked up and Holten-Pflug nodded. Graf edged into his firing position. He rested the end of his rifle on the windowsill, checking the cars in the sights. The first car approached, all the occupants wearing military uniforms.

"Hold your fire." Holten-Pflug moved his weight from foot to foot. "If you shoot at the first car, it might stop, and you won't get Churchill."

"Yes, sir." Graf set his sight on the next car.

The first car raised a cloud of dust as it passed, making it more difficult to see who was in the next car. Graf surveyed the area. "It looks like chiefs of staff. I can't see Dietrich in position in the street.".

"Let it go on." Holten-Pflug fidgeted with his rifle.

"The next two cars each have four men – none of them are Churchill." Graf set his sight on the cars.

"He must be in the last car... the one in the distance." Holten-Pflug felt his pulse race.

Graf steadied the long rifle. "Yes, I can see a fat man smoking a cigar."

The driver of the last car realised he had fallen behind the convoy and accelerated to catch the others. By the time he reached the spot Graf had picked out, the car was doing 65 miles an hour.

"Fire. Fire!"

A cloud of desert sand flew in the air. Graf could not see his target. The bullet skimmed across the roof of the car. It was still a tribute to his marksmanship, with the poor Russian rifle.

Back at the British Legation, Churchill sat and drew out a cigar in the back of a battered old army car Walter had found in the garage.

Walter put his hand out. "The cigar, sir – it's a dead giveaway."

Churchill grunted and passed it to his bodyguard.

The ancient army vehicle, with some old trunks strapped to the top, chugged through the back streets of Tehran on its own. The sentries were leaving their posts, their duty completed. In a few more minutes, after Churchill and Walter's car had passed, they would discover the dead sentry, but for now, no one gave the old car a second glance.

Walter remained on alert and saw everything. They were about to pass a bundle of rags lying in the dirt, in front of a smoking building and an upturned army jeep. Walter raised his hand. "Stop the car, George."

He jumped out and knelt in the gutter. The rags were worn by an injured man. "Keep guard, George."

Walter examined the man, lifting him up to the car. Blood oozed from a wound on his head. "Open the rear door, George. Sir, would you like to take the front seat?" Churchill grunted and moved to the front. Walter manoeuvred the man into the car and got in.

George handed Walter a medical kit from the trunk. "Let's go, George." Walter wiped blood from the man's head.

Churchill turned around to get a better view. "My word, it's Mr Downwood."

Walter checked Downwood's body for wounds. "You seem to have got your disguise from the wardrobe room of the pantomime *Aladdin*. But without it I wouldn't have recognised you again so easily."

***

As they boarded the plane later, Churchill looked at all the old trunks piled on top of the dilapidated army car. "Get the luggage, Thompson," he chuckled.

Walter smiled and handed the bloodied Downwood to Dr Moran and his assistants on the plane.

George sighed. "Oh, the good doctor made it."

The latest part of *Operation Long Jump* had been a failure. Holten-Pflug was not prepared to return to Oberg and report the fiasco – so he shot Graf in the head and decided to disappear. He had a suitcase full of counterfeit notes from various countries. The dangerous psychopath resolved to find the Iranian and secure a passage to South America – but what was left of the Iranian and Dietrich decorated the walls of the filthy cellar in the centre of Tehran.

CHAPTER 26
Luc – Traitors

11 December – St-Laurent-de-la-Cabrerisse, Corbiéres Hills, France

In the little bar facing the River Nielle, Luc stretched and lifted his glass to a portly man named, Xavier – the *Maire*. "Here's to you and your *Maquis*. I deliver my charges to you for a safe passage to Spain, *merci monsieur*."

Luc had returned from Switzerland and scouted out the house at St Genis. He was surprised to find the old couple still in residence. It was only a matter of time before the meticulous Germans would find they were not on their lists and arrest them. He looked over to where Henri and Gertrude were sitting by the window. Henri had half emptied the bottle of *Ricard*, while the water in the jug was almost untouched.

Sylvie, the barmaid, brought the old couple two hot dishes of *cassoulet* – a local dish of duck, sausage and beans. She looked over to Luc, "Would you like to eat your dinner at the bar?"

"Oui, merci." Luc was glad to have at last passed on the responsibility of looking after the old couple to others. Henri might have helped the group, but Luc had a strong underlying dislike of the man.

Later that evening, Luc came across Xavier as he was leaving the little church next to the bar. "Huh, I'm not quite sure if I want to help the man you brought me." Xavier spat on the floor.

Luc shouldered his rifle. "What do you mean? If it wasn't for him, I wouldn't have had a second identity. I've been hiding out in Switzerland for months. I thought I'd better save the old couple as the Germans are getting very organised, categorising everyone."

"The old lady has gone to bed, and the man is boasting about his forgeries."

Luc lit a cigarette. "Oh, yes, he is an excellent forger. He saved many of us by giving us good papers."

"No doubt. But he's drunk, and he's boasting about how he got rid of a love rival by making deliberate mistakes. A man called Martin."

"That *putain con!*" Luc threw his cigarette to the pavement and ground it. "Henri." He flung open the door to the bar. "What's this about making mistakes on Martin's papers?"

Henri cowered in the corner. "I didn't. I didn't." He fell to his knees, knocking over the jug of water.

Sylvie wiped the table with a cloth. "That's not what he said earlier."

"Show me your papers, Henri." Luc grasped Henri by the collar, pulled open his jacket and snatched the papers from his inside pocket. A vein pulsed on his temple. "Hand me a pen please, Sylvie." With a shaking hand, he opened Henri's identity papers and wrote across them in large capital letters the word *TRAITRE*. He flung the papers in the puddle on the floor and walked out into the cool night air.

Xavier was waiting in the street. "What do you want to do with him?" He offered Luc another cigarette. They stood there for several minutes, smoking. "All right, we'll deal with him for you." Xavier exhaled white smoke. "The old woman can live here with us. I'm glad not to have to go to Spain. The mountains are swarming with crazy, fanatical Nazi's looking for the holy grail."

"Thank you, I'm anxious to find my old friends in the Resistance and re-join the fight."

As they walked away from the bar together, Xavier shrugged and sighed. "I suppose the *Maire* will have to write up a report that he fell off his bike and fatally hit his head."

"And will the *Maire* do that?"

"I will."

1944
Invasion

CHAPTER 27
Walter – D-Day

5 June – Southampton and Churchill's apartments

Churchill stood holding his hat by the gangplank of *HMS Princess Astrid*. Seagulls called overhead and the air was fresh with salt from the morning tide. His team were standing in line beside him, Walter, George and Bunny. She looked stunning in a moss green suit and pill box hat.

Thousands of young men shuffled forward, in long lines, to board the ships. As the men passed their Prime Minister, they touched his coat.

Churchill looked every soldier in the eye. "Good Luck."

Troop carrying trucks lined the dock, waiting to be loaded. Each had a chalked slogan: *First Stop Berlin, Up yours Adolf* and *Save Hitler for me.*

Bunny smiled at each man. Some dropped their eyes and flushed with the attention. She reached over to Walter.

He gave her hand a little squeeze.

Churchill's eyes were heavy. He leaned against the handrail. During the last month he had toured the country, making certain all was prepared. He had been relentless, observing, making final checks and asking questions.

A bright-eyed soldier winked as he boarded the ship. "Got your free ticket for France, Mr Churchill, sir?"

"They won't let me go, Private or I'd already be aboard. I'll be there as soon as I can."

"We'll clear a path for you, sir."

"Thank you. Best of luck."

George opened a boiled sweet and offered one to Bunny. "We'd have been on board that ship if it wasn't for the King. The Old Man was determined to be in the first wave, but the King told him if he went, then he would come too. He was forced to back down – couldn't 'ave the King getting shot."

The last of the men, a private, stood on the gangplank and called out: "Mr Churchill, what did you think of our food yesterday?"

Churchill smiled. "I didn't think it was half bad. But what did you think of it?"

"A bit more meat next time, sir. You should've seen the faces of them cooks when you came in for a bite."

"Just doing my job – checking everything's working well. I'll try to get the men more meat." Churchill waved.

Orders were shouted and cranes creaked with the weight of tanks and trucks being hoisted aboard.

Churchill gave them the *V* sign and took out a cigar. Walter lit it.

The men responded with "Three cheers for Winston." Some gave cheeky *V* signs.

Churchill waved his handkerchief until the ship turned into the Solent. It joined the 5,333 ships waiting at a point by Spithead to sail to France. They were loaded with 156,000 men of all the Allied nations, thousands of tanks and trucks, hundreds of American tugs, miles of pontoons, dozens of concrete floating jetties, large floating cranes armed with guns, motor torpedo boats, and *queer ships* each with a secret new invention, designed to foil the German's defences. The biggest armada in history.

Churchill boarded a motorboat and toured the harbour, waving and giving the *V* sign. Hope … to every man. He leaned on his bodyguard as he disembarked at the dock. "Right then, Thompson – to the station and back to London."

As the train left Southampton, they steamed past a city of tents built for the embarking troops. Thousands of trucks and tanks lined the roads and filled the fields. Every warehouse was full of stores, ready to be taken to France.

Non-resident civilians had been moved from the area and service personnel held within a 20 mile radius. Participating troops were confined to barracks or ships – all leave cancelled.

Churchill smiled and gazed up at the sky from the carriage window as hundreds of American bombers flew overhead to clear a path for the ships. 10,000 planes would take to the air to support the invasion – tomorrow.

***

London – same day

Churchill was puffing and blowing at his desk – his head bursting with plans for the forthcoming military action.

Bunny sat waiting for dictation.

"So, Miss Shearburn, this is it. Send a memorandum to all Cabinet Members to let them know the plans have been put forward 24 hours because of the prospect of bad weather. Tomorrow is the big day – the invasion – D-Day."

Bunny returned to the desk in her small office and concentrated on her typing.

Walter opened the door. "I've never seen so many ships as I saw today in Southampton." He walked to the window and checked for anything unusual. "Did you hear the impromptu speech he made to the troops?"

"Yes – it was simple, but effective," replied Bunny. "Rather like me."

Walter fiddled with the blackout blind. When he turned, Bunny was standing right in front of him, dangerously close. She leaned towards him just as Downwood burst through the door: "Mr Churchill's calling for you, Miss … Oh, hope I wasn't disturbing anything…"

***

6 June – The War Rooms – D-Day

The next day, Walter rose early. He found a cup of tea and a biscuit waiting for him at his station. He drank it as he walked to the Operations Room, to discover what was going on.

286

The air was electric. Everyone was sharp and alert doing their jobs with skill – passing on urgent information about troop landings and enemy resistance.

Churchill stood on a rostrum and smoked his cigar.

George observed from the doorway. "The deception seems to have worked. I've been up all night watching it unfold. The Germans were not ready at all. They thought they 'ad another two weeks to prepare for it. Their main defence is still at Calais. Our cipher ship tells us the Germans believe the Normandy landings are a diversion. They've not moved their main armoured force. I can't believe it. Everything's going so well."

At the back of the library, an enormous table dominated the room, covered with a map of the French coast. Young women, wearing headphones were moving labels representing ships, aircraft and troop movements.

George waved at the map of France. "It's the biggest operation of all time – ever. All night long, we pounded their defences. The fighters have only set down to refuel. Then they've been back in the air, protecting the bombers and strafing the enemy. The Mulberry harbours are being floated now.... My God, I would love to be there to watch. Battleships are bombarding the beaches over a 50 mile stretch. The first to land have been the amphibious tanks. Next have been the Royal Engineers to clear a way through the mines. The Commandos, we saw off yesterday, are landing on the beach, hidden by smoke and scrambling across the sand to disable the German shore batteries. Some of the Commandos are going forward inland to support the Para-troops, who landed at midnight."

Walter stared at a label marked *54th Argyll and Sutherland* – Bernie's regiment. "How many casualties?"

"The orders are that the US Coast Guard Cutters are there to pick up injured men – on no account is any ship or landing craft to stop for survivors on the way into land. The tough objective is to get the men on the beach. The problem has been the German guns – there's thick concrete surrounding the installations and even direct hits from our ships are having little effect."

"Are we winning?"

"Yes, we think the Germans may already be short of supplies. Hitler is using obsolete French tanks to back up his *Panzers*. They've got *Panzers* making their way up from the South, the 2nd division, but the French Resistance have been asked to try and stop them."

"Do we know who are missing? The 54th there, how are they doing?"

George's face dropped. "We've lost 12 ships and 48 landing craft and a further 60 vessels are reported damaged – but we're making headway. The 54th are still intact or the girls would have taken their label off the map."

"Bernie's in the 54th…."

"Then he's on Gold Beach. The German guns have been disabled there. Can you imagine what it must be like? A vast fleet sailing across the English Channel, like nothing that's ever been seen before. Men scrambling off their landing craft into the water and firing on the enemy: parachutists, ships, planes."

"My sister's returned to France."

"But she's with the Resistance, isn't she? They were warned. I'm sure she's not in the way of this lot."

Walter fell silent, withdrawn behind his façade. He touched the paper serviette in his pocket, folded into a swan. *We're coming Stella – hang on.*

CHAPTER 28
Stella - A Costly Manoeuvre

6 June – A field near Limoges, France

At first light they heard a throbbing of turbocharged *Wright Cyclone 9* engines approaching from the north. Stella had been tapping out the *OK* message every 10 minutes in Morse code. She stood close to the hedge as a whole flight of US *Flying Fortresses* came into view. Everything had gone as she had hoped. It was a breath-taking sight, and the first time supplies had been dropped by day.

After her rigorous training with the SOE at Arisaig in Scotland, Stella was smuggled back into France by boat. She landed in Collioure, a small town on the Mediterranean and had been collected by Xavier and his men. Her first job was as a courier, cycling from place to place with messages or explosives in her basket. But now, everything was better organised and less amateur. The SOE had provided her with a new identity, as a widow bombed out from Brest, with the name of, Nathalie Boucher.

In March, the SOE sent her to take charge of a network based in Limoges. Soon after her arrival, she had linked up with Pierre and Nicole, both of whom were running smaller units there.

The *Maquisards*, the name given to her group, swooped down on the hundreds of containers dropping from the sky and loaded them on the waiting trucks. Stella tapped out the last *OK* signal when the operation was complete. She was about to disconnect the radio set when it started to receive a message. She grinned, clapped her hands and did a little dance on the spot. It was the one message she had been waiting for: *Action Stations. D-Day*. A twig snapped behind her, she felt for her gun, left the equipment and slipped into the trees.

"Put your hands up." She pointed her gun at the figure examining her radio set.

"Would you shoot an old friend?" asked Luc.

"Oh, Luc. Is it really you?" She pushed the gun into her belt and flung her arms around the tall, thin Frenchman.

"I thought it was time to come back and join the fight." Luc kissed her on both cheeks.

"Oh Luc – it's wonderful you're back. You couldn't have picked a better time. The Allied invasion – it's on."

"What, today?" Luc shouldered his long rifle.

"Yes – and we have a really important job to do. We've been instructed to delay the tanks, the 2nd *SS Panzer Division*, to stop them from killing our men landing in Normandy. The longer we can hold them up, the more men can get ashore."

"So, it's Normandy." Luc helped Stella pack up the radio.

"Yes, and we must hold up the *Panzers* for as long as possible, at all costs. I've been sent here by Churchill's Special Operations people to help organise the Resistance in backing up the Allied invasion."

"How many people do you have?" Luc picked up the heavy radio set and followed Stella to a truck parked in the shelter of the trees.

"I've got 3,000, but I hope to recruit more as news of the invasion spreads." Stella climbed in the driver's seat.

"What's the strength of the *Panzers*?" Luc placed the radio in the truck.

"There are 15,000 men, a crack division, 209 tanks and self-propelled guns. Incidentally, about a third of the men are French and from Alsace – what bastards. Oh Luc, you look just the same. Come on, let's get you to our HQ. It's an old cheese factory. Pierre, Nicole and many of our old comrades are there."

"You mean the good Father, Pierre still lives? Well, that must mean anything's possible."

***

8 June – Bretenoux, France

Two thousand *Maquisards* lay in wait for the German *Panzers,* at a narrow point in the road, where it cut though a small hill. Stella touched a delicate purple flower, growing from the rocks, where she hid.

"It's a wild orchid," said Pierre. "Apparently ten different varieties grow here. That one is called a military orchid – let's hope it's a good omen."

Stella pulled the stem towards her. There was no perfume. "We can't win against them, we're too lightly armed. But we can hold them up – delay them getting to Normandy. If we keep laying mines, we'll dent their morale."

Pierre had a stack of improvised bombs at the ready. "Make sure you give me good cover when I throw these."

Luc crawled to their position. "They're coming."

Stella raised an arm.

It was just before noon.

The rumble of diesel engines grew louder. And the unmistakable squeak of metal wheels on tracks, a sound only a tank can make.

An armoured car led the column. The ground trembled as it ran over the first landmine, shot into the air and burst into flames.

Stella raised her arm again and the *Maquisards* began firing at the infantry, who had been meandering between the tanks and armoured cars. The *Maquisards* benefited from the height advantage and the snipers killed 45 German infantrymen before they could take cover. The column halted as the tanks became stuck in the small gorge.

André, a fighter recruited by Pierre, ran forward with one of the anti-tank guns. The Germans mowed him down with machine gun fire before he could shoot. He twitched as he lay on the ground. Pierre crawled forward to try to reach him but was held back by enemy fire.

A wave of 20 infantrymen tried to scale the steep bank. Stella screwed up her eyes as the Germans were massacred. Blood sputtered in a pink mist from each man as bullets from the French machine gun emplacements tore through their exposed bodies.

Injured men gave out agonising screams for help – some called for their mothers as they died. Their comrades took cover behind the tanks trapped in the gorge. No one came to help the wounded.

The *Masquisards* were holding the Germans back.

Stella watched a bird land on a branch of the tree she was using for cover. It settled and began to sing.

The *Masquisards* let of a round of fire at a German head that appeared from the first tank.

The bird flew off.

Ten minutes passed.

Stella jumped as one of the injured German soldiers appeared directly in front of her. Luc shot him in the head.

The Germans were ordered to advance in numbers. Despite punishing machine gun fire a few scrambled to the top. Grunts and screams came from the men during fierce hand-to-hand fighting. But the *Masquisards* were experts with their knives. Blood spattered the rocks as each German lost his life.

The driver of the leading tank began to make small, sharp movements back and forwards to drive over what was left of the armoured car and escape the trap.

Luc understood his intention and dashed forward to recover the anti-tank gun from André.

Stella shouted at Pierre: "Quick. Give him cover!"

The tank began to move forward.

Luc picked up the gun, pointed it at the tank and pulled the trigger. It jammed. The tank's machine gunner saw his chance and sprayed bullets at Luc. Luc pulled the trigger again. This time the gun fired, hitting the tank far too high to disable it. When Stella looked through the smoke, the tank had lost part of its turret. The machine gun and its operator were nowhere to be seen. Luc was lying on the ground.

Stella blew her whistle to sound a retreat. She knew they must run to save themselves as they had no chance of winning once the Germans emerged from the little gorge. She looked back at the orchids; their purple flowers wore a new fragrance – death.

***

They ran to the waiting trucks and cars. Had they caused enough damage to ensure the 2nd *SS Panzer Division* would be delayed? They drove fast to the little town of Brive-la-Gaillarde, hoping to take cover in its narrow streets. Here, the *Panzers* would find it difficult to move their large turrets. Machine guns and other weapons were already in place in some of the houses.

***

9 June – Brive-la-Gaillarde

It was just after dawn and the mist was rising from the valley.

"There are German tanks coming up the street." Pierre called to Stella as they sipped water from their metal flasks.

Stella looked out of the post office's second-storey window at the approaching convoy. An armoured car led the procession. "What's that strapped to the hood of the leading armoured car?"

Pierre leaned out of the window to get a better look, then shrunk back.

Stella spat out her drink as she realised it was one of her injured men. She shouted the command. "Let those bastards have it, but leave the armoured car"

Pierre drew one shutter over the window. As the armoured car roared closer, he recognised his friend André tied prostrate to the front. Across the street, the *Maquisards* opened fire with a machine gun on infantry and tanks. A bullet zipped past Stella's cheek. Pierre closed one eye and held his rifle steady. He felt his index finger on the warm metal of the trigger and squeezed. A German infantryman who had spotted their position fell to the ground.

"Signal to Nicole," shouted Stella. "We can't hold them here." She was about to open the window that had one shutter closed. *Boom.* Splinters of wood showered the room. The floor dropped from under them. "Damn." She fell back on a rafter.

Pierre fired off one more shot from the window. "Quick, before we're surrounded." They started to run down the stairs. German artillery had blown a hole through the first floor. The stairs were on fire.

Luc appeared below them, his shoulder bandaged but still holding his rifle. He struggled to wedge a plank up to where they were stranded. "Slide down…."

"Luc. Oh my friend – I thought we'd lost you." Pierre began his decent.

"Lucky you've got rid of those stupid robes, *mon ami* – they'd get all caught up."

On the ground floor, Stella peeped around the door that led outside and checked the street. They raced away from the sound of the guns.

"If we get separated, meet me at the next rendezvous," shouted Pierre.

A dust cloud mushroomed over them as they ran. They were deaf for a minute and lifted along with the force of the blast as they escaped. Stella looked back and was pelted by tiny pieces of rubble – the post office was in ruins.

They ran to join the mêlée of dust coated, hysterical townspeople – screaming and running.

German infantrymen stood in the town square. Panic stricken women and children abandoned their possessions. Stella and Pierre weaved between the carts, bicycles and baby carriages, blocking the main road. They did not look at the troops. An explosion boomed in the next street. A *Panzer* tank burst through a small house into the square. People screamed. Pierre and Stella ran across the road. Luc waved to them and disappeared into a side street with Nicole. Pierre stopped, crumpled against a wall, gasping for air.

"Come on. Come on Pierre… you can make it."

"I'll make it… I'll make it… run on ahead."

They were in the northern part of the town. Stella had a stitch and was slowing. Pierre glanced into an alleyway.

A German dispatch rider was urinating against the wall. His motorcycle and sidecar were parked at the end of the alley. The engine was still ticking over.

Stella and Pierre looked at each other and drew their revolvers. They raced towards him, firing as they ran.

The first bullet hit the soldier in the arm, and he fell against the wall. The second bullet hit him in the shoulder, and he fell backwards.

Stella jumped on the motorbike and looked back at Pierre, his face red and sore with tears.

Infantrymen were at the far end of the alleyway. As soon as they caught sight of the dispatch rider lying in a pool of blood, they fired, and bullets flashed past.

Stella opened the throttle wide, and Pierre almost fell off the sidecar as he was climbing aboard. "Hang on."

Pierre looked up at her from the sidecar. He reloaded his gun. Before they had reached their destination outside Tulle, a German armoured car was behind them.

Stella headed for the sunflower fields to the north, where Nicole's group were waiting. She had already planned their retreat to this place, where the fields would provide good cover if they were overrun. Stella was relieved to see Luc had made it.

He massaged his shoulder and was clearly in pain. "Bullet went right through – I'll just need six weeks bed rest." He kissed Stella and Pierre. "I need a pistol. I got hit right where I hold my rifle."

Stella reached behind her to a gun tucked in her belt. "Here take my spare."

Pierre put his hand on Luc's rifle. "I'll take care of her – I know you've given her a name."

"Carla – it means one who possesses strength."

Red dust rose in the valley as two enemy trucks ground to a halt beside the German armoured car. A detachment of twelve infantrymen sprang from each truck and began combing the tall flowers.

Stella abandoned the motorcycle and sidecar. She ran into the fields with her comrades, coming face to face with the big yellow sunflowers, smelling of candy and sugar.

Stella crouched, hidden by the thick stalks. She withdrew a long, thin knife from a leather sheath concealed inside her trousers. The crackle of an infantryman coming up behind Pierre, alerted her. She slipped behind the German soldier. Her knife held to his throat. "Shhhhh...."

Pierre turned and put his hand over the German's mouth. They forced him to the ground. The man struggled. Pierre hit him a sharp blow to the head with the butt of his gun.

Stella took the German's gun and knife. "Leave him, Pierre, you've knocked him out." She crawled away to hide.

Pierre wasn't leaving anyone. He gripped the man's throat until his shallow breathing stopped. All the time, he thought: *Were you the bastard that killed André – strapped his injured body to an armoured car and drove around while he died in agony.*

Stella's face was lined with concentration.

The German troops were picked off one by one by Luc and the other Resistance members. When they had all been killed, seven *Maquisards* dragged the corpses of the German drivers and infantrymen into the road. They piled them into a makeshift barricade.

Pierre cut open the trousers of an *SS* officer, sliced off his testicles and stuffed them in the corpse's mouth. "That's for André." Pierre spoke with a murderous rage Stella had never seen before.

"André?" Stella touched Pierre's arm.

"Yes, the hero with the anti-tank gun." Pierre shook her off and spat on the ground. "He was my *special* friend. This will fucking hold the bastards up."

"Oh, Pierre. Would André have wanted us to sink to their level? We will move to the hills and engage the *Panzers* again at point four, as agreed." She pulled Pierre towards her.

"Leave me alone," he growled.

The *Maquisards* moved off to a nearby hill to watch the approach of the column. They lay together in the undergrowth and spied on the units of 2nd *SS Panzer Division* through field glasses.

SS-Brigadeführer Heinz Lammerding led the *Panzer* tank unit personally in order to reinstate morale. He wore the German cross in gold on his breast pocket, with the oak leaves at his collar. He looked tall and handsome as he stood stiff in the front of an armoured car. His lips drew into a thin line and he stopped the column, with a wave of his gloved hand, in front of the barricade of corpses.

The German losses had been slight, but their courage had been dented.

"Send some men to gather up the bodies. Turn around." Lammerding ordered his

Unterscharführer to drive to the rear. He passed each of his officers, barking new orders.

Lammerding surveyed the adjacent countryside, catching a sudden glimpse of reflected sunlight in Stella's field glasses. "Ha. I see them – they're up on the hill. *Scharführer*, take 50 men and assault the hill. Bring me some of them alive."

Pierre was the first to move. "My God, they're coming up here. Make a run for it." *The Maquisards* scattered deeper into the hills.

Stella hesitated. "Wait – something peculiar is happening." She was mesmerised by the whole column doing an awkward about-turn towards the town of Tulle. The brief joy of watching the German's halt their advance was replaced with fear. The enemy burst up the slope on motorcycles.

"Come on, Stella." Pierre slung Luc's rifle over his shoulder. "Everyone's gone."

Stella took hold of the double handles of the machine gun. "Save yourself, Pierre."

"No. Come on."

"Pierre, I've got the machine gun. Go. This is an order. The others need you. Go."

"You crazy girl." Pierre turned and ran down the other side of the hill towards a farmhouse.

Stella opened fire with the machine gun. The German bikes skidded to a halt. *Scharführer* Straub, a stocky career soldier knew the range of the weapon he was up against. He kept his men at the right distance and surrounded the machine gun.

"Get behind the gun." Straub waved his arm at his best man, indicating the rear of Stella's installation.

Each time she fired a burst, the man crept forward.

Discovering she was running low on ammunition, Stella decided to fire one more round and then make a run for it. She had given Pierre five minutes head start. She crouched and turned – straight into the path of the soldier. He pointed his gun at her head. She raised her hands. He snatched the pistol from her belt and then ripped her knife from its sheath. He pushed her forward towards *Scharführer* Straub who twisted her wrist as he marched her downhill to SS-*Brigadeführer* Lammerding.

"This is our enemy, sir." Straub threw Stella into the dirt.

Lammerding leaned forward and lifted Stella's face to his. "What, one French bitch? Take her to the town, *Scharführer*."

***

9 June – Tulle

The German column crawled in a line back to Tulle. An eerie mist rose from the steep valley sides. The mountains cast a dark shadow over the town. The river looked black and not one flower bloomed along its banks.

Stella circled her wrists to ease the bite of the rope binding her hands. She lay on the floor of German truck by the feet of the infantrymen. *Scharführer* Straub rested his boot on her back.

Lammerding stopped his armoured car outside the fire station. "*Scharführer*, get me one of the engines and tie the woman to the side."

Stella wobbled as she tried to balance on the black, rubber hoses strapped to the outside of the water tender. Her wrists burned from the rope attaching her raised arms to the top rung of the metal ladder.

"Drive the engine around the town, Straub. You will announce through the megaphone, for every German killed today, 10 Frenchmen will die."

Straub obeyed. 500 infantry men toured the streets – with hate in their hearts over the deaths of their comrades.

"*Raus. Raus.* Get out." The soldiers shoved an old couple out of their house into the street.

"Take him to the factory." The German officer in charge took a silver cigarette case from his jacket pocket as he gestured towards the elderly man.

"No, no." The old woman fell to her knees on the hard pavement, knocking the cigarette case out of his hand.

"*Dummkopf.*" The officer cursed and kicked the woman hard in the belly. "Take her too."

They were shoved and booted to the town square to join the other men, who were standing to attention at gunpoint.

298

SS-Brigadeführer Lammerding touched a serviette to his lips in the *Brasserie du Ville*, while his men turned the town upside down, searching for men to execute.

Straub opened the café door and reported, "Sir, we can't find any men. They've all gone into hiding."

"Then use *Gestapo* techniques." Lammerding, clicked his fingers for more wine. "I can wait. I have dessert to sample yet."

Behind the counter of the café, Claude, the owner squatted and trembled under a tablecloth, while the two women served the German.

Straub commandeered every house in the town to billet 15,000 troops before he stood at the doorway of the most elegant building in the main square. He turned to his *Korporale*. "We shall billet here." Marching through the front door and into the hallway, he waved with casual arrogance at a frightened woman and her two young daughters. "We will eat in 30 minutes."

The woman hurried away to the kitchen to rustle together what little food she had to make a meal for the Germans.

Straub looked at the certificates on the wall of the family dining room. *Rousset, A. – certified dentist. Rousset, M. – certified dentist.* "So, which are you?" he asked the woman as she entered the room with a basket of bread. "Rousset, A., or Rousset, M.?"

"M. – Madeleine Rousset." Her voice quavered as she left the bread on the table.

"And where is your husband?" Straub tore a piece of bread from the baguette.

"He's attending his mother's funeral in Toulouse." Madame Rousset scuttled from the room, not daring to look at the German.

The *Korporale* sat down at the table. "Well, *Scharführer*, how are we going to find any more men for *Brigadeführer* Lammerding?"

"We will eat, wait and listen," replied Straub, tearing off more bread.

After dinner, Straub demanded silence in the house while the Germans sat in different rooms smoking cigarettes.

There was a faint sound, as if someone needed to ease an aching arm or leg in a cramped space. Straub stood up and tiptoed into each of the other rooms, listening hard. He put his index finger to his lips and beckoned his *Korporale* to join him upstairs in one of the bedrooms. They both heard the noise this time.

"It's coming from under the floorboards," Straub said, smiling. The *Korporale* rolled back a small, patterned rug to reveal the loose boards and pulled them up. A man was curled up in a small gap between the joists.

"Get him out." Straub marched down the stairs. Madeleine Rousset was waiting in the hall, trying hard not to betray her anxiety.

"*Madame.* We found a man in your bedroom."

The *Korporale* dragged the man into the hall, a revolver at his head.

"Antoine. Antoine!" Madeleine choked on tears at having let his name slip so easily.

"You know this man?" Straub sneered.

Madeleine Rousset nodded, wiping her face.

"Take him," ordered Straub.

At midnight, one hundred men stood to attention and faced German guns in the courtyard of a factory in the town.

Women and children, holding hands, observed behind the blue metal gates. Some sobbed. Infantrymen with fixed bayonets on their rifles prevented them getting closer.

Lammerding watched through the restaurant window. He stood and the waitress handed him his hat and gloves.

The cook and waitress put up the shutters and locked the door as soon as he stepped into the square. "What will we do with Claude?"

Claude jumped when the waitress lifted the tablecloth. "Don't worry about me – I'll hide. You girls go home and lock your doors." He made his way down to the cellar and moved a cupboard – concealed behind was a small room with a camp bed. *I never thought I would need to hide in the same place I hid the Jewish families.* He lit a small oil lamp and closed the door. In the flickering light was a message scratched on the wall by one of the families: *Merci. Votre bonté ne sera pas sans récompense par Dieu.* It thanked him and told him told him his kindness would not go unrewarded by God.

Lammerding walked along the lines of Frenchmen. He studied each one. "You've got dirty shoes," he told one man. "You can't possibly be a law-abiding citizen."

"But major –" protested the man.

"*Scharführer.* Take him away."

"No, no," screamed the man. "Please. I was just working in my vegetable garden today. Please, NO."

The other Frenchmen began to surge forward, and 50 German infantrymen raised their rifles. The men shuffled back into line.

"No." The man struggled like a feral dog as four German soldiers put a makeshift noose around his neck. They strung him up from a telegraph pole.

He made guttural noises and his body jerked with uncontrollable convulsions. The crowd was transfixed as the man twitched on the rope until he died.

His wife dodged past the infantry men and lunged at the *SS-Brigadeführer*. "You German bastards…"

Straub shot her in the back of the head, and she fell at Lammerding's feet.

"Bring me the woman from the Resistance," demanded Lammerding.

Straub strode off to untie Stella from the fire engine. As soon as she was close enough, Lammerding grabbed hold of her hair and thrust her head into the face of one of the Frenchmen. "Is he with you?"

Stella rubbed her wrists and arms trying to restore circulation and did not answer.

"Is he with you, bitch?"

The man shook and tried not to meet Stella's gaze.

"No," murmured Stella.

"I think that's a *yes*," declared Lammerding. "Take him too."

Lammerding ordered his driver to park his armoured car in the street. He smoked while he watched *Scharführer* Straub continue the interrogations. Stella was dragged to face each unfortunate citizen, as they were condemned. By 02:00, there were 120 men of Tulle hanging from telegraph poles and balconies, like Lucifer's fruit.

Stella observed the Germans. *Lammerding's actions may have satisfied their desire for retribution, but it's delaying his schedule for reaching Normandy. Every hour he wastes here, more of our troops are making it up the beaches. What's more, the nerves of these troops are becoming frayed.* Stella calculated they looked like an army that could be defeated – not like the great victors they thought they were.

Lammerding yawned and stepped out of his vehicle. "Organise an escort to take the bitch to Paris," he instructed Straub. "I'm sure the *Gestapo* would like to talk to her."

***

19 June – 84 Avenue Foch, Paris

Over the next few days Stella was flung around in the back of troop carriers, supply trucks and cars. She was held in makeshift prisons or police stations each night. She observed everything she could about German troop movements and she tried to make friends with her captors. She chatted to ordinary German soldiers in her broken German. They fed her and treated her well as she was passed from one division to another.

In Orleans she was handed over to the *SS* and her treatment changed. The officer in charge pulled the rope tight around her arms until it broke the skin. When Stella cried out, he slapped her hard across her face.

She was shoved into a prison van which sped into Paris and stopped outside an ordinary looking five-storey house. Stella recognised it as the *Gestapo* headquarters. She knew she faced torture and interrogation. She wore a hard, blank expression.

Uniformed clerks and secretaries were dashing around the building, carrying bundles of papers. All talk seemed to be in sharp bursts. There was an atmosphere of panic as the *SS* handed her over to the *Gestapo*.

"This is Nathalie Boucher, she's sent to you with compliments of *SS-Brigadeführer* Lammerding. She was caught with the Resistance firing a machine gun outside Tulle. She is accused of atrocities to 24 soldiers in the Third Reich. Here is the report. *Heil Hitler.*" The *SS* officer gave a stiff straight-arm Nazi salute, clicked his heels together and passed the rope tying Stella's hands to the *Unterfeldwebel* in charge of the desk.

"Who do we have here?" Klaus Barbie picked up the report. "Now young lady, let's untie you and get you something to eat." Barbie undid the knots.

Stella held his gaze. She noted the cold, pale eyes that seemed to match the grey suit he was wearing.

Barbie handed the rope to the officer on the desk. "Put her in Room six. I will talk to you again later, my dear."

She was led upstairs and locked in a little attic room, a former maid's quarters. It had a wooden floor, a single metal bed with a filthy mattress, a metal table and a large skylight. As soon as the door was closed, Stella examined the skylight. It opened to the roof. The frame had been sealed by iron bars, which were bolted to brackets attached to the rafters.

She lifted the mattress and squatted to examine the iron bed to see whether she could use part of the frame as a makeshift screwdriver. Just as she was working loose a bolt holding the bed together, she heard footsteps. She lay on the bed, feigning sleep. The door opened. "Get up, *Madame*," said Klaus Barbie, with a smile as thin as a knife blade.

A young blond *SS* officer followed him into the room, bringing two wooden chairs.

Barbie took one of the chairs. "Please sit."

Stella pulled a chair away from the table and obeyed.

Barbie spoke in French. "Now, we already have a good deal of information about your activities and a number of your colleagues are already incarcerated in Fresnes prison. You can, of course, avoid joining them yourself, if you will freely give us the information we require. Let's start with something simple, such as your real name."

Stella stared past him. She breathed in the heavy smell of his *Tabac* cologne.

Barbie fingered Stella's false identity papers. "Oh yes, we found these stashed close to the machine gun you were firing. *Nathalie Boucher, widow.* No, I don't think so."

There was a stony silence from Stella. She had no illusions about this place, and was aware, whatever she told them, death awaited her. What she did not know was that this was the same man who had interrogated her husband.

Stella knew Barbie had captured Max, from the south of France. Barbie was said to have tortured the Resistance leader, placing hot needles under his fingernails and breaking his knuckles. His face had been beaten into a pulp, and he was whipped to within an inch of his life. But even though his face was yellow and his breathing heavy, Max still did not talk. When his bruised and broken body lay in a coma, the Nazis put his unconscious form on a chaise longue and displayed it publicly as a warning to other people accused of being part of the Resistance. That was the last time Max had been seen alive. Stella pictured him with his alluring smile and his trademark red scarf around his neck.

Barbie saw the smallest of movements at the corner of Stella's mouth as she remembered her good friend. "That's right, now just a few things to clear up. You will save yourself a lot of pain and trouble if we can talk together now."

But Stella did not reply. She stared into space. She knew from her SOE training she was only expected to keep quiet for 24 hours to allow the others time to reach safety. Ten days had passed since the executions in Tulle, but she had no idea how many of her comrades had managed to escape. She prayed the sacrifices of her group and the brave people of Tulle had been enough to delay the 2nd *Panzer* division from reaching Normandy in time to engage with the Allies. *Where are the Allies? How long will it be before they reach Paris? Have some parts of France already been liberated? I have questions too. Where will you run when the Allies take back France? Because I am committing your face to memory – oh and those ears.*

Barbie began again: "How is Mr Brown, in London?"

Stella followed her training and concentrated on something complicated to remember, she focussed on a Hebrew prayer and blotted out Barbie.

"I know you are English."

Stella stared at the wall.

"You mutter English words in your sleep, you know. Actually, would you prefer it if we spoke English?"

Again, he received no response.

He began again, this time in English. "Let's at least get the basic details straight. Shall we start with your correct name? That's nothing sinister, is it?"

Stella remained silent.

"I like to clear up these matters. Perhaps you can tell me about your education. I presume it was an English grammar school."

Stella still looked blank. She was reciting the Jewish prayer over and over again in her head.

"If you don't wish to recall your schooldays, maybe you would like to tell me where you trained to be a British agent working in France."

She did not hear the questions, just her prayers.

"Perhaps you would like to see one of your French friends? Or maybe your husband... you must be feeling lonely without any friends or relatives to see you. If you give us a few names, I am sure we can arrange for some of them to visit you here."

Barbie spent another 10 minutes trying to coax Stella into talking, then lost his temper. "Tomorrow you will be begging to talk to me. Take her to Fresnes. We will get you to identify a few of your friends there. If you don't want to talk to me, you can watch them suffer."

The young *SS* officer escorted Stella down the stairs where the staff were busy moving boxes into a waiting truck. A young woman carrying files tripped on the pavement, causing hundreds of papers to fly into the air. Stella's *SS* escort was distracted for a second and she pulled loose from this grip. Before she could run, he caught her, held her firm and shoved her into a waiting car.

The German officer was tall, slim and fair. Stella amused herself by wondering what he would be doing now in Germany had there not been a war. She found herself recalling memories of happier times – her wedding, the opening of Europe Express in Paris, Martin... Stella blinked away a tear from her eye as she realised she could no longer conjure up a clear picture of Martin's face.

The *SS* officer noticed her changed expression. "You will regret not talking to us, you know. Why not talk to me? We're about the same age. If there was not a war on, we might have been friends – or even lovers." He sat next to her and stroked her face as they drove on, but Stella maintained her silence.

The young officer commanded the driver to halt at the top of the hill on the outskirts of Paris, to allow Stella to see the prison. He liked to give the *Gestapo's* victims a good view of the daunting building they would be occupying. Its windows were black holes covered with mesh or bars, and the masonry was green and slimy where the damp had crept in.

Stella was not afraid: she had been here before – something Barbie could never have guessed. The secret knowledge made her feel strong and confident. She thought of Patrick with his red hair and his birthmark. *Is he still here? Can he help me escape?*

***

26 – 30 June – Fresnes prison

Stella was hurled into a small, damp cell with a high barred window and a concrete floor. The cell had a metal door with a peephole, a bucket in the corner and an iron-framed bed with no mattress. At dawn, there was the heavy stamp of boots on concrete, and the rattle of a metal trolley bringing thin coffee and a few ounces of bread.

The days were filled with screams from other cells. Doors crashed open and shut and the old prison echoed with sounds of torture. Prisoners were not allowed to sleep for more than an hour. The guards slammed open the peep-hole cover, flashed a light in the prisoner's face and banged it shut. Stella retreated into her faith and talked with her God amidst the horror.

After days of starvation rations, Stella heard different steps nearing her cell. *"Tribunal,"* announced the guard, pushing her out of her cell and into line with seven other gaunt women. Stella studied them. She thought some looked English, but said nothing. *If only Luc's cousin is still working here. Did he stay after we got Henri Leclerc out? Would he be able to help me?*

They were shoved into the tiny wire-mesh cubicles of a prison van, speeding them away from Fresnes and back through the streets of Paris.

Stella could see men and women enjoying coffee in pavement cafés in the bright sunshine. When the van came to a halt outside *Gestapo* headquarters, they saw an extraordinary sight. Stella flushed with a warm glow – there above the city were German bombers in the daylight chased by RAF *Spitfires*. There were gasps from the prisoners and all eyes looked at the sky.

While the guards were distracted Stella touched fingers with the women either side of her. The women followed suit, just for a second, with the women chained either side of them – a tiny gesture but an overwhelming sense of hope from the vision passing over in the sky.

Inside 84 Avenue Foch, the hurried walk of clerical staff seemed frenzied.

Stella was taken to the same attic room. *They are preparing to leave. Thank you God. Ha – they've removed the bed. So how can I escape? Oh, there's a slight draught where the ceiling joins the rafters.* She got on her hands and knees and felt along the floor. There was a short, loose floorboard and she began levering it up, undeterred by her broken nails and bloodied fingers. She knew much worse waited for her in a second interrogation. All at once, she succeeded in prising away a shard of board. She dug away at the soft damp plaster in the corner of the room next to the rafter. Droplets of blood from her fingers mixed with damp plaster. She scraped the pink mixture and hid it in the space where the floorboard had been.

The sound of heavy boots up the wooden stairs made her jump. Her hand shook as she replaced the board just in time and sat on the floor in the corner of the room, as the door was flung open. A guard appeared carrying a metal plate of fatty sausage and potatoes. Without looking at her, he placed it on the table and left. Stella's heart was thumping as she forced the food into her mouth. She was weak and needed energy for her escape.

During her stay at Fresnes, she had eaten starvation rations and not once glimpsed a familiar face. Where were they all – Pierre, Nicole, Luc and the others?

307

As soon as the guard closed the door, Stella tipped what was left of the food on to the table and began to bend the metal plate against its edge. She soon managed to crease the metal and working it back and forth, broke the plate in two. She admired her tool and she got to work chipping away at the plaster. She stuffed food from the table in her mouth as she worked.

Through a crack in the door she could see into the corridor. The clerks had almost finished moving paperwork prior to evacuating the building.

The frenzy had saved Stella from certain torture by Barbie. Another girl held in the same building was stripped naked and forced into a tub of freezing water, while Barbie pulled on a chain holding her under. She was only allowed to gulp air while Barbie demanded answers. As Stella dug, the girl next door, floated in the bath – her dead vacant eyes staring at the ceiling.

Stella was too frightened to talk to anyone in Fresnes, but she listened to the warnings shouted from the other cells. Stella hurried to dig out the plaster – she knew she was next.

She put another piece of sausage in her mouth and chewed while she worked. Soon, she had made a small hole, and could see daylight between cracks in the clay roof-tiles. She began working as if in turmoil – her life depended on it.

After half an hour she had created a gap big enough to pull herself through. She slid the table over and climbed up, but she was weaker than she realised. As she struggled through the hole, she slipped, cutting her bare arms on the jagged edges of the broken wood. She needed something else to stand on, but there was nothing in the room apart from a few of the roof tiles she had dragged through.

Stella looked at the tiles and began piling them up, fitting each one onto the grooves of the next to make a step. She reached out and took more tiles until her step gave her just the height she needed to haul herself through the gap and on to the roof.

Outside at last, Stella sat on the roof to regain her breath. She rubbed her aching arms and the summer sunshine soothed her battered body. In the street below, the German soldiers no longer had their usual air of boredom – instead, they were hurrying.

She studied the skyline. The four-storey building next door was close enough for her to reach, if she slid down the gable. She edged her way down the angle of the roof. The red clay tiles were warm against her back. She slipped, sending little pieces of mortar down to the street. She froze. Her body ached as she tried to mould it to the pantiles. No one shouted an alarm or even looked up.

Across at the adjoining building, there was an open window, but she would have to pass four other windows to reach it. *Take a chance. Sidestep... sidestep .... Sidestep ... made it.*

Stella looked at her trembling legs. *I want to die fighting, not slipping off a roof. A few more feet. Right, let's have a look and see who is in this office. Merde, German uniform. Well, he's got his back to me. No time like the present.* Stella tiptoed across the window ledge, unseen by the German officer.

Second window coming up. Who's in here? ...Oh good, no one. I can take my time.... It's very warm.... Next window... oh no. It's a typing pool. There must be 20 women in there. One will surely see me. What to do? ...Wait till dark? No, not an option, they will find I'm missing any minute. Right, chance it.

Stella peeped in again. There was stern-looking supervisor overseeing the typists. *Right foot, left foot... Slow down, heart... keep calm.... The last window. Urinals.* The hairs rose on her neck as she remembered the men's toilets in Vichy.

She climbed through the window and was shocked at her reflection in the mirror over the washbasin. With her short-cropped hair, she could pass for a boy. She splashed water on her face. *What a luxury, some soap.* She soaked the hand towel and bathed the cuts on her arms. She took off her filthy prison shirt and washed all over. A small man's raincoat hung on the back of the door. She slipped it on and stuffed her shirt into a waste bin. She filled the basin with water and washed her hair with the soap. As she dipped her head in the bowl to rinse her hair, the door opened, and an old man entered.

"Ah, there you are, Maurice, my boy," he said, not looking at her. "I'll just go in here and then we'll take the mail to the Post Office." He shut the door of a cubicle.

Stella pulled her head out of the cold water and parted her hair to imitate a boy's. She examined her clothes. The distinctive blue of her prison trousers would give her away in the street.

She went into the cubicle next to the man and stood on the bowl to look over the low brick partition. *This is like déjà vu. If only Martin was here....* A single tear dropped on to the man's head but before he could look up, she lifted the cast iron lid from the cistern and struck him on the top of his head. As he fell to the floor, she climbed into his cubicle and checked he was still breathing. *I'm so sorry – you'll have an awful headache tomorrow.* She unbuckled his belt and tugged off his trousers. They were too wide, so she rolled them over at the waist. She climbed back over the partition, leaving the man slumped on the floor inside his locked cubicle, with her rolled up prison trousers as a pillow for his head.

She looked out of the window and saw it was beginning to rain. She fastened the raincoat and walked along the corridor towards the stairs. She passed the post room – the door was wide open – empty. She picked up an armful of packages before starting down the stairs. Two men in suits ignored her.

Third floor, second floor, first floor, ground floor. The packages concealed her face. She walked confidently towards the outside door. A young woman held it open for her. The sign on the outside of the building read *Société Générale* – a bank.

Freedom. But where shall I go now? The light drizzle turned to a shower. She glanced along the street. *Our old apartment won't be safe. Pierre's apartment's not far away. He's not on any Gestapo index card as far as I know. So, if Pierre's concierge is at home, he'll let me in – after all, he was a Resistance sympathiser, as well as being very fond of Pierre.*

It was early evening, and Avenue Foch was crowded with men and women returning home from work, carrying umbrellas and dodging puddles. Spotting a German military van ahead, she slipped into a side street.

Two nuns were leading a group of schoolchildren along the pavement. Stella followed them, still clutching the pile of packages. The children hid her baggy trousers from passers-by.

"Bless you, sister," Stella addressed the middle-aged nun leading the procession. "Can you help me? I'm trying to reach a friend's apartment in the Avenue Bugeaud?"

"How can we be of service, my child?" asked the nun, examining the strange-looking person making the request.

"Could you please walk there with me?" Stella skipped a puddle. "I need to avoid German eyes."

"Praise be to God – are the Allies coming today?" The nun opened an umbrella.

"Soon Sister, soon…," Stella whispered.

"I don't see why not. It would only be a slight detour… Sister Thérèse, may I speak with you? The nun waited for the other sister.

"*Oui,*" replied Sister Thérèse.

"Could we assist this young person by accompanying her to her friend's home? It is only a little out of our way…."

"But, sister, it's raining." Sister Thérèse raised her eyes to the heavens for confirmation.

One of the children splashed his foot in a puddle, and the boy next to him laughed.

The nun in charge smiled. "Look, they're are enjoying the rain… it's just a little shower."

"Oh, I suppose it will be all right. Come along, *mes petits*, we're going a different way today." Sister Thérèse walked along the line of children re-organising them in pairs and winked at Stella.

Stella walked close to the sisters. She felt most exposed when they returned to the Avenue Foch and crossed the road. By the time they reached the Avenue Bugeaud, the children were growing tired and slowing down.

"Just another block." Stella held a small hand beside her. "I'm so sorry the children are getting wet."

As she arrived at the familiar building, she blew a kiss to the sisters and slipped through the door. The sisters giggled and the children marched on. She headed for the stairs.

"Psssst," hissed the concierge, a small, white-haired man with a moustache that seemed too large for his face. "Psssst."

Stella stopped and stepped back towards him as he waved at her from the door of his ground-floor apartment.

"Attention." he said, turning his gaze up the stairs. *"Gestapo."*

"Oh, merci bien, Monsieur Leblanc."

"Where have you been? There have been so many people trying to find you and Pierre. They have searched Pierre's apartment many times. My wife has been in and cleared up the mess. Now today, out of the blue, they arrive again and take the place apart. They are still up there. Come in here – wait until they go."

"They know about Pierre?"

"Someone informed on him – but we'll get the bastard. Come in… I'll ask my wife if she has some better clothes for you. She's in the bedroom."

Stella was glad to get in out of the pouring rain and she laid the packages on the sideboard. There was crashing from the apartment above and Stella dried her hair on a towel and changed into a knitted twinset and fitted wool skirt. Madame Leblanc, a round woman in her 50s with bright rosy cheeks, found her a large safety pin for the waistband and insisted Stella take her last pair of good stockings. She offered Stella a pair of expensive leather court shoes, but Stella chose a pair of Mr. Leblanc's boots as they fitted well, and she thought she would probably have a lot of walking to do to make her escape.

The banging from upstairs continued for over an hour and the three of them sat in silence and ate rabbit stew. Stella played with her paper serviette. All at once, the racket stopped, and they smiled at each other when they heard heavy boots descending the stairs.

There were muffled voices from the hall and then a hammering on their door.

"Open up. Open up!" The *SS* soldiers were trying to barge through the heavy wooden door of the concierge's apartment.

"Quick – hide in the bathroom," said Leblanc.

"No, you will be implicated with me. I must leave."

"You can't," the concierge pointed out. "There is no other door."

The pounding and shouting intensified. "Open the door, or we will smash it down."

"Oh, *chérie*, open the door." Madame Leblanc emerged from the bedroom, holding a raincoat for Stella.

Monsieur Leblanc opened the door and two *SS* officers barged in.

Stella had been searching through the kitchen drawers for something to use as a weapon. She grabbed Madame Leblanc from behind and held a knife to her throat. "Halt, or I kill her."

Madame Leblanc let out a shrill scream on cue and dropped the coat to the floor. The *SS* men stopped in their tracks.

The young fair-haired officer, who had been Stella's escort to and from the prison, strutted in like a peacock. "Put your hands up, or we'll kill her ourselves."

Monsieur Leblanc stood facing the Germans, his hands behind his back as he unfastened the window. Stella stayed motionless for a second. She shoved Madame Leblanc hard towards the young officer, unbalancing him, and darted for the window. *Monsieur* Leblanc threw it open and Stella dived through. Another two *SS* troopers were waiting on the pavement. They picked her up and twisted her around to face their officer as he looked out at them red faced.

"Damn you." The blond officer's neck puffed, and his hat was lopsided. "Arrest them all."

"Please, sir, I don't know these people." Stella squared up to the young officer. "They're nothing to do with me."

"Shut up – take them to headquarters."

A large black police van arrived, and all three of them were bundled into the back.

"I am so sorry, *Monsieur, Madame* – I fear I have caused you so much trouble."

***

The van brought Stella and the other prisoners to 84 Avenue Foch and deposited them in the reception area, where Barbie was just leaving. "I don't have time for these people. Take them to Fresnes."

Stella noted the *SS*, the *Gestapo* and administrative staff seemed to be in the final process of moving out of the building. A warm glow washed over her. *They are going. At last. They are leaving*

313

Paris. Thank you, Lord, it has all been worth it. She gave Monsieur Leblanc a little nudge.

Her smile would have been wider if she had known that on 6th June the Resistance destroyed 52 trains and blew up railway lines in over 500 places. Normandy was cut off to the Germans on 7th June with no telephone lines or electricity. Lammerding and his *Panzer* tanks wasted nine days in Tulle and never made it to the Normandy landings. Most of the men in her nephew's battalion would make it up the beach.

CHAPTER 29

Bernie - D-Day Plus 20, not D-Day Plus 2

26 June – Royal Victoria Docks, London

The tents at the Royal Victoria Docks hummed with the sounds of the thousands of young men. Every port in England was crowded with conscripts waiting to be sent to France.

Bernie put his hands on Johnny's shoulders as he stood in front of him in a long queue, leading to a marquee. "Calm down, Johnny, we're over on D plus 20 – not D plus 2, like our mates – you're going to be fine."

"Bern, I've never been abroad an' I don't wanna get killed."

"They're just gonna give us some occupation money and occupation rations. No one shooting at you today."

"Those poor buggers who took our place on D plus 2 got slaughtered, Bern. I hear 400 from our unit died on the beach – it must have been hell." Johnny fidgeted from foot to foot in the line.

Bob, their new friend waited in front of them. "Thank God we were needed here to shoot down those rockets Hitler sent over." He moved his arm in an arc and made a sound like a rocket exploding.

Johnny chuckled. "I have to admit, Bern, I was shitting myself last time we was 'ere. Can't tell you my relief when that nice Welsh Sergeant-Major shouted: Back in the trucks, lads. You're needed to shoot down the German flying bombs."

Bernie moved forward in the queue. "Those doodlebugs gave us a fright though. What about the flying bomb that hit our pub?"

Bob rubbed his arms. "Oh, to be back at the *Lamb.* The landlord was grateful for our help. But I'm still aching from clearing all that rubble and stacking the old beams."

Johnny sniffed his tin helmet. "I can't believe the taps still worked. At last a good use for this piece of kit. It's too bad we didn't get much time to enjoy all the free beer we were promised for clearing up the damage and getting the pumps working."

Bernie smiled as he summoned up a memory of the sign the landlord had erected outside the pub, which read:

Business as Normal – Thanks to the boys of the 54 Light AAK R.A. 9th Battalion Argyll and Sutherland Highlanders

He gave Johnny a nudge when he saw their truck, they named the *Gin Palace*, being swung on board the ship by a huge crane. Many of the other men in the battalion were curious as to why this truck was so special. A few had tried to sneak a look in the back.

The three comrades had made their truck as comfortable as they could – two small bunks had been fitted above the cab, and a large radio set took up most of one side. A bench and a small table occupied the other, which served as their kitchen. It wasn't much, but the gang considered it was their home.

When the young men reached the issuing point, they were each handed their survival kit: a sausage-shaped lifebelt made of canvas; a chemical-burning stove; tea, sugar and dried milk; matches; tins of meat; occupation money; and chocolate.

"Chocolate instead of cheese again." Johnny screwed up his nose.

"I don't mind. I like chocolate – my mum works in a chocolate factory with my girlfriend." Bernie pulled out a photograph of his mum, Iris and Stella. He was standing in the centre in boxing shorts with one arm in the air.

Johnny took the photograph and examined it. "What a great night that was. I was able to send me old mum a postal order for twenty pounds – that saw her right for a while."

As they left the issuing tent loaded with their provisions, Bernie spotted three women over by the barbed wire. "Come on, Johnny. Bob move your arse over here." He led Johnny by the elbow.

"Here you are, boys," said one of the women. She had a large enamel pitcher of beer in her hand and she poured them a generous measure each.

They drank the beer straight down before they could be discovered by the corporal and blew the women kisses.

"That's just what I needed," said Johnny. "A bit o' Dutch courage."

***

27 June – Liberty ship - Empire Pitt, Port of Tilbury

"More invasion money – or, should I say, card money." Bernie tapped his pocket, bulging with the strange notes.

"No one in their right mind is going to accept this stuff," said Johnny.

They watched as the heavy guns were hoisted aboard the *Empire Pitt*. This was one of thousands of ships built in a hurry from light materials and designed to transport troops for the invasion.

A lone Scottish piper stood at the end of the pier as they eased out of the dock and played *Cock of the North*. The men listened to the tune in silence as they sat on the deck and the ship moved towards France. Johnny rested a palm on his stomach, feeling a knot tighten. As the sounds receded into the distance, some of the recent recruits began to cry – certain they were going to their deaths.

"Sod this." Bernie jumped up and walked over to where the Argyll pipers were sitting near the lifeboat. He leaned forward and whispered something to them.

"Right – good idea," said the first piper. The second piper blew into his bagpipes. The instruments groaned as they came to life.

"How about *Brown Bear*?" Bernie pretended to tune his own bagpipes by holding his nose and tapping his index finger against his throat.

The men stared as Bernie led the pipers in a march along the deck. "Come on, lads – join in."

Johnny was the first to join the trooping. *Na, na, na-na na na. Na na na-na na....*

Soon, the conscripts were on their feet parading to the tune.

While everyone was having fun, Bernie smelled food. He guided Johnny and Bob to the stern of the ship, where lunch for the seamen was being served. Bernie looked at the meagre rations in his pack and then at the cook.

"Here you are, matey." The red-faced cook offered a plate to Bernie. "Best beef stew, roast potatoes and Yorkshire pudding going. Go on, take it – we've one over."

Bernie gave the cook a winning smile and took the plate. "I knew I should have joined the navy." He helped himself to mustard. "Thank you, cookie, you must be a mind-reader."

"I can spot a healthy appetite," the cook observed as he cleared away his trays.

"Grab a fork, Johnny, Bob – we'll eat a third each."

Johnny wiped gravy from his mouth. "Much better than our occupation rations."

"Ah, but not quite as good as the free beer we're missing at *The Lamb*," Bob said with a mouth full of food.

"But more filling than tea with the Presbyterians." Bernie put the last of the meat on his fork.

"I know where I'm going to be when the action starts," Bernie overheard a sailor saying to his pal.

"Where's that, then?" A naval rating looked around the deck.

"In the little triangular cabin on deck there – the one with all the ropes in. Safest place on the ship if we get hit."

His friend nodded in agreement, and the two sailors went about their duties. Bernie listened to all the conversations on the ship.

"Where's the lav?" asked Johnny.

"See those canvas tents slung out over the side?" Bernie pointed to the stern of the ship. "Well, they've got holes in them – guess what that's for?"

Johnny grinned. "Good job I only want a pee – looks like you'd need to be a trapeze artist for anything else."

Bob looked at the ocean and put his hands on his head and screwed up his face.

Bernie put his face in his. "What's up with you?"

"Can't swim, Bern…. What if ….?" Bob held his nose and mimed drowning.

Bernie pulled him up by his collar. "What about the swimming lessons we were given?"

"Never went. I had scarlet fever – was in the hospital for months," said Bob.

Bernie shook his head. "Well yer lucky your best mate's passed his lifesaving. If we end up in the water, stick by me and whatever happens don't fight me when I put my arm around yer neck. I'll tow you ashore – you great idiot – fancy not telling us before." He reached into his pocket. "Here's a couple of elastic bands, let's tie them to yer glasses, so you don't lose them in the water."

When night fell, the sailor went to look for his hiding place in the triangular cabin. There among the ropes were Bernie, Bob and Johnny, curled up fast asleep. Bernie opened one eye. "Come on in, Navy Boys – shove up, Bob, these two thought of this first – never forgive myself if we got hit and we'd stolen their safe spot."

The sailors joined the *Gin Palace* gang in the cabin, and they all drifted off to sleep.

During the night, there was an uproar from the aft hold. The young dispatch riders were larking around. Two of them held down, a tall boy called Shorty, and with clippers set to zero gave him a two inch wide parting from front to back. Later that night, the two culprits got a similar treatment, only diagonally.

The next morning the ship's company lined up for deck parade. The Welsh Sergeant-Major strutted along the lines of men. He stopped in front of the dispatch riders. "Caps off." He examined their heads. "Right finish the job – all off."

It helped to pass the day and take minds off from what danger might lie ahead in France. Roars of laughter came from the men as all the dispatch riders were given silly haircuts before it all came off.

The ship waited off the Isle of Wight – waiting for dark.

Bernie stood by the bow and called the others. "Come and look at this amazing, sight. There must be hundreds of ships; look big war ships, destroyers and frigates, loads of liberty ships like ours and tankers. That's funny, our company's three ships, *Empire*

Pitt, Sam Verne and *Sam Soaring* are anchoring right in the middle."

There was silence as night fell and the three ships provided music for the invaders. They each had a piper aboard, who took turns in serenading the others. It was a clear warm night and men of all ranks sat on deck and sang.

***

28 June – Normandy – Gold Beach, Courseulles-sur-mer

Bernie stirred with the arrival of dawn as his body realised the ship was no longer moving. The French coast sparkled in the warm sunshine. He rubbed his eyes and blinked at the sight of a multitude of boats surrounding the *Empire Pitt*. He called to Johnny. "Look at this lot."

Johnny squinted to bring the scene into focus. The sea boiled with hundreds of rhino ferries made from steel boxes joined together and powered by two huge diesel outboard motors. They were ferrying men and equipment ashore.

Bernie pointed out frigates, destroyers and gigantic battleships, and the flags of all the Allied nations. "Look, Americans, Canadians, Australians, Belgians, Czechoslovakians, French, Greeks, New Zealanders, Norwegians and Polish!"

He shielded his eyes from the early morning sun. "Bloody hell, this is some rescue party for Europe. I never thought I'd see so many ships or men. I hope we're not too late for…." Bernie didn't like to think of Stella; he had shut her out of his mind. His eyes misted as he allowed himself to say the words he had long been holding on to. "I hope we're not too late for… for Stella – and for Martin."

Johnny did not want his chum to become gloomy. "Hey Bern, I've heard the Froggies serve terrific grub."

They jumped off the Rhino ferry into the water and Bernie towed Bob with one hand and held both packs and guns out of the water with the other. He put his feet down and touched the bottom. "Stand up Bob. We can walk ashore. We're not out of our depth and take your own pack, I'm not yer donkey."

RAF *Spitfires* and American *P51 Mustangs* flew low along the coastline, protecting the wading men.

They held their rifles above their heads and sloshed though the last few yards of surf and clambered sodden through the sand dunes onto Gold Beach. Their woollen uniforms were dank and heavy with sea water.

Johnny tripped on a piece of shrapnel and his soggy uniform was dusted down one side in fine sand. "Good job the Gerries aren't here – I can hardly move."

Bernie twisted his beret and water ran from it. "What I'd give right now for one of those freezing showers at Colchester."

They found their Morris Commercial – on the dock at Courseulles-sur-Mer. Bernie took a piece of wet chalk from his breast pocket. He scrawled a few words on the board at the back of the truck: *THE GIN PALACE When in doubt – brew up.*

The other soldiers toiling up from the beach peered at the message and grinned.

Once the three friends had climbed in, Johnny started up the engine and was directed by the Red Caps through the dunes and into an orchard. "Cover yourselves with camouflage netting and disappear." The Military policeman waved them towards a high hedge.

While the *Bofors* guns were being deployed, they made camp. Bernie found a two-burner petrol cooker in a ditch, strapped it to the floor of the *Gin Palace* with a billycan on top of it and prepared to set up a mobile kitchen.

Johnny strung a rope between two trees, and they hung up their soaking uniforms. They sat in their underpants and drank tea from metal mugs. Bob collected their invasion money and pegged it to the line with the wet clothes.

Johnny chuckled. "Wish I 'ad a camera. 'Ere we are, the army of liberation in our Y Fronts."

Bob looked up at the money dripping over his head. "Hope no one thinks we just printed this."

The next day, in dry uniforms they got their orders.

Their regiment was assigned to protect the headquarters of the Canadian artillery from the *Luftwaffe*. Bernie was to be in constant radio link to all their regimental units as they set out on the road through northern France.

***

24 August – Elbeuf, Normandy, France

The Germans retreated, allowing the Allies to breakout from the Normandy beaches. Bernie's unit drove in a fast convoy across country to reach the front line. Their job was to report the location of the enemy and signal when they spotted planes. Each boy could recognise an enemy plane by its silhouette. They sent signals to the guns detailing what type of plane they saw, how many, the height and direction of flight. It was up to the guns to shoot them down before they could drop their bombs or machine gun the Allied troops.

"Driving this old truck is like fighting your way out of a sack of spanners. The gears are stiff and the suspension hard as a rock." Bernie rubbed his aching arm.

Johnny jumped every time they hit a pothole. "I don't wanna get killed, Bern. I 'ope these homemade sandbags I've made will do the job. Two trucks were blown apart, yesterday driving over landmines."

They swapped drivers without stopping. One boy would leap over the back of the driver's seat and hold the steering wheel while the other slipped into the passenger seat. One of the three always took a rest in the bunk. They travelled through Caen, Lisieux, Pont-Audemer and Bolbec and did not stop until they got to Elbeuf, on the banks of the River Seine.

Bob draped the Union Jack over the side of the truck before they started for the day. "We're a clear target to the *Luftwaffe*, but we're advancing so quickly and so near the front line, we're more likely to get caught up in a RAF attack. Let's hope their gunners see the flag. I've heard terrible stories of troops and trucks near the front line getting bombed by aircraft from their own side."

For six hours they sat and listened to the rain tapping on the roof of the truck. Without warning, the tapping was joined by the *click-click* of Morse code.

"Here we go, my lovelies," announced Johnny. "Here come the *Luftwaffe*. Expect to be under fire in one minute."

Bernie sat in front of the radio in the truck. He wore a huge pair of headphones. He spoke with a clear voice into a large, metal microphone attached to the *Twenty-One* set on the small, built-in communications table. His job was to warn the Canadian artillery units of the location of the German bombers, which were droning into view.

The first German bomb rocked the *Gin Palace*.

The Canadian Lieutenant, with mud splattered on his face, stuck his nose around the curtain at the end of the truck and stretched to pass Bernie a written order. "Quick – get this one off."

Bernie was calm, clear and precise. "Charlie Dog How Five calling Red Leader, over. Red Leader, over."

The response was immediate: "Red Leader, Charlie Dog How Five, over."

"Enemy in codes Baker Two Three Charlie One – under fire from Gerry, please assist. Charlie Dog How Five to Red Leader, over."

"Red Leader to Charlie Dog How Five, leave the target area. Repeat, leave the target area. Over."

"Wilco, Red Leader. Charlie Dog How Five, roger and out." Bernie removed the headphones. "Okay, let's get the hell out of here. Bob, pull down the Union Jack."

Johnny started the truck and headed out of the field. Bernie glanced out of the back. He was thrown off his chair as a shell exploded with a *whoosh* and a deafening bang, just where they had been parked a few moments before. He rubbed his bruised arm as he picked himself up and righted the chair. The *Gin Palace* was showered with mud.

"Fucking hell." Johnny accelerated the truck a safe distance away and Bernie and Bob bounced around in the back – hanging on. They found cover in some trees.

"We're well out of it then." Bob's voice trembled as he feigned a grin and rubbed his hands together. "Shall I put our flag back up?"

"Yes, four eyes, better let the RAF know who we are." Johnny handed Bob the flag. "I was talking to some wounded Canadians back at Caen. They'd been injured by the RAF attempting to fire on the Germans. It was bloody chaos. The ground troops were identifying their positions with yellow smoke. But the RAF know that yellow is the colour used to show up their target. The more the men tried to warn the planes away from their positions, the more the bombs were dropped. Anyhow, I think we'll be safe about here – so yes, if you wouldn't mind old chap, put the flag back." He pulled up the large handbrake on the truck.

"If in doubt, brew up, lads." Bernie lit the primus stove. His hand was shaking as he struck the match.

***

25 August – Haltwhistle

Emily sat at the dining table in Iris's mother's house, nursing a cup of tea as Iris turned up the volume on the radio set.

"This is the BBC from London. Here is the six o'clock news. The Nazi swastika has at last been taken down from the Eiffel Tower. After four grim years, the tricolour flies again, to tell all Parisians they are free. General de Gaulle entered the city this evening after the police went on strike at the Île de la Cité on the Seine. There has been heavy street fighting, and the Prefecture was taken over by the Resistance. General Eisenhower encircled the city and General Dietrich von Cholitz has surrendered. He has defied Hitler's order to destroy Paris."

Emily hugged Iris. "Where is Bernie? What has happened to Stella and Martin?" She wiped a single tear from her eye. "I wish Bernie would write."

Iris squeezed her hand. "Come on, chin up, the war might be over in a few weeks."

1–5 September – Northern France

It was hot and dusty along the advancing line of camouflaged trucks and guns, and the air was choked with diesel fumes.

Johnny crashed the gears of the *Gin Palace*. "I overheard the officer telling the Sergeant-Major we're needed to support the front line – and we're needed bloody fast. We've got to cover 50 or 60 miles at a time without a break."

After a few hours, Bernie noticed the boys on motorbikes were becoming fatigued. "They need to stop and rest, poor buggers."

The convoy droned on in a relentless line. The dispatch riders' faces were black with fumes from the trucks, except for where they wore small plastic glasses.

"Slow up, Johnny," Bernie called out. "Hey, Bob, I'm going to get Johnny to slow up to almost stop, and I want you to run alongside that bloke on the motor bike and jump on his bike for ten minutes while we give him a blow." Bernie called to the boy, "We're going to cover for you and give you a rest. Start to slow down when we slow down."

Johnny slowed to three miles per hour and the driver of the truck behind tooted his horn.

Bernie indicated with hand movements, they were helping the dispatch rider.

Bob leapt off the back of the truck, ran alongside the bike and the rider slipped off. Keeping hold of the handlebars, Bob jumped on the bike while it was still moving. Bernie grabbed the rider, who ran behind the truck, and hauled him in.

"I've got a nice cup of tea for you, mate... poor bugger can hardly talk. The fumes from the trucks and the long ride have exhausted him. Take those glasses off." Bernie washed the boy's face with soap and warm water and handed him some tea.

The boy sank into an armchair Johnny had stolen from a bombed-out house. After a few sips of the hot liquid, he spoke. "It really is a *Gin Palace* in here – thanks so much, you lot. Sorry, but I don't know your name."

"It's Bernie, and it's a pleasure. That's Johnny driving and Bob on your bike. How about a biscuit?"

The rider was soon refreshed. "You're a lifesaver, Bernie. My mate was killed on Wednesday – it was awful. He got tired and fell off his bike and was run down by the convoy. Thanks, everyone. I won't forget this. I'm Shorty by the way."

"Anything else we can do for you?" Bernie put the kettle on again.

"How about a pee out the back of the truck?"

"Watch out." shouted Bob from the bike, as he was almost showered.

"Go and tell your friends to follow the *Gin Palace*." Bernie helped the boy off the back of the truck. Before the kettle whistled, they had another tired rider in the back of the truck. Bernie's gang repeated the changeover operation all day, slowing down with Bob or Johnny taking turns to swap over with the next grateful boy.

***

It took four days for the convoy to reach their station. A blue flag hung out of the back of the *Gin Palace* as a signal for the next dispatch rider to approach.

They were just about to slow down when Bernie called out to Johnny, "Hold on a minute, keep your speed up."

Johnny obeyed. Bernie peeped from behind the curtain to see if the next rider was still there. It was the Welsh Sergeant-Major.

"What, don't I get the same treatment?" he called from his bike.

Bernie pulled back the curtain. "Slow down, Johnny – we have a VIP."

They gave the Sergeant-Major a warm reception. "Magnificent," he declared, and shook their hands as he left the truck.

After another hour of travelling in fast convoy, Bernie noticed the *Gin Palace* had slowed. "No need to slow down, we've had all the dispatch riders aboard now."

"Bern, take a look at this." Johnny called out as they reduced speed.

Ahead of them, by the side of the road, was a small man with a bicycle and a large metal box strapped to the handlebars.

"You don't think it could be, do you?" Bernie clambered into the front of the cab.

Johnny slowed the *Gin Palace* and leaned out of the window. "What have you got there, mate?

"Ice cream," a thin Frenchman with a brush-like moustache announced in broken English. "One ice cream for two cigarettes?"

The truck behind sounded its horn.

"Hold on, mate," Bob called out of the back to the soldiers gesturing at them to get moving.

"You're holding up the whole bloody convoy," they shouted.

"It's the ice-cream man. Two fags for an ice cream." Bob collected cigarettes from Bernie and Johnny, licking his dried lips as he took three ice creams from the Frenchman before Johnny drove on.

One by one, the trucks slowed in front of the ice-cream seller until his supplies were exhausted.

Bernie yawned and stretched when they stopped three hours later to make camp for the night. He parked the *Gin Palace* and the gang headed for the mess tent.

"I've double rations for you lot for your dinner tonight," said the cook with a cheery smile. "What's more, the Sergeant-Major's ordered all spare basic rations be given to you."

After savouring their army dinner, Bernie's gang left with armfuls of biscuits, tea, sugar, cheese and chocolate. As they strolled back to the *Gin Palace,* Bernie whistled *Kiss me goodnight Sergeant-Major.*

Johnny and Bob joined in singing:

"Now we'll 'ave something to feed our riders with," said Johnny, struggling to climb into the cab with ten boxes of biscuits. "And I thought you'd given away all my rations, Bern."

Bernie sat motionless in the front of the truck. He was far away, staring at an envelope he'd been handed with a Brighton postmark. Abraham Gold's handwriting was distinctive.

My dear Bernie,

I hope all is well with you and the brave boys in your unit. We are all well here in Brighton. As the days go by, we get more and more concerned about Martin and Stella. In your Aunt Stella's last letter, she said your Uncle Martin had been arrested. Then, as you know, she returned to England for a while, but has since disappeared. We think she has gone back to France. Your Uncle Walter seems to know something, but he says he can't speak about it.

I have tried to contact everyone about them. The Red Cross know nothing. The military seem to have no information. I can only appeal to you. You may be advancing towards Paris. You may be able to take some leave to look for them.

Please ask everyone you meet if they know of them. They were involved in some way with the Resistance movement. Perhaps they are hiding and plan to join the fighting as you boys advance.

Please write to me with any news.

God bless you,

Abraham Gold

Bernie bit his lip. He had no news. His unit was heading into Belgium and Holland. He did not know anyone who was going to Paris. As far as he could make out, it was mostly American troops sent to that part of France. Bernie searched his brain for what he could do to help. *Unless we are to get leave in Paris what can I bloody do? We're miles from there. I'm being sucked along by this huge tide called war, and I'm powerless to swim against it to help my family.* He folded the letter, replaced it in its envelope and tucked it down the side of the front seat.

"Bernie. Don't you want some of this grub?" Bob called out with his mouth full.

"And I didn't even have to nick it," said Johnny, laughing to himself.

Bernie snapped out of his depression at Johnny's magic words. "Grub? Who mentioned grub? Right, let's get the kettle on. *If in doubt, brew up.*"

***

"Charlie Dog How Five to Red Leader, are you reading me?"

A shell dropped just 100 metres from their position, exploding trees and blowing a crater in the earth.

"Fucking Gerry again. Let's move." Johnny leapt into the front seat of the *Gin Palace*.

Splatters of mud hit Bernie in the face. The earth trembled.

Bob pulled down his flag. "We're about to get blown to smithereens."

Johnny started the *Gin Palace*, but the truck did not move. It was dark and a lemon segment of the moon had set just after 17:00. Flares from the guns lit up the sky. Bernie slipped out of the truck to see what the trouble was. Both rear tyres had punctures.

"Both?" Johnny put on his tin helmet.

Another shell landed close by, covering the *Gin Palace* with branches from the hedge.

"Both." Bernie watched the others in his convoy begin a retreat.

Bob shouted above the deafening booms. "Bloody hell, the Gerries are just down the bleeding road."

"I know, I know." Bernie sprinted over towards the truck, where he knew he would find his Corporal. "Bit of a problem, Corp," he panted. "Two flats."

"Two? Well, you'd better leave it and go join someone else."

"Leave the *Gin Palace*?"

"Otherwise, you'd better beg, borrow or steal an extra wheel from someone – and make it quick, because the Gerries have got some heavy stuff coming up this road."

"Okay, Corp." Bernie ran down the line of trucks. "Lend me a spare wheel?"

"Sod off, there's no time to be changing wheels. Get in – we'll take you." The driver of the truck was about to pull away.

"No thanks," said Bernie jogging to the next truck in the line.

A dispatch rider caught up with him. "Got a bit of trouble?"

"Yes – the poor old *Gin Palace* has a couple of flats."

"Right. You start jacking her up. Me and my mates will get you another wheel." The dispatch rider accelerated off, throwing up mud.

"Blimey, thanks," said Bernie.

The shelling was growing unbearable, and Bernie could see across the fields the Germans' range was getting closer. The earth shook as shells exploded close by.

Meanwhile, Johnny and Bob were already removing the first of the back wheels to fix the spare they had. "Look at this bloody tyre. Bald," yelled Bob above the din.

The work was heavy and slow, but they were spurred on by the forbidding noise of the approaching enemy. Bernie and Bob finished changing the first tyre and crouched by the side of the truck to wait for the dispatch riders. The German aim seemed to be getting better. Another shell crashed in front of the *Gin Palace*, lifting the front wheels in the air. The truck listed to one side.

"We're going to have to leave her, boys. Come on you two – move yer arses." Bernie picked up his kit just as a shell exploded 550 metres behind them.

With no strength left to run, they walked in a bedraggled line along the side of the black, ash covered road. Shells crashed and exploded. Out of the smoke came three motorcycles. Their approach seemed to be silent, like angels. The engines were muffled by the continued whoosh and bang of the German artillery. They didn't hear the motorbikes approaching because of the din of the shelling.

"Jump on, boys," yelled Shorty.

They rode pillion for 20 miles before they arrived at their regiment's camp.

The dispatch riders pulled up outside a tent. "We've put this up for you, with some of our blankets inside and some of our rations – so you can have a picnic."

Johnny pulled back the opening of the tent. "Thanks, boys. That's more than decent of you."

Bernie, Johnny and Bob ate the rations left by the dispatch riders and drifted off to sleep as soon as they lay down.

***

In the morning, the reality of losing the *Gin Palace* began to take its toll on the morale of Bernie's gang.

"Fucking Gerry." Johnny punched the air.

They ate breakfast without speaking. The noise of a diesel engine broke the silence. Bernie stood up and peered over the hedge at the road. There was the *Gin Palace*, being driven by one of the dispatch riders.

"Oh, my angel." Johnny hugged Bob.

Bernie put his hand on the warm bonnet of the truck when it came to a halt. "I can't thank you enough. But you're not the lot that picked us up last night – what's going on?"

"We got the call from our mates. You've been a bit of a life-saver and you needed some assistance, so we got permission to get the *Gin Palace* back for you."

"That's bloody marvellous. Bloody marvellous." Bernie hugged the dispatch rider and climbed into the cab. He patted the steering wheel affectionately. "It's all still here. Who wants tea?"

***

14 September – Antwerp

Bernie drove the truck, avoiding potholes and boulders in the road. Local people lined the streets and smiled and waved at Bernie and his crew. When Bernie stopped at a junction a pretty young Belgian girl rushed forward. She gave Bernie flowers and stood on tiptoes and brushed a kiss on his sunburnt lips.

"Hey what about me?" Johnny leaned out the passenger window and an older lady, possibly the girl's mother, pulled his head towards her and smacked a kiss on his face.

Bob stuck his head through the window. "I'll wait 'till the young lady's done with Bern." He retreated to the back of the truck.

"Thank you," said Bernie, handing the flowers to Johnny.

The girl kissed him again. "No thank *you,* Tommie. Thank you and all the brave soldiers who have chased the evil Nazis away."

A truck full of strange-looking ammunition, pulled past them. "What are those new shells we've got?" Bernie asked as he blew kisses to the girl and put the truck into gear.

"It's some sort of high explosive called *RDX*. I've not seen them go off yet. Let's hope they give Gerry one right up his arse." Johnny slapped his side.

Bernie clapped his arm around Johnny's shoulder.

"Vive les Tommies!" shouted a woman. She held out her grubby, naked baby for Bernie to kiss from the cab.

He leaned forward and pecked the baby's soft cheek. The crowd cheered.

Without warning, there was explosion after explosion all around. The Belgians screamed and ran for cover as dust and debris rained down on them.

"Go back." Johnny waved the civilians back behind the bombed building.

"I can't go back – we've got the rest of the convoy up our rear end. I can pull off the road up here." Bernie manoeuvred the *Gin Palace* into a side street. "It looks like the Gerries have got mortars behind that block of flats. Come on, we'll leave the truck here." The gang abandoned the *Gin Palace* and took cover among the ruins of what had been someone's home. Bernie waved the civilians back further to a safe distance.

"Here – take this for the little 'un." He thrust his army blanket into the arms of the woman with the baby and pointed the way for her to escape. She hurried away, calling out, *"Dank U, Tommie."*

The mortar shells exploded in quick succession all around their position. Bernie pushed Johnny to the ground. "Keep your bloody head down, you idiot."

The air was sucked out from under Bernie's feet and he covered his face with his hands as he felt the heat of an explosion. An army truck rose in the air and burst into flames. The Welsh Sergeant-Major beckoned forward a small group of soldiers, carrying a *Bofors* gun. Bernie and Johnny rolled over in the dirt and choked as the German mortars fired at them again. Dust rose, but Bernie and Johnny could not move, their cover had been blown away and they were in danger of being injured by shrapnel. The Germans had them pinned down.

The Canadian artillery unit assembled the *Bofors* gun in less than a minute.

Johnny began to belly crawl away from the line of fire. "Fat lot of good that little gun's going to be. Look, the fools are aiming it at the building. Over the top, you idiots." Bricks and dust flew all around them as more mortar shells fell. Another truck was struck and burst into flames. The Sergeant-Major shouted the order for the men to fire the small gun. They aimed it at the front of the building, and a large hole appeared.

"Shit. Bernie, did you see that?"

The whole street shook as the little gun fired the new shell. The men fired again. Their aim was excellent: the second shell tore through the hole made by the first.

"Good shot." Johnny put his head up to get a better view.

"Get down, stupid. Keep moving." Bernie pulled Johnny back under cover of a low wall.

The German mortars replied. A garage crashed to the ground to the right of the Canadians with the gun.

Bernie put his hands over his face as they were enveloped in dust.

The small gun fired again, then there was silence. Johnny stood up, coughing and choking. The air was still thick with dust. As it settled, the building in front of them came back into view as an enormous pile of rubble.

"Those bleedin' shells are bloody dynamite." Johnny danced around, laughing at his own joke.

Bernie stood in awe of the drama in which he had just played a part. He walked back to the truck, thoughtful and hopeful.

A General from the Canadian headquarters sheltered behind the *Gin Palace*, observing the effect of the new shells. "Good God," he remarked. "That *Bofors* has developed into a useful gun now."

Bernie and Johnny were dumbfounded at being addressed by a General and stared at him open-mouthed.

"Carry on, lads," he commanded as he strode away.

"Do you think this might warrant a small celebration this evening?" Johnny asked, using the Canadian officer's accent.

"Bloody right, old sport," mimicked Bernie.

"I reckon those shells are about five times as powerful as the old ones," said Bob, popping his head out from the tarpaulin curtain at the back of the *Gin Palace.*

Johnny wiped dust from his face. "We'll have to celebrate with about five times as much beer. You been there all the time, Bob?"

Bob passed each boy a mug. "Couldn't leave the *Palace,* could I? – Kettle had just boiled."

***

15 September – Heading for the front line – Belgium

The tyres of the *Gin Palace* squelched through the mud as they pulled into a field made soggy by the soft drizzling rain.

"Park by the dispatch riders," ordered the corporal on duty. Bernie found a suitable spot by a hedge, where they stopped and made camp.

"What's that *horrible* smell?" Johnny sniffed the air like a nervous rabbit and leapt out of the truck, followed by Bernie and Bob. "Oh God, Bernie, look at this."

The mangled wreckage of a German anti-aircraft gun disfigured the meadow. "It's been hit by a rocket-firing plane – a Typhoon," said Bernie. "Look at the damage these things can do."

Johnny stared with an open mouth. A few other men came to look. Bits of skull, boots and bodies were all mixed up with the mutilated metal.

"We'd better do the decent thing and give them a proper burial," said Bernie.

The men fetched shovels and worked until they had dug seven graves. They placed the battered helmets they had found around the site on a stick at the end of each grave. The Sergeant-Major was informed, and he summoned the Chaplain. The soldiers stood with their heads bowed at the side of the first grave while he spoke a few words. Bernie glanced at the identity papers he'd been able to recover from one of the dead Germans.

"Well, they were the enemy, and they got what was coming," said Johnny.

Bernie held a picture of one of the dead soldiers in his hand. "He was 19. It says here '*Geburtsjahr 1925*'. Look at him – just like us. I'll give these papers to the Sergeant-Major."

That evening, the Welsh Sergeant-Major and the Abbe from the local monastery stood by the gravesides and sung acapella, in harmony – *Ave Maria* and *Abide with me.*

***

21 September – Antwerp

Johnny threw his canvas bag in the back of the truck and it landed with a thud. "Well that's the last of the supplies for now – couple of ounces of tea each and some tins of beef."

Bernie picked up the message in Morse he had just taken down for the Sergeant-Major. "We need to take another port. The only safe harbour is Cherbourg and it's about 500 miles away. We haven't got enough trucks and certainly not enough fuel for them even if we did. I've got another message here requesting, fuel, food and ammunition."

Johnny unloaded their meagre supplies. "Why can't we use Antwerp? I'm sitting 'ere looking at boats and cranes?"

"Take a look at the map. There's a good fifty miles of river before a ship leaving Antwerp can get to the sea. And guess who's got tanks on both sides of that river?"

"Fucking Gerry…."

"I've deciphered some very worrying messages the last few days. That little puffed up short arse General Montgomery, seems to have sent more than 34,000 air born troops to take the bridges leading into Germany. Only it's failed. It's possible only half of the men made it back. Some of the Canadian officers have been arguing about it. We're stuck here with no supplies doing bugger all instead of clearing the Germans from here to the sea – so Antwerp can operate as a port."

Johnny shrugged his shoulders. "We can 'ave some pork belly and eggs if you'll arm wrestle fatty the Chef."

***

10 October – Antwerp to Kloosterzande, The Netherlands

Bob arrived at the *Gin Palace* out of breath. "Bernie, Johnny, we've got to clear out our stuff from the *Palace* and give it over to the boys ferrying supplies."

Bernie was sitting at the Twenty-one set. "Well let's get to it and hope the *Palace* brings us back some decent grub."

They unloaded their gear into a warehouse at the port.

The Welsh Sergeant-Major came quick marching up to where the three boys sat on the quay skimming stones across the water.

The boys stood up and saluted.

"Stand at ease," said the Sergeant-Major. "I've got a special mission I need carrying out and I think your little team might be just the ticket." He produced some squares of grey fabric from a canvas bag. "The Germans are re-enforcing and supplying their positions along the river at night. Most of the roads are raised up over the low land – some pretty high in places. I'm looking for a team to go and place these patches in those places. You see it's a new material – it's reflective. Our search lights can pick it out – the material will light up and be the target for our gunners. If you take your portable radio, you will be able to talk to the spotters at the guns and they can look through binoculars in the day time and tell you where to place the material to cause the most damage. So how about it lads?"

Johnny raised a hand. "Is it behind enemy lines?"

Bernie clipped the back of his head. "We're not blowing up our own roads, Johnny."

The Sergeant-Major smiled. "This is mission is vital – I'm asking for volunteers."

"Good chance of ending up dead, Sergeant-Major? asked Johnny.

The Sergeant-Major nodded. He looked at the three boys in turn.

Bob stood to attention. "I'll go, if you boys will. It makes me sick to my stomach when I have to write down reports of our men getting killed."

***

11 October – by the side of the River Sheldt, Belgium

Bob drove the Morris Commercial C8 field artillery tractor as close as he could to enemy lines. In the back, Bernie and Johnny checked their gear, waiting for dawn.

Bernie blew on his hands. "Bob, wait over there for us and make sure you don't get bogged down in all this water – we might need to make a quick exit."

They climbed out and freezing sleet stung their faces. Johnny fastened the straps of the heavy radio on Bernie's back. He produced a hand towel from his kit bag and wrapped it around Bernie's neck. "Bend forward, Bern." He cut a hole in the centre of his ground sheet and threw it over Bernie's head, bending the twenty-foot-high aerial and passing it through the hole.

"Thanks, mate, that'll keep out the driving rain and keep the radio dry." Bernie put on his gloves. "Right, let's get going."

They trudged along the edge of a field keeping to the furrows made by a tractor, their boots becoming caked in the mud. The downpour was making it hard going. After about twenty minutes they saw the reflection of the rain on the hard surface of the road ahead. They followed the road until it crossed a dike.

"This is it, unstrap the radio will you, Johnny?"

Johnny lifted the radio set from Bernie's back, and they sat on the mud under the ground sheet. "Charlie Dog How calling Red Leader. Over."

"Red Leader, Charlie Dog How, can see your position. Picnic site five yards north. Over.

"Johnny, get the tent pegs and lay the first one another five yards along."

"Will, do Bern."

The boys repeated the exercise for another five patches. Johnny strapped the radio to Bernie's back for the final time, when it began to receive. "Red Leader – Charlie Dog How. Gerry coming to tea. 20 number infantry walking North on road."

Johnny picked up the handset. "Charlie Dog How – Red Leader. Acknowledged. Over and out."

Bernie crouched down. There was no good cover. All at once, Johnny leapt in the air like a gibbon. He snatched the top of the long aerial and fell on Bernie. "Sorry, mate it was sticking up above the dike – giving us away."

The two boys moulded themselves into the mud and tried to disappear as the Germans marched by on the road above.

"Red Leader - Charlie Dog How. All clear. Over."

They trudged back to where Bob was waiting. "Where the hell yer been?"

Bernie looked at the state of them both covered in mud. "Making mud pies. You have any trouble? We heard some wiz bangs."

"I came under fire but sat tight in this armoured beauty."

Johnny unstrapped the radio for Bernie. "This vehicle might look safe, Bob mate, but don't be fooled by its sloped sides – it's not armoured."

Bernie shook water from the groundsheet. "What was that radio nonsense about a picnic?"

Johnny took it from him and folded it. "Oh, Sergeant-Major called the operation *Teddy Bears* picnic'."

"So who are we – the three flaming bears?"

***

20 November – Kloosterzande, The Netherlands

Bernie's unit crossed the border into the occupied Netherlands at night, arriving early the next day. The new grey material, laid out on the dikes for the artillery, had proved successful. The gunners blew up the roads in just the right places when German convoys

338

were crossing. But over 12,000 British and Canadian personnel died securing Antwerp as the new port for supplies.

Antwerp was ideal for supplying the Allies because the cranes were still intact, and the Belgian White Army had disarmed all the bombs left by the Germans.

It was a long, hard battle along the river Sheldt for the Canadians and British fighting in mud. The weeks of torrential downpours made the going almost impossible. The Germans had already flooded the area by blowing up the dams.

***

The Sergeant-Major sat at a desk in the town hall organising the billeting of his regiment in the small town of Kloosterzande, founded by monks in the 12th century. Bernie was called forward and introduced to a smiling Dutchman, Mr Aarssen. "Welcome, *Tommie.* Follow me, I have my bike outside."

Bernie shook the Dutchman's hand. "Thank you, sir."

The Sergeant-Major handed Bernie a key. "There's a truck for you at the back of the building."

"Thank you, sir." Bernie felt the familiar key in his hand. He looked over to Johnny and Bob, still awaiting their turn. "See you later, for radio duty? Might have a surprise for you both."

The Sergeant-Major made sure the gang got the *Gin Palace* back – he knew it was good for the morale of the regiment.

Johnny gave him the thumbs up and was called forward and introduced to an old stocky woman for his billet.

Bernie glowed when he found the *Gin Palace* behind the building. "Here, let me." He lifted Mr Aarssen's bike into the back.

The Aarssen's terraced house was warm and clean. The family consisted of Florentin, or *Flop* to his friends, a thin, athletic man around 45, his wife Marta or *Ma* and their three children. Ma was a thin, cherry-faced woman with mousy hair. Elly, who was eight, was lively and cheeky; Grete was seven and more serious; and little pink Marritje just 18 months old. A large garage occupied the front of the house, which Flop used as a carpentry workshop for making furniture – although in wartime, the demand for coffins was much greater than for dining tables. Flop played the big drum in Kloosterzande's marching band and was also the local football referee. During the latter years of the German occupation, he had organised the delivery of the weekly underground newspaper, *De stem van de strijdend Nederland* – 'The voice of the fighting Netherlands'.

"Come in," said Ma Aarssen, kissing him on the cheek and ushering him upstairs. "This room is for you."

Bernie dropped his kit on the bed. "But isn't this your room?"

Flop slapped Bernie on the shoulder. "No, *Tommie*. This is for you – we insist."

"But sir, madam – I've slept in the truck for months, I don't need to take your bed."

Ma looked at his kit bag. "Have you got any washing in there you'd like taken care of?"

"Thank you," said Bernie. "But I really couldn't ask you wash my smelly socks."

"You can and you will," insisted Ma. "And I've heated water to run a bath for you. Leave me your smelly socks and everything else needing a wash and I will see to it while you're having your bath."

Bernie kissed Ma on the cheek. "I must stink. I can't remember when I last had a bath – oh yes I can – at mum's – 1941."

Flop laughed and waved his hand in front of his nose. "Come this way. We love you, *Tommie,* but we might have to evacuate the house if we don't get you some soap and water pretty quick. Here take this dressing gown and when you've had a good soak, put it on and come down to the kitchen for some food."

"It pleases me to see a young man enjoying his food." Ma Aarssen beamed at Bernie as he ate the pork and cabbage she had prepared him. "It's such a relief to meet an Allied soldier at last – even if the presence of the Allies on Dutch soil doesn't mean the whole of The Netherlands is free."

Bernie took another mouthful. "Are you really sure you can spare this food? I've heard about the *Hongerwinter* last year, when the Germans cut off food and fuel to your country for not helping the Nazi war effort."

340

"Don't worry about us – we'll be able to grow our own food again now. My brother's bringing us some chickens he's been hiding this afternoon – you'll have eggs for breakfast every day."

The Aarssens treated Bernie like a favourite son, spoiling him with the biggest servings, despite the fact they had few rations to share. Shortages of food and fuel were still severe, but Bernie helped them out with provisions, and Ma managed to produce a filling meal from the mishmash of odds and ends he was able to supply. Flop was grateful for Bernie's free weekly issue of 50 Players cigarettes.

CHAPTER 30
Stella - The Camp

Autumn – Ravensbrück, Germany

Madame Jeanne Leblanc approved of the clean, trim railway station at Fürstenberg, in the Northeast of Germany. They had travelled for over a week, and the journey was hard.

Stella felt responsible for her unfortunate companion. Seven days in cattle trucks, with no room to lie down, no food and little water, in the sweltering heat was taking its toll on the women.

Klaus Barbie had ordered Stella's execution at Fresnes, but Luc's red-haired cousin Patrick was still at the jail. He and his accomplices regularly moved prisoners from the *death cell* to another cell from where they would be shipped out of the prison. Patrick had not personally seen Stella, and no one knew they had met. A member of his group suspected Stella was English, and he made sure his German collaborator at the jail marked her in the file as a political prisoner and not a Jew. Political prisoners were treated better than the Jewish prisoners. The tide of events was turning. The smarter guards realised they might need a friend in a political prisoner to speak up for them when Germany lost the war.

Stella stretched as she felt a slight forest breeze across her back. It was welcome and cooled her tired body.

The women were assembled in lines – five across and marched along the road past neat cottages with manicured gardens.

"Perhaps I'll have to work as a maid in one of these nice little places?" whispered Madame Leblanc to Stella. She smiled at a German woman and her chubby son. They'd emerged from their front door to watch the daily spectacle.

"Jew." The little boy spat at Jeanne Leblanc.

"Filthy Jews." Insults were echoed by the neighbours who had come to stare.

"Holy Mother of God. What horrible people."

"Don't look at them," said Stella. "Come along, Madame Leblanc, I'll take care of you."

"Horrible, horrible." Jeanne hugged her handbag to her.

The wretched group of women marched for half an hour carrying the few possessions they had. Stella had the clothes she'd been arrested in and her papers marked *NN'* for political prisoner.

Jeanne Leblanc's heart sank when she saw the sprawling camp. It was surrounded by lofty stone walls, topped with four rows of barbed wire, charged with a high-voltage electrical current. Every 20 metres, there was a high wooden tower manned by two sentries with machine guns and high-powered rifles. She stared at the guards. "Do they think we are dangerous criminals?"

They trudged the last half-mile to the camp, where the huge double iron gates opened to engulf them in the despair that was Ravensbrück. To the right of the main gate was a mass of wooden huts with two tall, smoke-blackened chimneys. Hundreds of emaciated women, some with their children, appeared from their huts to gaze at the new arrivals.

The new prisoners were jostled and pushed onto the parade ground, then ordered to strip. 500 women stood in silence without their clothes but with all their dignity and nobility. The male guards sniggered.

Stella held Jeanne's hand and whispered. "Don't look at them. It is they who lack grace, decency and humanity."

After an hour, a small medical team arrived. The doctor shouted to the prisoners to come forward by name and by classification.

First, the women classed as criminals were called. They were given an anti-typhus vaccination and blue-and-white striped cotton pyjamas with a green triangle sewn on the jacket. All the women were given the same treatment, but each group was given different badges: yellow for Jews; yellow and red for Jews with children; black for prostitutes; and red for political prisoners, including Stella, Jeanne Leblanc and several more.

The guard looked at his list. "Boucher, Nathalie."

Stella stepped forward with her head held in the air as she thrust out her arm for the injection. Behind his gold-rimmed spectacles, the doctor's glacial grey eyes registered her attitude. He selected a large veterinary syringe, containing a saline solution, and plunged it into her breast. Stella fell to her knees and screamed. The doctor gave a slow, thin-lipped smirk and dismissed her.

The guards began to confiscate the prisoners' possessions, including their wedding rings. Stella removed her ring and handed it to the guard, smiling as she remembered how carefree she was on her wedding day.

"*Non, non.*" Madame Leblanc protested as she was forced to give up her own ring. She was about to struggle with the guard.

"Shh." whispered Stella. "It's just a piece of metal. They can't take away the love it represents."

"That's 35 years of bickering and arguing," said Madame Leblanc, and laughed. She was a good-natured woman who had forgiven Stella for having drawn her into danger. "*Ma chérie*, most of us have gone along with the Germans just for a quiet life. If it were not for people like you, we would have had to put up with them forever. Thank the Lord our arrogant invaders are on the run. And I shouldn't think we'll be here for long."

The prison guards were recruited from local women and a few men. The women were young but tough and muscular, dressed in grey uniforms with divided pleated skirts and high black-leather boots. With whips they herded the prisoners to their huts. Block 17 was for women whose papers were marked '*NN*'.

Stella helped Jeanne Leblanc to find a bunk. The hut, which had been built for 60, housed 300. It stank of human body odour and the buckets of urine at the end of each row. Crammed together were a hundred three-tier wooden bunks, each with a straw-filled, verminous mattress.

"Come, Madame, here will do." Stella indicated a top bunk that was free. As it became clear there were not enough bunks for all, Stella and Madame Leblanc decided to share the narrow bed. "I've been finding out about this place from the other inmates. It's a labour camp, of course, but apparently, it's better to volunteer for work than to be what they call a *floater*. Floaters tend to be given the worst jobs. There's a workshop making gloves for German troops on the Russian front, a clothing warehouse, and a workshop producing pots and pans."

Jeanne clambered up to sit on the top bunk. "Well, I was always rather good at needlework."

344

"Hey, watch where you're kicking." A thin woman in the bunk below tugged Jeanne's leg.

"So sorry, excuse me." Jeanne leant forward to acknowledge the woman below.

"Right then, you must volunteer for glove making. I will too." Stella climbed up being careful not to disturb the woman further.

A block attendant flung open the door to the hut. "Food."

Stella and Jeanne descended to join the queue for supper. It was a thin, watery vegetable soup, one slice of bread and a bitter-tasting coffee.

"Ugh. It's revolting." Jeanne pulled a face as she swallowed.

"Don't worry, I'm sure it will improve." Stella squeezed the other woman's arm.

The food did not improve. Breakfast consisted of a small measure of the peculiar coffee. Lunch was a portion of the watery soup, and supper was the same soup with the added luxury of a slice of bread. Fellow prisoners told them it was the same every day.

The first morning, they were woken at 5am and herded out of the hut by the hut commander. Cracking her whip hard, she forced the women to stand for two hours in long lines on the dry earth until their limbs ached and their hearts grew heavier. At 7am the commandant arrived and sauntered around the pitiful parade. He dismissed them with a toss of his head.

"Come on, quickly," said Stella. "We've got five minutes to get to our workplace."

Jeanne had a cramp and was having trouble walking as Stella tried to hurry her along to the glove-making hut.

"I've negotiated for you to work here. I'll be just in the next hut – the clothing store. I'll collect you at the end of the shift."

Jeanne nodded. "Thank you, *ma petite*. You do look after me, don't you?" Her soft rosy cheeks puffed up.

Stella gave her a hug and darted along to the next hut, arriving just as the guard was closing the door. The guard tapped Stella's calves with her whip as a warning. Stella found a space at a bench and sat down to begin sorting and mending the clothes taken from the women arriving at the camp. At midday, they were on parade again. Stella collected *Madame* Leblanc.

345

"Come on – we've got 10 minutes to return to our hut for some lovely watery soup."

Stella rubbed her neck and stretched her arms above her head. She noticed how lean and masculine they looked. *Fighting the Germans has kept me fit. I just need to keep us both well in this place until the Allies arrive.* She ran back to her hut for the second shift after seeing Madame Leblanc to her workplace. It was eight o'clock before they were allowed to rest and eat their soup.

***

1 November – Ravensbrück

A vicious wind whipped around the camp. Stella stood by the window. Illuminated by the moonlight were 500 pitiful new women prisoners, standing naked in the freezing air. She was eager to talk to them because she knew each batch of new prisoners brought news of Allied successes and hope for them all. It would be four hours before the women had their inoculations and were given their thin blue-striped cotton prison suits to wear. "Please stay strong, ladies. We'll all help to rub you warm once the evil guards dismiss you – stay strong…. More clothes to wash and mend and send to Germans," she muttered to herself.

"Don't worry, my dear." Jeanne Leblanc giggled. "Those Germans won't find any use for the gloves I've been making."

"Sorry?"

"They're destined for the Russian front, *n'est pas*? Well, when I noticed no one checked the quality of my work, I started to sew up the trigger fingers. Now I no longer make them with trigger fingers. And, *chérie*, every day I have been stealing a little of the sheepskin."

"Madame, you're a revelation. Where have you hidden the sheepskin?"

"You're sleeping on it."

CHAPTER 31
Walter and Bernie - Advancing and Retreating

10 November – Churchill's plane over Paris

The plane flew low, and Walter was relieved to see Paris had suffered little damage. Walter scoured the landscape. His eyes fixed on a point where he thought his sister's apartment would be. He found himself staring at the Parisian buildings, wishing he would spy Stella and Martin standing on a roof top waving a Union Jack.

Walter arranged for Churchill to stay on the Quai d'Orsay. Churchill reclined in an enormous golden bath, in the luxury apartment. He called through the door to Walter. "I promised General De Gaulle that one day we would go down the Champs Elysees together. Tomorrow, on Armistice Day, I intend to fulfil that promise."

***

Walter used every bit of spare time to make enquiries about his sister. People in her old apartment block gave him details of Pierre's address. Neighbours of Pierre described how the old concierge and his wife were taken away by the *Gestapo,* but no one had seen Stella or Martin.

"To be honest they could have been here," said a young girl in the apartment opposite. But we dare not open our doors and take a look. I can let you in the apartment if you're a relative."

Walter took out his warrant card. "I'm a police officer from London – will that do?"

Once in the apartment, Walter looked at the overturned dining table and chairs. There, among the broken plates, was a small paper serviette folded into a swan.

***

It was foggy. Bernie stared skyward. There was an eerie silence. "The planes will be grounded today. I won't be reporting any enemy bombers, unless they want to fly close enough for me to touch them."

The unit was bored. Johnny tapped out a tune on the desk with his fingers.

"Oh, I recognise that one," said the Welsh Sergeant-Major. "Is it *Little Drummer boy?"* He started to hum the tune. "Tell you what, let's have a bit of sing song. I'll sing the words and you do the chorus. It's easy. When I put my hand in the air you lot sing along with me.

The Sergeant-Major sang in his powerful voice and the boys joined in with the *rum pum pums.*

The *pums and rums* were silenced by the wild tapping of the Morse code machines. The men froze as they deciphered in their heads the terrifying reports flying around the division:

The Germans have broken through.

The Germans are advancing.

Field Marshal Rundstedt is taking a lunge at us through the Ardennes forest.

The Germans have rallied 24 divisions, 10 of them armoured.

Paratroopers dressed in our uniforms have dropped behind the American lines.

We've been caught on the hop and are weak in the middle.

Rundstedt has driven hard through the centre of our defences, making our overall command impossible.

Rundstedt has asked his troops to give their all in one final last effort.

They've got within four miles of the River Meuse.

They're after Antwerp and Brussels – we are taking huge losses.

The Germans were fighting back – HARD.

1945
All Roads Lead to Belsen

CHAPTER 32
Stella - A Hell for Innocents

3 January–8 March – Ravensbrück

Stella slipped down from the bunk. She left Jeanne the blanket and was comforted to hear her soft snores. She scratched the frost on inside of the window and licked the tiny slither of ice stuck in her fingernail. Through the slit she could see marquees on the parade ground. A pale winter moon shone a ribbon of light along the muddy path. Five hundred women and children were trudging into the camp.

The women and children waited in chilling silence. They all had the yellow Star of David sown into their clothing. A biting wind nipped exposed ears and ankles. The new arrivals turned the frozen mud of the path to slush.

Stella wrapped her arms around herself. She watched to see if the Germans would give them any food.

A small boy noticed her shadow. He was wearing a felt cap with a feather. He raised one finger and waved.

The guards began to scream at the crowd. Dogs on tight leashes gave low growls. The people moved into the tents. The canvas reflected shadows of the women and children huddled together. They sat on the frozen mud of the parade ground. Guards patrolled the grounds and still the new arrivals were given nothing.

At five o'clock in the morning the usual parade was cancelled. It was a blessed relief. Stella tucked her hands in her pockets – lined with Madame LeBlanc's sheepskin. She watched as the women and children were marched out of the camp and up the hill to some new blocks. Stella tried to spot the little boy with the feathered cap. There was a landscape of stooped heads labouring up the hill.

The tents were taken down. A rumour started around the camp – the women and their children had been gassed in the new blocks. Work was already beginning on another *special* building.

Madame Leblanc was sewing tiny pieces of sheepskin together to make Stella gloves. "Someone told me the new construction is a crematorium. But it couldn't possibly be. We already have one by the front gate, and fortunately it is sufficient to cope with the number of poor women who die here."

Stella washed her hands in cold water and tried on the finished glove. She kissed Jeanne. "These are wonderful, but we must keep them hidden." She lowered her voice. "Don't let any of the other prisoners see them. I just pray the Allies get here soon."

The next day it was minus five degrees and the women were on parade at five o'clock in the morning as usual. Jeanne Leblanc stamped her feet.

"No moving." Irma Grese, a vicious guard hit Jeanne with her whip, slashing her tunic across the back and drawing blood.

Stella helped Jeanne to her feet, all the time staring at the floor. She had managed to avoid the attentions of this particular sadistic guard who was known for singling out the young and pretty women.

The women developed their own ways of keeping warm by moving a finger or a toe, so they did not freeze. Jeanne supplied those she could trust with sheepskin stolen from the workshop. They used it to put in their pockets and shoes. But poor food, infestations and cold, meant many women became ill. There were more and more medical inspections, and those who failed the inspection were marched up the hill. The new high chimneys, belching acrid smoke, held no secret; it was the stench of burning flesh.

Stella held Jeanne's arm and led her towards the workshop. She cracked the ice on a water butt, dipped a rag into the water, and bathed Jeanne's wound until the bleeding stopped.

"Thank you my dear, I'll be alright." Jeanne hobbled towards her hut.

Stella kissed her as Jeanne joined the line and ran to her own workshop. On the step of the clothing hut was a scorched red feather. Stella bent forward and picked it up. She crumpled against the door frame. Waterless tears burnt her eyes.

Knowing Jeanne had been feverish all week, Stella could imagine only one thing as she heard the block leader screaming "*Raus! Raus!*" next door. Jeanne was being whipped again. As the block leader marched away from the hut, Stella arrived to see the old woman lying in her bunk, so motionless, and her face so pale…far too pale.

Stella stabbed her finger on a protruding nail on the bunk and pulled Jeanne's face toward her. "Come, let me help you." She smeared her bloody finger across Jeanne's cheeks. "There, you should easily pass the medical inspection today."

Madame Leblanc did pass the medical examination that day, but collapsed a week later. Stella knew there was only one possible outcome; Jeanne would be led up the hill with the others.

Stella sat on her bunk staring into space. She tried not to believe that Jeanne was dead. She slipped into the daily punishing routine that was the hell of *Ravensbrück*.

Starvation drew in her cheeks and desolation shrank her eyes into near-hollow sockets – her body and soul drained of all emotion.

The next day, she was sorting through the sacks of clothes that had just arrived. She emptied the first sack on the bench and was about to fold it and put it onto the pile, when she noticed a striped uniform still inside the sack. She reached in and pulled out a familiar-looking tunic with a red triangle sewn on the front. Her hand trembled as she turned it around to inspect it – there was the angry gash across the back. Stella held it to her face and breathed in the familiar aroma of her friend. Her eyes pricked with dry tears.

That night in her bunk, Stella wept for Martin – for herself – for all the women who had walked up the hill. She shed tears in silence, so the guards did not beat her. She mourned for the world. *Where has humanity gone?*

***

Max Koegel, the Camp Commander, was following the progression of the Russians towards Ravensbrück. He was concerned about the reports of what might happen if they got to the camp before the Allies. He was from Hamburg and found out about a camp near there that would take his prisoners. A rumour swept around the huts. Ravensbrück was to be closed.

"So, are they going to let us go home?" asked Paulette, a young French girl wearing a prison uniform with a red triangle.

"That would be nice," mused Stella. She was lying on the bunk, empty without Jeanne's comforting body. She sighed and massaged her legs.

Within days it was confirmed the camp would be moving deeper into Germany – away from the advance of the Russians.

Stella had heard tales of *death marches.* She decided to prepare for a long, long walk. "Take some of this sheepskin," she said to Paulette, pulling it out from her mattress. "Put it in your boots and in your pockets. It will help you to keep warm."

Paulette smiled and revealed she was wearing two uniforms. "I'll get you another one. It's going to be cold at night. Who knows where we will sleep."

When they were ordered out of the hut, Stella pulled Paulette to the front of the column. "They will march us and try to starve us to death. It's hard and selfish, but we need to be in the front of the column to make sure we at least get a ration of what might be on offer."

***

9 March – Menz, Germany

The prisoners covered 16 miles in the first day. The guards stopped them at the end of the *Roofensee,* a long lake surrounded by woods. There was no food. The guards took turns to go off into the town for dinner.

Stella undid the laces on *Monsieur* LeBlanc's boots and dipped her feet in the cold water. She rearranged the sheepskin lining the soles and added a little more from her pocket.

Paulette came to join her. "See any fish? You're so lucky to have those boots."

They peered into the lake. There was no food later that evening, but in the morning, they queued for bread and coffee before setting off again. Not one woman had attempted an escape. Most of them had no idea where they were, and few spoke German.

Stella brushed the leaves from her short hair and headed to the front of the column. Paulette followed. They were determined to get to the new camp alive.

***

14 March – Lager Hörsten, Germany

Days of marching took a severe toll on the women – many collapsed on the road and were bayoneted by the guards.
They stopped for the night at a farm. Stella was getting weaker. Paulette was among the first in the line for some soup. Her feet were blistered, her hair was matted, and her clothes filthy. Unobserved by the guards, she let Stella in front of her.

The guards were angry about the march and began to vent their frustrations on the prisoners. Stella and Paulette sat on a large, cold concrete block in the barn,

"Get up!" screamed Irma Grese, who was now in charge. She brandished a whip.

Stella stood up, her whole body aching. She looked the guard in the eyes. To her surprise, she found she was looking at a young woman with meticulous grooming – pretty and blond, with her hair in neat ringlets. She flinched as she anticipated the lash of the whip.

Grese was distracted by the arrival of some local men carrying old-fashioned rifles and the rumbling of a troop carrier. "I will deal with you later," she snarled.

Stella had heard rumours of how Grese terrified the starving Jewish women in the camp with her vicious dogs. A memory returned. This was the woman who had whipped Jeanne Leblanc and marked her for death.

The guards climbed in the truck and were driven to the town for their evening meal. The old men, who were forced to take over their duty, were uncomfortable and edgy. Stella sat down, in slow motion, so as not to alarm the men. One by one, the women followed, huddling together for warmth. Stella pulled Paulette close, on the cold hard concrete floor, and they escaped from their terror with a few scant hours of sleep.

CHAPTER 33
Bernie - Adopted by a Loving Family

15–19 March – Kloosterzande, The Netherlands

Bernie sat in the kitchen of the Aarssen's tiny terraced house, looking out of the window. The area of South Zeeland reminded him of Norfolk – vast and flat with intricate ridges of earth for coastal defences. The only breaks in the landscape were the river embankments, designed by a nation existing below sea level.
The many farms that dotted the countryside grew wheat, rye and potatoes. There were few cattle or sheep, and meat was scarce.

Bernie's signals unit set up their radio in the town hall tower. Their guns were deployed all across the low-lying polders. The dams looked quite different from the riverside. They were lined with concrete slabs interwoven with wooden stakes and wire, on the south bank of the river Scheldt.

"Back on duty at six o'clock?" Flop asked.

Bernie nodded, his mouth full of rabbit stew.

"Better eat up. I've made a blancmange for dessert," said Ma.

"I love your desserts, Ma – can I take a recipe home for Mum?"

Ma was already writing it down. "You'll have to put this in English for her. How did you pick up Dutch so quickly?"

"I don't know really. My uncle speaks several languages and when you talk among yourselves, well it just makes sense." Bernie finished his food and winked at Ma. "Lovely, thank you. Will I see you after night duty?"

"I'll have some coffee ready," said Ma.

Bernie appreciated his good fortune in his billeting arrangements, knowing that other *Tommies* were sleeping in barns. He soon fell into a new routine. He got up around midday to eat a generous breakfast – two bantam eggs and a slice of pork belly. He reported for duty at 18:00 and finished at 04:00.

Bernie was stationed at the town hall and there were fewer people about at night. Extra rations were easier to get hold of, with the help of *Slippery Johnny*. Pork belly was always available, but Bernie longed for bacon with his eggs.

The Aarssens loved English white bread, and Bernie made it his daily mission to find them a spare loaf from the army bakery. In return, the Aarssens made him toast for his breakfast.

Bernie was grateful for their love and hospitality. He made it his quest to attain all the meat, milk and fresh vegetables he could lay his hands on to help the family get back to good health. He was concerned about the children. They had only just survived on starvation rations during the occupation, and all three girls were small and skinny for their ages.

It was 17:30 and Bernie heard the *Gin Palace* pulling up outside the house. "What you got today?" Bernie approached the driver's side window.

"Some meat – might be pork; some apples, a cabbage and a wedge of cheese," said Johnny. He reached through the window and gave Bernie a prod. "But, you're gonna 'ave to fight Fatty the chef, and the other chefs will be betting on you – so get in shape, mate."

Bernie laughed and took the food inside the house to give to the Aarssens. He returned and got into the passenger side of the truck. "This old bus has taken us some miles."

"It seems like she's got a new top speed," said Johnny crashing the gears.

"Oh yes?"

"She now does 50 miles per hour – downhill. Only problem, there's no bleedin' hills."

***

20 March – Kloosterzande Town Hall

They parked the *Gin Palace* at the rear of the building and headed up the back steps to the operations room. It was large and airy, and Bernie took his position next to one of the radios mounted on a desk by the window. In the centre of the room was a large table with four telephones. The town hall was bustling with people changing shifts. Bernie whistled *Scotland the Brave.*

"Shut that noise and get this signal off," demanded the Corporal.

Bernie laughed to himself as he sent the Morse code to their headquarters. "Blimey, you'd laugh, Corp if I told you about *another* man who hates me whistling that song."

The whole regiment was upbeat. The Allies were advancing. They were winning and someday soon, they might even invade Germany and the war would be over.

Bernie sat at his desk and stared at the heavens through the huge, high window. A quarter-moon lit a clear sky. Bernie's mind wandered as he gazed at the constellation, remembering a special time when his father was alive.

They had sat together on the garage roof, learning the names and the myths surrounding all the configurations. He could see the Big Dipper, the Little Dipper and a moving star.

"Moving star?" Bernie's vision was perfect. His sharp eyes had seen the moonlight reflect on the wings of an enemy plane. He spotted more – ten *Messerschmitt* 109s heading towards them. To reach the town, they would pass right over the number 161 gun battery. It was linked to one of the four telephones. But 161's gunners would not be able to see the *Luftwaffe* coming because the dikes around the polders obscured their view. Bernie felt light-headed.

He picked up the telephone linked to the guns. "Fighters coming from the northeast, across the river."

Bernie's alert was relayed around the operations room.

"All guns take post," he read from the orders he'd been passed to transmit. "All stations report."

The reply was instantaneous. "One, six, zero; one, six, one; one six two, roger."

The alarm bells rang, and the gunners responded.

"Number-one gun, Roger and out."

"Number-two gun, Roger and out."

"Number-three gun, Roger and out."

"Number-four gun, Roger and out."

There was absolute quiet in the operations room. The planes were advancing in an arrow formation. Bernie waited, hardly daring to move.

Johnny opened his mouth and started to speak, when the sudden booming of the *Bofors* guns drowned out his voice.

The *Messerschmitts* were taken by surprise. They broke formation. The sky glimmered with the reflection of the flat watery land. The noise of the guns muted the aircraft. They looked like moths flitting and diving in front of a porch light. One aircraft shuddered, and a flame flashed from its tail. Bernie watched as the pilot struggled to land his damaged plane. From observing its descent, he knew exactly where he would find it.

Dawn was breaking when Johnny dropped Bernie off at the Aarssens' house. Ma had already put the kettle on the stove to make him a chicory coffee. After two mugs of the boiling liquid, he went to find Flop, who was in the garage. "Can I borrow your bike?"

"Of course, son." Flop wheeled the bike into the street.

Bernie smiled. It was a long time since anyone had called him *son*. "I won't be long." He checked his gun. "I might be bringing back a prisoner." He took the old bicycle and went out to search for the plane. It was a bumpy ride. The tyres were stuffed with rags. He cycled along the deserted road to where he expected to find the plane. In the distance, he spotted a jumbled mess of wreckage strewn across the fields. There were figures standing in the road. As Bernie approached, he recognised a number of local boys. The decapitated pilot was still sitting in his seat, with the rest of the aircraft laid out around him like small pieces of a metal jigsaw.

"Stop that, stop that!" Bernie shouted at the boys. They ignored him and continued kicking the pilot's head.

"Stop it." Bernie lowered his Sten gun.

The boys froze. The largest boy, who was about 16, stared at Bernie and kicked the man's head again. The rest backed off. They recognised the big *Tommie* who was billeted with their football referee.

"What if he tells Mr Aarssen?" whispered the smallest boy.

"He doesn't know us, and he can't speak Dutch." The oldest boy advanced on the plane.

But Bernie did understand them. *"Ik weet dat je yongeman, en deze partij."* Then he added in English, "Clear off, you lot – you're no better than the Nazis behaving like this."

"Let's run," yelled the youngest boy. They hurried back along the straight narrow road towards the town.

Bernie stood alone with the mutilated pilot and pieces of the plane. A chilling wind blew from the northeast. Bernie felt the hairs stand up on the back of his neck as he reached beside the pilot's body. He tried not to look at the congealed blood where the head had once been. He found the parachute and pulled it out. The material was soft and billowed in the wind. It was difficult to control, and Bernie had to find pieces of the mangled plane to pin the parachute to the ground. It took several minutes to arrange the material into a suitable shroud, but he was patient and ignored the cold until he had completed the task to his satisfaction.

Bernie released the body of the pilot from its safety harness and lifted it onto the shroud. It was awkward and he laid it on the silk, trying not to cover himself in blood. He wrapped what had been the pilot's head in a piece of the silk he had cut from the main chute.

Bernie noticed the pilot had no watch or boots. He looked along the road, where he could still see the boys as tiny dots in the distance and mumbled a curse. He cycled to where he knew he would find the chaplain – the pilot would have a proper burial.

***

21 March – The Aarssens' house

Next morning, Johnny was waiting for Bernie in the kitchen at the Aarssens' as the whole family sat around listening to the small radio, tuned into the BBC.

"After the Battle of the Bulge comes the Battle for the Rhine. Massive quantities of supplies and troops have successfully crossed one of Germany's last defences. A smart American

sergeant spotted a railway bridge at Remagen, which the Germans had failed to demolish. He raced across with his platoon, avoiding enemy fire. Booby traps went off, but the brave sergeant held the bridge until reinforcements could arrive."

They all cheered.

"The crossing took place last night after a 2,000-gun bombardment."

"Cor, I would've liked to 'ave 'eard that lot." Johnny poured himself a coffee.

"Commandos seized the town of Wesel and Canadians and Americans established bridgeheads on the flanks. Two airborne divisions were dropped behind enemy lines by 1,500 planes and 1,300 gliders. It was an operation on a scale almost equal to that of D-Day. General Montgomery is carefully planning every detail of his advance in the north."

"Do you think we'll soon be home, Bern?" Johnny asked.

"Let's hope so, old chum," Bernie looked with affection at his adopted family.

Bob arrived at the back door, panting. "Pack up, Bern. We're going to advance."

CHAPTER 34
Walter, Bernie and Stella – Finding a Family

22 March – Baker Street London

Walter padded up the stairs to the office of Major Brown. He strode past the secretary. "Excuse me, Inspector, do you have an appointment?"

Walter did not reply. He opened the door to Brown's office.

Brown was reading a file. "Ah, Inspector, good to see you." He indicated to the chair.

Walter remained standing.

Undeterred, Brown continued, "We have made some enquiries. We can't tell you much. There was one possible sighting of your sister at Fresnes prison by one of our agents who later escaped, but to be honest old boy, it is a bit of a long shot."

"What can we do?" Walter pulled a cigarette out of a packet.

"Well, if it was her, we can ask the Germans officially if she is being held. But that might only draw attention to her and make her more interesting to them. It's a bit tricky, really."

Walter turned the cigarette over in his fingers. "What about the people she was working with?"

"Some were killed. Some have gone home since the invasion. To be honest, they're scattered."

"Keep trying, Major Brown, please…." Walter replaced the cigarette in the pack.

"Of course, Inspector – we'll let you know."

Walter left the office and almost knocked a bald man over on the stairs. "Excuse me."

"Inspector Thompson?" asked Anthony Downwood, extending a hand. "Coming to join the elite force?"

Walter did a double-take at Downwood's head. "No. I'm bloody looking for my sister." He pushed passed Downwood, ran down the stairs and burst out into the street.

"I just wanted to…" Downwood called after him "…thank you, Inspector." He spoke to the empty stairwell.

Brown shut the file in front of him marked, *Stella Gold* and placed it in the tray marked, *archive*.

***

13 April – 10 Downing Street

10 Downing Street was bathed in weak, spring sunshine. Bunny started work early. Her typewriter keys clicked against the platen like castanets. Every day, the reports she typed brought good news. There was hope in every communique, the war would soon be over. But all was not well with the Prime Minister.

Walter waited by Bunny's desk, where the sound of sobbing could be heard coming from Churchill's office.

Bunny gazed at him wide-eyed, wondering if they should say or do anything to offer assistance to the Prime Minister.

Walter placed his hand on her shoulder. "I think it's best if we all leave him for an hour or so with his grief. I wonder if anyone will ever know what President Roosevelt meant to the Old Man?"

Walter was wrestling with his own worries about Stella.

Bunny looked at Walter and waited for him to speak.

Walter looked out of the window at the back garden.

"I'm typing something for him to say. To be honest, I couldn't get it all down because his voice was so quiet, so I'm making it up. I hope he doesn't scold me."

Walter glanced at the page in the typewriter, feeling his eyes sting as the words Bunny had written for Churchill's tribute to President Roosevelt leapt out: *rapier wit… dynamic… gracious… kind… humility.* He realised those same words could be applied to his beautiful and daring sister, Stella.

Bunny pulled the paper from the typewriter. "It's as if they worked in a special sort of harmony."

Walter took the typed speech and returned to Churchill's side.

***

Bernie's unit travelled at just 30 mph. His radio signals were now supporting the British Armoured Division as they advanced into Germany. It was a damp, muggy day, and the trucks were covered in grime from the mud on the road. The sky was monochrome. Bernie slowed the *Gin Palace* to a stop in front of an area surrounded by barbed wire.

There was a noise like someone cracking a whip.

"What the bloody hell was that?" Johnny dived for cover.

"Sounded like a single gunshot," muttered Bernie, cramming as much of his large frame on the floor of the cab as possible.

Bob poked his head through the curtain. "What now?"

"Wait for instructions, I suppose," said Bernie.

The Sergeant-Major wasted no time in assembling a dozen soldiers. Hidden within the undergrowth, they made for the fence then cut their way through the wire. They disappeared.

Five carrion crows, with wings unfolding like black rags, lifted off a solitary leafless tree.

Bernie, Johnny and Bob waited.

Bob sniffed the air. "Can you smell something, Bernie?"

There was a faint odour of something sweet and sickly. "Yep… but I can't quite make it out." Bernie shuddered. "I've got a horrible feeling about this place."

The advance party returned, accompanied by an *SS* officer. They stopped beside Bernie's truck and reported to the Sergeant-Major. Their eyes appeared odd and unfocused.

"Sir, it is a concentration camp," the soldiers reported. "They say they have typhus. They want us to skirt round the camp and leave them to deal with their sick."

"*Sturmführer* Kramer," interjected the *SS* officer. He gave the Sergeant-Major a stiff-arm Nazi salute. "May I speak to one of your officers?"

The Sergeant-Major nodded and led the German away.

Bernie called to one of the soldiers in the advance party. "What's going on?"

The soldier approached the *Gin Palace*. "It's a bloody hellhole. Jesus, I have never seen anything like it. I hope we'll advance and leave this job to the medics. The Gerries want us to move on – they say they're no threat to us."

"But how many more will they murder if we leave them to it? I've heard rumours about these places," said Bernie. "I hope we can go in and give 'em hell."

They waited in their truck for word to come back down the convoy, watching as the German *SS* officer strutted back alone towards the camp.

Their orders came: "Wait here for the night."

They set up the mess tent. Bernie approached one of the blank-eyed men who had been inside the camp. He noticed the man wasn't eating – toying with his food.

Bernie sat down next to him. "What's going on? Why aren't we going in?"

"We've rejected the Gerries' terms, but given them a truce," the man replied. "Tonight, their troops will withdraw, and their guards will disarm. We're waiting for more men to come, but this is hardly a job for us – you'll see what I mean when we go in tomorrow."

Bernie lay awake that night worrying about what was in the camp. He had heard rumours of people being treated like animals and a strange lethargy seemed to be seeping from the place. When he succumbed to sleep, he was aware of his own heartbeat, but woke several times in the night covered in sweat. *We should be going in, we should be checking the people the Germans are holding there are alright.*

***

15 April – Bergen-Belsen, Germany

In the morning, Bernie heard the rumble of trucks. The infantry had arrived. They wasted no time getting into the vehicles and pressing on to the camp.

As they went through the gates, a blackened, bloated body hung from some gallows.

"Cut him down," Bernie shouted.

An ambulance pulled up and two medics began to lower the body.

Johnny shut his eyes and opened them again to try to make the sight in front of him disappear. "What the hell is this place?"

What looked in the distance to be a huge pile of black logs turned out to be thousands of naked, dead bodies. Skeletal beings were lying on top of dead bodies, and everywhere there were putrid corpses in various stages of decay.

"Oh dear Lord, those people over there – the ones on the very top of the pile – they're still alive!" Bernie dry retched. "How can we help? Where do we start? There are too many of them."

Thousands of bedraggled people came out of the compound to greet them. A man dressed in rags, looking like no more than a walking carcass, took Johnny's hand and kissed it. Johnny's face was taut. He clasped the man's hand in his own as the man sank to his knees and lay down. Johnny bent over him, still holding his hand as the man took his last breath.

Bernie could not speak. He held his hand over his nose and mouth, the stench was overwhelming. He could not have imagined such a shocking picture of human misery, even in his worst nightmares. This was a living death. Never before had he seen so many faces lost in unimaginable grief and hopelessness. Thousands of human beings had been tortured, starved, beaten and overworked in this place. Many had withdrawn into their own worlds, their minds unable to cope with the force of this inexplicable horror.

Bernie swung into action, helping to unload supplies from the trucks. He set up a temporary storeroom in the back of the *Gin Palace*, where he found all the food he had stashed away and started handing out his rations to the desperate people surrounding the truck. They took and ate anything he gave them – even the butter, jam and sugar – but even these morsels of food could not help save their poor emaciated bodies. It was too late… death had already marked them.

At dusk, Bernie and Johnny left and set up camp with the rest of their unit in a nearby field. The contrast of their routine army life with the scene they had just left proved too strange and no one could find any comfort in returning to ordinary tasks. There was a numb quietness in the mess tent as the men spoke in solemn whispers about what they had seen. They picked over their food, few of them able to eat. Even battle-hardened veterans were silent.

The men had been so full of fresh hopes at the prospect of returning home victorious from the war. The entire meaning of life had been demolished in one stroke as the sights and sounds of Belsen were forever etched on their minds.

Bernie reflected on the contrast between the crisp, starched *SS* uniform of *Sturmführer* Kramer and the filthy, half-naked prisoners. He ran from the tent towards the woods and held on to a tree while he vomited until there was nothing left in his stomach. Questions tormented him over and over again. All he could do was run and run – across the fields, into the low hills and the forest. But no amount of exertion could blow away the horrific images in his head. Exhausted, and staggering about in the dark, he came across the Chaplain's tent. There were voices coming from inside. He slumped, leaning on a guy rope, and listened.

"Sir, we estimate about 35,000 corpses and about 30,000 living, although many of them are barely alive – they are really *living corpses*. I don't think we can save the majority, and if we could, they would spend the short remainder of their pitiful lives in a lunatic asylum."

There was a brief pause before the voice continued: "We have three categories here. The easiest to help are the healthy. They may have just come to the camp and have managed to keep themselves decent. Some are disoriented and have typhus. Then we have very sick being cared for by friends. We can help some of these. A vast number look as if they have been living in hell. Over a hundred died today when the camp was liberated. One young woman told me they died of joy."

Another man's voice came in: "I need to get in touch with the rabbi. We'll conduct joint services."

Bernie was about to draw back the front sheet, but he realised it had gone silent inside the tent. Through a gap, he observed the Chaplain and the Sergeant-Major on their knees in front of a collapsible wooden table. It was covered in a white cloth, with a small wooden cross in the middle.

Bernie walked back to the camp, kicking stones.

The regimental pipers climbed a low hill by the camp and blew into their bagpipes. The battalion watched their silhouettes as they slow paced in the moonlight, playing piobaireachd, *Lament for Mary Macleod.*

***

16 April – Bergen-Belsen, Germany

Johnny spent a fitful night in the truck, and in the morning joined a group of men assigned to help in the camp.

The *SS* men and women who had been guarding the camp were put to work. They were pushed into a line, and a British Corporal addressed them in German. "Today, you murdering bastards will clean up this place. You will dig graves and you will respectfully place corpses in those bloody graves until you drop dead. Is that understood?"

"Yes, sir," replied the Germans.

Angry shouts accompanied a crowd of prisoners who rushed the line of Germans.

"Get back," the Corporal called out. "Fix bayonets," he ordered his party of men. "Go away."

The prisoners took a few steps back, ready to pounce on the Germans if the British troops withdrew.

All day long in the drizzling rain, the Germans loaded decaying bodies onto trucks. When the trucks were full, the Corporal forced the former guards to ride on top of the loaded corpses. One soldier saw his chance, jumped off the truck and tried to disappear into the crowd.

"Halt." The Corporal's shout rang out and the throng parted. One of the British soldiers opened fire, and the German fell to the ground. He was rushed at by the mass of murderous-looking people, who kicked and beat him. The Corporal fired his gun into the air several times and they dispersed, leaving the dead man on the ground – eyes staring ahead.

Johnny was assigned to help with provisions. When they arrived inside the camp, the only food they had found was a pile of stinking, rotten carrots. So he got to work setting up a store to dispense milk to the children.

An emaciated woman with a baby in her arms, wrapped in a filthy cloth approached him. "*Mleko, mleko*," she muttered, pointing at the large jug of milk in front of Johnny. He parted the cloth to look at the baby. Its tiny body was black and shrivelled – dead for several days.

"*Mleko, mleko*," she said again in a small voice, looking at the jug of milk.

Johnny's lip quivered as he poured a little milk into the palm of his hand and dribbled it off his fingers onto the baby's mouth.

The woman smiled, black teeth.

"Women and children," he shouted at the Germans, who had been organised into a work party to assist him. "Women and children – what the bloody hell. How could they possibly be a threat to you? Here I am, look at me – I'm your enemy. I am a professional soldier; fight me – not women and children."

He aimed a punch at a German guard, and one of the men in the Corporal's party caught his arm.

The German stood tall and stared Johnny down.

Johnny lunged at the man, kicking, punching and biting him. It took five men to pull him away, although not before he had succeeded breaking the haughty guard's nose. Johnny fought on, punching out his fury at the British soldiers.

"Take this man back to his unit and get him a drink," ordered the Corporal as the soldiers pinned Johnny's arms to his sides.

"Yes, sir."

***

As the men escorted Johnny back to the unit, they passed a thin woman. She had a shaved head and was filling her bucket with water from the standpipe, erected by the engineers.

The cold water burned her skin as she washed. A young girl, sitting on an upturned supply box, handed her a powder compact. It opened, revealing a tiny mirror in the lid. The shaven-headed woman had not looked at her reflection in a year and did not recognise the face she saw. Her high cheekbones appeared as though they were about to pierce her fragile ashen skin, and her lips were pale and colourless.

"Go on – have some lipstick," said Paulette. "I stole it from the SS stores." She had been new to Ravensbrück when the guards had forced the inmates to walk almost 400 kilometres to Belsen. She was not half starved when the walk began, unlike Stella.

Stella stared at the lipstick as though in a trance. The words barely trickled from her mouth. "I'm frightened." Applying the lipstick would make her different from the 20,000 women in the camp with the same gaunt faces and identical striped cotton pyjamas.

"I've got some clothes too – and boots," offered Paulette. "Would you like to try some on?"

Stella moved towards the heap of clothes. She gazed at them, and without any consideration, picked up a dress from the top of the pile.

Paulette took the oversized dress from Stella and handed her another. "Not that one – it's far too big. Here, try this one."

The flimsy cotton felt soft and clean. It had small burgundy daisies printed on a beige background. She wondered to whom it had belonged.

"Come on, I'll help you," said Paulette.

She assisted Stella to remove her dirty striped uniforms.

Stella's bare inner, left arm revealed a number tattooed halfway on her soft thin skin between her wrist and her elbow.

Paulette revealed an identical mark as she had done every day since they met. "Still sisters," she said, smiling.

Stella was in awe of this tireless child who was taking charge of her and helping the other bedraggled women in the hut.

"Are you really French like me?" Paulette held a dress up against her body, dropped it and chose another.

"No, I'm English," replied Stella.

"I knew it. You talk in a different language in your sleep. Hey, the English are here. They might be able to get a letter to your husband or relatives."

With the stone of guilt about Martin still heavy within her, Stella pressed at her stomach.

Paulette took hold of Stella's hand. "Come on, I'm relying on you to help me with the children later." The hand did not give way.

"Are you alright? Here let me check your back. My mother was a nurse and if you've got typhus, there'll be a rash." Paulette turned Stella around.

The rash was raw.

"Oh Lord, you've been scratching. Those horrible lice bite you and then shit on your skin. I told you if you scratched, you'd get infected.

Stella stroked the child's spiky hair. "Can you wash the lice off me?"

"Well, I can try but I need to get some de-lousing powder. Wait here, I'll see what I can beg or steal."

***

Bernie lay in his bunk. He put the pillow over his head. Below him, Johnny punched the side of the *Gin Palace*. He rambled: "My mum would never believe what I've seen today… Not that I'm ever going to tell my mum. Not that I'll ever tell anyone... I just want to leave here. I want to forget about this.... I wish I'd joined the navy, or been somewhere else…. How could they do all that? And this isn't even the only camp – there are others that are meant to be worse. But how could anything possibly be worse than this?"

Bernie did not hear Johnny talking. He was exhausted and sank into a dreamless oblivion, where at last he felt safe.

***

Stella vomited beside the hut, and lay down on the dry earth, her frail body exhausted from the effort.

Paulette looked through the wire fence. The military were building a tented hospital outside the camp. Please 'elp me," she said in her broken English to an English solider who was busy unloading supplies. "My friend, English... need 'elp."

"What? An English woman here in this camp?" Bob put the last crate outside the makeshift canteen.

"*Oui*, yes, please 'elp."

Bob looked round; there were no officers in sight. "Right love, where is she?"

"Come, come," said Paulette, pulling on Bob's sleeve. She dragged him over to the place where Stella had fallen to the ground.

Bob bent down to examine her and held his nose. "Are you English, love?"

Stella opened her eyes and double blinked. It was the first English voice she had heard in years. "Yes. I'm English."

Bob paused. "What to do? What would Bern do? Take her to the hospital? Right, come on love." He scooped her up in his arms.

∗ ∗ ∗

Bernie's unit worked through the day, without breaks, feeding prisoners and cleaning up the camp but more and more people died each day.

It was decided it would be more hygienic to move all those whom they thought could be saved to a new Displaced Person's Camp. It was being set up to provide toilets and clean water for the prisoners. Each person was fumigated as they entered, in order to rid them of fleas and lice, and so prevent the spread of disease. Some were terrified of moving camps. They still thought they were prisoners being led to their deaths.

371

Paulette made sure she was one of the first to enter the new camp, and when she got there, she went to look for Stella. The sign on the gate read, *Dust Spreads Typhus – 5mph*.

Stella was in the hospital. Her tiny frame lost among the clean white sheets and pillows propping her head. She was delirious with fever and rambling – lost inside her head, while a whirl of thoughts and images sped round in a blur. *I see everything, feel everything, I breathe everything – the march, the nights, the blunt coldness of the air, the whip, Jeanne's dress, and the cruel slit in the dress. André, Pierre's friend. André's lovely body, prostrate on an armoured car, or was it a tank ... or a car? Martin, Martin, Martin – we didn't get to say goodbye but I am coming to meet you, my love, I feel you holding me, your breath on my neck, pressing yourself against me until I am not there anymore – dissolved.*

***

28 April – Chequers

Bunny looked up from her typing and opened her eyes wide. "Mr Downwood?"

"Er, yes, Miss Shearburn, good morning. I've come to find Thompson." Downwood touched his thin moustache and glanced around the office as if he might find Walter in the filing cabinet.

"Inspector Thompson?" Bunny studied Downwood's strange bald head.

"Yes, quite right, Inspector Thompson." Downwood shifted his weight from foot to foot.

Bunny put her head to one side. "May I give him a message?"

"No, er, well yes, er… hand me a sheet of paper and a pen, if you would, please…." Downwood stood at the side of her desk and wrote two important words on the paper. "Do you have an envelope, Miss Shearburn?" He slipped the paper in, sealed it and wrote *Thompson* on the front. He held it out for Bunny, but before she could take it, he laid it back on the desk and added *Inspector*.

***

2–4 May – Lüneburg Heath, Germany

The yellow gorse bushes were still in flower, and the grass whispered as the warm spring breeze wafted across Lüneburg Heath.

Johnny stopped the *Gin Palace* so Bernie could climb out to view the encampment. In the valley was a city of marquees and bell tents erected by the Royal Engineers. This was the headquarters of the 21st Army Group. Today was a big day – the day that would mark the end of the war.

A Corporal directing traffic waved like a windmill at Bernie, indicating he should get back into his truck and continue moving with the convoy.

Bernie was in no hurry to obey his superior. He saw the world in another way – a bigger picture where evil people would submit others to unimaginable cruelty just because they were different. The war was over, whatever he did now made little difference, including hurrying along for a corporal. The Corporal began quick marching towards the *Gin Palace*. Bernie returned to the truck and sat in the passenger seat. Johnny saw possible trouble ahead and put his foot hard on the accelerator. He viewed the Corporal in his rear-view mirror, standing in the road, and shaking his fist.

"Bloody hell. Did you see who that was? Only Corporal Blue Gums." Johnny turned the corner before Bernie and Bob could get a good look.

"Blimey," said Bob, "I had that bastard too – let's park well away from wherever he's billeted."

Johnny pulled up in a meadow, high above Lüneburg Heath. "Yesterday, I heard a good word from the Yanks that describes what we are now."

Bernie nodded.

"We're just bleedin' *gofers*. Go for this and go for that – now they don't need us for signals anymore."

Bernie stretched. "Tea anyone." He put the kettle on the stove.

In the valley The Royal Engineers were making large crosses and arrows, using white tape. This area had been cleared to serve as a runway for the arriving peacemakers.

A large marquee had been erected at the end of the tent city, guarded by military police. Two plain trestle tables and six simple wooden army chairs awaited the signatories.

Field Marshal Montgomery arrived first – a very small man jumping out of a light aircraft. He had come to represent the British.

The *Gin Palace* was parked at a good vantage point above the plain to watch the show. Motorbike outriders came into view, leading a long line of staff cars. They flew the flags of Britain, America, France and Germany.

"Who's going to sign the peace agreement, if Hitler's dead?" asked Johnny.

"I'm not sure," replied Bob. "I think it's one of their admirals."

"Look, there's Monty," shouted Johnny, waving at Field Marshal Montgomery.

A booming cheer went up from the battalion. "Who's the American?"

"Bedell Smith, Eisenhower's chief of staff – over there getting out of the car," said Bernie, talking for the first time. "He's signing on behalf of the USA. We'd have been stuffed without the Americans coming to join the fight. The Germans have held up signing in order to allow as many of their men as possible to give themselves up to *us*, rather than to the Russians. They think the Russians are going to give them a hard time."

Bob climbed up on the front of the *Gin Palace* to get a better view. "It all seems so simple. Thirty minutes to sign a piece of paper to end the war, after everything we've all been through. After all the training we did, after all the bombs that fell and the innocent people killed, after D-Day, after all the fighting we saw in France, Belgium and The Netherlands, and… after Belsen."

Johnny was silent. He had seen enough of war. He didn't want to talk about Belsen.

"Time to go home lads and to try to make sense of the world again." Bob took off his beret and waved at the peacemakers.

***

5 May – Lüneburg Heath, Germany

The next morning, Bernie woke up with an ache in his stomach.

"Ugh. My bleedin' guts." Johnny held his middle.

From the back of the truck, Bob moaned, "Oh God, I've got the shits."

Johnny made his way to the mess tent for some water and returned ten minutes later, slopping the water can as he walked. "The whole unit has a stomach upset."

Bernie and Bob lay in the back of the truck doubled up with pain.

"What's that, son?" Corporal Blue Gums, overheard Johnny's comment and opened the door of the cab. "Oh, so it's you lot again. Right, get up. What do you think you are doing lying around in there when there's work to be done? I've got a job for you. Come on – on your feet."

Bernie, Bob and Johnny groaned and climbed out of the *Gin Palace.*

"Stand to attention. You heard me – stand to attention when you are addressed by an officer." The corporal smiled at them, revealing a set of badly fitting false teeth and blue gums. "Right then – a number of my men are suffering from a little tummy upset, and I need some latrines dug over there, do you understand?"

"Yes, Corp."

"Right then. I'll be back in an hour, and I expect to see you've done a good job." The Corporal executed a smart about-turn and marched off.

Bernie, Bob and Johnny trudged towards the spot near the trees, where the Corporal had indicated.

"I think we should have got some shovels." Bernie held his middle.

"What? Oh, right, yes. I'll go get them." Johnny began to walk back to the *Gin Palace.*

"What's up?" asked a dispatch rider.

375

"That bleedin' Corporal – making us dig a latrine for his men, when it's their food that's given us all the shits. To be honest, it's where I'll need to be soon myself with this bellyache. How come that nasty Corporal never gets the guts?" Johnny clambered into the back of the truck to find tools.

Bernie and Bob sat together on a log, crossing their legs. Johnny joined them and bent over double in pain.

Six dispatch riders dug out the latrines whilst whistling Bernie's favourite tune, *Scotland the Brave*.

"We don't forget a good turn," said Shorty.

Bob nursed his abdomen, "I think I could be your first customer – and pretty soon."

None of them were feeling too well by the time the tent was erected around the long-stripped sapling, supported at each end by sturdy logs.

Bernie unbuttoned his fly as he stepped into the latrine tent. "Thanks, chaps. I'm afraid I'm going to have to use your nice new convenience, and it won't be very pleasant."

"You're not going to be alone," retorted Bob. "Whatever I ate has gone right through me, too."

"Hold on, hold on, my need is greater," said Johnny.

"No, mine is." shouted another of the men.

The whole party raced for the latrine. Shorty lifted the awning and handed each man a copy of the *Daily Mirror*. "Blue gums had ten delivered. He sits on them so we can't get a look. Read them and use them to wipe your arses boys."

"Right then, where are you – let's be havin' you," screamed Corporal Blue Gums.

Johnny peeped through the awning. "Bleedin' hell, it's Blue Gums, in person."

The Corporal pulled back the front of the latrine tent. "Right lads – make way for the Corporal."

"Sorry, Corp," Johnny tried to supress his laughter. "All the stools are taken."

***

"There are huge crowds outside. They want to hear from the Old Man. Can't he tell them anything? Everyone knows the Germans have surrendered." Bunny looked out of the window at all the people standing in the street, awaiting confirmation from the Prime Minister that the war was over.

Walter joined her at the window. "I don't know – I'll go and ask him. I think he is waiting for Marshal Stalin and President Truman to give him the go-ahead before he makes the announcement." He returned a few seconds later, smiling. "He says he's going to announce tomorrow will be VE – Victory in Europe – Day."

Bunny jumped up from her chair, flung her arms around Walter's neck and kissed him hard on the lips.

Just at that moment, George opened the door, and raised his eyebrows.

Walter flushed, removed Bunny from him and held her at arm's length.

Bunny's face and neck reddened. She stood for a second glaring at Walter. She pushed him aside. She turned to George, kissing him on both cheeks. "It's over. It's really over."

George gave her a bear hug.

Walter's heart was pumping. *What the hell's the matter with me? Move over George.*

Churchill marched in to make an announcement.

Bunny stopped him in his tracks and held his face and kissed him on his chubby left cheek.

Churchill glowed. "Tomorrow then, let's get organised for the big day, our job is done, and thank you Miss Shearburn."

***

377

Bunny watched from her office window. The crowds were amassing. A wave of excited chatter surged along the human river. There would be an official announcement at three o'clock from The Prime Minister.

Tens of thousands of people had gathered in the streets of London. Outside number 10, Downing Street, their cheerful voices emitted a low buzz. The broadcast had to be brief as the cheering from the crowd grew to a crescendo.

Churchill spoke into the microphone set up in the Cabinet Room. Loudspeakers were set up all over the country in preparation for his speech. There were more than 100,000 people gathered in Trafalgar Square, standing shoulder to shoulder in solemn silence as he delivered his message. He ended his speech with the resounding words: *"The German war is therefore at an end. Advance Britannia. Long live the cause of freedom. God save the King."*

Walter picked up the telephone in the hallway. "Send the cars round will you please, George – we're taking him to the Ministry of Health in Whitehall, because it has a first-floor balcony."

Uniformed police cheered along with the throng of delirious people as they made a path to allow Churchill to reach his open-topped car.

Churchill had a huge smile for everyone and waved his hat. Walter stood on the running board and observed every face – all adoring fans – not a frown to be seen. When they arrived at the building, Churchill shook every hand and was almost knocked over by people patting him on the back.

The Old Man stepped into the light on the balcony and the roar from the crowd deafened him. He laughed and put his hands over his ears. "Thompson, where's my cigar? I must light one – the people expect it of me."

Walter stepped out of the shadows, handed him the silver case and produced his Zippo lighter.

The crowds became ecstatic, cheering and dancing on the spot as Churchill puffed white smoke from his trademark cigar.

George took a cigarette from his own case and offered one to Walter. "I don't think I've ever been so 'appy – will this cheering ever end?"

The band of the Guards struck up, *for he's a jolly good fellow* and 100,000 cheering voices sang along. After ten choruses the huge crowd became hoarse.

Churchill picked this moment to raise his hand and the crowd hushed in expectation. Never forgetting the art of oratory, he began in a low voice, taking time over every word. "The lights went out on England...."

There was an accidental theatrical effect – the floodlights went out on Churchill. The people roared with laughter, and the lights came back on.

"This is your victory," shouted Churchill.

"No, it's yours," a voice called back.

His last words were drowned out by the sound of crowds roaring all over Britain.

The band played *Land of Hope and Glory*, and London sang out again.

A blaze of flags and floodlights lit up the capital. The joyous revellers shook hands, hugged, blew whistles and formed the world's biggest *hokey cokey* line dance around Queen Victoria's statue, outside Buckingham Palace.

Across the nation, people were joining in street parties. The licensing laws were suspended. The population was about to get drunk and celebrate.

Churchill shook more hands as he returned to the open-top car. They travelled first to the House of Commons, then to Buckingham Palace. There was no need to switch on the engine as the car was moved by the masses – George had only to steer.

When they returned to Downing Street, Walter sent the open-top car away and was about to search for Bunny.

But Churchill was back at the door in his siren suit – an all in one battledress he often favoured for public occasions. "Where is the open car?" he asked.

"It's gone, sir." Walter looked beyond Churchill hoping Bunny would come with them.

"All right, I'll walk, Thompson." Churchill headed for the door.

Walter blocked his path. "It's impossible, sir. The crowd is too thick – they're standing shoulder to shoulder out there."

"Then I shall walk between two cars." Churchill pushed Walter aside.

"If you wait a moment, I'll get the car back and call the mounted police."

But Churchill was out of the door in seconds. Everyone was patting him on the back and shaking his hand. He climbed on to the rear bumper of one of the cars, crawled across the roof on all fours and sat on the top with his legs dangling over the windscreen.

The crowds cheered him as the car was pushed into Whitehall. Walter hung on to the side and glanced up at Bunny's office, but she was nowhere to be seen.

On the balcony of the Number 10 Annexe, Churchill recited a verse of *Rule Britannia*. As he finished, he raised his arm and the crowd began to sing the chorus.

Walter felt a surge of warmth for the Old Man as he watched him wave and blow cigar smoke at the cheering crowd. They had worked together since 1939. It felt like their little team had become a family – Walter, the Old Man, George, and …Bunny. "But where is Bunny?"

He knew she was offended he had not returned her kiss. There just had not been the opportunity to talk to her alone during the commotion of the day.

Bunny stood in the deserted street outside 10 Downing Street and glanced up to the black, blank windows of the empty office, where her letter of resignation rested on Churchill's desk. She thought about the kiss and touched her chest to ease the brick lodged there.

The noise from the crowd outside the houses of Parliament resounded in the abandoned street. It masked the *click click* of her good shoes as she walked along the pavement, carrying her small leather suitcase. She turned left into Whitehall just as Churchill's car turned in to Parliament Street propelled by the following crowds.

From his high position on the top of the car, Walter spotted Bunny's lone figure at the end of the street, walking away. "Sir, do you mind if I...?" he asked. But Churchill was too busy bathing in the adoration of the crowds.

George saw Bunny too – with a suitcase. "Go on, go on, we'll be OK."

Walter jumped off the car but the crowd following the car held up his progress. "Sorry. Sorry," he shouted as he pushed through the throng. "Excuse me. Sorry. Please let me pass." But it was hopeless – Bunny was gone.

***

Same time: 8 May – Town Hall, Kloosterzande, The Netherlands

Flop leaned out the window on the first floor and connected the wire to the last loudspeaker. He adjusted it, ensuring the huge crowd gathering outside the town hall would be able to hear. He fiddled with the radio and nodded to his wife as he attempted to get a clear signal from the BBC.

Local people carried British soldiers on their shoulders through the town. Flop's band played every English and American tune they knew, and then played them all again – *Alexander's Ragtime Band* was a particular favourite.

An American corporal gave a hilarious rendition of Irving Berlin's: *This is the Army, Mr Jones.* The crowds fell about laughing.

Despite their impoverishment, the townspeople managed to produce a street banquet to which everyone was invited. Flop's children waved homemade Union Jacks and tried to teach the British soldiers everything they knew about Dutch folk dancing. The British, who were getting drunk, performed this very badly, taking the women's parts of the dance – much to the amusement of the locals.

The folk dancers looked proud in their traditional Dutch costumes. The women wore large white hats and long dresses with white aprons, while the men wore waistcoats, flat hats and red cravats. They all wore heavy wooden clogs that clacked against the floor of the wooden stage, erected in the middle of the square. Everyone enjoyed clapping along to the clog dancing and feasting to celebrate the end of the starvation they had all had suffered in this part of the country.

As a final tribute to mark their joyous celebrations, the Canadian Artillery Regiment let off their spare shells into the clear night sky. Flop's children stared open-mouthed at the fantastic fireworks display, which went on for an hour. When the noise subsided, Flop's band began to sing the lyrics of *Het Wilhelmus,* the Dutch national anthem:

Shouts of *Oranje-Boven – Up the orange*, a reference to the Dutch national colour – ended each verse.

***

8 May – Lüneburg Heath, Germany

The *Gin Palace* gang sat on the hill overlooking the heath and listened to the scratchy voice of Winston Churchill as it was broadcast to the waiting troops.

"The German war is therefore at an end. Advance Britannia. Long live the cause of freedom. God save the King."

A huge roar went up from the troops in the valley. Bob embraced Johnny, Johnny clapped Bernie on the back and Bernie hit Bob on the arm.

"Ouch! Mind my typhus injection." Bob rubbed his arm.

"How come you got another injection?" asked Bernie.

"Oh, I was asked to take a woman at Belsen over to the hospital. She had severe typhus – so I had to have another jab. You know, I wasn't sure, but I meant to tell you – she might have been English." Bob's last few words were drowned by the sound of the British artillery letting off their spare shells.

Bernie hugged Johnny and Bob. "God, we've spent almost every minute together since 1941."

"All hail to Bernie – our leader." Johnny gave Bernie a sharp salute and Bob followed. "Now just get us out of 'ere will yer mate?"

Bernie grinned and saluted back. "I can't wait to see me mum. But I'll miss you boys. Who's gonna get the kettle on? If in doubt brew up?"

Johnny jumped off the back of the truck. "Forget the tea – follow me." He led the gang to the hedge and uncovered a wooden barrel. "Fill yer boots, boys."

"Good evening, lads." The Welsh Sergeant-Major looked over Bob's shoulder. "What do you have there?"

Johnny covered the barrel. "Nothing sir…."

"Did you steal it, Private?"

"No, sir, but my mate might have to box the local tavern owner's son – in a fair fight in the morning."

"Well then, did you get a tap with that?"

Johnny withdrew a wooden tap from his pocket. "Of course, sir."

"Well get it open then – we've all got some celebrating to do." The Sergeant-Major accepted a tin mug of ale and began to sing. Before long the dispatch riders, smelled the ale and were joining in. They struck up a chorus of *Roll out the barrel.*

Bernie filled his tin mug and walked along to Corporal Blue Gum's tent. "Here you are, Corp. All forgiven, war's over."

Blue Gums accepted the mug. "I just wanted to toughen you boys up you know. So, you'd make it through the war."

They had begun the war as boys, and had ended it as men, learning how to survive the daily routine of life away from their mothers. They were an efficient team on the signals, and they went about the business of war with consideration for others, recognising the plight of the dispatch riders and honouring their enemy's dead soldiers. They learned how to live with a new family in The Netherlands, and how to be compassionate to those innocents caught up in the tide of war and imprisoned in Belsen.

These shared experiences had tied them together forever… they were the *Princes of the Gin Palace.*

***

383

There was not much for the signals unit to do once the signing was over. They just had to keep the 30,000 German prisoners behind the wire and the 3,000 *SS* officers and *Gestapo* locked up inside a makeshift prison.

Johnny sat at a desk and beckoned the next German forward. He looked the man up and down and at his papers. *Very young, tired and hungry – this one wasn't in the SS.* He stamped the boy's papers. "Right over there, get a travel warrant and a packet of food." He turned to Bob at the next desk. "Just the Japs to beat now."

"They won't be a pushover." Bob looked at the man in front of him and at his photograph again. "What do you think, Johnny? He doesn't look like his photograph. I don't like the look of this one. Too clean, well fed and he has an attitude. Corporal, sir.... This one might be for you."

The Corporal ordered two infantrymen to take the suspected Nazi for further questioning. The German soldiers were questioned one by one. Once cleared of any involvement with the *SS* or the *Gestapo*, they were free to return home. Bob and Johnny were easy going with the German prisoners as they drove them to the railway station. They had been briefed by their Sergeant-Major that these young men had been conscripted and forced to fight, and most of them were decent human beings. Not so the *SS* troops. They could be identified by a tattoo of their blood group in their left armpit. These prisoners were considered hardened, unrepentant Nazis, and so were taken away to local prisons to await news of whether they were accused of any war crimes.

Since the first day of June, the weather had stayed warm and dry. All the prisoners had gone, and there were no longer any signals to send. Doing little or nothing in the hot, sticky weather became tedious for the *Gin Palace* gang.

Bernie drove The *Gin Palace* back from their last run to the station. To his left he noticed a cool, clear lake.

"Come on, Bernie, it's time for a bit of recreation." Johnny turned to Bob, "Fancy a swim?"

The small lake seemed secluded, and the boys stripped off their clothes to splash about naked in the water. They laughed and joked like schoolboys.

After a while, Johnny noticed someone spying on them from the opposite side of the lake. "Look, someone's trying to find out what the Argyll's have under their kilts. Let's pretend we haven't seen them and jump out and show 'em."

They leapt out and made a rush for the shore, grabbing pieces of clothing to wave above their heads. They whooped a Highland war cry as they advanced on the snoopers. Four startled nurses jumped out from behind a bush and ran squealing back to the hospital building, hidden from view by the trees.

The naked *Gin Palace* gang chased the nurses up a long sweeping paddock. They all arrived breathless in the middle of a manicured lawn, surrounded by convalescing patients. Most remained oblivious to the sudden appearance of wet and naked soldiers in their midst.

Bernie gave a fleeting glance around, checking for officers. In the corner of his eye, he saw someone who looked familiar – *could that be a very thin Martin Gold, asleep, with a bandage around his head?* The resemblance was there, but he could not be sure.

Johnny covered his private parts with his hands.

"You'd better cover your faces," shouted Bernie. "If there's an officer, he may recognise our faces, but he's hardly going to ask for a parade of our meat and two veg."

The gang covered their faces and ran naked and laughing back to the *Gin Palace*.

***

The next day, Bernie was alone when he went to the village post office to collect the mail. The officers had pinned photographs from Belsen in the front window with a notice in German explaining the horrors of the camp.

Bernie picked up the sack of mail for the regiment. The bag was getting lighter each week as more and more members of the battalion were sent home. Five German boys stood outside the shop, laughing.

"Look at that one." A tall boy pointed to one of the horrendous pictures and pulled a face.

"Just another horrible Jew who deserved to die." His friend tapped the photograph with a short stick.

Bernie's neck puffed red. He drew his gun and screamed at them to put their hands up. "*Legen sie Ihre Hände in de Luft.*"

The tall boy drew a knife from his belt.

Bernie snatched it away and slapped the boy hard across the face.

"Put your hands in the air!" Bernie repeated and the boys obeyed. Bernie felt a bubble of murderous fury rise in his chest. He quick marched the boys with their arms in the air to the local police station.

"Do something with these boys," he shouted at the German police sergeant, his voice quivering with rage. "They seem to find Belsen something to laugh about."

"Damn Hitler Youth," said the policeman. "Let me have them. A few nights in the cells and a discussion with some rubber truncheons might bring them to their senses."

Bernie shoved the boys forward, relieved the German policeman had agreed with his actions. It was clear that despite their former obedience to the Nazi regime, some of the Germans were divided in their attitude towards the camps.

"Will it ever be over? The evil, the sickness, the hatred?" Bernie asked aloud as he walked back to the *Gin Palace*, kicking stones. He booted a few of the stones for several hundred metres and had kicked away most of his anger by the time he returned to the camp.

As he approached the *Gin Palace*, Bob ran up to him. "Bern, where've you been? Sergeant-Major's looking for you."

"He doesn't want to see you or Johnny?" Bernie looked in the wing mirror of the truck and adjusted his beret.

"No, he just sent a corporal to get you. If it's about our naked swim – well, we seem to have gotten away with it, but maybe someone recognised you."

"Ha. That's what comes of being so well-endowed and having to share showers," said Bernie. "Well, don't worry, I won't break under interrogation." He marched off towards the Sergeant-Major's tent.

As he pulled back the flap, the tall, figure of his uncle was unmistakeable. Bernie smiled and then felt awkward as he did not know whom to address first or how.

The Sergeant-Major took the lead. "Inspector, is this private your nephew?"

"Yes, sir, he certainly is," Walter replied, extending his hand to Bernie.

"Well, I will leave you two to your business. Private, here is a 48-hour pass, and you may make use of your truck." The Sergeant-Major smiled at Bernie and quick-marched out of the tent.

Bernie gave his uncle a quizzical look. "I thought I was coming here for a roasting. Uncle Walter, what are you doing here? And how the devil are you? How's my mum? Any news of Aunt Stella and Uncle Martin?"

"I'll explain everything along the way," said Walter. "But right now, I understand you can drive a truck, so let's go and find it – we've got a lot to do in 48 hours."

"So where are we going, Uncle?" Bernie started up the *Gin Palace*.

"Bergen-Belsen."

"Oh no, you don't want to go there. There's a terrible concentration camp, where I saw the most awful things – things I don't want to talk about or even think about, ever again."

"Yes, I know – I've heard about it." Walter withdrew the slip of paper from his inside pocket – a message Downwood had left him. "I got a tip-off that your Aunt Stella might be there, and that's why I'm here."

"For crying out loud, no, no. She couldn't have been there. None of the inmates spoke English. Uncle, it must be a mistake."

"Well, on one hand, I hope you're right, but on the other, it might be our only chance of finding her. You know the way there?"

"Yes, but you better prepare yourself. It might not even be there anymore. It was so infested with bugs and disease, we set fire to most of the huts before we left." Bernie drove as fast as the *Gin Palace* could go. At first, the going was easy on the new A7 *autobahn*, but then they had to use country roads, avoiding bomb holes, debris and burnt-out army trucks along the way.

It was dark when they reached the camp. The smell of death was still in the air, and Bernie was reluctant to get out of the cab.

Walter opened the passenger door. "Is that the commanding officer's billet?"

Bernie pulled up his lapel against the chill even though it was almost summer. "It was, but it looks deserted."

Walter got out of the truck.

Bernie stayed in the cab. He watched his uncle enter the building and the flash of his torch across the ground floor windows.

Walter was back in a few minutes. "There's no one there. I'm going to take a look around the camp."

Bernie shook his head. "No, let's wait 'till morning. I'll make a brew." He climbed into the back of the truck and stopped short because there, asleep in his bunk, was Bob.

Bob opened one eye and reached for his glasses as Bernie nudged him awake with his boot. "What the hell!"

"Look, Bob – sorry mate, I should have checked the *Palace* before I took her on a field trip. Just go back to sleep. I'll have you back to HQ in the morning." He covered Bob with a blanket and lit the primus stove.

Walter found another large brick building at the back of the officer's quarters and switched on his torch as he entered. The

388

first room seemed to be filled with small white peas. *Oh my lord... those are teeth, gold teeth. This is sick – and there are thousands here! You were right Bernie – I don't want to see any more.* He walked back to the truck. "Looked like we passed an American base, a few miles back down the road. Let's go and see if they know anything."

"Look in the back," said Bernie. "We've kidnapped my mate Bob. I'll have to get him back by tomorrow, or he might be in trouble."

Walter pulled back the curtain to reveal Bob curled up in the bunk.

The sentry at the American base was helpful, but reluctant to let them enter the base. "This is a hospital, and a displaced persons camp," he explained. "I can call over and ask if the officer in charge will come out and talk to you, if you like."

After about ten minutes, Lieutenant Owen ambled over to the *Gin Palace*. It was clear he had been woken. "Raise the barrier, corporal," he called to the sentry, and waved to Bernie indicating a place to park the truck.

Walter and Bernie got out. Walter saluted the Lieutenant and handed him his warrant card.

"Inspector Thompson of Scotland Yard. How can I help you, buddy?"

"I am searching for a woman," said Walter, taking the single sheet of paper Anthony Downwood had left for him, from his breast pocket. "Her name is Nathalie Boucher. She was on a list of inmates compiled by the British when they liberated the camp. She's my sister."

"Let's go to the office," said Owen. "We've taken over those lists." He showed them into a long hut. The walls were lined with files. "Boucher, you say?" He opened a book. "B ... O ... U ... C ... Ahh, here we are – hut 19."

"Thank you," said Walter, turning to leave.

"Oh, but Inspector – she won't be there now." The Lieutenant replaced the book on the shelf.

"Where can I find her, then?"

Owen let out a sigh. "I'm so sorry, Inspector, but most of the inmates in that part of the camp were in a terrible state. It took us a while to get them the medical attention they needed. Let me check to see if she was admitted here." He pulled out book after book, searching the pages for her name. He closed the final ledger and shook his head.

"May I?" Walter held his hand out for the books.

"Of course, Inspector. Do you mind if I get some shuteye? I'll ask the sentry to let you out of the compound when you've finished."

Walter sat down at the lieutenant's desk and Bernie took the chair opposite. "Look for Stella Gold, Stella Thompson and Nathalie Boucher."

It was 03:00 a.m. when they had finished checking every ledger twice. They found no record of Stella. "Well, let's go and check where we last know she was seen - hut 19."

"For Christ's sake, Uncle…." Bernie began, but Walter shot him a look.

Bernie drove back to the camp, around the muddy tracks, trying to avoid potholes, until the headlights revealed a sign that said *HUT 19*. A faint moon outlined the camp. Walter slipped out the truck and illuminated his torch.

Bernie turned the truck around and Bob stirred when the *Gin Palace* hit a pothole and stalled.

Bob stretched and hopped out of the back of the truck. He let out a loud long scream and could not stop. He was rooted to the spot.

Bernie jumped from the cab and ran to where Bob was hysterical. "Stop, Bob, it's all right, they've all gone. Look most of the huts have been burnt down. Stop Bob, Bob. BOB."

Bob thought he was having a nightmare, and slapped his own face trying to wake himself.

"Bob, stop it." Bernie hugged Bob tight to his chest.

Bob took off his glasses. He aimed a punch at Bernie. "What is this, you sick bastard? Why the fuck am I here? You sick…."

Bernie held Bob at arm's length so he could talk to him without being hit. "We're looking for my aunt. We've just been told she was here. Can you believe it? So, we have to try and find her. Get back in the *Palace*, and I'll make a brew. My uncle's out there searching the huts."

Bob nodded and climbed back into the truck while Bernie re-lit the primus stove.

Walter stepped into Hut 19. It had been partially burnt. He put his hand over his face, the stench of rotting straw and human detritus was overwhelming. It was crammed with bunk beds like shelves – four high. He shone his light on each one, hoping to see some human form.

Bernie and Bob were drinking their second mug of tea by the time Walter returned. "Can I offer you a brew?" Bernie asked his weary uncle.

"Thank you," said Walter, accepting a mug of warm liquid and wrapping his hands around it.

Bob threw the dregs of his tea out the back of the truck. "Can we please get the hell out of here? I can drive, since I have slept. You two can get your heads down, and with any luck we will get back before the morning parade."

Bernie and Walter nodded, and Bob started the engine. After a few miles, Bernie joined Bob in the cab. "I suppose it was a bit of a long shot, expecting my aunt to still be alive. I don't suppose there were even any English people in the camp."

"I think there might have been one," said Bob. "Well, her friend, who was French, had said she was English. I took her to the tented hospital outside the gates, that time when I told you I had to go and get another typhus jab. The poor thing was light as a feather."

Bernie slid into the passenger seat. "My God, Bob, what was her name?"

"Don't ask me, she was delirious, so I signed her in as Mrs English."

"Turn the truck around!"

"Don't be daft. The chances she is your aunt are... well... the chances she survived, are... well...."

"Bob, mate, stop the truck. If we don't go and check, my Uncle will never forgive me. The tented hospital was moved to the American Displaced Persons Camp. We have to go back there. But don't worry. You can still make the morning parade."

Bob pulled the *Gin Palace* up sharp and Walter put his head into the cab.

Bernie explained: "Bob here helped a woman who spoke English. We're going back to the Americans."

"Well, it was just one word," said Bob. "I asked her if she was English, and she said 'Yes'. It might have been the only word she knew."

By the time they pulled up at the camp, the guard had changed, and the new Corporal was not so obliging. Walter got out of the back of the truck and marched up to the sentry box. After a heated discussion, the Corporal used the telephone, and Lieutenant Owen was summoned for a second time that night.

The Lieutenant was sympathetic. "I know if it was my sister, I would want to check every possibility, too." He led them into the long hut and pointed them towards the relevant journals.

Walter, Bernie and Bob began the job of checking through the names once more. This time, they searched for *English.* After an hour, they closed the final book, and Walter used the telephone to contact Lieutenant Owen. "Thank you again, Lieutenant, but we've had no luck."

"I am sorry, Inspector," said the Lieutenant. "I didn't like to discourage you, but I haven't heard any of the patients speaking English. Most of our nurses have been brought in from France – so I hear quite a bit of French."

"My sister does speak French. Just one question - there's lots of different writing in the ledgers, so who would have recorded the information?"

"Well, an administrative nurse completes the records on arrival. But the different writing is perhaps because many of the persons admitted here were incoherent when they first came. Once they can tell us who they are, the duty nurse will enter their names in the book."

"And the nurses are French?"

"Yes, all of them are French, Inspector."

"I'll call you back," said Walter. He dashed back to the wall of files once again and selected the book marked *A.* There, with an admittance date of 18 *Avril,* were the words, *Madame Anglaise, number 24736, Ward C.*

Walter put his hand to his chest. "Ward C, Ward C."

Bob looked at a plan of the hospital on the wall and pointed to a building, marked Ward C.

The three of them raced to the door. The dawn was glowing yellow and orange through the trees as they ran together to a brick building marked *C*. There was no one else around.

***

8 June – Displaced Persons Camp, Belsen, Germany

Stella stirred from her sleep, and for the first time in weeks, felt hungry and thirsty. She was still weak and raised her head and screwed up her eyes, trying to refocus. She had just dreamed her brother was standing at the side of the bed, holding her hand.

"So, you really are English," said Paulette, dressed in an orderly's uniform. "Excuse me, gentlemen," she said, pushing past Bernie and giving him a cheeky smile as she held a beaker of water to Stella's lips. Stella sipped the water and sat up in bed. She held out her arms, and both Bernie and Walter leaned forward to embrace her.

Bob stared hard at the woman, trying to recognise her. "Yes, this was the woman I carried. She has some hair now and has put on some weight." He looked at Paulette. "I remember you – you are her French friend."

"*Oui*, and you are the *Tommie* who 'elped her."

Walter pumped Bob's arm. "Thank you, oh thank you."

Paulette returned with some breakfast for Stella.

Lieutenant Owen and a young doctor joined them next to her cot. The doctor took Stella's pulse. "What she needs is rest and building up. We don't really have the facilities here, but in my opinion, she's not strong enough to travel back to England yet."

Bernie scratched his head. "There's a military convalescence hospital with a lovely lake, that's close to Lüneburg Heath." He nudged Bob.

"My sister was in the SOE," explained Walter, "So I imagine, she's entitled to be transferred to that facility."

393

***

9 June – Belsen to Lüneburg Heath, Germany

Telephone calls were made, and the next day, the boys carried Stella in her cot to the *Gin Palace*. Walter spoke to the Sergeant-Major and requested Bernie's pass be extended another 24 hours and explained they had kidnapped Bob.

Bernie crashed the gears as he drove. *Should I say anything about who I might have seen in the hospital.* Walter leaned forward from the back of the truck and put a reassuring hand on Bernie's shoulder. "It's okay, young Bernie, I understand about Belsen. I've heard they are burning the place down today."

Bernie said nothing, but forced himself to drive like an ambulance driver rather than a rally driver, even though he couldn't wait to get there. As they approached Lüneburg Heath, he realised he was unsure of the way. The last time he had approached the hospital, it was from the road by the lake. He did several U-turns before coming across the drive to the large country house being used as a hospital.

Bernie stopped the *Gin Palace* outside the imposing entrance. "Uncle, can you do the paperwork? I just need to check out a hunch...." His words were lost as he was already through the front door.

"Can you please stay with Stella?" Walter asked Bob, who nodded.

Bernie ran through the corridor of the house until he found the huge French windows leading to the lawn. He spotted the man he was looking for and ran over to him. *Oh thank the Lord! It's Uncle Martin.*

Martin was asleep in his wheelchair, in the shade. Bernie punched the air and ran back to the *Gin Palace*, taking an empty wheelchair along the way. Bernie and Bob helped Stella into the chair and went to meet Walter in the reception area.

The administrator completed her paperwork. "Mrs Gold can go to room 19."

Walter leaned over and kissed Stella. "We'll have you better in no time."

Bernie could hardly contain himself. "May I?" He took hold of the wheelchair handles. Walter and Bob followed on while Bernie wheeled Stella away from room 19 and towards the French windows.

Bernie stopped when he came to the nurses' station. "Can you all please wait here?" He turned to the nurse, "Excuse me, the man in the wheelchair over there, has he got anything wrong with his heart? Will he be okay if he gets a bit of a surprise?"

"Let me see," said the nurse, checking her records. "Oh, the Captain – quite the hero. The Americans brought him here, having picked him up in Belgium. He was part of the White Army there – the Belgian Resistance. He acted as a scout while the Allies advanced. They were so taken with his bravery; they shipped over a brain surgeon from New York to remove a bullet lodged in his head. He's recovering very well. We did not know Captain Thibault had any family, he lost his memory but he's remembering more and more things each day. He had his operation 10 days ago, and he's healing nicely. We are building him up. So yes, I think he can cope with a surprise. Please excuse me. I need to start my drug rounds."

Martin was dreaming again, although he had lost his memory after being shot in the head. Madeleine and Marcel had nursed him back to health, and they had a small amount of food on the farm they had hidden from the Germans. They also hid Martin, from everyone, including their relatives and neighbours, even when he was recovered. It was not until the Allied troops advanced into Belgium that the Belgian Resistance visited the farm. Martin remembered his name was Martin Thibault but nothing else and he came out of hiding. "Well, I'm already dead," he'd told the Resistance, "so let's go and kill some Germans."

Martin began remembering his old life, now the bullet had been removed, with a little coming back to him each day. He felt the soft sun on his face as he daydreamed. He smiled as he thought about *charoset*, the traditional Jewish apple-and-nut dessert and he remembered he was Jewish, and that the beautiful girl he saw so often when he shut his eyes, was his wife.

Bernie couldn't wait to see what would happen as he wheeled Stella, towards Martin and bumped the chairs together. He skipped back to Walter and Bob. "I just lit the blue touch paper. Now watch." Bernie nudged his uncle, who stood with his mouth open while Bob scratched his head.

Martin opened his eyes and looked at Stella, who was sitting beside him.

Stella had spotted Martin the minute they had passed through the French windows.

He reached out his hand to her. "Stella. My *Neshama.*"

"Yes, my darling, I'm here, I'm here…." Stella kissed his hand and held it to her face.

"And boom, fireworks," said Bernie. "Well a few sparklers at least."

The two invalids leaned across their wheelchairs and tried to kiss.

"Shall we give them 15 minutes?" Bernie waved across to Martin.

Walter took a step forward and then a step back. He gave a little wave to Martin and smiled when Martin lifted his hand in acknowledgement. "I could do with a cup of tea. I've just noticed there's a canteen in the library. I just can't believe we've found both of them."

The three of them sat in happy silence over their tea. Bob added three sugars. "I'm in for the high jump. Will they shoot me for going AWOL?"

"AWOL? I'm going to make sure you get a medal for finding my sister. Don't worry, Bob. I'll explain everything to your Sergeant-Major and if he won't listen to me, he'll listen to Mr Churchill."

"I thought your duty with him was over now the war is finished?" said Bernie, stirring his tea.

"Oh, it is, but we're still friends. When he found out I'd been given a *name* by the secret service – one used as an alias, by your aunt Stella, he organised my flight out here."

"What will you do, now?" Bernie checked his watch for the time.

Walter's gaze dropped to his tea. "I don't know."

"How's that Miss Shearburn? I got the impression, she rather liked you."

"I've no idea," said Walter with a sharp edge to his voice. Realising his tone might be misunderstood, he added, "I was hoping to talk to her and clear something up before I left, but she disappeared on VE day and has since vacated her flat. I've no idea where she's gone."

"She once gave me her sister's telephone number."

"Ah well… no doubt you've lost it."

Bernie winked. "Oh, yes, years ago. But I have your photographic memory, Uncle – Mayfair 891."

***

16 June – Downing Street

George knocked on the door to Churchill's private study.

Churchill's voice boomed from beyond the door. "Come in."

George stood in the doorway. "Sir, I've just come to say I'm off."

"Ah, Sergeant. Well, come in, man. Any news from Thompson about his mission?"

"No, not yet, sir"

"Well, what are you going to do now, then?" Churchill looked over his glasses.

"Well, frankly sir, I don't quite know."

"Well then…." Churchill smiled.

George shrugged his shoulders.

"Why don't you stay with me, man?"

"Because the rules say I am too old, sir."

"Of course, you're too old, but not if I employ you privately. What do you say about that then, detective?"

"Sir, I'd be honoured, thank you."

Churchill had a sparkle in his eye. "Good man. No need to start until the morning."

***

Walter sat with his back to the wall in the café stirring his tea. *Is she late? No, I'm early.* He looked up at the clock on the wall. He caught his reflection in the café window and straightened his favourite blue silk tie – the one given to him by President Roosevelt.

He gazed at his tea and smiled as he remembered Churchill arranging for him to fly out to Germany, and the moment Stella had looked up at him from her hospital bed. "My wonderful reckless sister." He smiled, realising he had spoken the words aloud.

"Who's reckless?" Bunny appeared in front of him.

"My sister," Walter stood up.

She took a seat beside him.

They said nothing for a few seconds, and both started to talk at once. "How are you?" They laughed.

Walter touched Bunny's hand. "Sorry, you first."

"I'm well, thank you – a secretary at the BBC. How is your sister and her husband?"

"Oh good, Stella is recovering, and Martin is up on his feet. They're due to return to Brighton next week. Young Bernie is being demobbed and will also be coming home. Martin's father is looking to retire from the coach business so Martin and Stella will be taking over. Bernie, and my sister Emily want me to come to Brighton and open the garage – but I'm not sure about that."

"Motorbikes was it? The garage in Brighton?" Bunny grinned. "I've always fancied myself on the back of a bike."

"I didn't have you pegged for a girl who would ride pillion."

The tea arrived and Bunny poured two cups. "Gosh, how did you ever keep up with him – the Old Man?"

"Oh, I don't know, maybe my training with the police athletic team helped. He seemed to work you pretty late hours, too."

"Yes, but I liked the work. He did have some funny quirks, though."

"Surely not. Really?"

Bunny tapped her nose. "I'm not sure if I should tell you."

"Let me guess – pins and paper clips?"

"We had to remove everyone and secure all the papers with legal tags. He had some funny ways."

Walter laughed. "I once smoked a pipe. How he hated that. Nearly as much as he hates whistling."

Bunny giggled. "Just before I left, he asked me to lean out of the window of Downing Street and tell a citizen in the street to stop whistling."

"What did you do?" Walter remembered the day, in what now seemed so long ago, when the Prime Minister had shouted at Bernie for whistling.

"I told him it was a public highway, and the man was entitled to do what he pleased within the law." Bunny grinned and took a sip of tea.

"And what did he say to that?"

"He grunted and carried on with the dictation." Bunny laughed and spilled a little of her tea in the saucer.

"One day, I will have to tell you a story about my nephew and whistling… I have kept all my notebooks of everything that happened."

"Perhaps… if you like… I could type it for you."

"I would have thought you had had quite enough of typing."

Bunny's head dropped and she focused on stirring her tea.

Walter took both her hands and looked into her eyes as he spoke. "But first, I'd like to ask you about those mystery sandwiches and cups of tea… oh, and that kiss. But not here. I've got the bike outside. Would you like a trip to Brighton? Do you like the seaside?"

***

25 September 1945

Walter lifted Bunny's chin and kissed her soft lips. The Registrar gave a little *excuse me* cough, leaned across the desk and shook Walter's hand. The clerk slid the book across to Bunny and she signed her name. Walter followed suit.

"Oh, can you complete your address just there, sir?" The clerk passed the book back to Walter.

Bunny smiled at Walter. They had no address, their service with Churchill had finished. Walter winked at Bunny and wrote: *10, Downing Street, London SW1.*

The low early sun blinded Walter as he pulled back the heavy door of Westminster registry office.

"Surprise!" shouted Emily, George, Bernie, Stella, Martin and Bunny's sister, Kitty. They laughed and threw confetti at the couple.

"How did you know?" Walter brushed himself down.

"So, you think you're the only detective in the world." George shook Walter's hand with vigour.

"Kitty." Bunny kissed her sister.

Kitty held on to her hat in the light breeze. "Oh, this young man called round to see me and let me in on your *secret.*

Bernie gave Walter a hug. "Congratulations, uncle, Mum and George have arranged a lunch for us all in *The Ship and Shovel* in Craven Passage."

"Mum and George? When did you two get to know each other?"

"Oh, Walter, your Sergeant came to see me back in '41 when Bernie was conscripted, and you were away somewhere with Churchill. I must say it was lovely to meet someone with such a hearty appetite. We've been meeting up since I got back from Haltwhistle."

George rubbed his tummy. "Your sister makes a wonderful rhubarb crumble, better than Churchill's cook. She just happened to be making one when I called, so I've had to take her out for a few meals since – you know just to thank her…."

"George – you cheeky basket." Walter gave his friend a warm smile.

Emily handed Bunny a bunch of yellow roses. "It's a *Peace* rose, a hybrid tea. It's been grown especially for the end of the war, to celebrate the peace. George got me some bushes for the back garden."

Bunny put the flowers to her face. "Oh they smell wonderful. Thank you so much, but there are so many roses here, you can't have any left in your garden."

"I'm so glad you like them. They flower and flower all summer." Emily kissed Bunny.

Walter hugged and kissed Stella. "Let me look at you. My *skinny blister* – let's get you to the pub and feed you up some more."

Martin pumped Walter's hand and kissed Bunny: "So you thought to leave us all out of this eh? I'm hoping we've got lots to talk about concerning a certain garage in Brighton.

***

Walter and Bunny sat at the head of the table in the pub, surrounded by the family. A few extra guests sat at the end.

Luc had his arm around Nicole, who was heavily pregnant. "Nicole wants a girl," he told Stella and Martin. "We're going to call her, Carla."

Bob and Johnny sat either side of Paulette – both of the boys, hopeful.

Downwood, with a strange haircut – was flirting with Pierre.

Walter turned to George. "Downwood?"

"Ah, he's not so bad – we spotted him downstairs in the bar and Stella's friend Pierre invited him along. What could I say – if it wasn't for him, you wouldn't have got to your sister so quick."

"What is that on his head?"

"His hair fell out after the explosion in Tehran. It's a *syrup.*"

Walter smiled and stood raising his glass: "A toast to all of you – my flawed but treasured family. You're all so precious to me – the toast is – being together again."

They stood for the toast. "Being together again."

After several hours of drinking and stories, Walter was anxious to catch the eight o'clock train to Brighton. He had bought two first class tickets and booked a room in the Grand Hotel.

After prolonged goodbyes, Walter opened the door of the banqueting room leading to the upstairs corridor. Bunny waved to the guests, while holding her flowers.

They stopped, looked at each other and smiled. Were their minds playing a trick? Or, in the hallway, was that the lingering aroma of the Old Man's favourite, *Romeo Y Julieta* cigar?

EPILOGUE

Dad dips his head under the water before coming up for air. I watch as he emerges and bobs back down under the surface. He looks happy and I don't want to upset him.

But the questions I want to ask are burning in my head. I think better of it and clamber back into the pool to swim another length to give him more time.

The other swimmers have gone, and we are alone.

He draws in a huge breath of air and turns to face me, throwing the question back at me: "What did I *see* at Belsen? I've spent 50 long years trying to block those sights out of my head...."

I reach for his hand. He looks down to study the water, as if trying to glimpse memories in the swirling blue. "Bodies, hundreds of them, blackened and stacked like logs. The sadness in the eyes of one naked man still alive among the dead, the hopelessness of the medics trying to lift him from the pile."

He ducks under the water again to dissolve his tears before resurfacing, the red streaks still raw on his face. "Thousands of starved people forced to live like animals – too sick for us to help. There were rooms full of people's teeth. Rooms full of human hair. Filth everywhere. Local people pretending they knew nothing about it. People who lived close by but who never asked, 'What's the terrible smell, or why does the town keep getting covered in grey ash?'"

I reach for him, but he is already gone, swimming fast lengths under water. I can't see his tears, but I can feel their vibrations as waves in the pool. I become worried he has been down too long, but then he comes up noisily at the deep end. "Why the hell do you want to write about all this stuff?" He smacks his hand down on the water.

I swim towards him. I know this is hard for him, but I believe in my mission. "Because it is important. Because your history is part of who I am." I fling my arms around his strong neck. "Because all of the families who survived the war are connected. And

403

because I am proud of you – you are my big strong dad, my John Wayne, and I love you."

Mum appears from the shower in her dressing gown. "Bernie? Are you all right?"

Dad softens when he sees her. "Well, if you are determined to hear all about this, please be a love and go get us some fish and chips." He lifts me up in the water and catapults me backwards, so I land with a hard slap on the water.

***

After dinner, I wait in silence for Dad to begin. His voice is low, and I try not to disturb him as I take my notes.

"Where do I start?" Dad looks down for a moment. Well, before the Second World War, we Thompsons were just an ordinary, happy, working-class British family. My dad – your granddad – had been a sergeant in the Great War, and one of his jobs was to recover the dog tags from the men left dead in the field. Little did he realise the mustard gas stayed in the clothes, so when he undid the dead men's collars to take their identities, he breathed in a little bit of the gas each time, which eventually killed him 17 years later.

"After he died, my Uncle Walter took on the fatherly role for my Aunt Stella, his younger sister, and me. I was a gangly, freckly teenaged boy, and Stella was 25 years younger than Uncle Walter, so he was like a father to her, and she was like an elder sister to me. People said my Aunt Stella was a great beauty, but personally, I couldn't see it – she was far too skinny."

"It was Uncle Walter who held us all together with his presence and personal charisma. If you really want to know Uncle Walter's story, you'll have to read his own version of the events – it's all written down in his policeman's notebooks somewhere – I am just not sure where."

For the rest of the night, I listen with fascination as Dad tells me the amazing story of how he, my great uncle Walter and my great aunt Stella all contributed to the downfall of the Nazis. But I don't forget his words about my great uncle's notebooks.

***

10 July 2000 – My house, Bishop's Stortford, England

Bernie takes a moment to compose himself. It has been an exhausting day for him talking about the war.

At last, I feel I understand who he is. He reaches over and touches my hand. "Put the kettle on then, there's a good girl."

"*If in doubt, brew up,*" I josh.

"Yeah, something like that," he says with a warm smile. "I suppose you want to know what happened to them."

I nod, pouring out two large mugs of tea.

"Well, your great uncle Tommy and great aunt May were married in September 1945…"

"Hang on! Hang on! Uncle Tommy was Walter and Aunt May was Bunny?" I can't believe this little old couple were the heroes of Dad's story.

"Ha ha. They never went back to work for Churchill again, though he became Prime Minister again in the 1950s, but Walter refused to come out of retirement a second time. Churchill was mad, and when your great aunt typed up Walter's memoirs. He was threatened with losing his pension if they were ever published. But in 1956, Walter was short of money, and he took an offer of three thousand pounds for his story from a Canadian publisher, *I was Churchill's Shadow*. Oh, they had a wonderful time. The book was also published in the United States and called *Assignment Churchill*. They went on tour around the country telling their tale. The Americans were fascinated with his personal insight into Winston Churchill. After that, they had enough money to enjoy their retirement."

"What about all the other people in this story?"

"Oh, I don't know love. I've blotted all this out for 50 years – you'll have to go and look them up yourself."

***

405

Two years later, in July 2002, I discover a small leather suitcase hidden in the attic of a Somerset farmhouse. Inside, 700 pages of my great uncle Walter's notes record the details of what happened to him and Churchill during the war.

I slowly piece these events together with everything Dad told me about his involvement in the war. I hope I have done them all justice. They were all heroes, and they all make me proud.

THE END

ACKNOWLEDGEMENTS

I should like to thank the following people, without whom I could not have finished the book:

First, my agent, Jacqui Stevens. Her coaching and advice - second to none. Her encouragement and friendship have made me want to write more. Her partner, Andrew has also been so helpful with his artistic design and suggestions. Her lovely Dad, Daryl Stevens and her brother, Paul Stevens have also made excellent suggestions.

A huge thank you to Robert E. Towsie, for his amazing editing. He has written two books, where Winston Churchill is a character. I laughed all the way through. You will be intrigued.

Thanks to Dennis Guilmette for being so helpful and supportive.

Next, I gave the book in its various raw forms to friends and acquaintances to read. Thank you to my long-suffering husband, Gordon who has listened to me read the whole book aloud on more than one occasion. Those of you that commented and helped are:

Kimberley Stoker – who could easily have a third career in editing. Her ability to enhance my dialogue and create 'toffee apple moments' was outstanding.

Tara Oester – who read the whole book on her holidays and then followed up by reading the complete 16 episodes of the TV series.

Edwin Coombes – who really should write his own book.

Jessica Robinson who saw the book from a young person's perspective and gave me great feedback. Thanks for saying it is 'epic'.

Great comments were received from Julie Juliff, Dave and Lynne Evans, Lesley James, Janet Cutmore, Helen Andrews, Charlotte Bridger, Peter Henocque Yeun, Eileen, Maggie Pontin, Pam and my mum, Beryl Dow. Even my hairdressers, Shelley, Emily and Steph have listened while I read parts to them.

Others have made small but vital contributions. Benji – thanks for 'cretin'. Even Emma, who hates to read, has thrown me the odd helpful word. I can't wait for my grandchildren to be old enough to read it.

Charlotte Mottram – thank you for the marketing advice.

This year some super people have been inspiring and helpful. Laura King – great organiser, David Gandy – so nice you read my other books, Lisa Bentinck – so smart, organised, professional and energetic, Dasha Abramovic for letting me see her wonderful home, Johnny Pigozzi for kindly inviting me to his party, Simon Howley helping me get it all together for the future project.

Linda Stoker

NOTES

7 December 1941

The Japanese attempted to wipe out the American Pacific fleet which was resting at Pearl Harbor in Hawaii. There were 22 Jones killed in the attack on Pearl Harbor. 2402 casualties are listed. 48 were civilians. One was a baby girl of three months.

8 July 1943

Jean Moulin (codenamed 'Max'), the leader of the French National Resistance Council, was tortured and murdered by the *Gestapo*.

30 August 1944

Carl-Heinrich von Stülpnagel – who took over as military commander of France from his cousin, Otto, was tried and hanged for treason in Berlin. He had been part of the plot to kill Hitler and for his part had rounded up all the *SS* and *Gestapo* officers in Paris and put them in prison. When the plot failed, he tried to shoot himself but only succeeded in blinding himself before he was arrested by the *SS*.

23 May 1945

Heinrich Himmler committed suicide after being arrested by the British. He was one of the most powerful men in Nazi Germany and one of the persons most directly responsible for the Holocaust.

September 1945

Irma Grese was tried and hanged at Lüneburg by British executioner, Albert Pierrepoint, for crimes against the Geneva Convention and murder. She was a warden at Ravensbrück, Auschwitz and Bergen-Belsen and inflicted terrible cruelty on her charges.

December 1945

Cherche Midi Prison, France – Otto von Stüplnagel committed suicide. It was thought he may have had a nervous breakdown after being replaced by his cousin as head of occupied France. He was focused on Germany winning the war and did not agree with activities that did not directly impact on this – like murdering Jews.

6 February 1948

Walther Schellenberg testified against other Nazis in the Nuremberg Trials. He was sentenced to six years imprisonment, during which time he wrote his memoirs, *The Labyrinth*. He was released in 1951 on grounds of ill health. He was referred to as the *Scott-Free Nazi* as he never paid for his crimes. He died of cancer in 1952.

30 November 1964

Sir Winston Churchill celebrated his 90th birthday and was dead 56 days later. His body lay in state in Westminster Hall in the Houses of Parliament for three days. His old seat in the House of Commons was left vacant as a tribute. Each member of his wartime chiefs of staff gave watch over the watch at the catafalque as their own mark of respect. Walter often visited the small village churchyard, near Churchill's ancestral home at

Blenheim Palace, where Churchill was laid to rest.

13 January 1971
Heinz Lammerding was tried for war crimes in 1953 for the hangings in Tulle and for atrocities at Oradour-sur-Glane. He was sentenced to death in absentia by the court of Bordeaux. But for some peculiar reason he was not returned to France by West Germany to pay for his crimes, instead he resumed his career as a civil engineer in Dusseldorf and died of cancer at the age of sixty-six. I would really like to know – why?

18 January 1978
My great uncle, former inspector Walter Henry Thompson, died of carcinomatosis and carcinoma of the bronchus at the age of 87. Most of his story is true. A good non-fiction account can be found in *Churchill's Bodyguard* by Tom Hickman, or in the excellent Nugus Martin documentary TV series of the same name.

17 April 1978
Walter's second wife, Mary Shearburn (aka Bunny) died just three months after him, also of carcinoma (and perhaps of a broken heart).

September 1973
Martin Bud, my Jewish boss, lent me the money to buy my first house. I named Stella's fictional husband Martin as a tribute to him and his generosity.

18 May 2004
My father, Bernie Dow, died on his 81st birthday. Most of his story is as he told it – except he never worked in his uncle's shop.

He married my mother, Beryl in 1952. She was one of the faces in the crowd outside Buckingham Palace on VE Day. She said she was standing beside my grandmother, Edith and my great-grandmother, Lily.

Dad was 75 when he told me about Belsen. I miss him every day.

My mother still receives Christmas cards from the Aarssen children in The Netherlands.

The character, Johnny is based on my father-in-law, Jim Smith. He told me much about his army career, but the most important fact was he met Paula in Belgium and married her after the war. I am lucky enough to be married to their wonderful, son, Gordon.

The Germans were never punished for shooting down Lesley Howard's unarmed civilian plane.

Printed in Great Britain
by Amazon

59574434R00251